THE
PERSUASION

THE
PERSUASION

IRIS
JOHANSEN

GRAND CENTRAL
PUBLISHING

NEW YORK   BOSTON

Jacket design by Flag. Paper background by Herman Estevez. Male figure © NikKeevil/Trevillion Images. Image in type © Getty/RF. Cover copyright © 2020 by Hachette Book Group, Inc.

Grand Central Publishing

Hachette Book Group

1290 Avenue of the Americas, New York, NY 10104

grandcentralpublishing.com

twitter.com/grandcentralpub

First Edition: June 2020

Grand Central Publishing is a division of Hachette Book Group, Inc. The Grand Central Publishing name and logo is a trademark of Hachette Book Group, Inc.

The publisher is not responsible for websites (or their content) that are not owned by the publisher.

The Hachette Speakers Bureau provides a wide range of authors for speaking events. To find out more, go to www.hachettespeakersbureau.com or call (866) 376-6591.

Library of Congress Cataloging-in-Publication Data has been applied for.

ISBNs: 978-1-5387-6296-7 (hardcover), 978-1-5387-5217-3 (large print), 978-1-5387-5340-8 (Canadian trade paperback), 978-1-5387-6295-0 (ebook)

Printed in the United States of America

LSC-C

10 9 8 7 6 5 4 3 2 1

THE
PERSUASION

CHAPTER

1

MACDUFF'S RUN
SCOTLAND

The portrait of Fiona MacDuff shone on the wall of the private gallery like a star lighting the darkness.

Yes!

Russell Davron stood for an instant focusing the beam of his flashlight at the painting, admiring the technique of the artist as well as the beautiful face of the woman he had managed to capture with such accuracy. The long, wavy red hair, the hazel eyes shining with such vitality and humor, the hint of recklessness in the curve of her lips. Fiona MacDuff had been dead for centuries, but she looked as if she could step out of that portrait and take life by storm, molding it to whatever she chose. It was no wonder that John MacDuff, Earl of MacDuff's Run, chose to keep her portrait here at the gallery of his primary residence rather than at one of his other estates. While researching the painting, Davron had wondered why MacDuff hadn't sold it during the years when he'd been tottering on the verge of bankruptcy. Of course, the painting was unsigned, which made it less valuable, but somehow Davron doubted if that had even made a difference to him. Because even now after MacDuff had managed to save his family fortunes, that portrait still had a place of honor in this castle. In good times and poor, the earl hadn't been able to let his Fiona go. Davron was beginning to see why . . .

"Why the *hell* are you just standing there?" Stefano Luca hissed as he came up behind him. "Take the painting and get out of here. That relief sentry should be reporting in another ten minutes. He's going to wonder where the other guard has gone. If you've made trouble for me, you'll pay, Davron."

Davron felt a chill as he moved quickly toward the painting. He had a very good idea what payment Luca would demand if anything went wrong. Luca wasn't the same man who had recruited him all those years ago. Or perhaps he was and Davron had chosen to ignore it because it was safer and more profitable to close his eyes. "I only took a minute," he whispered. "I'm sure you disposed of that guard's body with your usual skill. We'll be gone long before they find him." He carefully took down the painting. He probably should have been more cautious. These days it wasn't safe to argue or displease Luca in any way when he was this on edge. It would be wise to try to soothe him. "And I was only appreciating our lovely *Fiona*. I'm sorry I argued with you when you told me that she was worth retrieving. I was thinking only of the monetary value." He didn't add that this was also what Luca was usually concerned about. "Your eye is obviously better than mine. You must have seen something else in her."

"Stop *talking*. Just get it out of here." Luca was stepping closer to the empty wall where the portrait had been hung. "Stash the painting in the truck. I'll be there in a minute. I just have one more thing to do here."

And Davron had an idea what that last thing would be. Luca was carrying the stainless-steel container he had lately started to bring to every job like this. But it was no longer empty as it had been in the truck. He jerked his eyes away from the canister. Well, what did he care? Luca might be a bit mad, but he'd furnished him with a fine living for years and Davron had learned to live with the ugliness and fear that went along with it. All Davron had to do was take care of business, obey orders, disable all the security systems at the galleries, and act as a beast of burden when Luca made his choices. It seldom involved anything in the least violent. Luca liked to handle that himself.

As he had done tonight.

But Davron couldn't resist looking curiously over his shoulder as he moved quickly across the gallery toward the door.

Blood.

It was no surprise. There was usually blood these days, Davron knew. Luca liked to leave a signature. This time he had a brush in his hand and was dipping it into the container and then painting the wall with a huge bloody cross. It was probably the blood of the guard he'd stabbed outside the gallery. Davron had wondered why Luca had sent him ahead to grab the painting while he cut the man's throat.

He'd needed time to take the blood.

The cross was finished now, and Luca should be following him soon. But he wasn't coming. He'd reached into his pocket and was pulling out something and fastening it to the center of the bloody cross.

It was a photograph, Davron saw in surprise. This was a new addition to Luca's usual routine. Davron couldn't make out the details of the photo from across the gallery but it was definitely the photograph of a woman.

A woman with long, wavy hair that he thought might be as red as Fiona MacDuff's in this portrait he was carrying.

But Davron couldn't really be sure with all that blood flowing over the photograph . . .

———◆———

KENDRICK CASTLE
WALES

"Wake up, Jane."

It was Michael's soft whisper, Jane MacGuire realized drowsily as she opened her eyes. It was still dim in the tent, though she could see a slit of daylight at the opening. Her brother, Michael, was no longer curled up in his own sleeping bag across the tent but sitting next to her, fully dressed and with legs crossed. Was something wrong? Probably not. She could see that his chestnut-brown hair was a little rumpled, but those amber-colored eyes were sparkling with the boundless vitality usually present only in a ten-year-old. Still, better check. "Hi. You okay?"

"Sure." He lit his flashlight and smiled cheerfully down at her as he saw that she was fully awake. "You were just restless so I thought I should wake you up. Did you have a bad dream?"

"I don't think so." She yawned, sat up, and looked at her watch. "I don't remember if I did." But it was six thirty and almost time to get up anyway. All the volunteers and students participating in this archaeological dig at the grounds of Kendrick Castle usually met down at the mess tent for breakfast at seven thirty. Michael always looked forward to mixing with them and finding out what they'd discovered the day before. It had become almost a ritual during the three weeks she and her brother had spent together sharing the work of the dig and the other experiences connected with it.

But that wasn't supposed to happen today.

She frowned as she gazed at Michael's jeans, blue T-shirt, and white tennis shoes. "Hey, why are you dressed to go to work? Your mom and dad are going to be here this afternoon. And after we have tea, they're going to take you back to London for the weekend. Did you forget about it?"

He grinned mischievously. "Gee. Yeah, that's what happened, Jane. I just can't keep track of everything on my social calendar. It didn't occur to you that that's hours away from now and I can hang out with my friends and maybe do some digging?"

Of course he hadn't forgotten. Michael never forgot anything. And sometimes what was behind that little boy's sunny smile was not at all what it seemed. "Don't be a smart aleck." She reached out and tousled his hair. "You wake me up and then make fun of me?" Her gaze was suddenly searching his face. "And, as I said, I don't remember having a restless night." She paused. "Did *you* have a nightmare, Michael?"

"I never have nightmares. Maybe I was a little restless." His smile faded. "Because when I woke up, I got to thinking that it would be great if you could come back to your apartment with us instead of staying here at the dig for an extra day. Why couldn't you do that?"

"Because I have work to do." But she could do it if she chose. She had been very tempted. This opportunity to see Eve and Joe would be very brief, and then they'd be gone again. They had been in Maldara, in Africa, for the last four weeks because of Eve's forensic sculpting project. Eve Duncan was one of the foremost forensic sculptors in the world, and this job had been both difficult and heartrending for her. Not to mention taking place in a country recently torn by civil war that was a hazard in itself. That had been the primary reason Joe Quinn, Eve's husband, had insisted on putting his own career as a police detective on hold to stay with her. They were only returning for this weekend visit because they hadn't liked the idea of leaving Michael for this long. Then they would have to return to Maldara for another two weeks for Eve to finish her reconstructions before they'd be able to stop by here again to pick up Michael and return home to Atlanta.

And then Jane would lose them all for heaven knows how long again, she thought glumly. Because her paintings were principally sold by a gallery in London, she'd rented an apartment there and didn't get back to Atlanta nearly as often as she'd like. Which meant she didn't get to spend nearly enough time with her family. Every minute with them was precious to her.

But Eve and Joe's time with Michael was also precious after all those weeks away from him, she reminded herself. She ignored Michael's pleading expression and forced herself to shake her head.

"I haven't finished the sketches of the dig that I promised to give to Lady Kendrick to put in their advertising brochures. She *needs* them, Michael. Kendrick Castle is like dozens of other properties here in Wales that are struggling to keep from going bankrupt. Lady Kendrick's made a big success of this architectural dig, but a little publicity will help her. My working just one more day on the sketches should do it." She got to her knees and started gathering up her clothes to take down to the shower room in the common area of the dig. "I promise I'll be there in London tomorrow. Besides, don't you think that your mom and dad deserve to have you to themselves for at least one day? There's a slight chance they might have missed you. After all, you're their only son." She added teasingly, "Though I don't know why they'd ever miss a brat like you."

He didn't return the smile. "But they've missed you, too." He frowned. "You do that all the time, Jane. You're always telling me how important family is and then you take a step back as if you don't belong. I don't like it."

"Don't be silly. What an imagination." She looked over her shoulder. "I just have a few things to—" She broke off as she saw his expression. She hadn't realized that he had noticed her slight withdrawal every now and then. But she should have known that he would see and be bewildered by it. He was the most loving child she had ever known, and his instincts were remarkable. Okay, she had always tried to be honest with him and she wouldn't let this be an exception. She turned to face him. "We are family and that *is* what's important," she said quietly. "But sometimes family members come together at different times and periods in their lives and it makes them different, too. I came to Eve and Joe when I was about your age and they took me in off the streets and gave me a home. But I'd already gone through too much to ever be a child again." She met his eyes. "Yet that didn't stop me from being able to be their friend and it didn't change the love I felt for them. It just made it a little different." She smiled gently. "But then you were born and you gave your mom and dad the son they'd never had and me a brother. We all had you from the very beginning. Win-win situation."

He shook his head. "Not if you keep stepping back."

Good heavens, he was stubborn. "I just want them to enjoy every minute they have with you this weekend. Sometimes life seems to fly by, and your mom and dad work so hard. Your experience with them is totally different from mine, and I want you to all explore it for this little while." She smiled. "Hey, I can afford to step back and give my friends and family a little extra time together." She reached out and touched his cheek with her index finger. "When you've all given me so much. Understand?"

He nodded soberly. "I always understood, Jane." He made a face. "But all that does sound pretty sappy, and you're wrong. You should go with us. I don't want to leave you here alone."

"I won't be alone. Not all the volunteers go home on weekends. There will still be plenty of campers here."

He kept frowning. "It's not the same."

"No, it won't be. I'll miss you, but I might actually get some work done. And you'll have a terrific time with Eve and Joe tonight." She gave him a quick hug and jumped to her feet. "Tomorrow, I promise, I'll hog all the attention the minute I walk into that apartment." She undid the ties on the door and opened the tent to the sunlight. "Now let me get dressed so we can go down to the mess tent and have breakfast. Can't you see it's going to be a beautiful day?"

Michael looked outside at the ancient towering castle in the distance, then at the stone bridge over the brook that led to the slowly waking camp—a veritable tent city on the hills surrounding it. He slowly nodded. "Yeah, maybe." His brow was still wrinkled in thought. "Didn't you tell me that Seth Caleb was going to come and stay with us here for a few days? Why don't you ask him to come down today? He could keep you company until it's time for you to go to London tomorrow and maybe come with you."

She stiffened. Where on earth had that come from? Michael hadn't mentioned Seth Caleb since she'd told him a few weeks ago that he'd been forced to cancel his plans to visit. She hadn't told him that she'd been profoundly relieved to send a message to Caleb and tell him there was no need for him to come after all. She'd promised Eve she'd ask Caleb here to act as bodyguard to protect Michael from a kidnap threat that had not materialized. "You can't just drag Caleb down here from Scotland because it suits you, Michael. I know you like him, but he has a life."

"He'd come if you asked him." Michael was still looking out at the castle. "And I bet Mom and Dad would be glad to see him. Mom likes him a lot. She told me once that he'd saved her life when she was pregnant with me. He probably did all that really neat stuff he can do with controlling the blood flow in—"

"Caleb can be very appealing," she interrupted to stop the flood of words. She hadn't even known that Michael was aware of exactly how rare a gift Caleb had. She was sure that Eve had not gone into details to Michael about Caleb's rather bizarre abilities. Had Caleb told the boy himself? Possibly. You could never tell what Caleb would do. Or maybe Michael had just sensed it in his unique way, which was as unsettling as it was accurate. "But you don't impose on people because they're interesting to be around." She gave him a gentle nudge. "Go on down to the mess tent while I go shower and get dressed. I'll meet you in fifteen minutes."

"He wouldn't think you were imposing." Michael was moving reluctantly toward the door. "He really likes to be around you. I can tell. And he's lots of fun, don't you think?"

She looked away from him. "'Fun' is not exactly the word I'd use."

Blazing heat. Electricity. Sexual eroticism in all its forms. She could almost see Caleb standing naked before her. She drew a deep breath. *Don't think of him.* Difficult. When he always seemed to be—

Her phone was ringing. Saved by the bell. She glanced down at the ID.

Michael had stopped at the door and turned hopefully back to her. "Caleb?"

"Did you think wishing would make it so?" She made a face at him. "But at least you're in the right country. It's Lord MacDuff calling from MacDuff's Run. I haven't talked to him for over six months. I thought he was still in Spain." She punched the ACCESS button. "Hello, MacDuff. When did you get home?"

"Just a little while ago. I flew in early this morning." MacDuff's tone was very casual. "I thought it was time I'd touched base with old friends and I thought of you. How are you, Jane?"

"Fine. I've spent the last few weeks at a dig here in Wales with my brother, Michael. Eve and Joe have been in Africa while Eve did several reconstructions, and I grabbed the chance to take Michael to this castle in Wales. We've been playing in the dirt and searching for ancient Roman artifacts. It reminded me a little of that dig we did at Cira's castle in the Highlands." She chuckled. "And it's been almost as unproductive. We should have known your very extraordinary ancestress wouldn't hide her treasure in such an ordinary place. The Roman troops here in Wales were much more boring, and we're not expecting treasure. But searching for it has been great fun, and Michael and I both learned something from doing it."

"That's good. Even if those little bits of artifacts you probably found aren't on the scale of our Cira's treasure, knowledge rules, doesn't it? So are you both going back to Atlanta soon?"

"Michael will be going back in a few weeks with Eve and Joe. Then I'll have to go back to London and get ready to do an Italian tour. I spent most of the last six months painting in the Italian lake country. They seem to like my work in Rome."

"They like you everywhere. I bought one of your landscapes in Portugal. Though I prefer your Scottish paintings."

She chuckled. "Of course you do. You're a Highlander."

"Seth Caleb isn't a Highlander, and he likes your Scottish landscapes, too." He paused. "Is he in Wales with you?"

Curious...She was silent a moment before she answered, "No. I haven't seen Caleb for months." And this was not like MacDuff. He was a consummate sophisticate who would normally never be so rude as to display this curiosity. Particularly since Jane was sure she hadn't succeeded in hiding from him how tumultuous those last months with Caleb had been for her. He knew her too well. "Is everything okay, MacDuff?"

"Why wouldn't it be?" he asked lightly. "I'm home here at Mac-Duff's Run. It's my favorite place in the world, and there's no place I value more. Just wanted to check in with you. Take care, Jane."

The next moment, she realized he'd pressed DISCONNECT.

Strange...She slowly lowered her phone. The call had been short and filled with questions. He'd done a good job of seeming casual, but she still felt as if she'd been interrogated.

"Is Lord MacDuff okay?" Michael asked.

"He said he is," Jane said. "He likes being back at MacDuff's Run." But that had been a little unusual, too, that he'd called this early on the same day he'd gotten back to the estate instead of settling in and waiting until later in the day or even tomorrow. "He's always loved the Run. I can't blame him, I really like it, too. It's like stepping back in time into a scene from Rob Roy."

"But you're not going there to see him, are you?" Michael asked quickly. "Who needs Rob Roy? You need to stay here. After we come back from London, we'll just ask Caleb to come visit so that you won't be bored. That will be much better."

"What?" She stared at him. "You're being weird. Where did that come from? I haven't been bored for a minute since we've been here. I think we're a great team." She frowned. "I thought you thought so, too. Haven't you been having a good time? Was I wrong?"

"No." He was suddenly across the tent and sliding his arms around her waist, hugging her. "It's been awesome. *You're* awesome. I just didn't want you to have to put up with a kid like me for the last couple of weeks you're here. Like I said, Caleb is kind of fun."

There was that word again. She immediately crushed down the previous vision it was bringing to mind. "I'm very happy to be putting up with you." She cradled his face in her two hands to look down at him. "It's always too long between visits for me." She gave him another hug and then kissed the tip of his nose. "Caleb would just get in the way."

"But you won't go to Scotland to see Lord MacDuff?"

"No, I will not." She chuckled. "For your information, I wasn't invited. Not everyone wants my company, Michael. You're stuck with me."

"Good." But he was smiling mischievously again as he backed away from her. "Caleb would want your company, though. And I bet he'd like to go to the dig with us and see how all those old Romans lived. He thinks stuff like that is cool, and he'd be great at it. I could call him for you."

"Michael." She was trying to hold on to her patience. "Believe me, Caleb would not find anything interesting about how those ancient Romans lived. And you might think he's perfect, but he's not great at everything."

"Well, maybe not everything." His lips were still twitching as he turned away. "Just a thought. I'll see you at breakfast." He ran out of the tent.

She shook her head ruefully as she reached for her toothbrush. Lord, she was going to miss him when he went back home to Atlanta. Yes, living with Michael was filled with all sorts of challenges, but he was also loving and brimming with curiosity and humor, and she was crazy about him.

But he was very persistent, and that persistence had fastened on Caleb this morning. She'd thought she'd squashed it before she got the call from MacDuff, but that only seemed to have revived it. Because he definitely hadn't wanted her to go to MacDuff's Run. Oh, well, not to worry. Once he was with Eve and Joe, maybe he'd forget everything but them.

No, he wouldn't. Sure, that was what an ordinary kid might be expected to do. But Michael didn't forget anything; he just filed it away and brought it forward when he found a use for it. As he'd done when he'd brought the conversation back to Caleb to try to keep her from going to MacDuff's Run.

It was odd that it had seemed to be so important to him...

MACDUFF'S RUN
SCOTLAND

"She's fine," MacDuff said curtly as he turned to Scotland Yard inspector Rob Tovarth, who was standing at the gallery entrance. "And I could tell she knows nothing about this particular bit of nastiness." He gestured at the bloody wall. "I shouldn't have even let you talk me into calling her. Jane is too honest not to blurt something out if she'd had even a hint about the *Fiona* being missing. It's crazy to assume she'd have anything to do with the theft of my painting or the killing of that guard."

"You'll forgive me if I call your attention to the fact that she has very much to do with it, my lord," Inspector Tovarth said mildly. "You said that Jane MacGuire is the image of Fiona MacDuff, the woman in the painting." He nodded at the photograph pinned in the middle of the cross painted on the wall. "And her photo is hanging there instead of your painting. I'd argue that there had to be a reason why any killer would do that. It was only sensible to bring her into it." He shook his head. "But may I remind you I also asked you to bring her here to be interrogated?"

"She's in Wales with her younger brother. There's no reason to involve her," MacDuff said as he strode over to the wall where Fiona's portrait had previously hung. "The bastard was fond of blood, wasn't he?" he muttered as he gazed at the photograph. "Shock value?"

"Probably. But he definitely wanted you to make a connection between Jane MacGuire and the painting. What is she to you? A relation?"

"Friend. I've known Jane for years. She was only seventeen when I first set eyes on her." His lips twisted. "Though I admit I've tried to claim her as a relative since that first meeting. I'd lived with that painting all my life, and after one look at Jane I knew that she was our kin. I even offered to send detectives to investigate and establish a claim for her." He grimaced. "But Jane would have no part of it. She'd been adopted by people she loved when she was only ten and she said that she had no need of any other family." He shrugged. "I was a bit insulted at the time. Not many people would turn down a connection to the MacDuffs."

"Aye, very odd." Tovarth nodded. "But people have a habit of changing as time goes on. There's always the chance she might have later decided she wanted the portrait."

"And killed my guard to get it?" MacDuff said impatiently as he whirled to face him. The inspector was a tall, well-groomed man in his thirties and had seemed to be both meticulously polite and efficient since he'd arrived here. But at the moment, even his politeness was annoying MacDuff. "Don't be a fool. I would have given her that portrait if she'd asked. I owe her a hell of a lot more than that. I tell you she had *nothing* to do with this. I only agreed to make that call because I was afraid something might have happened to her. That photograph was obviously meant to send a message."

"You might be right," Tovarth said. "That blood on the photo does look to be a threat. But it's my business to be suspicious of everyone until they're eliminated."

"As far as I'm concerned, Jane *is* eliminated. She was never a suspect." MacDuff gave him a cool look. "Now drop it, Tovarth."

"Certainly, sir," the inspector said as he met MacDuff's eyes. Then he abruptly shook his head. "Or perhaps not, my lord. I realize you're very upset, and you're a man who is accustomed to running everything and everyone around him." He smiled. "Perfectly natural. You're a very important man, or the Yard would never have sent me here even though you requested we become involved. Earl of MacDuff's Run, former war hero, influential mover and shaker in the halls of Parliament. You deserve to have your opinions listened to with respect. I will gladly do so." He paused. "As long as our investigation doesn't bring up any information regarding Jane MacGuire that the Yard might find disturbing. Then I will *not* drop it. I feel obligated to do my best to give you all you need from us."

MacDuff frowned. "I've just told you what I need you to do. Jane's not to be——" He broke off, and suddenly a warm smile lit his face. "You're right. I'm being an overbearing ass. You're only doing your job. That guard was with me for years and I'm angry that he was butchered. Plus that painting meant a lot to me. So does my friend Jane. Shall we start over?"

"Starting over would be a waste of time, my lord." Tovarth gestured at the forensics team, who were streaming into the gallery. "You've already helped enormously by identifying the photo and calling Jane. As I said, I respect your opinion. I just wanted to point out that you might consider I'm paid to have opinions of my own." He went on quickly, "However, if we're to assume Ms. MacGuire might be a possible target, we should act accordingly. Does she have adequate protection? Perhaps I could assign a man to——"

"I'll take care of it," MacDuff said. He took a step closer to look at the photo. It was a casual close-up of Jane, a warm smile on her face, the wind blowing her red hair. Vibrantly alive and every bit as beautiful as Fiona in the painting she'd replaced. She was wearing a white shirt, and there was a lake in the background. How often had MacDuff seen her like that during the time when they'd been hunting for Cira's treasure? Perhaps it had even been taken there at Cira's Loch Gaelkar. It might narrow the field to find the sons of bitches who had done this if he could trace the location. He turned back to Tovarth. "You just concentrate on finding who killed my guard Jack Binarth. He had a wife and family. You're Scotland Yard; use all those DNA databases and Interpol connections you have at your disposal to get me a name."

"I have every intention of doing that, sir." Tovarth hesitated, his gaze following MacDuff's to the photo. "But I'd prefer to also arrange protection for the lady. There's a certain savagery connected to the way the killer used that blood. You're sure that you have someone competent enough to handle it?"

"I said I did," MacDuff said curtly. He drew a deep breath. *Keep calm. You asked them for help, now use them.* Tovarth was now impressing him as being sharp, determined, and only wanting to do his job. And he was right: The killer had made sure of situating Jane's photo so it appeared to be almost drowning in blood. He had received a chill himself when he'd first seen it on his arrival this morning. "No problem, Tovarth." He was reaching for his phone as he spoke. "I have a man in mind who is most certainly capable of handling any threat to Jane MacGuire."

"Indeed? May I ask his name and qualifications?"

Firm, but polite, MacDuff thought. Tovarth wasn't going to give up his input on the case if he could help it. "His name is Seth Caleb. He's an old friend of Jane's." He smiled crookedly. "But I really wouldn't delve into his qualifications if I were you. He doesn't encourage curiosity."

"Seth Caleb?" Tovarth stiffened as he repeated the name, his eyes suddenly intent. "The Hunter? You're bringing *him* here?"

"You've heard of him?" MacDuff could see that he had. It shouldn't have surprised him. He was aware Caleb was probably known by most of the leading police and intelligence agencies in the world. And despite his passion for privacy, Caleb was a figure who caught the imagination and held it. The excitement in Tovarth's expression told its own story. "I take it Scotland Yard would consider him acceptable to watch over Jane?"

"I've heard of him. There are rumors that he sometimes works with MI6." He made a face. "Or that MI6 sometimes works with him. He has the reputation of liking to be in total control." He added, "And I don't know if my superiors would consider him to be acceptable or not. His reputation is...questionable. We do know he has had amazing success hunting down and disposing of murderers, felons, and terrorists who have caused us a good deal of trouble over the years. But some MI6 in authority regard Caleb as more of a renegade ninja type. I think it best that I stay and meet him, if you don't mind."

It wasn't hard to guess that it was more pure curiosity than professional efficiency that was driving the request, MacDuff thought. Some of the details that Tovarth had heard about Caleb must have been damn intriguing to arouse that response. He shrugged. "I don't care as long as you stay in the background. Though I don't believe you'll have a choice. We'll both disappear for Caleb as soon as he sees that photo."

"I'll be discreet." Tovarth paused, his glance sliding away from MacDuff's. But after a short pause, he suddenly asked, "Is there any truth in what they say about him? There are a few ridiculous stories circulating at MI6 that he has some kind of weird psychic control over the blood flow of anyone near him. That he can even induce fatal heart attacks if he chooses. Foolish, right?"

MacDuff just looked at him.

Tovarth added quickly, "I know that most countries and law-enforcement agencies are exploring their own psychic investigative programs, but I'm afraid I'm too pragmatic to accept it. Still, it's interesting. Particularly since there's another rumor I've heard that Seth Caleb can do some other rather bizarre mental hijinks with changing perception. Some of the MI6 agents actually seem to be very wary of him." He paused. "Have you heard about that?"

Anything MacDuff answered would only whet the inquisitiveness that was nagging the inspector. "One always hears a good many stories about Caleb. You can be sure quite a few of them are true.

Why don't you ask him?" Then as MacDuff began to dial Caleb, he had second thoughts. His own coming meeting with Seth Caleb might be explosive enough without bringing another element into the mix to annoy him. "No, don't ask him. That would definitely be a mistake. He might be in the mood to demonstrate. And I've changed my mind, it's best you don't even stick around to meet him."

11:45 A.M.

"Where is it?" Seth Caleb slammed the door of his Range Rover and started across the courtyard toward the stone front steps, where MacDuff was waiting. "Why didn't you call me before this?"

"You knew three hours after I did. I was in Madrid and had to fly home in the middle of the night when the police notified me," MacDuff said grimly. "Have a little courtesy. I didn't have to call you at all. I was very tempted not to." He turned on his heel and entered the house. "And where do you think it would be?" He gestured down the hall. "The gallery. The photo on display isn't the same as the copy I emailed you. You won't find it quite as gory. The inspector insisted on having forensics take the original to headquarters to test it. So I had them make me a copy."

But Caleb was already striding down the hall, intense, totally focused. "You knew you had to call me. You knew what I'd do if you didn't."

He was almost giving off sparks, MacDuff thought. But when didn't he appear to be on the verge of an explosion? MacDuff had always found him amusing, interesting, and ultra-complicated when he wasn't near that volatile flashpoint that could be triggered in a heartbeat. After he reached that point, he was still interesting but no longer amusing and completely deadly. Today MacDuff had no intention of containing that volatility even if he could. "Yes, I didn't need you barging into my home and disturbing my staff when you heard about it. They're already upset about Jack Binarth's death. He was a good man." He watched Caleb as he entered the gallery and halted in front of the bloody cross. "And he didn't have to die. The medics said he'd already been knocked unconscious before his attacker cut his throat. It was either a warning...or the killer just wanted the blood for his damn exhibit." He leaned against the doorjamb and crossed his arms, his gaze on Caleb. He was staring at the photograph, and MacDuff could see by the taut line of Caleb's shoulders and back that he was getting very close to that explosion. Push him a little bit more. "Which do you think? You're an expert in that area. I thought I'd get your opinion."

"Are you enjoying this, MacDuff?" Caleb's voice was silky smooth. "I wouldn't advise you to go down that road. Unless you're accusing me of doing this?" He suddenly swung to face him. His dark eyes were glittering, his lips tight. "And I thought you knew me better than that. I'd expect to hear that stupid bloodlust bullshit from someone less intelligent, but you've known me long enough to realize that's not who I am. Why are you trying to make me angry?"

"Because *I'm* angry," MacDuff said harshly as he straightened. "I don't like what happened here last night, and I don't like it that Jane was showcased as a part of it. And the minute I saw how that bastard used that blood, I thought about you. Hell, yes, I know you're no vampire wannabe, but I also know you have that bizarre talent of controlling the blood flow of anyone near you. With a result that can be either healing...or fatal."

"Then I'd hardly need a knife to cut that guard's throat, would I?" Caleb asked mockingly. "Why be angry with me?"

"Because Jane told me that several years ago your sister Maria was killed by some weird cult that was trying to duplicate that talent you possess in such abundance. They thought it might be an inherited talent and drained her of her blood. Jane said that you went on the hunt for the members of that cult and destroyed them." His eyes were narrowed on Caleb's face. "And I'm wondering if they were all destroyed. I was thinking that perhaps someone who knew about your relationship with Jane might have thought putting pressure on her would be a way of getting to you. What do you think?"

"I doubt it." Caleb added harshly, "For Pete's sake, do you think I haven't been monitoring that cult to make certain it never becomes active again? I have another sister, Lisa, who could be targeted. There's no way I'd let anyone get near her. There's been no sign of those snakes raising their heads again."

"Doubt?" MacDuff repeated. "But you're not sure?"

"No, dammit, I'm *not* sure," he said fiercely. His eyes went back to the photo on the wall. "I'm not sure of anything right now. But it's not likely, and I'll make sure. However, I think we should look in another direction. It's much more likely that Lisa would be targeted than Jane if that was the purpose. After all, Lisa is a descendant of the Ridondo family. That's why they chose to kidnap Maria. They evidently thought I might be too much of a challenge." His lips twisted. "So think of another motive. Providing that you didn't just bring me to your palatial estate to accuse me of killing your old retainer. I don't believe that was your sole motivation."

"I didn't accuse you, I was just questioning. It seemed a logical supposition. I'm still thinking about it. I admit I'm relieved that Lisa is more likely to be a victim of those ghouls than Jane." He gestured at the photo. "But that's a clear threat. I *won't* have anything happen to Jane. I thought you might feel the same way." He paused. "Unless your relationship has definitely faded into the horizon. She told me several months ago that she wasn't seeing you any longer."

"Did she?" Caleb's voice was noncommittal. "I admit she's having a few problems with me. But situations have a way of changing, don't they? I drop in on her occasionally to remind her of that." He turned away from the photograph. "And this situation has just had a radical change. It's time I reminded her again." He stared MacDuff in the eye. "Instead of worrying about a cult, we should wonder why that painting was taken. I understand that it had an intimate connection both to Jane and to your family. Did Fiona MacDuff really look exactly like her?"

"Yes." His brows rose. "You've never seen it?"

"No. Jane has always been a little wary and had a tendency not to permit me too close to that part of her life. Though she did make the attempt at one time." He smiled wryly. "So I can hardly blame her if I scared her off. But I admit I did want to see it. I called your agent last year and told him if the painting ever went on sale, I'd meet any price."

"You wanted to own it?"

"It was Jane." He shrugged. "Everything about her...interests me. Yes, I wanted to own it."

And not only the painting, MacDuff thought. Caleb's voice was cool, but the intensity in his expression was electrifying. "Past tense?"

"No, not past tense. When I get it back from those thieves for you, maybe you'll be so grateful that you'll be willing to sell it to me." He gave one more glance at the photo over his shoulder as he headed down the hall toward the front entrance. "I'll let you know about the cult. Keep me informed if you get any other information from the police. You won't have to worry about Jane. I'll take care of her."

"I talked to her only this morning. Hadn't you better ask me where she is?"

"No, I know where Jane is," Caleb said. "I always know where she is."

The front door slammed behind him.

———◆———

Caleb was pulling out his phone and dialing his sister, Lisa Ridondo, the minute he got in his Range Rover.

He'd be lucky if she answered him, he thought. And if she did, she'd probably only do it to make him suffer. Well, let her get her pound of flesh. She deserved it. He'd been ignoring her calls and messages for the last few months and she'd been totally bewildered. She'd gone from not understanding, to hurt, to anger, to bitterness, and then back again. There wasn't the slightest doubt she thought she'd been treated abominably.

And she was right, he thought wearily. And this conversation might not ease the pain he'd caused, nor the pain he'd felt himself.

Providing she even answered his call.

She picked up the call on the next ring. "You son of a bitch." Her voice was shaking with anger. "What were you trying to do to me?"

"I told you that I would have to take steps if you didn't make me that promise. It was necessary."

"The *hell* it was. You cut me off. You've always been there for me. You're my *brother*. Ever since I was a little kid, I always knew if I reached out you'd be there. You taught me everything I needed to know. Whatever went wrong, you'd make it right. Then you just...left me."

"And now I've taught you the final lesson," he said softly. "That it doesn't go two ways. I could tell that you were going to try to step in and follow in my footsteps and practice a little control of your own. That wasn't acceptable, Lisa."

She was silent. "It is if I say it is. I'm not a child any longer, Caleb."

"No, you're a willful, intelligent, beautiful young woman who causes me no end of trouble. Do you think I liked not being able to contact you? I hoped that we might come to an understanding."

"Because you knew how much it would hurt me when you did this."

"Yes, you weren't listening."

"And you had to get your own way."

"That was definitely high on the agenda."

She was silent. "I *hated* you."

"I don't doubt it."

"You hurt me."

"Yes. I knew I would."

"All you had to do was just let me help you a little. You never let me give you anything. It's not as if I do that kind of thing all the time. Would that have been so bad?"

"Extraordinarily bad. Because you like Jane very much, and you've told her you consider her your good friend. You would have been outraged if anyone had tried to do that to you."

"Maybe not."

"Lisa."

"How do you know?" she said defiantly. "You haven't seen me in almost a year. Of course, that wouldn't have mattered if you'd just contacted me, dammit."

"It mattered. But it's not as if I didn't know what you were doing. You were down in the Caribbean working with Margaret Douglas at Summer Island. Did you enjoy yourself?"

"Yes. It was interesting working with the dogs." She was silent. "Okay, I might have felt guilty about Jane." She rushed on, "But I might not. Because I do like her very much, but I love you, Caleb. It could have been worth it."

"Past tense?

"Unless I change my mind."

"Not good enough."

"I promise," she said grudgingly. "And that hurt, because I'm definitely the injured party here. I would never have done anything like that to you, Caleb."

"No, because I am the son of a bitch you called me when you picked up my call," he said wearily. "You're lucky I haven't hurt you before this."

"Bullshit. You'd never really hurt me. I was just angry." She added quickly, "But don't do it again."

"I'll certainly try to restrain myself," he said mockingly. "Now tell me if you've done anything that would intrigue me since you've been with Margaret. Met anyone new or interesting?"

"No."

"Any side trips?"

"Jamaica."

"Why?"

"Because I'd never been." She paused. "Why are you asking me questions? You're never one for chitchat."

"But I've been without your chitchat for too long. Perhaps I missed it."

"Perhaps," she said slowly. "And why did you call me out of the blue when you let me go for weeks without a word?"

"Same answer." Time to end the conversation. Lisa was getting too curious. "But I'll be happier when you're not island-hopping in the Caribbean. I'd prefer you to stay closer to me."

"Then you'll have to prove it by picking up the telephone or reaching out to me. You can't have it all ways, Caleb."

"I can try." He chuckled. "I did miss you, Lisa. Think about abandoning the puppies at that clinic and coming to see me. I'll call you next week."

"You'd better."

"Count on it." He pressed DISCONNECT.

It was the truth. He had missed her terribly. But he would never have made the move to call her until he was sure she'd had enough time to realize that he had meant what he said. Lisa was emotional, passionate, and usually sure she knew what was best for everyone. It had been too dangerous to take a chance when she'd focused on Jane. He hadn't been absolutely certain that this wasn't still too soon. But he'd had to check on what she was doing and if there was anyone suspect in her life right now. Plus add a few words that might lure her back where he could keep an eye on her.

He was relieved that everything appeared to be safe and entirely normal where she was located right now with Margaret Douglas.

Lisa was very smart, and he'd made certain she could protect herself if a threat presented itself. He'd taught her that she might never be completely secure after her sister had been murdered, but he'd decided there had been no need to frighten her by telling her about a possibility that might have nothing to do with the monsters who had killed Maria. Yet he'd felt as if he had to cross every *t* after MacDuff had been so obsessed about the blood.

The blood.

Not that Caleb wasn't obsessed; the blood had been both his heritage and his curse all his life. It had defined who he was and what he could be. But he wouldn't allow it to dominate him . . . or anyone he cared about.

So think, get moving. For the time being forget about the blood and go down another direction, as he'd recommended to MacDuff.

He drove out of the courtyard and headed south toward Wales.

———◆———

KENDRICK CASTLE

"I'm ready." Michael grinned at Jane as he tore into the tent and turned around in front of her. "All clean and spiffy so that Mom won't think you're letting me get away with anything while she's gone."

"And early." Jane glanced at her watch. "We have another forty-five minutes before we're supposed to meet your mom and dad at that tearoom. I'm impressed."

"Well, the guys got bored down at the dig, so I thought I'd come back up here and hang out with you." He plopped down on his bed-roll. "So could you tell me why Caleb wouldn't like to dig for those Roman artifacts with us? He likes doing cool stuff like that."

Caleb, again. She'd hoped the past hours with his friends would have distracted him. But evidently he'd only taken a deep breath and gone straight back to Caleb. "Because Caleb comes from a very old family who lived in northern Italy many centuries ago. It was a small village called Fiero, but the family was pretty interesting themselves." She added dryly, "However, I doubt if Caleb would think the ancient Romans had anything to teach his family or him."

"Why not?" Michael's gaze was narrowed on her face. Then he snapped his fingers, immediately jumping to a conclusion. "That neat blood thing he can do?" He continued eagerly, "Could they all do it? Was it like having the same color eyes?"

She should have known that she couldn't just hint vaguely at anything with Michael. He had gone exactly where she didn't want him to go. Okay, be honest, but back up and try to get out of it. "A little bit like that. But it wasn't every member of the family and eventually it was only passed down very infrequently." She smiled. "Satisfied? Now can we talk about something besides Caleb?"

Michael was studying her. "Why don't you ever want to talk about him, Jane?" he asked quietly. "He used to be around a lot when I came to visit. I think you're like Mom and Dad and not telling me everything because you think it might worry me. Why would it worry me? I like Caleb." He paused. "And I think it's really important that you tell me about him. You said he wasn't perfect, but he doesn't have to be. I think maybe being perfect would be boring. He's just...Caleb."

She stared at him in shock. Of course Michael had noticed everything about the cautious way he was treated by her and the rest of the family. She supposed she should be grateful he hadn't zeroed in on her evasions and half-truths before this. How the hell was she supposed to handle this confrontation? "Well, he's not boring. But as you already know, he's a bit unusual. Why is it this important to you to know any more?"

"I'm not sure, but it is, Jane." His brown eyes were fixed intently on her face. "And usually when I feel like this, there turns out to be a reason."

And how was she to know what that reason was when everything about Michael had always seemed to be a mystery in itself? All she could do was play this one by ear. "Okay." She dropped down on the campstool beside his bedroll. "You're clearly fascinated by Seth Caleb, so I'll give you his entire story as far as I know it. Though I'm not sure that anyone really knows everything about Caleb. He never talks about himself. What I've learned was through his sister, Lisa." Her lips twisted. "And if you think perfection is boring, I guarantee that neither Caleb nor any of his family tree was ever boring. So sit back and I'll tell you what I know about him. Then you decide for yourself." Was she doing the right thing? He was a kid. No, he was Michael. Just obey her instincts and hope for the best.

"Before the Ridondos settled in Fiero, they lived in Spain at the compound of the Devanez family. The members of the family were known to have had various psychic talents, like Caleb, that made them very unpopular with their neighbors. So unpopular that they had to flee from Spain to keep from being turned over to the Inquisition for witchcraft. But even after the Ridondo branch moved to Italy, they decided that in order to survive they had to protect themselves from informers to the church by terrifying all the villagers into silence. Two of the brothers Ridondo decided to do that by using their so-called blood arts to make them seem to be demons of darkness. It was easy for them since all they had to do was concentrate on the death-and-pain side of the gift, and not the healing." She glanced at Michael to see how he was taking all this. No fear. He only appeared totally fascinated. "And Caleb said that maybe they came close to becoming demons in the beginning. The power of the blood talent might have been too much for them to resist. But they must have gotten sick of all that blood and terror after a while, and they moved from Fiero Village into a castle in the country. Time passed, new generations came on the scene, the Ridondos became wealthy and respectable, the blood talent became something to hide. Simple enough, because the talent appeared only rarely in family members as time went by. But of course that blood taint couldn't be entirely erased. Rumors occasionally surfaced from their old home in the village about the dark past of the Ridondos and their reign of terror. Foolish, exaggerated stories about wizards and vampires and that power that had terrified those villagers for decades."

"Silly," Michael said, disgusted. "They should have known it was only a really cool talent. Bad or good, that was all it was."

"Well, that wasn't the popular opinion even among family members," Jane said. "There were problems through the years. I don't know exactly what they were. It had something to do with the fact that it seemed the physical blood talent was often accompanied by a mental ability to twist and alter the truth, change opinions and perceptions. Evidently that could be even more difficult to accept for anyone in the family who didn't possess it themselves. After a while any child who was born with the blood talent was considered an outcast, a monster to be shunned by the family. Caleb himself was forced to change his name when his parents sent him away to be raised by his uncle in Scotland. He was only a few years older than you at the time." She added quietly, "Not everybody in the Ridondo family thought it was as cool as you do, Michael."

"Stupid." His brow wrinkled in a frown. "So they thought Caleb was some kind of a monster? You know he isn't. Anyone can see that."

"Can they?" She glanced at him. "I just told you a story about his family that was rather terrible in some ways. I wasn't sure I should give you all those details. I didn't want to frighten you." She paused. "Do you believe there are monsters out there, Michael?"

"I know there are monsters." His voice was sober as his gaze shifted to look out the door. "I *know* it. Maybe not like wizards or vampires, but people who are real, real bad inside. That's why there have to be people who can fight them. And I know that Caleb isn't a monster. So maybe he has to be one of the others . . . someone who can kind of . . . balance things."

"You have a good deal of faith in him." She smiled faintly. "I guarantee that Caleb would laugh if he heard you describe him like that. More of a dragon-fighting knight than a monster?"

He nodded. "But you don't think he's a monster, either."

"No, of course I don't. Not for a minute. He's just... unusual and definitely marches to his own drummer. But then I've seen how often he goes to hospitals to help heal patients when no one else can do it." She grimaced. "Not that he'd ever let anyone know if he could help it."

"And that makes you angry. You seem to be angry with him most of the time." His gaze shifted back to her. "Why?"

"Personal reasons that I have no intention of discussing with you," she said firmly. "There's such a thing as allowing people to maintain their privacy. I gave you what you wanted from me today, now drop it."

"Okay." He was smiling mischievously at her. "I'll figure it out."

She was afraid he would, but she hoped it wouldn't be for another few years. "But, truth or fantasy, all this talk about Caleb's family has nothing to do with you. I only told you what you wanted to know about Caleb because it always seemed you wanted to find out everything concerning him. The only important thing you have to remember is that Caleb regards you as his friend."

"I know he does, Jane." His smile faded as he added absently, "But maybe that's not the *most* important thing."

"It's all we're going to discuss at the moment," she said firmly as she stood up and pulled him to his feet. "It's time we left to go meet your mom and dad. Stop frowning, you know we're going to have a fantastic time."

"I was just thinking..." There was a sudden bounce in his step as he moved quickly toward the door. "Of course we are. Being with Mom and Dad always makes everything wonderful..."

CHAPTER

2

C ome with us," Eve Duncan urged Jane after they'd finished tea. "You're not making sense." She slipped her arm affectionately around Jane's waist as she walked with her through the lobby to where Joe and Michael were waiting in the parking lot. "I fully agree with Michael that there's no earthly reason why you shouldn't just jump in the car and head back to London with us." She made a face. "He said you gave him some story about how you needed to give us time to be with him. Ridiculous."

"No, it isn't," Jane said cheerfully. "You only had two days with him when you visited right after all the smoke and furor settled down in Maldara. You wouldn't let me opt out then, but you have to do it now." Her smile faded. "Look, I adore Michael. But he's a very special child and you've had an almost psychic connection with him since the day he was born. I know what you're doing with the reconstruction of those children in Maldara is necessary, but the separation has been hard on all three of you during these weeks. You need this time alone together."

"We need *you*, too."

"But that's different. I had you to myself all those years before

Michael was born." She added softly, "Wonderful, wonderful years. It's Michael's turn now."

"You always did think you had to take care of everyone in the family." Eve sighed and shook her head as she gazed at Jane's expression. "You're not going to change your mind?"

"It's only one day. I'll see you at my apartment at noon tomorrow. Maybe we'll go to the zoo or something. Then Monday morning, Michael and I will take you to the airport and come back here to the castle and do some more digging. It will work out fine."

"Stubborn." Eve wrinkled her nose. "I don't know why you won't—"

Jane's phone rang, and she glanced at the ID. "Lisa Ridondo." She frowned. "That's weird. I haven't talked to her for months. There might be a problem. If you don't mind, I'll take this and tell her I'll call her back."

Eve nodded. "Go ahead, talk to her. I'll wait." She grinned. "From what I remember about Lisa, she was always unique, but very interesting." Her smile faded. "And absolutely adored her brother, Caleb." She dropped down in a chair in the lobby of the tearoom and waved her hand. "Take your time."

"Thanks." Jane was already turning away and accessing the call. "Lisa? I haven't heard from you for a while. How are you doing?"

"Well enough," Lisa said. "It took you long enough to answer the phone. I was feeling a bit rejected." She added ruefully, "Of course, I could be getting a little paranoid. Caleb has been tutoring me on how actions reap consequences. I was afraid I was getting the same treatment from you."

"I don't know what on earth you mean." Jane hesitated, then added, "And it's not likely that Caleb and I would get together on any course of action. I'm sure he told you that we're not seeing each other any longer."

"He did." She added fiercely, "I thought you were incredibly stupid. What woman wouldn't want Caleb? He's fantastic."

"Then he'll have no trouble finding someone less stupid than me to agree with you. But no one can say you're unbiased, can they? Did you want anything else, Lisa? Eve is waiting for me to get off the phone."

"Eve? Tell her I said hi. She's very cool."

"She likes you, too. But the word she used was 'unique.'"

Lisa chuckled. "She's right. I'm glad she appreciates that. What are you doing with Eve?"

"Having tea at Kendrick Castle in Wales. Michael and I are at a dig while Eve and Joe are in Africa. They have to go back there on Monday, but we're having a great time while they're here."

"Then everything is okay with you?"

"Of course. As I said, we're having a great time." She paused. "Why did you phone, Lisa? Something gone wrong in your world? May I help?"

"No." Silence. "And now you're making me feel guilty. I was just mulling over something Caleb said and thought I'd phone and tell you that I really do like you and I only thought it was for the best." She added defiantly, "And it might have been. But I'm sorry if you might think it wasn't exactly what I should have done." She let out her breath in a sigh of relief. "And now I've got that out and I'll hang up."

"What?" Jane was trying to decipher the pieces of the bewildering statement. "I have no idea what you meant by all that. Would you care to explain?"

"No, not particularly." Lisa suddenly laughed. "I got the satisfaction of offering an apology without being heaped with blame. I feel better. And I'm still pissed off at you about Caleb, so I don't really want you to feel better. I figure we're through here." She hesitated. "After you tell me if everything seems well with Caleb?"

"I wouldn't know. It sounds as if you might." But she couldn't leave it with that if this bewildering call from Lisa had anything to do with Caleb. He was Lisa's entire world. "I'm sure he's fine. I've never seen a time when Caleb wasn't fine and in complete control of everything around him. I'm certain you haven't, either." She turned back toward Eve. "I have to go now, Lisa. If there's anything I can do for you, let me know."

"I will. I'm working on it." Her voice was cheerful again. "Goodbye, Jane." She cut the connection.

"Sorry, Eve." Jane slipped her phone in her pocket. "It didn't seem to be anything important." She frowned. "Or maybe it was. Sometimes it's hard to interpret Lisa. I believe there was an apology involved somewhere along the way, and I have no idea why she would feel it necessary." She shook her head wryly. "For such a brilliant woman, she can be very convoluted."

"Woman," Eve repeated and shook her head. "I always remember her as the teenager whose life you saved all those years ago. It's difficult to think of her as a grown-up."

"Sometimes it's difficult for her, too," Jane said dryly. "And it's not as if she wasn't there to help me later when I was in trouble. I would have died in that desert if Lisa hadn't stepped in. Tit for tat. I definitely considered the score even by the time she took off and decided to go climb some mountain in Chile."

"Maybe not quite so even," Eve said quietly. "As I recall, your trouble all had to do with Caleb, and Lisa would have done anything for him regardless of whether you were involved. Has that changed?"

She shook her head. "He's everything to her. She skips all around the world learning skills and getting involved in all kinds of causes, but they always keep in touch." She frowned as she suddenly remembered Lisa's last question about Caleb. "I'm sure that wouldn't have changed. They take care of each other."

"Relationships do change." Eve glanced away from her. "Michael told me that Caleb didn't come down to the dig a few weeks ago as you said he would."

"Once everything quieted down in Maldara and you told me

there was no longer a threat, he wasn't needed. So I called and told Caleb not to come." She stared Eve in the eye. "I didn't lie to you. I know you feel safer about Michael when he's with Caleb. Who wouldn't? Caleb is fairly fantastic as far as the protective factor is concerned. He's the Hunter, the man every agency and organization tries to hire when they come up with zeros. I would have brought him here if it was necessary."

"I know you would," Eve said. "But you were relieved not to have to do it, weren't you?" She answered herself. "Of course you were. Caleb can be very . . . difficult. But he's also completely charismatic. You've always had a love-hate relationship with him." She hesitated. "You've been in and out of each other's lives for years. Lately I thought that there was something very . . . strong. I admit I believed that you had a chance of working it out. It must have taken a lot for you to give him his walking papers."

"You might say that." Even though Caleb sometimes pretended as if their breakup had never happened, Jane thought wearily. "But I assure you that he took it very well. When I told him I wasn't going to see him again, that it wasn't working for me, he didn't even try to argue with me. He just smiled and said he understood and would give me a little time."

"And did he?"

"Yes. I saw him very seldom after that, and never alone. Though he'd occasionally drop in at one of my gallery exhibits." But she'd always been aware that he was somewhere out there, waiting. And the nights after he'd found a reason to see her, as he had at that gallery exhibit, she'd lie in bed burning, aching, remembering what it had been like to have him in her body. She could feel that burning now just at the memory. Lord, she didn't really want to talk about Caleb right now, but this was Eve and she wouldn't shut her out of anything. Eve wouldn't have mentioned Caleb if she hadn't been concerned about her. "I admit he has a tendency to drive me crazy," she said lightly. "Let's just say we don't want the same things in life. The sex was great, he's super intelligent, he's amusing, but I was never sure how he actually felt about me. He certainly never told me, he never mentioned anything beyond what we were together in that moment. No future, very little past, just the present." She shrugged. "I always felt as if I were caught in a whirlpool and I never knew where it was going to take me. Or where he wanted it to take me. And being around him was so intense on so many levels, it got so that I wasn't certain if I really cared what he felt for me." Her lips suddenly tightened. "But I *do* care. I've seen what you and Joe have. I can't live with the way Caleb makes me—" She broke off and then said, "It's just better if we keep distance between us." She smiled. "And it isn't usually hard to do. My work keeps me very busy. And some government agency or mega corporation is always begging Caleb to go on the hunt for some scumbag no one else can bring down. So don't worry about me." They'd reached the car, and she smiled at Joe as he turned toward them. "Sorry I kept Eve. I had to take a call." She gave him a hug and a kiss before he got in the driver's seat. "Bye, Joe. Enjoy your evening." She glanced teasingly at Michael in the backseat. "If you can manage to do it. Michael's been saying that he'll have no trouble beating you at chess now that he's had all that practice every evening with me."

"I'll manage to survive." Joe grinned. "If I have trouble, I'll just start teaching him the Chinese board game Go. That should keep his ego in check."

"Go?" Michael leaned eagerly forward, his arms draped on the back of the front seat. "I've heard it's super complicated. Why don't we start out with that one?"

Jane groaned as she reached over and gave Michael a hug. "I don't know if I'm up to a complicated Chinese entry into our game nights. Go back to chess, Joe."

"Too late," Michael said with satisfaction. "Either come with us or you're toast for the next week or so."

"Well, you seem to be cheerful enough about it," Jane said. Come to think of it, he had perked up and been cheerful for the few hours they'd been at the tearoom, she thought. "I detest blackmail. I believe I'll leave your chastening up to your dad." She tilted her head and asked softly, "Everything okay, Michael?"

He nodded. "It's going to be all right now." He smiled slyly. "Until we come back and I start beating you at Go."

"Brat." She kissed the top of his head and took a step back. "I'll see you all tomorrow."

She stood watching them drive out of the parking lot and then up the road.

It had been a lovely tea and she had been with the people she loved on a great sunny day. What could be better? Except for that rather weird call from Lisa, there had been nothing disturbing since she'd walked into this charming tearoom. But even that call had not been so much disturbing as confusing. And Michael had evidently jettisoned that peculiar mood that he'd been in since the moment she'd opened her eyes this morning. That was important as well. Now to get back to the castle and start working on those sketches that she'd told Michael she was going to do for Lady Kendrick.

She got into her car, backed out of the parking spot, and headed back toward the castle a few miles down the road.

And screeched to a stop just before she reached the castle gates.

Dammit!

Seth Caleb got out of his silver Range Rover, parked on the side of the road opposite the front gates, and strolled across the road toward her. "You look wonderful," he said quietly. "I always liked you in teal. It sets fire to your hair. That's a nice little tearoom up the road. I assume you've been having tea with Eve and Joe?"

"Yes, I have." Caleb was wearing black jeans and a casual navy-colored shirt, and he looked just the same as the last time she'd seen him. Of course he did, she thought impatiently as she braced herself. It hadn't been more than a few months since he'd dropped into the gallery for her last showing. And the moment he'd entered the door, she'd been aware of him. How could she help it? She was always aware of him. During the months they had been lovers, he'd somehow tuned her every physical and mental response to know him, *need* him. And even though he'd deliberately stayed in the background that day, he'd attracted his usual attention from the other art patrons. But then he was always high-impact and totally magnetic. The strand of dark hair falling over his forehead, the slight brush of silver at his temples, the full sensuous lips, and just the hint of an indentation in his chin. Still, it was more the high intensity that seemed to burn inside him that caught and held attention. She could feel that intensity now . . . Her hands clenched on the steering wheel. "What the hell are you doing here, Caleb?"

"I've come for a visit." He smiled as he strolled around her car and leaned to look in the driver's window at her. "You promised me one a few weeks ago and then reneged. That wasn't fair, Jane. I was disappointed."

"I told you it was no longer necessary." He was too close. She could feel the heat his body was emitting. And that clean, smoky spice scent that always clung to him was drifting to her. "I sent you an email thanking you for agreeing to help, but things worked out very well for Michael without you. We didn't need you."

"Oh, I understood that. But emails can be so cold." He added solemnly, "Though I did appreciate that you added the thanks. That made it a little warmer." He opened the car door for her. "But I was looking forward to seeing Michael again. It's been a long time since you had him in London for a visit. After thinking about it, I decided I wasn't willing to give that up."

"That wasn't your choice to make." She didn't get out of the car. "And Michael is on his way to London right now with Eve and Joe. If you really want to see him, perhaps we can arrange another time and place."

"But not if you have your way," he said softly. "Right, Jane?"

She met his eyes. "Not if I have my way. I've said what I wanted to say. And I don't believe you missed Michael that much, Caleb."

"You should." He grinned. "I'm telling the truth. Just not all the truth." He took her hand and pulled her out of the car. "But that's going to change right now. Come for a drive with me and I'll tell you why I'm not going to let you send me away this time."

She hadn't wanted him to touch her. She could feel the pulse in her wrist pounding. "I don't want to go for a drive with you."

"But you'd like it less if I drove into the castle campgrounds and forced a discussion there. That's your territory, where you feel safe. You don't want me invading it."

Lord, that was true. "I don't have to have either," she said coolly as she tried to jerk her wrist away from him. "Back off, Caleb."

"Yes, you do. Pick and choose." He added coaxingly, "Because Michael will be disappointed when he calls me back later and I have to tell him that you tossed me out and you're alone here. He wouldn't understand."

"What?" Her eyes widened. "I'm the one who doesn't understand. Why should he call you?"

"He didn't want you to be alone. And he wanted to be sure everything would work out to his satisfaction. Haven't you found that Michael can be very thorough?"

"Yes," she said absently. Then the anger sparked as she thought she understood. "None of this makes sense. Did you call him, Caleb?"

"I really like the boy, and I wouldn't involve him in our business unless I was forced." His hand tightened on her wrist. "But then I might use any means necessary. However, that time hasn't come. I was surprised when Michael called me a couple of hours ago and asked me to come and keep you company this evening. He appeared to be quite determined about it."

Her jaw went slack. She could tell he was telling the truth. No wonder Michael had been so serene when he'd said goodbye.

"Sometimes Michael gets an idea in his head and just won't let go. You should have told him that you couldn't do it."

"But I *could* do it. Why would I lie to him? I was almost here by that time anyway." He gestured to the Range Rover. "Give me twenty minutes to let me talk you into keeping my promise to Michael. Then I'll bring you back and I can tell him I did my best. Because he *will* call and check, Jane."

"I know he will," she said grimly. "And I want to talk to him when he does." She hesitated. This was the last thing she wanted to do, but it was only twenty minutes, and Caleb always kept his word. *Get it over with.* She strode over to the Range Rover. "Twenty minutes. But it's a waste of time. I don't know why he's so concerned about me being alone today. It's not as if I'm not accustomed to it."

"I don't know why, either." He closed her door and then went around to the driver's seat. "But we both know that the boy is a little fey, and I'd just as soon not go against him in this. I didn't argue with him."

"Well, you should have. And he's not fey. I always think of an elf living in a hollow tree when I hear that word. Michael just has certain strong...instincts."

"Very strong. And closer to the psychic category than instinct." He held up his hand as she opened her lips to speak. "I know you like to hide his talents under a bushel. It's safer for him. But when I'm with you, I'll use any word I choose. I'm not insulting him. On the contrary, I consider him a brother. We share both a gift and the risk of being ousted because of it at any given moment."

"Michael would never have to worry about being ousted by anybody."

"Yes, he would, if he didn't have his family to protect him." Caleb's tone was matter-of-fact. "Then he'd be on his own."

As Caleb had been alone when he was growing up with parents who didn't understand either his gifts or that he wasn't a monster just because he was different. Lisa had been furious when she'd told

Jane about that time, but when Caleb did it was without a hint of self-pity. Still, it hurt Jane to think of it.

"Look at you." He was gazing quizzically at her. "Have I depressed you? The chances of your Michael having to face anything like that are practically infinitesimal considering everyone he has in his corner." He added lightly, "And if you all fall by the wayside, I'll swoop down and teach him all he needs to know about surviving. The two of us would do fine together."

Yes, they would. She had seen the love and care he'd given his sister Lisa when she was in need. Caleb could be ruthless, but he could also display an incredible understanding when you were forced to face tremendous odds.

And now she was remembering all the things she had learned about him that were good and splendid and completely sympathetic. Not about the manipulations, the dominance, the times she had felt more like an erotic harem girl than an independent woman. Not about that swirling whirlpool that never let her get really close to him.

Stop it. Push it away. It would be far too easy to let her slip back into that sensuous haze. "That wouldn't happen. I have no intention of falling by the wayside. Michael will definitely be okay." She added grimly, "As long as we all can keep him from trying to run our lives." She looked at her watch. "You now have fifteen minutes. Start talking, Caleb."

"Pressure. Pressure." He pulled over to the side of the road. Then he turned off the car and reached for his phone. "But the pressure is genuine and so should be the reason for letting me stay and take care of you tonight." He dialed up a photo, enlarged it, and handed the phone to Jane. "This was the picture I received early this morning from MacDuff together with a short message. I was on the road to his place three minutes later."

"MacDuff?" She slowly took the phone and gazed down at the photo. At first, she couldn't understand what she was looking at.

Then her gaze narrowed on the photograph in the center of the bloody wall.

She inhaled sharply. "What the hell is it?"

"You." He paused. "Blood."

Her gaze flew to his face. "And MacDuff's message?"

His words came fast and brief. "The painting of Fiona MacDuff was stolen. A guard was murdered and his blood used to form the cross. Your photo was substituted for the painting."

She felt a chill. "Incredible."

"Not incredible. It happened," Caleb said curtly. "And it told its own message."

She was trying to think through the shock. "But perhaps not necessarily aimed at me just because of the photo. It all happened at MacDuff's Run. MacDuff's estate. MacDuff's portrait of one of his ancestresses. The guard was an employee of MacDuff's. I don't really have anything to do with MacDuff's Run. MacDuff is just my friend. All this madness really could be focused solely on MacDuff. We should be worrying about him."

"And how are you going to explain the photo?" Caleb said. "Or the fact that it was dripping blood?"

"I'll have to think about that." She tried to smile but found her lips were shaking. "It does seem macabre."

"A threat," he corrected. "Ask MacDuff. He didn't think the threat was toward him. It was clear he was concerned about you. The first comment he made when I went into the gallery was about what an expert I am in blood. The next was about the cult that killed my sister. And I was the first one he called when he saw your photo in his gallery. He was definitely making a connection between the blood and you . . . and me."

She stared at him, shocked. "But he *knows* you. He wouldn't think you'd hurt me."

"Wouldn't he?" His eyes were glittering in his taut face. "I don't think he would, but what do I know?" He was smiling recklessly.

"A choice between someone he knows and respects, who helped him retrieve a family treasure? And a weird freak whom everybody knows might do anything to anyone if he takes the notion."

"He's smart. He'd know better. So stop accusing him."

"Because he's your friend."

"Yes, and because you're being idiotic. You're in a nasty mood."

"That I am." Then he shook his head and made a face. "It's been a bad day for me. I didn't like seeing that damn photo. It shook me."

"Nothing shakes you." She paused. "But I don't like it, either. Why would MacDuff think that the cult would have anything to do with it?"

"He's jumping at conclusions and hoping to hit it right." His lips twisted. "If he hadn't put me on the defensive, I would have done the same thing. But he had the advantage of having me standing there in front of him, and you'd already told him about the cult. The connection was irresistible. He could probably smell the blood."

"I told him because he was my friend. I wanted him to get to know you, to reach out to you. You never talk to anyone about yourself." She made an impatient gesture. "And now you've put *me* on the defensive. Could the cult actually have anything to do with all this?"

"I don't think so. I had a list of all the cult members responsible for selling my sister to Kevin Jelak, that psycho who murdered her. I was very careful about hunting every one of them down. I assure you it was none of the members in the main cult," he said grimly. "And I've had the village of Fiero monitored by my people ever since to make sure there weren't any new players on the horizon. But you can bet I'm going to find out."

"Kevin Jelak," she repeated slowly. "I haven't thought of that name for years. The first time I met you was at the lake cottage when you were hunting for him. I was sorry for you that you'd lost your sister, but I had no idea what a horror he would be to my own family. He almost killed Joe." Her gaze flew to his face. "But Jelak could have nothing to do with this, right? Eve told me she'd seen you kill him."

"Jelak is dead," he said flatly. "Whoever is responsible for what happened at MacDuff's Run, it's not Jelak. And Eve gave me no problem about it. She was too glad to have Joe back."

"That photo." She moistened her lips. "If it *was* the cult, would MacDuff have been right about why they put it there?" She looked at him. "Because it was some kind of weird message to you?"

"I don't know why else." He made a face. "I'm the obvious connection. I'm always the obvious connection. I'm used to it. But there's no proof yet that a cult had anything to do with the theft. Maybe someone just knew how much MacDuff loved that painting and wants to ransom it back to him. So stop worrying about it."

"I'm not worrying about it. I just think that I have to find out. I need to know if it's me or MacDuff who is the target." She grimaced. "*Then* I'll worry about it."

He was silent. "Shit." Then he suddenly chuckled. "I'd suggest you start worrying a little ahead of that. Let's make it a team effort of finding out who the target is and combine it with keeping you alive."

"Whatever." She was frowning thoughtfully. "But I think I have to go to MacDuff's Run and see that photo on the wall."

"And MacDuff and I both want you to stay away from it. That's why MacDuff didn't tell you about the theft when he called you. A man died last night. As far as we know, the estate might still be watched."

"And why would they do that? They've got what they want. You sound paranoid."

"I'm not certain they did get what they wanted. Not with that damn bloody cross that would draw anyone to look and see your photo right in the middle of it. Not with taking the portrait that looks just like you. It's more like an invitation." He drew a deep breath as he saw her expression. "You're going to go to see it, aren't you?"

"It's not real to me." She shook her head. "I have to talk to MacDuff. I need to *see* it."

He was silent. "Okay," he finally said. "You want to go? Then I'll take you." He started the car. "Right now."

"Now?" She was gazing at him, startled.

"No better time. Why not? If I don't show you what you want to see, then you'll find a way to go without me."

"Exactly. There's no reason for you to come along. You're not involved in this, Caleb."

"I couldn't be more involved." He shrugged and said wryly, "After all, I'm the major suspect."

"That's totally ridiculous." She added, "And if it wasn't, that would be another reason why I shouldn't let you go with me."

"But you said it's ridiculous, which means you trust me not to indulge in mayhem on the way." He leaned toward her. "Look, you're going to fight letting me spend the night on the castle grounds as Michael wanted me to do." His lip turned up at the corner. "He even generously offered to lend me his sleeping bag so that I could share your tent."

"What?"

He started to laugh. "You can see why I wouldn't give up easily, and you'd be very upset by the time you found a way to toss me out. So instead, let me take you to MacDuff's Run and you'll get something accomplished that you do want to do. You can talk to MacDuff and look at that damn bloody cross." His smile ebbed as he added grimly, "And let anyone on watch get a good look at you and show them you came when you were summoned."

She thought about it. "It's not a bad idea. Except that it's already almost five in the afternoon."

"But you're tempted." His eyes were narrowed on her face. "Now, what can I do to seal the deal..." He thought for an instant, then said, "I'll call and have a helicopter waiting at the private airport about twenty minutes from here. That would almost assure you that we'd arrive at MacDuff's Run by sundown. Then, after you're satisfied, I'll fly you to London to be with your family. You'll probably not get there before midnight, but it will make them happy that you're going to be there earlier than expected. Michael said that you were planning on arriving at noon tomorrow."

"Michael evidently managed to confide quite a bit about my plans," she said dryly. "How much did he contribute and how much did you ask?"

"It was about even this time, as all conversations tend to be." He paused. "I admit it's not always like that. He's an excellent source and I have to know what you're doing."

"You *used* him?"

He shook his head. "Michael knows that we have problems. But he likes me and he believes that I can take care of you. He's amazingly protective for a youngster. That appears to outweigh his respect for your privacy."

"Well, it doesn't outweigh mine. How long have you been 'chatting' with him?"

"Whenever it was necessary or whenever I wanted to touch base with my friend." He met her eyes. "Or whenever I felt as if I needed to have someone tell me what you were saying and doing, so that I'd feel closer to you."

She couldn't breathe. She couldn't look away from him. She could feel her heart begin to pound again. She couldn't tell whether it was from sheer sexual readying or if he was making the effort to create that sensation. She knew the slightest adjustment of her blood flow could do that, too. "Don't do this to me, Caleb. Or I'll make you pull over to the side of the road and let me out."

"O ye of little faith," he said softly. "It's not me, it's you. I admit I have a tendency to fall from grace on occasion. It's natural, since I've had this passion for you for much too long to claim it's anything but an obsession. But you can't blame me for everything, Jane."

"Yes, I can." But she couldn't blame him for her own weakness; she could only try to stay away from him until she could banish it. "And you and Michael shouldn't have had this . . . this . . . collusion."

"You're changing the subject. Are you going to let me take you to MacDuff's Run?" he asked. "Suppose I throw in the offer that I'll be incredibly nonthreatening until I hand you over to Eve?" His lips quirked at the corners. "But I won't make the same offer if I have to take Michael's place in your tent."

"For someone who didn't want me to go to the Run, you're being very proactive about it."

"I don't want you going there without me." He took out his phone. "The helicopter?"

So much for staying away from him, she thought wearily. But since she was being forced to face this bewildering and frightening puzzle, she would have to deal with it any way she could. Who knew? It might actually prove to be a way to cut down the contact with Caleb as much as possible after she let him have his way in this.

Which seemed totally illogical. Everyone knew going cold turkey was always best.

Screw it. She'd do what she could. She needed to go to MacDuff's Run. She turned away from him and looked straight ahead. "The helicopter."

<hr />

MACDUFF'S RUN

The setting sun was casting silver-blue lights over the crashing surf as Caleb landed the helicopter in the courtyard of MacDuff's Run.

Beautiful, Jane thought. She'd have to remember to paint that particular view the next time she was here. She'd already painted the castle many times, but there was always something different to discover and beguile her here. She'd grown to love everything about

MacDuff's Run when she'd first visited all those years ago. The place was full of mystique and atmosphere and seemed to breathe of the Highlands and the generations of Scots who had built their castle on this craggy coast.

"Spectacular." Caleb was looking at her expression as he set the helicopter down. "It's no wonder you like to visit here. I hate to think that the memory of last night's murder might mar the thought of it for you."

"It won't." Jane saw MacDuff coming across the courtyard and opened her door. "I first came here because I was tracking the history of Cira, who created the dynasty of the MacDuff family. But I learned a good deal more by the time I left. This place has seen centuries of battles and death and mayhem. It's all woven into the fabric of what it is. You just have to accept it, avenge it, and start all over again." She jumped out of the helicopter. "Memories should be kept alive only if they're happy or they teach you something."

"Oh, I agree." Caleb grinned. "I just didn't think you'd be quite so willing to embrace that philosophy. You're usually a bit more gentle. Perhaps you *are* Fiona's descendant."

She shook her head adamantly. "Don't get MacDuff started on that." She was walking toward MacDuff as she spoke. "Eve and Joe are all I'll ever need." But she was smiling at MacDuff, and the next moment he was enveloping her in a warm hug. "You should have told me about this, MacDuff," she said when she broke free. "It might be weird and scary as hell, but I had a right to know."

"Not weird enough to keep you away from here," he said dryly. "I thought Caleb might have the sense not to tell you about it. I gave him too much credit."

"I wanted to see it," Jane said soberly. "It's crazy, MacDuff. Why would anyone . . ." She trailed off. "But we'll have to find that out." She turned and headed for the front door. "No one was able to identify the people who did this?"

He shook his head. "Two sets of footprints and the treads of a van in the dirt outside the gate. We're checking out the rest. Inspector Tovarth said the theft was very well planned, the timing impeccable, very professional, so he's researching similar thefts worldwide. He's also looking into the possibility of bribery to the staff. Though I told him that's hardly likely with *my* staff." He followed her into the hall. "But no one appears to have seen the thieves, and there's no hint of the real reason why the *Fiona* was taken and not one of the two Sargents in my collection."

"Except that they wanted you to believe it had something to do with me." She smiled. "And you promptly attacked Caleb."

"He survived it." He shrugged. "Caleb always survives. It seemed a possible direction. That blood was . . . disturbing."

"And so am I," Caleb said as he caught up with them at the door of the gallery. "Understandable that you made the connection. No hard feelings. Well, maybe a few . . . " He looked at Jane. "Ready?"

"That's why I'm here." She braced herself and entered the gallery.

The blood on the wall was darker than it had seemed in the picture on Caleb's phone. It was dry now and not dripping around the photo in the center of the cross. Caleb had told her this photo wasn't the original one he'd shown her in the car. The knowledge should have made it appear less horrific, but somehow it didn't. Neither did the blood spattered on the wall. It only reminded her of one of those Rorschach inkblots that were supposed to reveal the personality of the observer. She said it out loud. "Rorschach inkblots."

Caleb nodded. "Maybe. Only an artist would have seen that possibility. But then what's he trying to say about your personality? Or his own?"

She shook her head. "I've no idea. It just occurred to me. He stole Fiona's portrait. She looks like me. Maybe he thought I was trying to steal her thunder." She glanced at MacDuff. "Do you have any disgruntled relations running around who might have thought they should have a portion of your august heritage?"

"Not to my knowledge. Until recently all my kith and kin were running the other way because of the taxes on the estate." MacDuff grimaced. "Just as you were, Jane."

"Not because of the taxes," Jane said. "Because I already have a family I love. And anyone with a right to this place would be crazy not to want it." She added softly, "It's a magical place, MacDuff."

"I think so," he said teasingly. "But it's good to hear you admit it at last. You've been very snooty about your precious American upbringing. And they say we Scots can be arrogant."

"And so you are." Jane took a closer look at the photo. "But I don't think this photo was taken here in Scotland." She was frowning. "I recognize that lake . . . I think I did a sketch of it last year."

"Where?" MacDuff asked.

"Italy. The lake country. I spent several months there."

And someone else had spent time in that beautiful countryside at the same time, she thought as cold iced through her. Someone with a camera, watching her, aiming, shooting that photo. How close had that murderer been to her? Had he been planning on how he was going to layer that blood onto the photo—

"Stop thinking about it." Caleb's hand was on her arm. "Don't worry. We'll track him down and find out who took it. You stayed in Mantua, didn't you?"

"Yes." Of course Caleb knew that. Michael had probably told him, she thought with exasperation. "But I wouldn't bet on us finding out who took it. Everyone has a camera these days. It's the world of the iPhone."

"I will bet on it," he said. "Because it's also the world of databases and a zillion high-tech methods to find the answers." He added grimly, "As well as a few more ancient methods guaranteed to extract information. I'll get on it right away."

"It's good to see you so eager," MacDuff said silkily. "I wonder why? It's positively inspirational."

"Enough," Caleb said. He turned to Jane. "He just wants to remind you that my family home of Fiero has been located in that section of Italy for centuries. In case you'd forgotten that my sister was kidnapped from Fiero by the cult."

"I hadn't forgotten." Jane glanced at MacDuff. "Caleb and I talked about it before I came here. I'd never forget a tragedy like that. But Caleb had nothing to do with it, just as he has nothing to do with what happened here last night. So back off, MacDuff."

"Such loyalty." MacDuff tilted his head. "I've heard you can be very persuasive, Caleb. But I felt I should bring it to Jane's attention that sometimes coincidences are not coincidences." He took Jane's hand and smiled down at her. "And let her know I'm keeping my eye on you."

"I don't need you to do that." She pulled her hand away. "I don't know why you'd even think I did. He saved Eve's life when she was pregnant with Michael. He even helped when we were searching for Cira's treasure. There's no way he'd hurt me."

"Drop it, Jane," Caleb said quietly. "He's only exploring possibilities. He realizes sometimes people change or react differently to situations." He shrugged. "Or have the skill to fool individuals who are gullible enough to permit it. I believe he's putting me in the latter category."

"I'm not putting you anywhere, Caleb. I'm just being cautious with someone I care about." MacDuff turned back to Jane. "And since you've chosen not to see him recently, it occurred to me you must have also found something about him that made you uneasy. As Inspector Tovarth told me earlier, he even manages to make the agents at MI6 take a step back." He changed the subject. "Are you going to stay the night? Have you had dinner?"

"Only tea." Her gaze was fixed once more on the blood. "I'm not hungry." She moved her shoulders, trying to shake off the chill. "And Caleb's taking me to London tonight to drop me off at my apartment. I'm going to spend some time with Eve and Joe before they go back to Maldara."

"I'm glad. Seeing Eve is always good for you." His eyes followed

Jane's to the photograph. "And you need to forget this ugliness for a little while. We're working on it. I have Scotland Yard and Interpol following up." He glanced at Caleb. "And perhaps *he* might even come through for you. We'll have to see."

"Yes, we will." Caleb's smile was tiger-bright as he headed for the door. "I'll wait for you at the copter, Jane."

"Were you *trying* to irritate him, MacDuff?" She shook her head as Caleb disappeared out the front door. "That wasn't smart. He was very close to exploding."

"But he didn't do it," MacDuff said cheerfully. "I regard that as an excellent sign. I imagine he was holding on to his temper to please you. Most of the time I've noticed he doesn't give a damn." He held up his thumb and forefinger. "He's just this close to being a savage, you know."

"Wrong." She could feel the anger spark as she started down the steps. "And I wish you wouldn't speak of something you know nothing about. How can you expect Caleb to be anything but what you always expect of him? All his life, he's been told that everyone would be afraid or hate him because he had that blood talent that ran in the Ridondo family. It's incredible he's managed to turn out as normal and civilized as he has." She could see Caleb waiting by the helicopter, legs parted, staring at them with mockery and defiance as they started crossing the courtyard. Then he turned on his heel and headed for the cockpit. "Though I don't know why I'm arguing," she said curtly. "He'd probably agree with you."

"Perhaps because somehow he's made you feel he's a victim?"

"Never." Her eyes were blazing. "Lisa said he wasn't a victim even when he was a child being punished by his parents because they considered him a monster. He fought them and came out on top. I just don't want anyone else to be unfair to him."

"Then I'll be certain to treat him gently." MacDuff's eyes were twinkling. "However, it might bewilder him." He stopped as they reached the helicopter and he opened the door for her. "Have a good time with Eve and Joe. I'll let you know if I find out anything about *Fiona*." He looked at Caleb. "Take care of her." He slammed the door and took a step back. The next moment he was striding back toward the house.

"Well, I have my orders," Caleb said as he reached out to switch on the helicopter. "Naturally, I'll humbly obey. One must not irritate the earl at any cost. It would be—" His phone rang and he glanced down at the ID. "Michael." He pressed ACCESS. "You wanted to talk to him. Go ahead and do it. He wants reassurance that all is well with his plans for you. I'm not in the mood to reassure anyone of anything at the moment."

"I can see that." She took the phone from him. "Hello, Michael. I'm *very* upset with you. I had my own agenda set up for today and you had no right to interfere by calling Caleb. I told you that you don't try to control the world to suit yourself. People have lives and wishes of their own."

Silence. "You're mad at me."

"Of course I am."

"But you're still going to let him stay with you tonight? You shouldn't not do that just because you're mad at me."

"No, he's not going to stay with me," she said curtly. "We're not even at the encampment right now. So much for your fine, convoluted strategies. We're just leaving MacDuff's Run."

"No," Michael said sharply. "Caleb shouldn't have taken you there. I didn't want that. I thought that he'd stay with you at the dig."

"Well, things don't always turn out the way you want them to, Michael. People have the right to make their own choices. That's what I've been trying to tell you."

"I know. I'm sorry you're angry with me. I thought it would be better if you—"

"Listen to me. What part of this aren't you getting? It's my choice."

"I'll remember." He added quickly, "But you said you're leaving

MacDuff's Run right now? Where are you going? How are you getting there?"

"That's my business, Michael."

"Please, Jane."

She probably shouldn't indulge him, but he sounded troubled, and what he'd done was because he'd been concerned about her. It wouldn't hurt to put his mind at rest. "Caleb rented a helicopter and we're flying straight to London. It seemed more convenient than going back to the castle. Caleb's dropping me off, and I should be at the apartment a little after midnight." She paused before adding sarcastically, "I hope that meets with your approval."

"Yes." His voice sounded abstracted. "And you're leaving now?"

"As soon as I get off this call." She should just hang up, but she couldn't say goodbye to Michael in anger even when she wanted to shake him. "Have you had a good time with your mom and dad today?"

"Yes, we just got back from dinner and I came back to my room to call Caleb. We're going to play Go. That should be fun."

"Don't be too sure. Your dad never lets you win. You have to earn it. It's always a teaching lesson. That's how you learn what's important."

"Like you're trying to teach me now?" Michael asked. "But sometimes it gets confusing for me. I'm never sure what's more important. This time I thought having Caleb there with you was more important. But I'm sorry if I made you mad."

"Just remember next time. Bye, Michael. I'll probably see you for breakfast in the morning."

"Yeah." His voice was suddenly thoughtful. "What should I tell Mom and Dad about why you're coming here tonight instead of tomorrow? They'll want to know if there's a problem." He suddenly chuckled. "Besides me."

"Yes, besides you." But she wasn't sure what she wanted him to tell Eve and Joe about what had happened here at MacDuff's

Run. She certainly didn't want to discuss that ugliness with Michael. Hell, considering how weird he'd been all day about her going to MacDuff's Run, she wasn't sure that he hadn't already been getting vibes about it. "Just tell them I decided to come early. But not to stay up to wait for me."

"Okay. I'll just tell them the truth. That you missed us."

Evidently he thought that her explanation needed embroidering to be acceptable. Well, it was the truth. And she'd decide what else she wanted to say to them later. "I did miss you." She added, "But I'd miss you more if I didn't have to worry about keeping you in line."

"I'll remember. I didn't mean to—" He broke off. Then his voice was suddenly rushed, urgent, as he continued, "You should leave there now. Right *now*. Goodbye, Jane. Tell Caleb I'll call him."

He cut the connection.

She handed Caleb his phone. "We have his permission to leave. He said he'd call you. I hope you'll reinforce what I said to him. I don't think my lecture did any good."

He was starting the rotors. "I'm sure we'll talk about it."

"How noncommittal can you get? You'll do exactly what you want to do." She added in frustration, "Which is also what Michael will probably do."

He smiled faintly. "But you have a chance that you'll get what you want. Because, in our own individual ways, we both want to make you happy."

Before she could answer, all sound was drowned as the helicopter lifted off.

◆

"Can we leave now?" Davron asked, his eyes fixed nervously on Luca as he lowered the binoculars from his eyes. "They're taking off now and we shouldn't even be here. What if someone sees us? We should have left the property after we stole the painting instead of hiding up here in these hills. I don't know what you were thinking."

"That this is exactly where we should be," Luca said coldly. He knew it was only because Davron was frightened that he'd dared to question him. But he was beginning to annoy him, and he wasn't sure that he might not be better off ridding himself of the fool. He'd brought him into his plans because he had the contacts and security background to make the thefts easy to pull off. But the first stage of his plan had now been accomplished, and he doubted if the squeamish bastard had the balls to be of any value as he moved on. "And I'm thinking that I wanted to see her and how she'd interact with Caleb. What do you think I've been waiting for all day? I wanted to see *her*."

And Luca *had* seen her, watched the way she moved, the way she smiled, the way both MacDuff and Caleb reacted to her, the vibrant vitality that was so like the woman in the portrait in the back of the truck. And even though that interaction had been more with MacDuff than Caleb, he was still satisfied. He'd been uneasy for the last weeks. He hadn't wanted to admit even to himself that all his plans could crash down around him if the situation wasn't what he'd believed it to be.

But he felt better now. Because he'd seen Seth Caleb's face when he'd stalked out of that house and gone back to the helicopter. He'd studied him long enough to know that he seldom let his emotions show, but the anger and passion in his expression as he'd left Jane MacGuire only a few minutes ago had been a revelation.

"Was it what you wanted?" Davron asked. "It played out just as you said it would. It brought her here right away and Caleb actually went to get her to make sure of it. That must mean he thought she was valuable. So do you think we can use her?"

Luca didn't speak as he watched the helicopter lift and bear north over the cliffs. He was mentally replaying that moment when he'd seen Caleb stride across the courtyard, every step generating that bold electricity that was his trademark. And then the tight, shuttered look on his face that had still revealed so much as he'd watched Jane MacGuire coming toward him with MacDuff. "Oh, yes, Davron," he said as he carefully put his binoculars away. "I believe we can definitely use her."

CHAPTER

3

J ane waited until they'd gained altitude and turned south toward London before she spoke again, "MacDuff was upset. He didn't really mean that he thought you were guilty of doing anything that was—"

"Yes, he did," Caleb interrupted. "He might not have believed it was true, but he thought it was worth running up the flagpole and seeing if he could stir up a little trouble." He glanced sideways at her and smiled mockingly. "And he got a very defensive response from you. I was quite touched, if a bit surprised." He gave a half shrug. "I admit he did manage to push a few buttons with me I'd forgotten were there. MacDuff is very good."

"He didn't have to do that." She was still irritated with MacDuff, but she wanted to forget about those buttons that must have been excruciatingly painful if there was still lingering pain after all these years. "You actually think that you can find out about that photo?"

He nodded. "I'll get to work on it after I drop you off. I'll start with calling Dimak Palik, my info agent, and get him busy on the Mantua connection." He smiled faintly. "Why don't you curl up and try to nap? You've had a rough day, too. It will be a little over three hours to get to the heliport and then another forty minutes to take a taxi to your apartment. As promised, I'll fly you straight to London and not take any interesting side trips." He paused. "But you might spend a few minutes trying to decide if you're going to tell Eve about our visit to MacDuff's Run. It could have...ramifications."

Yes, it could, and she didn't want Eve to have to worry about her when she was back working in Maldara. Eve had enough problems dealing with the politics of a country that had recently gone through a horrendous civil war while still completing the forensic sculpting she'd promised to do there. On the other hand, Jane hated the idea of not telling her the whole truth about anything. Honesty was important. Either way, she would have to make a decision before she arrived in London. She leaned back and closed her eyes. "I have a little time. I'll think about it..."

———◆———

Four hours later Caleb was punching the button of the elevator at her apartment house. "What did you decide?" he asked. "Yes or no."

"No. Unless Michael has already told them I was at MacDuff's Run, I guess I'll just let them assume that I came straight from the dig." She made a face. "But that's still almost a lie. I hate to lie."

"I know you do." He was gently nudging her down the hall toward her apartment. "And this time I'd almost rather that you did tell them. I'm going to have to go to Italy for at least a few days. I like the idea of Joe Quinn staying here and keeping an eye on you when I'm not around."

"It doesn't matter what you like or don't like. I'd appreciate it if you can tell me about that photo, but I can take care of myself, Caleb. Joe made sure of that from the time he and Eve adopted me." She looked straight ahead as she unlocked her door. "And I've done just fine without you for these last months."

"Have you?" His voice was thick, dark, sensuous. "I haven't done fine without you, Jane. I *need* you." His fingers were suddenly touching the hair at her nape, rubbing, caressing the sensitive area. "Don't go in there. Come with me. I can make you need me, too."

Melting heat. Tingling electricity. She couldn't *breathe*. Don't look at him. She had to get away from him.

No, stand your ground. She couldn't keep running away. She couldn't let him do this to her. "I'm sure you could, if I let you." She kept her voice steady. Then she deliberately turned to face him. "Sex is terrific and you know all the tricks, Caleb. It's really not fair that the talent you have lets you also manipulate the mind and imagination. You can make me pretty dizzy." She moistened her lips. "But it's not enough for me. I tried it before and I need more than you can give."

She saw a flicker on his face that might have been hurt. Then it was gone and he was smiling mockingly. "No, you don't." His voice was soft, his dark eyes glittering. "You haven't even touched what I can give you yet. Because I never used anything connected to that talent from the moment you came to my bed. I made you a promise I wouldn't go down that road and I kept it. I was actually trying to be what you call normal, but I guess I couldn't pull it off." His fingers were touching her throat and the skin was burning, her breasts tautening. "Do you feel that? I can make every part of your body come more alive than you've ever known." He reached out and touched her nipple. She inhaled sharply. "Feel the throbbing? Feel the heat? Feel the flow? You gave up on me too soon. Isn't this enough to content you until I find a way to work this out for us?" He rubbed back and forth over her breast, his fingers delicately plucking.

The heat...

The swelling...

The muscles of her stomach were clenching...

Her entire body was pulsing...

The sensation was incredible, and she instinctively moved catlike against him.

"See?" he whispered. "We can do this, Jane. What we had before was only a beginning. Maybe I handled it wrong. I'll take you in another direction. Just give me a chance. I can make it happen."

He probably could, she thought dazedly. Her body was ready for him after only these short seconds. But how would she feel afterward? Caught in that same whirlpool of feeling she'd fled all those months ago?

She wouldn't know, because she couldn't let it happen. She took a deep breath. Then she pushed him away and took a step back. She was shaking, she couldn't get her breath. "Go away, Caleb." She was fumbling to open the door. "You're wrong. We're wrong for each other. How could I trust you when I don't even know who you are? It's too late."

"The hell it is." His eyes were narrowed, his lips tight. "Okay." He drew a deep breath. "Get the hell inside before I change my mind. I don't want to blow it. Everything's crazy right now. I knew I'd have to take a step back until we could find out what was happening at MacDuff's Run, but it's only a step back. Just realize I'm not letting you go." He turned away. "I'll call you tomorrow, Jane." He was striding back down the hall toward the elevator.

She watched him get in the elevator. She was still shaking, and she hoped everyone would be asleep when she went inside the apartment. She didn't need Eve to know how vulnerable she was at this moment.

Maybe not so vulnerable.

She had made Caleb take no for an answer.

When she'd only wanted to say yes . . .

———◆———

"Are you still mad, Jane?" Michael whispered.

She turned over in bed and gazed at him standing in the doorway of her bedroom, silhouetted against the light of the hall. "For heaven's sake, it's one thirty in the morning. I've just gotten to bed, Michael. Did you stay up just to ask me that?"

"Yes." He padded barefoot across the room and plopped down on the foot of her bed. "You said to tell Mom and Dad not to wait up. You didn't say anything about me." He was wearing his blue-and-white-striped pajamas, but he sounded as wide-awake and alert as he had this morning when she'd opened her eyes and found him sitting beside her sleeping bag. "And since you just got to bed, I knew you wouldn't be asleep. I figured it would be okay. I just wanted to make sure you weren't still angry. That way we'd both sleep better."

"I'd sleep better if I knew you weren't going to pull this kind of stuff again," she said dryly.

"I'll try, but it's hard to promise. It just kind of happens when I get worried." He added gravely, "I was worried today, Jane. I wanted to *do* something."

And she couldn't ignore the soberness of his voice. "Why, Michael?"

"I just woke up scared and I didn't know why. I thought something had happened to you, but I saw you were still asleep." He bit his lower lip as he looked down at the sheet. "But it didn't matter, it was still about you. So I started to think about ways to make sure you stayed safe."

"Caleb."

He nodded. "But it didn't work out like I thought. He shouldn't have taken you to that place. It gave me a bad feeling." He raised his head and looked at her. "Did you have a bad feeling when you were there?"

What could she say? She wasn't about to tell him why she'd consented to go to MacDuff's Run. "Yes. But it wasn't because I wasn't safe. I wasn't alone or frightened."

"No, you weren't alone." He was silent a moment. "Someone was *there*."

She inhaled sharply as a chill iced through her. His meaning was unmistakable. "My, how spooky you sound. If there was, he wasn't close enough to make me afraid. And you just had a feeling. It could have been imagination. Right?"

Another silence. "No, he wasn't close."

"And it might have been imagination?" she repeated.

He nodded. "I guess so. But it worried me."

And the fact that he'd sensed someone close, threatening, worried Jane. She wanted to dismiss it from her mind, but she knew Michael too well. Just because it was weird and mysterious didn't mean there wasn't some basis to his words.

"And that means I'm not going to get my promise from you," she said ruefully as she leaned forward and touched his cheek with her fingers. "Then I can't promise not to get angry with you again. You can't keep doing this."

"But you're not mad now?"

How could she be? He was part fey, part boy, all wonder. She'd have to fight every day to maintain any kind of anger against him. "Not at the moment. But don't get cocky. I meant what I said."

"I won't." He jumped to his feet, dived forward, and gave her a bear hug. "I'll try. I really will. Good night, Jane." Then he was running toward the door. "I'll think of something really fun for us to do tomorrow. See you in the morning." He skidded to a stop. "Is Caleb going to be here?"

"No, he has something else to do." She added quickly, "And don't call him after you go to bed."

"I won't." He was frowning thoughtfully. "I think maybe what he has to do is really important stuff... I'll talk to him later."

The door closed behind him.

She settled down more comfortably and pulled the sheets higher. She still felt a little chilled.

Someone was *there*.

———◆———

"Where are you?" Caleb asked Dimak Palik when he answered his call. "Tell me you're not in Russia again."

"I wish I was," Palik said sourly. "I like the Russians. My jobs for them are much simpler than for you, Caleb. Just in and out, gather the information and pick up my cash. With you I need hazard pay."

"You're paid well. I just demand my due." He repeated, "Where are you?"

"Greece." He sighed. "Where am I going?"

"Italy. Mantua. Right away. I'm heading for the airport now. I'll meet you at the San Girano Hotel. It's good you're fairly close. You'll be able to work on getting me what I need before I get there."

"And you'll expect me to have the entire package to give you by the next day."

"Maybe. At least the initial information." He paused. "There is an urgency this time."

"Always." He was silent a moment, and Caleb could almost hear the clicking of his thought processes. "Italy. It's not one of your damn hunts?"

"Not of the usual type."

"None of them are usual," Palik remarked. "You go on hunts for armies, governments, police, personal family vendettas, or just because you've found someone who particularly deserves to be killed. Why is this one different?"

"Jane MacGuire might be involved in the fallout."

"Shit. Who was stupid enough to do that to you?"

"That's what you're going to find out. I'm going to send you a current photo of her taken in Mantua. I need to know when it was taken and who did it. She was probably stalked in the hotel itself, and some of the hotel staff might have noticed her being photographed. If you get even a nibble, check all the security cameras and follow through on it. I need a name. Use bribery or force but get me the answer."

"I'll use bribery. I'll call you to instigate the force. You're infinitely better at it than I am. Anything else?"

"Fiero Village. Contact the people you've hired to monitor it. I have to know if there's been any change in status."

"Fiero?" Palik gave a low whistle. "I would have been told. You've made that a top priority."

"Just check it. Any change, no matter how small. Is there any problem with my sister's surveillance?"

"You would have known about it if there had been. I received a report two days ago."

"Check it again."

"I'll contact Haverty. But I don't think that—"

"Don't think," Caleb said harshly. "Just get me answers fast. I want to get back here in the next two days."

"You'll have them," Palik said. "And you'll pay handsomely for them. You'll remember that speed is always expensive."

"How could I forget?" he said dryly. "You're always so willing to remind me." He cut the connection.

HEATHROW AIRPORT
LONDON

"It's been a fantastic two days." Eve had to clear her throat as she gave Jane a hug while waiting to follow Joe through security. "But I'm tired of not having you at home. This globe-trotting has got to stop. Georgia does have some beautiful areas for you to paint, too."

"I know. But you're the one who ended up in Africa this time," Jane said. "And it will only be a couple of weeks before you come back through here."

Eve made a face. "And I hope that two weeks won't stretch out any longer. We're going direct from the airport to the royal palace for the inauguration of the interim president, and it might be a day or two before I can get back to work. We'd skip it, but he's a good man trying to keep that country afloat." Eve gave her another hug. "But relationships and families have to be kept afloat, too. Start planning on ways we can do that, and let it start in Atlanta. Think about it. Okay?"

"I always do." She blinked back tears as she watched Eve and Joe start through security. Eve was right: It had been such a good two days that she'd managed to almost forget both Caleb and that visit to MacDuff's Run that had been so unsettling.

Almost.

"I wish they'd been able to stay longer, Jane." Michael's wistful gaze was following her own. "There never seems to be anything to worry about when they're around, does there?"

Jane didn't like the sound of that. Michael had told her he'd been worried and had a bad feeling that night she'd come back to the apartment. The last thing she wanted was to have him feel depressed or anxious during these last two weeks he was under her care. She was having enough problems keeping her own attitude positive. "That's because they're your mom and dad. That's how you're supposed to feel. But now we're on our own again, and we'll get along fine." She smiled down at him. "Ready to go? We probably won't get back to the castle before dark. Want to stop and get a bite to eat?"

Michael shook his head. "No, I'm not hungry." His gaze was still on Eve. "She was right, you know. We should all be together. Particularly now." He turned away and started walking toward the exit. He was silent until they began crossing the parking lot. "It will be good to get back to the castle. I like the idea of searching for treasure." He frowned. "I know it wouldn't really be our treasure, but we'd be the ones who found it. Like the way you discovered Lord MacDuff's family treasure and saved his family fortune at Loch Gaelkar. That was very cool. Mom said that he might have lost his estate except for you."

"MacDuff is smart; he would have found another way to save it. And it wasn't only me. It was a joint effort. Just the way it is for all the volunteers at Kendrick Castle."

He didn't get in the car but stood there, gazing at her. "You said Caleb was one of those people who helped MacDuff at Loch Gaelkar where you found Cira's treasure. He probably did a real good job, didn't he?" He added gravely, "I bet he could help Lady Kendrick, too."

Caleb again. That was another clear hint that she should invite him to the dig. Patience. Everything always seemed to lead to Caleb where Michael was concerned. However, verbally attacking him would only upset the boy. Maybe she could get her brother to look at Caleb a little more objectively. "Caleb usually does a very good job. But he's not perfect, Michael. Believe me, he'd be the first to admit that." She paused. "What do you like so much about him?"

Michael was silent, and for a moment she was unsure if he would answer. Then he finally said, "He *sees* me, Jane."

She looked at him in bewilderment. "Sees you?"

Michael was gazing straight ahead as he nodded. "From the first time you brought him to meet me, I knew he could see me. And he never pretended he couldn't, not once. Everyone else pretends because they know Mom and Dad like them to do it. But Caleb never has and it makes me feel . . . good inside."

She stared at him in shock. His words had come out of nowhere, and she wasn't sure that she knew what he was talking about. But she had an idea that she might, and it was scaring her. Because how the hell was she supposed to handle it? Yet she knew this could be the most important conversation she'd ever have with him. She couldn't blow it. "What are you talking about, Michael?"

"Sometimes I know things other people don't know," he said simply. His gaze shifted back to her, his amber eyes clear and steady and his expression grave. "And you *see* me, too, Jane. You always have, but you do pretend. Because you love Mom and Dad and you know they're more comfortable if you do. They believe they're keeping me safe by doing it, and maybe they are." He smiled. "So I pretend, too. After all, most of the time it doesn't really matter."

"I think you're wrong." She had to swallow to ease her tight throat. "I believe it must matter. Because why else are you talking to me like this in the middle of the airport parking lot? This is a very weird conversation. Either you're serious and trying to get through to me about something really important to you or this is a very bad joke." She paused. "But it's not a joke, is it?" She gestured for him to get into the car. "So let's discuss it and get it out in the open." She went around the car and got into the driver's seat. She braced herself for an instant before she turned to face him. "Okay, talk to me. Why did this come up now?"

"Because I think it's time." He stared directly in her eyes. "I got scared the other day and I couldn't *talk* to you. And lots of times you don't really answer me when I ask you questions. You leave stuff out because you're afraid I'll worry." He moistened his lips. "That was the way it was that day you went to see Lord MacDuff. I could *feel* it. Everything was all mixed up. I knew you wouldn't listen to me. And you wouldn't tell me things I needed to know." His expression was troubled. "And I was afraid it might happen again and keep on happening. So I decided that I couldn't let it."

She was staring helplessly at him. Those words had tumbled out, stunning her. She tried to think, but her mind was a jumble. "And what am I supposed to say to that? You're a kid. You still have rules and lessons to learn, and right now I'm in charge of you. If I don't explain everything in triplicate, it's because I want to protect you." She drew a deep breath as she realized how lame that sounded. Because everything he'd said had struck a chord, and she'd realized it was only the tip of the iceberg. She supposed she'd always known this time would come. She'd gotten a hint of it when he'd spoken so frankly to her about Caleb the other day. Time now to be honest and confront it. She tried to smile. "Okay, so you've got a lot of psychic stuff going on in that brain of yours that I've tried to ignore. Because I guess I don't know how to handle it, and it's not really my responsibility; it's Eve's and Joe's. Only now you're making it my responsibility." She shook her head. "So what do we do about it?"

"Gee, how do I know?" Michael's expression was suddenly no longer sober. His eyes were twinkling, his face was alight with laughter. "I'm just a kid."

She scowled at him. "Don't joke. I want to shake you, brat." But that moment of mischievous humor had made her feel less helpless and bewildered. This was still Michael whom she loved and needed to protect and guide. That would always be fixed and firm in her life. Providing he needed either of those services from her, she thought ruefully.

Of course, he did. They just had to find the right way to broach this new era in their relationship. She said brusquely, "Okay, then we'll work it out somehow. I just want to be clear that I'll still be the one running things. Just like I was before."

He nodded solemnly. "Right. Just like you were before."

She gazed at him suspiciously. "If you grin, I'm going to take you back in the airport and put you on that plane with your mom and dad."

"No, you won't." He was grinning broadly now. "That's a bluff. You'd be worried about all those jungles and the wild animals."

"I believe I could make the adjustment."

"No need," he said gently. "I'm just teasing. I don't want to cause you any trouble. Like you said, I'm a kid and I don't know all the answers. Everything's going to be just the same as far as I'm concerned. I just need you to listen to me when I'm worried about you. Please don't close me out." He shook his head as he added jerkily, "Because sometimes that gets pretty lonely, Jane."

She could see that it would. That last comment had almost broken her heart. This very special child trying to make his way in a world where he couldn't admit that he was different or face being ostracized. In a way, it must be a little like what Caleb had gone through growing up. "I promise I won't close you out." She reached out and gently touched his cheek. "And you'll have to tell me if you ever feel lonely around me. I might forget and you might have to remind me, but that will never be my intention. I'll do my best not to let it happen."

He cleared his throat. "Yeah, I know." He grabbed her hand and squeezed it hard. "Well, I guess we've got that settled," he said gruffly. He released her hand and fastened his seat belt. "That didn't go so bad, did it?"

He sounded as awkward as Jane felt. That conversation had been super difficult for both of them. "It depends on how you look at it. Not bad, just disturbing. You'll have to take it easy on me until I have more time to recover." She was feeling almost shell-shocked by both the new aspects of their relationship, and the promise she had made to him. She had an idea that she would constantly be questioning how to balance that promise with remembering Michael was a child, and that his childhood must never be ruined because of how very special he was. She could fully understand Eve's and Joe's dilemma. Even now she was questioning the wisdom of what she had just promised him. Oh, well, all she could do was use her instincts. But she did need time to absorb and assimilate.

"It's going to be okay, Jane." Michael was gazing gravely at her face. "We can get through this together."

Affection, understanding, reassurance, and that strange wisdom that had been with him from the moment of his birth were all there in his expression.

She felt a rush of love as she slowly nodded. "Yeah, no problem. We're a great team." *The balance*, she reminded herself. *Remember to strike the balance.* She changed the subject. "Now, did you learn enough about that game Go from Joe to be able to teach me when we get back to the castle?"

It was fully dark by the time they were approaching Kendrick Castle, but Jane could see the lights of the tent encampment on the hills surrounding it gleaming up ahead.

Her phone was ringing. Caleb.

She hesitated, glancing at Michael, who had been curled up asleep on the seat next to her for the last half hour. She didn't want the ring to wake him. This trip had been a little exhausting and emotional for both of them. Besides, it didn't matter whether she answered the call or not. Michael would find out a way to contact Caleb when he wanted to anyway. She pressed ACCESS. "Hello, Caleb."

"Were you disappointed I didn't call you yesterday as I promised?" he asked mockingly. "I decided to spare you the decision of whether or not to take the call."

"How kind of you."

"Sarcasm? Besides, I was too busy anyway. I left for Mantua that same night. I just arrived back in London a few minutes ago. But I wanted to call and make certain you'd reached the encampment safely. Are you there yet?"

"No, the castle's right ahead." But she couldn't resist asking the question: "Mantua? You went there yourself? Did you find out anything about the photo?"

"Not enough. But we're on our way. Palik's been acting like a whirling dervish scouring the entire town for the photographer who took it. It's good that you're beautiful and attract a good deal of attention. The staff of the hotel and the waiters at nearby restaurants had no trouble remembering you. They just had to be prodded a little to remember the people around you and anyone who seemed particularly interested. Particularly one who was taking photos. Palik finally found one he thought was a likely candidate."

"Who?"

"You made a lot of sketches while you were sitting on the

fourth-floor balcony lounge overlooking the lake. There was a man who was there almost every day that you were. He never sat at a table close to you, but he was *there*. He was always at a table half-way across the balcony reading his newspaper. Late thirties, fair hair, swarthy complexion. Muscular, well built."

She was trying frantically to remember anyone of that description. But when she was sketching, she was always almost totally absorbed. "Are you sure?"

"Oh, yes, because the waiter who waited on him also noticed he had his phone out on the table all the time he was reading his paper. He would occasionally seem to take a shot of the lake, which was coincidentally in your direction. The security cameras got several shots of him during those days. I'm going to send you one now to see if you can identify him."

She could hear the ping as she received the photo. She quickly accessed it. The description was exactly as Caleb had said, but he hadn't mentioned that the man's features were classically good looking or that those dark eyes were cold and the expression on that swarthy face totally unrevealing. He was wearing an elegant dark suit that was impeccably tailored. "I don't remember ever seeing him. He's good looking so I suppose I should have noticed him. He looks...like a banker...or an executive. And he seems...cold."

"It would take someone very cold to cut a man's throat just to use his blood to decorate your picture."

She shivered. "It doesn't make sense. Do we have a name? Can you find out who he is?"

"Palik is looking into it. The man wasn't staying at your hotel. We're checking other hotels in the vicinity because his stalking of you was over a period of several days. He paid his bar tab in cash and tipped his waiter well. The only other things we know are that he's obviously well dressed, soft-spoken, and tries not to be noticed."

"Several days," she repeated numbly. "Not just one day to get the photo. Why? And why wouldn't I notice him?"

"Why would you expect that you were being followed if he was that unobtrusive." He paused. "And everyone who was questioned about you said that you seemed intoxicated by the town and totally absorbed in your work. I admit I was a bit jealous. I wanted to show you Mantua. It's one of my favorite towns. It can be an Arabian Nights city." Before she could reply, he went on brusquely, "And it was clear that he wanted to establish more than a one-night stand with you. He was watching you, thinking about you, savoring the connection."

Savoring. The word made her feel dirty. She looked down at his photograph again. She could see the surface coldness—yet perhaps that wasn't the correct word. There was also an intensity, a total absorption, as he'd stared at her. "How can I find him?"

"I've already sent the photo to MacDuff to give to his Inspector Tovarth to process through the Yard and Interpol. With Palik and them both working on it, we should have answers soon. I'll get back to you as soon as I can."

"Thank you," she said stiltedly. "I'd appreciate you doing that, Caleb."

"For God's sake, Jane. Do you think I won't—" He broke off. "Be as formal as you like, it's not going to keep me away. I'd be on my way down there right now except I'm waiting for Palik to get back to me with an answer on another question I asked him to follow up on. I thought I'd have it by now. He's been damnably slow."

"Don't come. I told you I don't want you here at the castle."

"You might have had a chance of me listening if I hadn't just spent almost two days tracking a son of a bitch who's been following you around like a hungry hyena." His voice roughened. "You don't have any chance at all now until I bring the bastard down."

"The hell I don't. I can take care of myself. Joe was a SEAL, remember? He taught me from the time he and Eve took me into their home. I don't want you here, Caleb. The gates of the castle are right ahead of me. I'm going to drive through them and go to my tent. If you show up anywhere on the grounds, I'll tell Lady Kendrick you're harassing me. She's a strong woman, and she won't tolerate that crap." She put on her brakes as she came down the hill toward the gates. "You can't have everything your own way. How many times do I have to—"

Her windshield splintered!

Screech—

What on earth was happening?

Then she realized exactly what had happened as another bullet plowed into the top of the seat next to her!

Dear God, that bullet had been so close to Michael...

"Down, Michael!" she shouted as she fought his seat belt and tried to jerk him lower on the seat. He was waking up, but she was scared to death he would straighten and become a target because he still didn't realize what was happening. "Keep down!"

Another shot!

Piercing the back door.

The castle gates were straight ahead. She honked her horn to get someone to open them for her.

No one was there.

A bullet hit her left back tire, sending the car skidding sideways!

"Jane..."

Michael was wide-awake now, reaching out as if to help her.

But she was the one who had to help him. He was pinned in place by his seat belt; he couldn't move away from any bullet aimed at him.

And the right front tire had just been blown, sending the car careening directly toward the closed front gates.

She stomped on the brakes as hard as she could, then jerked open her seat belt at the same time that she threw her arms over Michael's body to cover him.

Pain.

"Jane. Wake up." Michael's voice was frantic. "You're bleeding."

He was scared, she realized dimly. She wanted to comfort him, to tell him that she was all right. But she couldn't get the words out...

Darkness.

What the hell had happened?

Caleb punched in the number of the main line of Kendrick Castle again.

No answer. *Son of a bitch*, what was going on? From the moment Jane's phone had gone dead he hadn't been able to reach anyone. Okay, call the local police and see if there was—

His phone was ringing. He glanced down at the ID. It was Michael.

He punched ACCESS. "Are you okay? What happened to you, Michael? Is Jane all right?"

"Hi, Uncle Caleb, I'm okay. I just got a little bump when the airbag went off." His voice was shaking a bit. "But they want to take Jane and me to the hospital because she didn't wake up yet. I told them they'd have to get your permission since my folks appointed you my guardian if anything happened to Jane. I knew you'd want to be there with her...she was bleeding. You know about stuff like that."

"Bleeding," he repeated. *Keep calm. It might not be anything.* "An accident? Is there a doctor there?"

"Not yet. There's only a guy who knows first aid who works for Lady Kendrick at the castle. The ambulance is on the way," Michael said. "But I thought you should talk to Lady Kendrick and let her know what to do. I'm just a kid and she wants to speak to a grown-up. I'm going to hand my phone to her now."

"Lady Alice Kendrick here." The woman who came on the phone was clearly upset, her voice fast and breathless. "I understand from your nephew that you're in charge in case of emergencies while his parents are out of the country. Is that true?"

"Absolutely. How serious are Jane's injuries? I understand she's bleeding? How badly?"

"I believe they told me that it's stopped now. Hopefully that wound wasn't serious. But she might have a concussion. The tire blew and her car crashed into the gate. Naturally, we'll have to have her examined. The police are insisting on it anyway. I have your permission to transport her to hospital?"

"Of course. But don't do anything radical without my permission. I'll be on my way as soon as I hang up. I should be there in no more than two hours."

"Fine. Thank you for your cooperation. We'll take good care of both of them. Such a dreadful thing to have happened. It must have been some hunters trespassing on the estate. I just can't understand it." She took a deep breath. "I believe Michael wishes to speak to you again. Such a brave boy. And so very clever. He stepped right up to help when I was trying to reach someone in authority to help his sister."

"Yes, very clever." Michael had evidently arranged everything about this nightmare to suit himself and what he considered best for Jane. *Uncle* Caleb? He'd even added the family touch. Caleb didn't give a damn. The only thing that mattered to him was that Michael had included him in the scenario he'd constructed. "Thank you, Lady Kendrick. I'll talk to you later."

"You're coming?" Michael asked when he came on the phone. "Right away?"

"As fast as I can get there. Is Jane still unconscious?"

"I think so. She seemed to be moaning a little, but she didn't open her eyes. They've got a kind of brace around her neck that won't let her move."

"Good. That means somebody knows what they're doing. What about you? Nobody seems to be worried about you. But are you certain you're okay?"

"Yes, Jane didn't loosen my seat belt, only her own after that first bullet. She was trying to cover me with her body."

Caleb froze. "Bullet? There were bullets?" He didn't wait for an answer. He'd find out everything that had happened later. Right now he had to stop asking questions and get to her. "Lady Kendrick mentioned police. I thought it was just because of the accident. Listen to me, Michael. I want you to stay close to those policemen until you're at the hospital. And make certain someone is near Jane until that ambulance arrives. Can you do that for me?"

"I thought that would be what you'd want me to do," Michael said quietly. "I told Lady Kendrick I wanted to sit with my sister until I was sure she was all right. Lots of policemen are in there with her. So we'll all be together." His voice lowered to a whisper. "But get here soon, Caleb. They *hurt* her."

"I'm on my way." He cut the connection.

First things first. He dialed the number to arrange for the helicopter service he always used. That took five minutes, and while he was walking toward the terminal he was calling MacDuff so that he could have him find out from Inspector Tovarth what the hell had happened at Kendrick Castle.

But he knew enough to feel the rage within him ignite.

They hurt her.

———◆———

UNIVERSITY HOSPITAL OF WALES
2:40 A.M.

Darkness.
  Her head was throbbing . . .

That was all right, just go deeper. Nothing could happen to her in the darkness.

"No, you don't," Caleb murmured, his hand tightening on her own. "I'm not done with you yet, Jane. No deeper. Stay right where you are. I have a little more repairing to do on you. Then I'll let you wake up."

He didn't understand. That wasn't what she wanted. She needed to let the darkness take her away. The pain would only grow if she woke up.

"I understand. Now don't be a wuss. Do you think I'd let you get away from me that way? You did a little too much damage and no one's paying enough attention to it. I've just got to fix it and then let you wake up and have those doctors compliment themselves on how brilliant they were to just let you regain consciousness on your own instead of doing surgery."

But it wasn't what she wanted. It would take too much effort and pain to do what he wanted. Why wouldn't he listen to her? Caleb never listened to her.

"Shh. I'll listen to you after you wake up. I can't do it now. And I can't let you go deeper. But trust me, you won't care after a minute or two." *Something bright and warm and loving was hovering, coming closer.* "You won't even remember . . ."

CHAPTER

4

Darkness.
  Terror!
  The windshield shattering!
  The bullet had been so close to Michael!
  What if the next one—
"Michael!"

She sat bolt-upright in bed and swung her legs to the floor. She had to get to—

"It's all right, Jane." Caleb was beside her, holding her still, as she leaped from the bed. He muttered a curse beneath his breath. "I had enough trouble getting that Dr. Rabine to let me stay with you. If he thinks I'm causing you to go into convulsions, he'll try to kick me out, and I won't let that happen." His grip tightened as she kept struggling. "So stop causing trouble. I'm fixing everything, dammit."

The words were rough, but she was vaguely aware his hands were gentle and stopped struggling. But how could he fix everything? That bullet had been so close to—

"Michael!"

"Shh. He's fine. He's in the waiting room with one of the

policemen Tovarth sent down when I called MacDuff. But he'll be better when he can come in and see that you're awake." He added dryly, "If a little out of your head. Now will you lie back down and let me take care of you?"

Relief. Caleb wouldn't lie to her. Michael must be safe. And now that the first panic was subsiding, she was beginning to be able to think again and feel a faint stirring of resentment. She looked around the room. Hospital. She must be in a hospital. That's right, Caleb had said something about a doctor and as usual he was trying to maintain total control of the situation...

"I'm not out of my head. I was scared." She pushed him away and then quickly sat back down on the bed as she felt her knees weaken. "You're sure Michael wasn't hurt? They checked him over?"

"The entire ER was waiting on him hand and foot when I got here a few hours ago. If he'd had as much as a hangnail, they would have treated it with loving care. All the nurses wanted to adopt him."

"Of course they did." Michael, the beloved. Michael, who might have died if that bullet had been a few inches closer. "He always has that effect."

"Well, it was in full force last night." He swung her legs back on the bed and drew the sheet over her. "How do you feel?"

She thought about it. "My head aches a little." She reached up and touched the back of her neck. "And I'm a little stiff here. But I'm okay, too." Her gaze flew to his face. "Aren't I?"

"According to the doctor, you suffered a blow to the head that caused a mild concussion, wrenched muscles in your neck, and received a laceration on your left temple. He didn't believe that any of them would prove life threatening." He added grimly, "Though he didn't like the fact that you remained unconscious for the last several hours. Neither did I."

Caleb's displeasure was very obvious and she didn't feel up to dealing with it. "Well, I'm awake now. So that doctor must have been right."

"Better than you deserve," he said with sudden harshness. "You could have broken your neck, besides that concussion that had everyone worrying." He touched a bandage at her temple. "Plus that bloody cut that had Michael panicking and calling me to fix. You should never have unfastened your seat belt. Michael said you threw yourself on him in that last minute."

"What else was I supposed to do?" she asked fiercely. "Dammit, stop yelling at me. I didn't know what was happening. But I did know that when that airbag went off, Michael would be pinned in place like a target for that bastard who was shooting. I couldn't risk the next bullet hitting him. I had to make sure that—"

"I know you did." His arms were suddenly around her, his voice guttural, his lips buried in her throat. "I know you couldn't do anything else. Not you. And as usual I'm screwing everything up. Well, what did you expect? I'm not your kind friend MacDuff, or understanding Joe Quinn, or Trevor, that perfect lover you loved and lost. You'll probably never see any of that in me." He drew a deep breath and then released her. He backed away and dropped down in the chair beside the bed. "You'll have to forgive me. I've had a few bad hours myself since Michael called me." He added mockingly, "And everyone knows I always come first in the scheme of things."

"Maybe not always." She thought she'd seen a flash of genuine pain beneath that mockery. But who could tell with Caleb? She reached up and touched the bandage on her temple. "And evidently you came when Michael called, so you didn't think of yourself then."

"Wrong. I was being totally selfish at that point." He shrugged. "But it's best we don't discuss that at present. I've already upset you enough, and now I have to smother all my more savage instincts and try to behave properly. You're probably confused and frightened and need to know what's been happening."

"That would be an excellent guess," she said. "You might start with why someone was shooting at me." She moistened her lips.

"And Michael. But why would anyone try to shoot a little boy? It had to be at me, didn't it?"

"Presumably. Who knows? We don't know much at present. According to the police who were investigating the shooting, the shots came from the hill across the road from the main gates. There were six shots fired from an automatic rifle. One shattered the windshield when you were approaching the castle, that was probably the one that came closest to hitting you or Michael. The other shots appeared to be aimed at almost random targets, the tires, the roof, the rear door...It was as if the shooter wasn't trying to aim at you personally, it was more to frighten or play with you."

"*Play* with me," she repeated. She felt sick as she remembered those minutes of terror. "Why would anyone do that? And there was a child in my car. You'd have to be insane to endanger a child."

"Yet there are all kinds of insanity present in the world today. Most of it starting with selfishness or power. Perhaps he thought it would add to his excitement...or to your fear."

"It did that." She closed her eyes for an instant as she recalled the stark fear at the thought of Michael dead. When she opened them, she said, "Tell me they found out who would play a sick joke like that. Did they catch the bastard?"

"No, after your car crashed into the gates, the shots stopped. By the time the authorities got up the hill, they found only some shell casings and tire tracks leading down the other side of the hill." He added, "And two sets of footprints in the dirt where the shooting took place. The shooter was being incredibly careless in this day of technology. Picking up the casings would have been the smart thing to do. But he didn't seem to care." He paused. "The entire episode was bizarre. And a little coincidental after what happened at MacDuff's Run." He met her eyes. "No other car or driver was attacked at the castle last night. Just Jane MacGuire. It must have occurred to you that this was a bit odd."

"It might have, if I'd been able to think clearly." But she realized the thought had been hovering phantomlike since she'd regained consciousness. "You'll understand if I'm a little bit behind, Caleb. I'll worry about it later."

"Don't bother." He smiled. "I'll handle it. I had Tovarth send those footprints to the lab to compare them with the ones they found outside the walls at MacDuff's Run. If they match, we'll have something to follow up on. It might not take long at all. Since the bastard is so careless, he'll probably be easy prey."

Prey.

And Caleb was an expert hunter, she thought. But she didn't want that deadly skill to be used because of her. "That's the job for the police. Stay out of it."

"Oh, no," he said softly. "I'm taking this very personal. I brought MacDuff's Inspector Tovarth into this because of convenience, but I won't let him cheat me. You could have died. Michael could have died."

"You said that shooter might have only been playing with me."

"But he still could have killed you. He didn't care. So he's mine, Jane."

"Stop arguing with me," she said wearily. "I won't let you do it. Now be quiet. My head's beginning to ache again and you're being foolish."

He blinked. "Heaven forbid I cause you to have a headache." Then he threw back his head and laughed. "We'll discuss it another time."

"No, we won't. You always say that when all you mean is that you're going to go around and attack from another direction. Will you go get Michael so that I can talk to him and he can see that I'm okay?"

"By all means." He got to his feet. "And I'll waylay the head nurse and make certain she doesn't come in before you're ready for her." He was heading for the door. "But while you're waiting for Michael, you should consider that he might not have been an accidental target." He paused to look back at her as he reached the door. "It could be that they chose to attack you on this trip because they knew you'd have Michael with you. What could have frightened you more? Anyone who knew how much you cared about the boy would realize what his death would mean to you."

She inhaled sharply. "What the *hell* are you saying?"

"I'm saying that you can't count on being sure of anything right now. Someone sat on that balcony in Mantua and studied you for a long time. And I don't believe he'd only concentrate on your wonderful sketches. He wanted to know you." His lips turned up in a crooked smile. "I'm not trying to frighten you, I'm only trying to be very clear. Because I'm not certain we have the time to be anything else. We don't know why or how you might be targeted yet. I could waste time trying to find out, but I'm a simple man who'd prefer to remove the attacker regardless of the reason. So you just think about it and decide whether you actually want to keep me from doing what I do best."

Before she could answer, he was gone.

And Jane was left lying there gazing at the door. He was so reckless, so deadly, so different from her. Yet he was smart and canny and he might be right about Michael also being a target.

And he was the Hunter who would go into action in a heartbeat and any threat would go away. All she had to do was say the word and the nightmare would start.

But once it started, how could she make it end?

———◆———

"Caleb said that you're practically okay now." Michael ran into her hospital room and over to the bed. He stopped and tilted his head, gazing critically at her. "Well, you look better than you did when they brought you in here." He gave her a hug. "But Caleb probably only said that so I wouldn't worry."

She grinned. "But you told me he didn't pretend." She made a weighing motion with her hands. "Lie. Pretend. That comes pretty close, doesn't it?"

"Yeah, but it's different. And you're smiling now and that makes you seem *almost* well."

"And you don't want your buddy to ever be wrong?" Her eyes narrowed on his face. "You weren't hurt?" When he shook his head, she said, "Then we're both doing great. We'll be out of this hospital in no time and be able to go back to work at the castle."

"Yeah." He was silent. "But maybe not without Caleb. Lady Kendrick kind of expects him to be with us from now on."

"What?"

"I didn't want anyone to worry Mom and Dad, so I told Lady Kendrick that Caleb was supposed to be my guardian if anything happened to you."

Her jaw went slack. "Now, that wasn't anywhere near pretense. That was a huge whopper."

"But it made Lady Kendrick feel better, it kept Mom from worrying, and I knew Caleb would be able to take care of you if anything went wrong." His hand tightened on hers. "I was scared, Jane, and there was no one but me around to do stuff. I knew Caleb could help if I got him here."

She melted as she looked at him. "I was scared, too. But I don't believe your fib was quite the way to solve the problem."

"It worked," he said simply. "Anything else would have been too confusing. Caleb said I did good."

"That doesn't surprise me," she said grimly. "Then we'd better have Caleb explain that web of lies to all and sundry. Starting with Lady Kendrick. She's our hostess, and this entire episode must have been a complete nightmare for her."

"Maybe at first," Michael said. "But Caleb spent a couple of hours with her while you were in the ER. She really, really likes him. She said I was lucky to have him for an uncle."

"Uncle," Jane repeated carefully. "No, I don't believe I want you to elaborate on that. And that's when she said she wanted him to join us at the encampment?"

"Only she invited Caleb to stay at the castle."

"Of course she did." Because Caleb had no doubt revved up that *persuasion* gift at which he was so skilled. Lady Kendrick would have probably given him the damn castle if he'd asked her. It was suddenly too much to handle. From the moment Jane had opened her eyes, it had been to frustration and confusion. Now she had to deal with Michael's intricate manipulations and Caleb's subtle *persuasions* as well. "Then I believe we'll let them do whatever they wish for the time being. I'd rather not be involved in it until I feel a little better."

He was frowning. "You're not happy. Do you want me to tell Lady Kendrick the truth? I will."

"I know you would." She lay back on the pillows. "But I think I'll wait and decide how to go about this with the least amount of hurt possible. I'm tired, Michael. All I want to do is rest now. Is Caleb outside in the hall?"

He nodded. "With Nurse Haback."

"Then why don't you have him get you something to eat and come back later? Maybe I can see the nurse and the doctor and then get a little rest."

He was still frowning. "If that's what you want."

She leaned forward and gave him a hug. "That's what I want."

He went to the door and then stopped to look back at her. "But Caleb does have to be there, Jane," he said soberly. "Bad things happened last night, but it could have been worse. The doctors were worried about you, but Caleb told me that he'd take care of it."

"What?"

"Don't you remember? I think he did some of that stuff like he did for Mom."

"No, I don't remember." Or did she? If she did, it was almost too vague to determine. "Perhaps you're mistaken."

He shook his head. "He came and he fixed everything that was bad."

It could have been worse.

Sometimes I know things other people don't, Michael had said.

And she had believed him. She believed him now. But she had no special talent like Michael, nor that damnably powerful *persuasion* Caleb used that could seem to turn night to day. She didn't know anything right now. She had to let everything sink in and decide what to do.

And how to contend and hold her own with both of them. Because there was no way she would allow herself to be controlled, or be persuaded to do something she didn't want to do.

She closed her eyes. "We'll talk about it later, Michael."

She knew he was still staring at her. He wanted to say something more to persuade her to his way of thinking. She could feel him hesitate. "Have a nice meal." She added firmly, "See you later."

She kept her eyes closed until she heard him leave the room. She would have liked to just keep them shut and doze off again. She hadn't been lying about that headache. But she didn't know how much time she had to find a way to cope with what had happened tonight. Hopefully Michael would keep Caleb occupied until she was ready to deal with them both again.

So forget about the damn headache and just try to think . . .

"Oh, dear, you do look better. I'm so relieved."

Jane opened her eyes to see Lady Alice Kendrick standing in the doorway. A gray-haired woman in her late seventies, she was still fit and energetic with a great sense of humor. Jane had always liked her. "You're very kind. I do feel much better. I'm sorry I was so much trouble. Would you like to sit down?"

Lady Kendrick shook her head. "No, I just popped in to say hello and assure you that neither you nor any other volunteer will have to worry about anything like this happening again. I'm doubling the sentries." Her lips tightened. "I don't know what happened, but I won't have my property used as some kind of shooting range. Life is too difficult for idiocies like that. Please forgive me."

"You've never been anything but thoughtful and gracious. There's nothing to forgive."

"Well, I also had another reason to stop by to see you." She motioned to someone in back of her. "My secretary, Nigel, was concerned that he might have done something to hurt you. He was the one who administered first aid before the ambulance got there." She stepped aside to let a sandy-haired young man in his twenties come into the room. "You see, Nigel, she's doing very well."

He nodded, his gaze on Jane's face. "I'm very glad. You looked so...pale lying there. I was frightened."

"Thank you so much for taking care of me."

He smiled shyly. "I'm glad I could help."

"I told him that he was foolish to worry. The EMTs said he did a wonderful job." Lady Kendrick smiled affectionately at him. "I can't tell you how often he's patched up the scratches and bruises of my students working in the digs. But now we'll run along and leave you to heal, won't we, Nigel?"

He nodded and ducked quickly out of the room.

Lady Kendrick was about to follow him when she looked back over her shoulder. "I saw Seth Caleb and Michael as I left the elevator. He's such a charming man and I can't wait to have you both for dinner." She smiled, lifted her hand, and then swept out of the room.

It was going to be difficult to avoid interacting with Lady Kendrick when she was obviously so smitten by Caleb, Jane thought.

Her headache was beginning to feel much worse.

———◆———

"Jane's upset with me." Michael was frowning as he walked down the hospital corridor with Caleb. "But more with you, I think. How can we fix it?"

"We don't." Caleb smiled down at him. "There are times when it's best to leave a situation alone. We do what Jane wants us to do and then wait for developments. She's very smart, you know. And she's different from us. That part of her that makes her wonderful also makes her difficult. If you try to get rid of the difficult, you might destroy the wonderful. You wouldn't want that to happen."

Michael shook his head. "But I got scared and I thought maybe I should do—" He looked at Caleb's expression. "No?"

"No." Though taking action was exactly what Caleb wanted to do, he thought wryly. Who was he to give advice to this kid when he was always on the verge of explosion where Jane was concerned? "Interfere and you might blow it. Let me handle it." Good advice if he could abide by it himself. But Michael was looking up at him with that steady, searching gaze that always saw too much. "Yes, it was bad and should never have happened to her. We'll keep it from happening again. I'm working on it." His hand grasped Michael's shoulder. "You can help by watching Jane and everyone around her. Okay?"

He nodded shakily. "But I probably won't see him. He's not here anymore," he murmured. "He got what he wanted."

Caleb stiffened. "What?"

"The man who was shooting. He just wanted to hurt her. He wanted the blood. He thought the crash would do it."

Caleb's grasp tightened on the boy's shoulder. "How do you know that, Michael?"

"He was *there*. Right before the crash." He swallowed. "I could *feel* him. It was so strong...He kept thinking about the blood and making her hurt. He thought it was much better than the photo at the gallery."

"Did he? What else, Michael?"

"He thought it was enough. It didn't matter whether or not he'd almost killed her. It was a risk he'd had to take. She had to know how it felt. Now he could move on to the next step...You're hurting my shoulder, Caleb."

"Sorry." Caleb's hand dropped away. "I would have liked to have known all this before, Michael."

"I would have told you, but it didn't seem as important as you getting Jane to wake up. I was worried about her. Besides, they aren't here anymore."

"Do you know where they are?" he asked carefully. "Providing you believe it's important enough to tell me?"

He shook his head. "They're just not here. Maybe they went back to MacDuff's Run."

"Back? That's where they came from?"

He nodded. "I told you, he was thinking about the other blood on the photo." He paused. "I was wrong about you getting Jane well being more important?"

"No, you were entirely right. It was perfectly natural that you thought of her first. But next time you might remember to tell me everything instead of categorizing in order of what you think important."

"But there's not going to be a next time." His eyes widened in alarm. "You said we can't let it happen again."

"I wasn't talking about Jane." He punched the elevator button. "But even though you're certain that she's safe at the moment, I believe we'll eat in the hospital cafeteria instead of finding a restaurant."

He nodded gravely. "So I can keep watch."

"Exactly. And maybe relax and think about what happened before you hit those gates. Anything else that might occur to you. A name would help enormously."

Michael shook his head.

"There were two men on that hill. Didn't you get either name?"

"Two? There was only one." He shook his head in confusion. "Or, if there were two, the other person wasn't important, he kind of didn't exist."

"How depressing for him."

"Well, that's how it seemed. I guess I'm not helping much," he said, dejected.

"I wouldn't say that," Caleb said. "You've already helped by confirming that the man who was taking potshots at you and Jane was the same one who was at MacDuff's Run." He pressed the button for the cafeteria. "Now I can call MacDuff and tell him to have the inspector concentrate on combining the investigations. I'll do it while you're having your snack." He smiled at Michael. "And because of you, we can move on to the next step, too."

Michael smiled back at him. "You just want me to feel better about making a mistake. It won't happen again, I promise. It's hard keeping everything straight. Sometimes I get mixed up."

"I imagine you do." All the emotional and psychic conflicts must be a constant challenge for this boy. Caleb could definitely empathize. "You'll work it out."

Michael nodded. "Right." His smile had suddenly become mischievous. "I just didn't want you to think I was perfect. Jane told me that there was no way you were perfect, and I didn't want to make you feel bad." He walked ahead of him out of the elevator and into the cafeteria. "Do you think they'll have pizza here?"

———◆———

The call from Palik came through while Caleb was watching Michael eat his fruit salad for dessert.

It was about time. He'd expected the call last night, and it was almost six in the morning now. Caleb got up from the table and turned away from Michael so the boy wouldn't hear how pissed off he was. "You're late," he bit out. "Why? What's the word?"

"Stop barking at me," Palik said sourly. "I've had enough trouble since you called me. I had to make sure I had the right information. Will you calm down and listen to me?"

Caleb took a deep breath. "I'm listening."

"I had trouble contacting Enrico Donzolo at Fiero Village. He was the man I hired to keep an eye on the area to make sure there wasn't any cult activity. His phone was going straight to voicemail. So I called his sister and she said that she hadn't heard from him, either, that he'd left a note saying he was taking his sons up to his cabin in the mountains on a fishing trip."

Caleb began to swear beneath his breath.

"I didn't like it, either," Palik said. "And I knew you wouldn't. Very unprofessional. You pay Donzolo very well to keep an eye on what's going on in Fiero, and he's always been reliable reporting."

"Until this time," Caleb said grimly. "Did you send someone after him?"

"I went myself. It was a great sacrifice. You know I abhor leaving the city for all that fresh air and boring nature crap. And it turned out that he wasn't even at the fishing cabin. So I started looking around the property. It took me most of last night to find him." He paused and then said softly, "He didn't go fishing, Caleb."

———◆———

"You're looking much better," Caleb said as he strode into Jane's hospital room late that afternoon. He looked her over critically. "Rested. No circles. More color." He smiled crookedly. "And not nearly as tense as when you threw me out to go watch over Michael."

But Caleb was more than tense, she recognized instantly. She had seen him like this before—he was generating a reckless electricity that was almost tactile. She automatically warily braced herself. "I wasn't tense, I'd just had enough. I was beginning to feel as if you both were ganging up on me." She looked him in the eye. "So I had a nap and then I started to think how I could keep you from overwhelming me."

He tilted his head. "And what did you decide?"

"Just to dig in my heels and walk away if you try to run over me."

"That sounds like a great plan. I know you consider me as disposable. But how can you walk away from Michael?"

"I can't. Michael is the problem." She added, "And neither of you has made it any easier by those stories you told Lady Kendrick. I feel guilty as hell about going along with a lie, but if I don't, she might contact Eve and get her all upset."

"That was Michael's thought exactly."

"And you patted him on the back and told him what a good job he'd done."

"He did an excellent job," he said coolly. "The truth is often over-rated when it comes to keeping the peace. Michael has an amazing grasp of how to obtain the greater good."

"And he went directly to the right person who would back him up."

"Yes," he said quietly. "And I always will. The rest of you can stress complete honesty to him. I'll balance it with being honest when it doesn't hurt the people you care about. And you don't have to worry about talking to Lady Kendrick. I've taken care of most of that business. I'll follow up, and by the time you get out of the hospital, she'll think Michael referring to me as his uncle was just a title of kinship because I'm so close to your family."

She wasn't about to go into that prevarication. "So much for Lady Kendrick. I suppose you've also got a plan for what I should tell Eve about what happened here?" She made an impatient gesture. "Don't answer that. I'm not going to invent a lie for the greater good."

"I wouldn't think of attempting to change you in any way. As I said, I'm very skilled at the greater-good concept. I'm at your disposal."

"That's my intention," she said grimly. "Because I sure as hell won't send Michael to Maldara to be with Eve and Joe. That country is a second Rwanda, and Eve would worry all the time if she had to expose Michael to all that corrupt bureaucracy and criminal elements. That's why she was happy to leave him with me. The only other alternative would be for them to cut short her work on those reconstructions and go home. That would put them between a rock and a hard place." She stared directly into his eyes. "So you *are* at my disposal, Caleb. But not to lie to them. I'll have to tell them what happened eventually. But I figure that I might be able to stall them until the police find out what's happening here, so that they can make an informed decision. Eve and Joe were going to be very busy for the next few days at that inauguration business, and that might be all the time we need. I texted them on the road last evening that we were almost back at Kendrick Castle. They were going straight from the airport to the swearing-in of Interim President Gideon, and then there was some kind of festival scheduled."

His eyes were narrowed on her face. "What are you getting at?"

"I was terrified when I thought that Michael might have been hurt last night. I can't let that happen. But I can't send him to Maldara, either." Her lips curved in a bitter smile. "You agreed to help protect Michael a few weeks ago, and I backed down when I thought it wasn't necessary. That's all changed. I think we both agree that it's definitely necessary now." He wasn't answering, and she went on quickly. "Just Michael. Naturally, I'll take care of myself, but I need someone to keep him safe. No one can do that like you. Everyone knows the things you're capable of. Eve was so happy that you were going to take care of him during that emergency before. It would make her feel even better if she finds out what's happening here. I think that—"

"Hush." He put his fingers over her lips. "Of course. You know I will." He took his hand away. "On the condition that I have total control of Michael from this moment on. He's mine. No arguments."

She hadn't expected that stipulation. "That's a bit overbearing. I don't know if—"

"I won't have you arguing about how I care for him." His voice was clipped. "I know you don't trust me, but this time you're going to have to. You've asked me to keep him safe; now you have to trust me not to screw it up."

That tough, hard recklessness was back, as if his moment of softness had never been. He wasn't going to back down. And heaven knew she needed desperately to keep Michael safe. "We'll see how it goes."

He shook his head. "All the way, Jane."

She sighed. "Okay. But you'd better do it right."

He smiled. "He belongs to you. It will be my way, but in the end you'll have no complaints."

And she had no right to complain since she'd been the one to go to him. Anything to keep Michael safe. "Where is Michael now?"

"Still being cared for by Tovarth's policeman. He's down in the game room by the gift shop. I had a few things to discuss with you and I didn't want him around for a while." He dropped down in the chair beside the bed. "Though I wasn't anticipating one of them being Michael himself. I know how possessive you are."

"Not possessive. I just always want the best for him and hope that I can give it to him. This time it seemed that was you." She lifted her chin. "Though I thought you might be more reasonable."

"And give you what you want?" His smile was suddenly purely sensual. "I'd do that without question. Just not in this arena. When are you going to get out of here? The head nurse said that Dr. Rabine had signed off on you a couple of hours ago."

"He did. He said that I was fine but not to push it for a few days. But then I had to give a statement to the local police officer handling the case." She grimaced. "Not that it did him any good. It read like a trip on a roller coaster . . . without the seat belt. I didn't know what was going on at the time." She added, "And Lady Kendrick dropped by for a few minutes and expressed her disappointment and dismay that I'd been hurt. She spoke highly of you. Why am I not surprised?"

"You shouldn't be. She's an intelligent woman." He paused. "You still want to stay at the castle? You'd feel safe?"

She nodded. "Michael loves it here. And I've always felt safe at the encampment. There are patrolling sentries, dozens of students are around at all times of the day and night, and the gates are locked at ten every night. According to what Lady Kendrick said, she's even going to double security from now on." Her lips twisted ruefully. "You'll notice the only time anything happened to me was when I was *outside* those gates." She gazed at him curiously. "Where else would we go?"

"I'd have to think about it. I just don't like the thought that someone was on that hill across the road peering down at you. But I'll arrange for one of Tovarth's men to be stationed there." He paused. "However, Michael might have lost his enthusiasm for the dig after yesterday."

"What?" Her eyes widened. "Did he tell you that?"

"No." He added, "But he told me that he knew the man who shot you wanted to hurt you. He could feel that the bastard thought the blood might be enough even if he didn't kill you."

She inhaled sharply at the words. The shock lasted only for an instant. It would have been natural for Michael to confide in Caleb. "He could *feel* it?" She shivered. "He told me that he sometimes knows things other people don't." Her lips were trembling. "He didn't tell me that monsters sometime came to call and murmur in his ear. How frightened he must have been."

"Only for you," Caleb said. "And he said that the murderer at MacDuff's Run was the same man who was shooting at you here. He could *feel* the blood. It was all about the blood. I called and let MacDuff know."

"That Michael told you he was communing with murderers?"

"No, I'd protect Michael's specialness even from MacDuff. I merely mentioned that I'd run across a connection between the two attacks." He smiled crookedly. "No one would think that weird for me. Certainly not MacDuff. Who's more weird than Seth Caleb?"

Was there a hint of bitterness beneath that mockery? She found herself saying quickly, "But he'd know how valuable you are. Maybe you *are* weird, but I chose you to take care of Michael, didn't I?"

"Reluctantly."

"Bullshit. If I was reluctant, I'd never have asked you to take care of him at all. Michael's too important to me."

Caleb just looked at her.

She tried again. "And it's your fault I never know what you're going to do or who you really are. It's like swimming in the dark. Anyone would be uneasy."

"Swimming in the dark," he repeated. "Never knowing if there's a shark below you?" Then he smiled. "But I'm not a shark, I'm definitely hot-blooded." His smile faded. "I didn't mention to MacDuff another piece of information that I gathered today. I decided to save it for you in case you wanted to go back to MacDuff's Run and tell him yourself."

"Why would I do that?" She was aware that the dangerous recklessness she'd first noticed when he'd walked into the room was back in full force now. "What's wrong with you? Are you enjoying this?"

"No, quite the contrary. I'm pissed off because I fell into a very dark hole. It's going to be difficult to climb out of it." He leaned back in his chair. "I heard from Palik today. He was very late getting back to me on an assignment I'd given him. I was angry, because everything else seemed to be going down the tubes, too. But he had a good excuse, so I forgave him. I'd asked him to check on Enrico Donzolo, a man he'd hired to keep watch over any problems or signs of cult activity in Fiero Village." He smiled crookedly. "You remember Fiero? Such a fine village, with such unique citizens."

"Of course I remember. Your sister Maria was kidnapped from her husband's estate near there." She could feel herself tensing as she gazed at him. "And you said you later found it was a hotbed for that cult that was responsible for her death. You said you hunted down all the members of that cult and eliminated them."

"And it was true, but I'm a careful man. I wasn't going to risk them rising from the dead to plague me again. Cult members have a habit of being like rabid animals, biting and infecting everyone around them. So I had Palik arrange to have one of the villagers, Donzolo, keep watch." He shook his head. "But when Palik called him to check on the present status, he was told he'd gone fishing in the mountains with his sons. His phone calls went to voicemail. When Palik went up to the mountains to check on him, he wasn't at his cabin. There was no sign of him being there, so he set out to check the property. It took almost two days for him to find him, but only because he was looking too close to the cabin. Once he went beyond the lake, he had no problem locating him." He met her gaze. "Because they wanted him to be found. They'd spread a trail of blood directly to the cave where they'd left him."

"A cave?" She swallowed. She'd started to shake when she'd heard the word "blood." She couldn't look away from him. "Why was he—" She broke off as Caleb handed her his phone.

"A picture is worth a thousand words," he said harshly. "Look at it. The cabin was too close, but this cave was just right. It protected him from the elements, and it took a little effort and time for Palik to discover him. I believe the timing was thought to be important."

She slowly looked down at the photo on the camera.

She flinched.

Blood.

Everywhere.

So much blood.

A gray-haired man had been pinned to a wooden crucifix fixed to the cave wall. His dark eyes were wide open and stared into nothingness. His throat had been cut, and his blue shirt was soaked with blood. But so were the crucifix and the cave wall behind him.

"The blood . . ."

"That's what I asked Palik," Caleb said. "The human body has only so much blood. This was excessive." He added curtly, "There were two other bodies in the cave as well as this dramatic display of Donzolo. They'd murdered his two sons, nine and twelve years old, and took their blood, too." His lips were tight. "After all, they had to have a sufficient amount to complete their exhibition properly. They'd gone to such a lot of trouble to send their message."

"Three deaths..." She shook her head dazedly. "What message?"

"Look closer. His shirt is so soaked in blood that I didn't see it at first. How disappointed that would have made them if they'd known."

She knew what she was going to see even before she slowly enlarged the photo.

There in the center of Donzolo's chest was a photo, streaked, almost hidden, by the blood on his shirt.

"Me...again," she said hoarsely. "It looks like it was taken at the same lake as the other one. Why?" She looked at him as a sickening thought occurred to her. "And did his sons have one of those—"

"No," Caleb interrupted. "No photos. Evidently the boys were killed just to supply the blood, not to send a message." He added, "To each his own, Jane. And this message was very effective and pointed, wasn't it?"

"It...seems to be." She ran her shaking fingers through her hair. "Effective at least. If you mean scaring and bewildering me. Though I don't understand why it appears the threat is aimed specifically at me." She met his eyes. "I think you might have it all figured out. I could feel the lightning striking all around you from the time you walked in here today."

"Well, you're accustomed to that, aren't you?" he asked. "But you might remember that I've never let it strike you in all the time we've been together. Though it's come very close." He smiled crookedly. "But this time I might have to work harder at it. I can't believe I really have to enlighten you why you're a target. You were fighting MacDuff hard enough to protect him from maligning me. You just didn't want to believe it." He inclined his head mockingly. "Which is very kind considering how wary you are of me. I didn't want to believe it, either. But I'm nothing if not a realist. These attacks have nothing to do with MacDuff except as a conduit for reaching you...and me. This last Donzolo attack points directly at Fiero and the attempts I've made to keep my family protected from any cults. And Palik said that there were more than two sets of footprints in that cave. The ground where the bodies were found had been trampled by over a dozen people." He paused and then said flatly, "Which means that I've failed. The cult is back. I'll have to go after them again."

"I'd say they're...going after you." She was looking down at the photo of Donzolo pinned to the crucifix. "You hired Donzolo and they deliberately went after him to show you that you couldn't stop them. My photo was probably only an afterthought."

"Wrong. I agree that I'll still likely be the main target this time. But you're far more than an afterthought. They've been watching you. They want to make certain I'm fully engaged with the idea you're in their sights, so that they can use you to play their games with me." He tilted his head. "It all points to you. First the theft and murder at MacDuff's Run, then the attack on you and Michael. They'd probably already committed the murders of Donzolo and his sons at Fiero Village by then. I'd think they'd almost be ready to make a major strike."

"Against me?" She shook her head. "That doesn't make sense. If they've been watching me as much as you think, they have to know that we're past history. We've hardly seen each other for months, and then only in public. You haven't been to my apartment or taken me out to—" She had a sudden thought. "Lisa!" she said, panic-stricken. "She's your sister. It wouldn't be me. They'd go after her, wouldn't they? We have to call Lisa."

"Easy. Lisa wouldn't be a prime target for the cult. I've made sure of that. Besides, it's already taken care of. She's at the animal clinic on Summer Island in the Caribbean working with Margaret Douglas. Palik's already sent someone to the research facility on the island to pick Lisa up and bring her back here."

"Thank God." She drew a relieved breath. "Margaret Douglas?

Lisa didn't mention her when she called me the other day. That's strange, she knows what good friends we are."

Caleb's eyes flickered. "She called you? You didn't tell me."

"It was the same day you took me to MacDuff's Run. I was a bit concerned about other things at the time." She shrugged. "And it was a confusing call anyway. I don't really know why she bothered to phone me. It was something to do with an apology that really wasn't an apology. I was with Eve or I might have asked more questions." She frowned. "She seemed her normal self. The call wouldn't have anything to do with this... atrocity, would it?"

"No, if she appeared normal, I'm sure she was just pursuing her own agenda," he said casually. "We all know that can be a many-splendored thing on occasion."

"Good. But I'm glad you're bringing her here." She went back to something he'd said before. "And why wouldn't she be a prime target?"

"Because the cult killed her sister only after trying to experiment with her blood and finding it didn't have the power they wanted. Everyone in the cult knew that. It was natural for them to assume it was because she was female, and that using Lisa would have the same negative result." He smiled sardonically. "While I was on the hunt for those sons of bitches, I might have dropped a few words to the effect of how incredibly stupid they'd been when I was the only one in the family who had the blood talent."

"You used that *persuasion* thing?"

"Of course. Rumor can become truth if handled correctly. I had to make everyone believe that Lisa had no power whatever. And if she was being watched, they'd also realize that she'd displayed no powers all through her teen years."

"Because you'd made her promise not to use them." Jane had been present when Caleb had first let nineteen-year-old Lisa renege on that promise, and it had been a nightmare scenario for all of them. "Did you think she was being watched all through those years?"

"Not by those bastards. I hoped that nightmare was over when Maria was killed. But Lisa was just a young kid. I'd gone through enough to know how anyone different can be ripped apart." His lips tightened. "I wasn't going to let it happen to her."

Jane had been aware there was no chance of that happening. She'd never seen a relationship as strong as the one between Caleb and his sister. "I know you always took care of her. "

"She belongs to me." He grimaced. "Even if she can sometimes make life difficult." He held out his hand for his phone. "Just as you can, Jane. Don't let this be one of those times."

She gave him the phone. "Are you threatening me, Caleb?"

"God, no. I wouldn't dare at the moment. I'm feeling very humble that I made a mistake that put you at risk."

She blinked. "Humble?"

"I know. Enjoy it. It will be gone soon." He leaned forward and took her hand. "I'm just asking you to work with me and not against me, dammit. That murdering bastard *will* try to use you. You may not think that he'd believe we still have a relationship, but I do. He's researched you. He's watched you. He's watched us together." His hand tightened on hers. "And I guarantee he'd know that it's not over for me."

"You're just guessing." She should move her hand, but she couldn't do it. Everything about him was alive and electric and so totally intense that she could hardly breathe.

"Maybe. I'm not Michael who gets psychic messages from these goons. But I know how I feel, and I've probably been transparent where you're concerned. I feel as if I am. Look, just work with me. I'll clear this up as soon as I can. It's my fault, and I won't let anything happen to you. I promise." His voice was hoarse and fierce, his dark eyes glittering. "Palik will get me a name and I'll find him. He'll be very, very sorry that he decided to use you against me." He released her hand and got to his feet. "Now I'll get you checked out of this hospital and take you and Michael down to your tent. I'll camp outside by the fire to keep watch and make sure that those grounds are as safe as you say they are." He headed for the door. "And I'm feeling so chastened that I won't even remind Michael he offered to lend me his sleeping bag and a place in your tent."

———◆———

"They found Donzolo a few hours ago." Davron pressed DISCONNECT on his phone. "Pietro said that Caleb's man, Palik, made a call to him from outside the cave. Then he went back down to the village to Donzolo's sister's house."

"To break the sad news," Luca said derisively. "And perhaps have her contact the police so that Palik and Caleb won't be involved in the local investigation. Donzolo's sons were only youngsters and their deaths could arouse a certain . . . indignation."

"It might have been better to not kill the boys." Davron was nibbling at his lower lip. "I didn't see why you had to take them, too."

Davron's squeamishness was increasing steadily, Luca thought. He'd known it would happen as time went on, but it still made him impatient. "Of course you didn't. You never see beyond the tip of your nose. I knew I'd need to make a show of taking their blood." He frowned. "And Pietro and Alberto and the others needed to see me take it. For the past few years, they've only been playing at being what I wanted them to be. Going to their stupid cult meetings and pretending to have the guts to make that final step. It's all very well to talk about making a sacrifice, but it's another thing to see some-one who has the guts to do it. They had to be fully committed, and killing those children would do that. As they stood there and watched, they became not only witnesses, but part of the process. They'll never be able to go back. Now they know I'm the one they have to follow." He added softly, "As you do, Davron, but I don't appreciate you disagreeing with me. I hope you didn't express those opinions to anyone else at that gathering."

"No!" Davron's eyes widened in alarm. "You know I'll do anything you want me to do. Didn't I help you with luring Donzolo to the cave?"

"Not without an argument."

"Only because I thought it was a risk. You can trust me."

Trust? As if Luca would trust anyone but himself when he was getting this close to the finish line. He could feel the excitement stir within him as he remembered that exhilaration and power he'd known in those final moments in the cave. Of course, the blood really meant nothing to him. It was only a symbol that he found fascinating, he assured himself. It was just a part of the plan he'd been carefully crafting over the years. The blood had its place, just as those fools in the cave did. He was nothing like those bloodthirsty savages. Just as he was nothing like this wimp, Davron, whom he was getting closer and closer to eliminating.

"I do hope I can trust you," Luca murmured. "Because I think that I might let you have an even more personal involvement as we move forward toward bringing Jane MacGuire into the fold..."

CHAPTER

5

KENDRICK CASTLE

Michael was asleep at last.

Jane gazed at him curled up in his sleeping bag across the tent. He'd been positively wired for the last hour after they'd left the hospital and arrived here at the encampment. He'd been chattering to Caleb and helping him build his campfire at the bottom of the slight slope on which their tent was located. Then he'd settled cross-legged beside it still talking to him. It was only when Caleb had sent him into the tent to go to bed that he'd reluctantly settled down for the night. Even then he'd tried to talk longer to Jane until the practically sleepless night he'd had before had caught up with him.

Jane was glad that Caleb's presence had managed to give Michael that sense of adventure and excitement. After what he'd gone through in that car last night and the stress afterward, he might have gone into depression instead.

She had a sudden thought.

Unless he'd been prevented from falling into that pit by less-than-conventional means from Caleb.

She sat straight up in her bed. Would he have done that to Michael?

She was out of her sleeping bag and heading toward the tent entrance the next minute.

Caleb was lying on his back in front of the fire, with his arm beneath his head, still fully dressed in the jeans and black shirt he'd worn earlier in the day. "Is there a problem?" He studied her face. "Yes, I think so. What have I done now?"

"I don't know. Maybe nothing." Was this a mistake? She'd acted on impulse and now standing here gazing at him she was having second thoughts. "I'm never sure. I just had to check." She moved closer to the fire. "Michael seemed so excited and happy tonight. Did you—" She stopped. "When I asked you to watch over him, I didn't mean— Michael has enough problems without dealing with—"

"My corrupting the poor lad with my devilish talent?" he finished for her. "I don't wonder that you're suspicious. What a terrible thing that would have been." He raised himself on one elbow and said softly, "To give the boy a few hours of pleasant distraction before he has to face cold reality again."

"Did you use that damn *persuasion?*"

"No, I did *not,*" he said with cool precision. "Just because I'm able to do something doesn't mean I automatically choose to do it. I'm very careful with that particular talent. The effects can be too lingering. I would never do it to Michael unless it was to save his life. When you put him into my hands, I told you that you had to trust me." He shrugged. "But that didn't last long, did it?"

Had she hurt him? She thought beneath the cynicism she might have pierced that armor. The thought brought a rush of guilt and regret in its wake. "I said I just had to check. I don't know anything about that *persuasion* business I've heard you can do. I only know I feel responsible for Michael." That wasn't enough. "I'm sorry."

"Was that difficult for you?" He suddenly smiled. "I'm sure it was, but you deserve it."

Maybe she hadn't hurt him. He'd recovered quickly enough. "I'm not entirely certain about that," she said dryly. "If what you say is true about that *persuasion*, you weren't equally careful about using it on me. I remember a few times that you had no compunction about exposing me to it before I told you I'd never put up with it."

"Oh, I was exceptionally careful with you. That's why I let you stop me before it really began. But then you were always special." He sat up and linked his arms around his knees. "And since you were wrong this time, too, and I saw signs of genuine regret, I think I should let you make it up to me."

She stiffened warily.

"I'm not a fool, Jane." He chuckled. "But I find I'm in need of company. Will you sit down and have a glass of wine with me?" He nodded at his backpack. "I'll even let you wait on me."

She hesitated and then sat down. "You can get it for me. I'm not that sorry."

He sighed. "I should have taken longer to play you." He got to his feet, went over to the backpack, and got out a bottle of wine and two glasses. "But I'll take what I can get."

"You came prepared." She looked at the label on the bottle. "I don't think you picked that up at the hospital gift shop."

"Lady Kendrick was happy to supply it when I told her that it was to celebrate you getting out of the hospital. Though I was tempted to fib and tell her it would help heal your wound." He poured her wine. "But she's smart and would realize the cut on your head is only a scratch."

"It frightened Michael."

"It frightened me, too." He sat down in front of her, cradling his glass in his two hands. "And I hadn't even seen the wound when he told me about it." He added, "That's why it can't happen again. I have such a delicate nature." He looked down into his wine. "I've been thinking about it and I'm going to arrange to have MacDuff set up additional protection for you and Michael with Scotland Yard. It will please Eve and Joe, and it's only sensible. I'll be here, of course, but just in case there's a slip-up and I'm not, it would be—"

"A slip-up?" Her eyes were wide with alarm. "Nothing's going to happen to you. You said you'd be here for Michael. You promised me."

"And I'll keep my promise," he said quietly. "This is just a backup." He was silent. "I know these cults. They're total fanatics. They won't stop. I watched them kill Maria. I won't watch them kill you. But there might be...problems."

She stared at him in disbelief. She was feeling an icy chill. "You're saying that those crackpots might be good enough to take you down? That's bullshit."

He laughed. "I appreciate the vote of confidence, but accidents do happen. I'm just acquiring additional insurance with you as beneficiary. After all, this is purely my battle. It wouldn't even exist if I wasn't who I am."

"And I'm supposed to accept that?" she asked fiercely. "Don't be crazy. Nothing can happen to you. So stop this nonsense."

"I will. After I get MacDuff to do what I need." He finished his wine with one swallow. "I just wanted to tell you so that you won't get edgy if you see anyone following you." He was studying her face. "It will be fine. Nothing is going to happen to you or Michael. I didn't mean you to worry. But you're always telling me that I'm such a secretive bastard."

Her hand tightened on her glass. "You are. Look at this damn bottle of wine. Who else would con Lady Kendrick into doing this?" She lifted her eyes to his. "So that you could tell me that you might die and you have to have your blasted insurance?"

"It was a bit overdramatic." He smiled. "Probably nothing will happen, and I admit it was done in my usual taciturn fashion."

"Of course nothing will happen. Why would you even think of it now?"

"I suppose because of the cult," he said simply. "When you've been told from childhood that you're a monster whose fate is to be either killed or used, you tend to believe your destiny is carved in stone. And when a cult of crazies pops up that could hand you either fate, it strikes a certain resounding note. When I bring these sons of bitches down, I'll be back to normal." He smiled crookedly. "Whatever that is for me."

"Heaven help us." She held up her hand. "I'm joking."

He was laughing. "And it just goes to show how much I've shaken you that you think you have to explain. I thought we'd gotten closer than that before I was thrown into outer darkness."

"You didn't shake me. Or maybe you did. I've grown to think of you as invulnerable. I *like* to think of you like that. So don't start talking about having any Achilles' heels. That's for other people. And anyone who made you think anything else was an asshole."

"If you say so," he said solemnly. His eyes were twinkling. "I assure you it was only a temporary aberration. Maybe I just wanted to lure you back to bed. Did I play it solemn and desperate enough?"

And he could have been doing just that, she realized. When did she ever know if he was truly sincere? But the moment when she had thought about even the possibility of him dying had shocked and panicked her. "Caleb!"

"You have to make up your own mind about me," he said softly. "That's the way it's always been. I can't help you with it."

"You never have," she said curtly. "And it's no wonder that I don't understand you. But how well do you understand me? Did you really think I was only concerned about Michael and myself? Maybe you did, how do I know?" She jumped to her feet. "Well, screw you, Caleb. I'm not going to have anything happen to you. I wanted a protector for Michael, not help for myself or a damn sacrifice. We're all going to come out of this alive." She headed for her tent. "And I'm not going to sit around twiddling my thumbs. You may think this is your battle, but I'm not letting those bastards take anything away from me. Understand?"

"Absolutely. You couldn't be more clear." She looked over her shoulder to see him sitting there, the glow of the fire touching his dark hair, his eyes narrowed on her. "And I know you don't want to encourage me, but I'm afraid you have. I believe I actually detected a hint of possessiveness in that last statement. It was something of—"

His phone rang.

"Sorry." He pulled the phone out of his pocket and glanced at it. "I've been expecting this call from Palik. Since I wouldn't want to force you to twiddle your thumbs when you're being so proactive, I'll turn on the speaker." He punched ACCESS. "How soon will Lisa be here, Palik?"

"There's been a slight problem," Palik said hesitantly. "I'm not quite sure what her ETA is at the moment." He went on hurriedly, "But I'll know within a very short time. As soon as I get a call from—"

"What the hell are you talking about?" Caleb said with soft violence. "I told you that I want Lisa here *now*. You were sending someone to pick her up on Summer Island and put her on a plane."

Lisa? Jane slowly turned away from the tent and moved back toward Caleb.

"I didn't think there would be any trouble, but we can't seem to locate her. We knew she was at Summer Island until two days ago. But when I sent my agent to go pick her up, Margaret Douglas told him that Lisa had left the island to fly to Miami the day before and *might* be back soon. Damn casual. And we couldn't trace her after she got off the plane. We're still trying."

"Miami!"

"We'll find her," Palik said quickly. "Do you think I don't know what you'd do to me if we didn't? My best man, Haverty, is on this. He said that he questioned the flight attendants, and your sister didn't appear to be traveling with anyone. Though she could have met someone in Miami. I would have flown to Miami myself if I hadn't been mired in big problems here."

"You don't have any bigger problems than this, Palik."

"I had to delegate, dammit. You told me I had to search Fiero

Village until I got a name for you. I had to make a choice. There's no proof yet that your sister was taken by any of those ghouls."

"Is there any proof that she wasn't?"

"No, but Haverty thinks he has a lead. He promised to get back to me in the next hour or so. I'll let you know as soon as I do." He paused. "I don't suppose you'd be interested that I'm close to getting the name of the man who nailed Donzolo to that cross?"

"Not until you can tell me that he hasn't already butchered my sister." He cut the connection.

Caleb was breathing hard. His face was taut and pale, the features knife-hard. She could almost hear the thunder crackle as he turned toward her. "A little more than I expected," he said curtly. "You don't want to deal with this. Go on to bed."

"The hell I will." She came to stand beside him. "I'd say it was a little less than expected. You were sure that Lisa would be here. You told me that earlier. How did it all go wrong? Can't you phone her?"

"I tried earlier today to let her know I was bringing her home. She didn't answer me."

She frowned, puzzled. "But you can still always reach her when you need to. It's part of that bonding thing you have between you."

"I couldn't this time," he said curtly. "It didn't worry me because she's been a bit temperamental lately and I thought it might be a response to a disagreement we had. I knew Palik's agent would be picking her up today anyway."

"Then why couldn't he do it?"

"If I knew that, I wouldn't be ready to kill Palik," he said harshly. "He should have found a way to learn what Lisa was doing. No one is permitted on Summer Island but the employees of the research facility, so I couldn't have anyone watching her on the island itself. I thought that might also be a safety factor, because no one else could get in. But no one can prevent anyone leaving there, either. If the lure was enticing enough, Lisa could have been persuaded to go to

Miami. But why would Margaret Douglas make a decision like that so casually?"

"Why wouldn't she?" Jane asked. "I've known Margaret for years, and unless she's changed considerably she's closer to being a Gypsy than anyone I know. She wouldn't think of questioning Lisa about a little jaunt to Miami—it would probably be exactly what she'd do herself. That's why they always got along so well."

Caleb muttered a curse. "Letting the two of them cohabit even in the same hemisphere was a gigantic mistake."

"Not usually." Jane frowned. "Maybe this time. At any rate, you had nothing to say in her decisions. She's not a child any longer."

His dark eyes were glittering. "She's *my* sister."

"And Palik said that he'll get back to you soon. You said he was very efficient."

"Not efficient enough." He turned away from her. "I told you to go to bed."

"Yes, you did." Why didn't she just walk away as he'd told her to? She'd been trying to back away from him for months, and this might do it. But she couldn't do it this way, not when he was in pain, not after all they'd gone through together. "And very rudely." She crossed to the bottle of wine that was still lying by the fire. "But I might forgive you considering the circumstances." She filled his glass with wine and brought it back to him. "Though you definitely need mellowing." She held the glass out. "I'm not sure this is going to do the job, but it's the only game in town. It might help a little. Drink it."

He was staring at her without expression. Then he took the glass and drained it. "Satisfied?"

"No." She handed him the bottle, then went over to the fire and dropped down before it. "It didn't touch you. Maybe if it was vodka or whiskey."

He stared at her for another moment. "That wouldn't touch me, either." He walked over to stand before her. "I don't want you here.

I want to be alone. I'm very upset. I don't want to take it out on you, but I will. Get away from me, Jane."

She shook her head. "You're stuck with me. So you might as well sit down and talk, instead of growling at me."

"I don't want to talk."

"Because it might reveal you have a few feelings tucked beneath all that fire and brimstone?" Her glance shifted to the fire. "You're safe with me. I'd never tell. Because as far as I'm concerned, the next couple of hours aren't going to exist. When they're done, we'll be going right back to where we were before. But, one way or another, we've been together a long time, and I can't leave you when I can see you're hurting. So suck it up, Caleb."

He stood there for another instant, then dropped down on the ground beside her. "Pity?"

"Shut up. Nothing is ever black and white. No one should know that better than you. Your life has been all the colors of the rainbow, but mostly black and blue. I need to be here, whether you need me or not." She paused. "You think you made a mistake. You think those creeps went after Lisa because they thought she had the power they needed, or they wanted to use her to get to you. You believe she wasn't as safe as you thought, that she was a prime target after all."

"Are you finished?"

"Except to say that you're very smart and you wouldn't make a mistake like that if there was any way to prevent it. It's not as if Lisa has ever been easy. She's a rebel through and through, and the only person she's ever paid any attention to is you."

"Then it seems I didn't handle her well, doesn't it?" His lips twisted. "Maybe I should have furnished a luxurious dungeon for her at my place in Scotland instead of letting her roam the world."

"Yeah, that would have worked," Jane said sarcastically. "She would have found a way to get a truckload of C-4 and blow the place up." She added, "Though I did wonder why you didn't keep her closer to you after that day she saved my life in the desert. She was terribly upset when she was forced to stop the heart of that killer, Santara. Even I could see it." Jane could still see it, feel it. Lisa tackling Santara, her body covering him, pulling him close, her expression fierce, intent, as she concentrated on exploding his heart. And then afterward, broken and numb as she'd gazed in horror down at the man she had killed as Caleb lifted her to her feet and gently held her.

"Of course she was upset," he said roughly. "It was her first kill. She'd never used the blood talent before." He paused. "And she's never used it since."

Her gaze flew to his face. "What?"

"Surprised? All that passion and self-will...I was shocked, too. I tried to help her through the aftereffects of the kill, but I admit I expected that after she became accustomed to the idea, it might begin to intrigue her. All that power..." His smile was bitter. "After all, that's why the Ridondo family became hunters when they gave up the darker...amusements. It helped to stave off the temptation. And look who she had for a brother. But evidently she didn't feel the pull—or if she did, she resisted it." He added harshly, "That's another reason why I was certain she wouldn't be targeted. Only the one kill that I made sure was kept secret, and no pattern that would lead anyone to doubt the entire scenario I'd set up to keep her safe."

"The entire scenario..." Her eyes widened. "That's the reason you didn't keep her close to you. Lisa adores you, she would never have left you voluntarily. You sent her away so that there would be no chance she'd be thought guilty thanks to her association with you. It was another way of protecting her."

"Nonsense," he said coolly. "She was nineteen and it was only natural she'd want to explore everything the world had to offer. I just encouraged her to do it."

"She would never have gone. But she was used to doing whatever you wanted her to do." Jane was ignoring what he'd said and trying to work her way through to the truth. "You weren't just her mentor, but also the only family member she trusted. You'd taken care of her and kept her safe since her sister was killed." She repeated deliberately, "You did send her away, Caleb."

He shrugged. "Think what you like. At the moment, I'm not in the mood to argue with you. I just thought you might like to know that Lisa had only the one kill. Things like that tend to mean something to you."

"But that one kill was the one to save my life," Jane said slowly. "I'm glad she never had to kill again, but if it traumatized her to that extent I'm wondering if it hurt her even worse than I imagined."

"First you worry about her having to kill to save your life. Then you worry about Lisa being traumatized by not being able to kill anyone else. There's something very bizarre about you embracing that contrast." He added mockingly, "Be careful, maybe you're being drawn under the spell of my wicked influence."

"We're not talking about you, we're talking about Lisa. And I didn't really mean..." She gave it up. It was all too complex. He was being his usual enigmatic self. Besides, she had found out entirely too much tonight about Caleb...and Lisa, and she didn't know where it was leading her. "But anything that will keep her from being noticed now would be a good thing." She glanced at him. "And maybe no one did notice her. Maybe all that stuff you did worked, and Lisa just went to Miami to get a suntan."

"Maybe she did." He added grimly, "However, suntans are no longer considered healthy."

"Okay, then you'll have to lecture her about that when you see her." She yawned. "But I'm tired of arguing with you and I won't do it any longer. If you did make a mistake, then we'll fix it and get her back. But I doubt you did. You've kept her safe all these years; I can't see you screwing up now. That man Palik will probably be calling you and telling you that soon."

"I didn't say I'd made a mistake. I believe those were your words."

"I stand corrected." She shifted over beside him and put her head on his shoulder. "But all the rest is true. You know Lisa, and you shouldn't have panicked. So we'll just sit here and wait."

He went still. "By all means, make yourself comfortable."

"I will. I'm tired. I just got out of the hospital."

"Then go to bed."

"We've already gone down that path." She yawned again. "You were never really angry at me. Maybe a bit annoyed because you weren't getting your own way and you were scared about her. But I think you've got some of that frustration and worry out now. Can't we just sit here and be quiet for a little while?"

She could feel his breath move beneath her cheek as a little of the tension left his body. "Why not?" He pulled her into the curve of his shoulder. "I guess we could do that, Jane..."

◆————◆

"Shh!" Caleb's hand clamped down abruptly, covering Jane's lips and jarring her from sleep. "Not a sound." His gaze was searching the darkness, focusing on the tents down the hill and to the left. "I don't like this..."

Jane had frozen. It was more than clear Caleb didn't like what he sensed was out there in the darkness. Every muscle in his body was sleek, tense, powerful, ready for attack. She shook off his hand, her eyes straining to see what had alerted him. "A couple of the students?" she whispered.

He shook his head. "One person. Moving carefully. He doesn't want us to know he's heading this way." He reached in his jacket pocket, pulled out his Glock, and handed it to her. "I think I'll have to go ask him why. So much for how safe you are in this encampment. Stay here and take care of Michael."

Before she could answer, he'd faded out of the glow of the campfire into the darkness.

And she had his gun in her hand, she thought in frustration. He might not need it if he got within arm's distance of the man, but what if he didn't and that other man was armed?

Stop worrying. Caleb was the Hunter, an expert. Her job was to protect Michael. She moved closer to the entrance of the tent, but she was still staring desperately down the hill. Caleb must have reached that lower tent area by now, but she didn't hear anything.

No sound of struggle.

No outcry.

She didn't want to stay here tucked away with Michael. She wanted to *be* there for Caleb.

She went still. She had just heard...something...

"Son of a *bitch*!" A black-garbed body was tossed like a sack of garbage on the ground beside Jane and rolled down the slope toward the fire! "That wasn't necessary. You *hurt* me, Caleb."

Lisa! Jane knew that voice very well. She stared in shock as the girl rolled over and glared at Caleb, who was now striding down the slope toward her.

"I could have killed you." Caleb was glaring down at his sister. "Which is what I'm tempted to do now. What the hell do you think you're doing here, Lisa?"

She lifted her chin. "I wanted to come. You said it might be time I came back the last time I talked to you." She added defiantly, "Not that I cared what you thought. I make my own decisions now. I was just getting bored on the island and wanted a change."

"You almost got more than you bargained for," he said grimly. "Why did you just hop on a plane without letting me know? And why didn't you answer my calls?"

"I didn't want to talk to you yet. I would have gotten around to it. You always want everything your own way. You might have decided to send me back." She scrambled to her knees. "And stop standing over me as if you were going to tell an executioner to lop off my head."

"It's a thought."

"A very bad one." Jane couldn't take this any longer. She was striding down the slope toward them. There was something very poignant and vulnerable about Lisa in this moment. It had been a long time since she'd seen Caleb's sister, but she didn't look any older than that lovely dark-haired nineteen-year-old who seemed to light up every room. And the half-defiant, half-pleading way she was gazing up at Caleb was also the same. It was making Jane's heart ache for her. "Give her a break, Caleb. She's here now and no damage done. She's right, this was really entirely her own business."

Caleb didn't look at her. "Damage could have been done."

"Then it probably would have been your fault for keeping her in the dark all the time. Stop blaming her." She thrust the Glock he'd given her at him. "You're lucky you didn't have this to shoot her with."

"It wasn't his fault." Lisa suddenly turned fiercely on her. "Don't be stupid. He was trying to protect you. He'd never shoot me. Didn't you see how good he is? He took me down so quietly that no one down there in the tents even knew what was happening."

"Lisa," Caleb said quietly.

"Well, it wasn't all your fault." Lisa drew a deep breath. "I knew you weren't going to like it when I came here." She turned back to Jane. "Thank you for trying to step in and keep him from being angry with me, but you should have kept out of it."

"I'll remember that next time," Jane said dryly. "Along with the fact that the two of you are so close that you can almost finish each other's sentences. Forgive me for trying to even out the playing field a little." She took a step closer and started to examine Lisa's arms. "You said you were hurt. Where?"

"Nowhere. Not much. I was angry. I said it for effect." She stared balefully at Caleb. "But you *could* have hurt me."

"Not likely. You're tough."

She smiled at him. "Yes, I am."

"Good," Jane said as she started to turn away. "Then if you're not hurt and I'm obviously in the way, I'll go back to my tent. I'll let Caleb fill you in on a few things that might explain why he was a bit upset when he'd lost contact with you."

"No, don't go." Lisa took a swift step forward. "I didn't come here to see Caleb. Why would I do that? I didn't know he was here. As far as I knew, you were still being as ridiculous as you were when I talked to you on the phone. I came to see you."

"Why?"

"I thought I had a good reason." She glanced warily at Caleb and added quickly, "Just to talk, nothing else. But when I arrived at the airport, I called the castle to see where I could find you out here on the dig. They told me you were in the hospital and wouldn't be back until later tonight." She frowned. "I didn't like that. You were fine when I talked to you."

"I'm fine now."

"I thought I'd come and see for myself." Her gaze was on the bandage on Jane's temple. "I was kind of worried." She turned to Caleb. "Is she okay?"

He nodded. "Concussion, but there will be no problems if she doesn't do anything foolish. The cut was nothing."

Lisa breathed a sigh of relief. "Good. Then we should be able to handle it. Those people at the castle were all weird and tense and wouldn't answer any questions."

"I'm handling it, Lisa," Caleb said.

"No, I'm here. You might not like the way I showed up, but that's your problem. Did you know that I spent six months last year getting EMT training at a hospital in Dallas? It was fascinating. I'm actually overqualified to keep an eye on her." She smiled cheerfully. "So make use of me."

"It's not quite that simple," he said quietly.

"No?" She was gazing searchingly at him as her smile faded. "Tell me why not."

"I'll see you later, Lisa," Jane said as she turned and headed back up the hill. "You might give her a glass of that wine, Caleb. She might be tough, but she could still have a few lingering nightmares hovering over her."

"What does she mean?" Lisa turned back to Caleb. "What nightmares?"

Jane glanced at his face. It was going to be okay. Suddenly all the hardness was gone from his expression as he took Lisa's arm. There was only the love, the closeness, the boundless compassion and bonding that always existed between them.

"Not anything you can't handle." He picked up the bottle of wine on the ground. "But we'll pamper Jane and let her think we'll follow her advice. Sit down and I'll get you a glass."

———◆———

"Could I talk to you, Jane?" Lisa whispered. She was standing at the door of the tent with the glow of the firelight behind her outlining her slender figure. "Caleb said tomorrow, but I can't wait." She glanced at Michael still asleep across the tent and lowered her voice even more. "He said you might be asleep by now but I didn't think so. It's only been a couple of hours. I'll try to be quick."

Lisa was right: No way had Jane been able to drift off. The scene between Caleb and his sister had been too charged with emotion that Jane found contagious. Jane put a finger to her lips, then got up and moved quickly toward the door. The next moment she was outside the tent and fastening it behind her. "Caleb could have been right. Tomorrow might have been better," she said as she sat down a few feet away. "It's been a busy night for all of us."

"Caleb is usually right," Lisa said as she sat down beside her. "And I'm impatient and inconsiderate and you're just out of the hospital. All that is true, but it doesn't change the fact that we'll all sleep better once we talk." She threw out her hand in disgust to indicate Caleb, who was now sitting beside the fire talking on his phone.

"Except him. He's trained himself to sleep like a rock under any circumstances. After he finishes with that call, he'll roll over and go right to sleep. I could slap him."

"No, you couldn't," Jane said flatly. "A couple of hours ago you were attacking me just for hinting that he might not be totally perfect."

"That was different." She made a face. "I can't help it. It's instinct. I'm sorry I said you were ridiculous. I've been a little upset with you lately." She shook her head. "No, a lot upset. And I can't let it happen again. I can't let Caleb get angry and send me away." She reached out and took Jane's hands. "You've got to help me."

"He's your brother, Lisa. I have nothing to say about it. Speak up for yourself."

"You have everything to say about it. Caleb told me about the blood and the photo and all the rest." Her hands tightened. "Those monsters are back." Her voice was shaking. "They killed my sister. And now they're going to try to kill Caleb. He's the one they always wanted." Her face was pinched and pale. "Did you really think that giving me a drink or two would make that particular nightmare go away?"

"No, I just wanted to remind Caleb that everyone isn't as resilient as he is." She added gently, "But there was no need. I could see that he'd tell you everything in the gentlest way possible."

"Resilient?" She looked at her incredulously. "Why shouldn't he have been? He had all the practice in the world. I've told you that he went through hell from the day he was born. He just refused to show it. When we were kids, I watched our parents call him a monster and punish him for any little wrong." Her eyes were blazing. "Bad blood, they'd say. It was no wonder he made everyone around him afraid. Naturally he was blamed for anything that went wrong." She drew a deep breath and tried to regain control. "And he listened to them, took everything they said and did to him, and just walked away. And then later, when he was older, there were always real monsters out there in the world who wanted to destroy him." She drew a shaky breath, trying to recover her composure. "But I won't let anyone else punish him ever again."

"I can see how you'd feel like that," Jane said gently. "But I've never seen anyone as strong or clever as Caleb. If he ever was a victim, every trace disappeared a long time ago." Wise words designed to ease the girl's pain. Yet Jane had moments when she felt the same fury at injustice that Lisa was feeling. But this was not the time to do anything but soothe and distract. "He can take care of himself. He doesn't need you, Lisa."

"Well, he's got me." She was smiling recklessly. "Whether he wants me or not." She lifted her chin. "And I'll make him want me. I'll show him I can be useful. He has no idea all the things I can do these days. Every place I've gone, every job I've taken, I've learned something."

"I believe he probably does have a good idea," Jane said quietly. "Just because he wasn't with you doesn't mean that he didn't keep track. I bet whenever he talked to you on the phone, he ended up knowing exactly what you were doing."

"Maybe." She nodded. "Probably. I always tried to make our conversations interesting for him. Well, then it may be easier for me to convince—" She stopped, frowning. "No, you'll still be necessary. It wouldn't be enough."

"Necessary?" Jane repeated warily. "What are you talking about?"

"You have to convince Caleb that I should stay with you and help you." She held up her hand as Jane opened her lips to protest. "And you can't let him bring in any of those people he was talking about to stash me away someplace. They'd just get in the way."

"And might save your life," Jane said dryly. "I agree with Caleb that that's an end much to be desired."

"But Caleb doesn't even believe I'd be a principal target." She grimaced. "He carefully explained that to assure I'd be safe now, he could tuck me safely away. It seems that the cults have been convinced that I just don't have what it takes as far as their needs are concerned. What a blow to my ego. And I did so want to grow fangs or give them all my blood as Maria did."

"Not amusing, Lisa."

"That wasn't amusement, it was bitterness. Or perhaps I'm just jealous because I wasn't even on the list to act as bait for Caleb this time. Caleb said it's clear that everything they've done, the photos, the attacks, are elaborate setups to warn him that you're the chosen one." She made a face. "Those ghouls evidently think that sex and whatever else keeps him coming back to you will be the weapon they need to bring him down." She added fiercely, "And they don't even realize that you don't *care* if they kill him."

Jane felt a jolt of shock that turned to outrage. "That's not true, Lisa. And I won't allow you to say it. I know you're in pain, but that's no excuse." Then she saw the tears running down Lisa's cheeks and the anger melted. "Shit." She pulled her into her arms and held her close. "Maybe a *little* excuse. But don't you dare do it again."

"I won't," Lisa whispered. "I know it was a lie. You don't want him to die. You just might not do everything I'd do to keep him alive. Maybe no one would. I should have been the one they chose." She pulled away and wiped her cheeks on the back of her hands. "I told you I was bitter. And I'm acting like an adolescent. I promise I'll make it up to you." She swallowed. "I'm scared, Jane."

"And that's the last thing Caleb wanted. That's why he intends to surround you with Palik and his men—to protect you."

"As he has all these years?" She shook her head. "I was sitting there beside the fire listening to him give me all the reasons why I'd be safe from the people who'd killed Maria and wanted to kill him. He was very matter-of-fact and perhaps didn't realize the picture he was drawing for me. But I'm not a fool. Everything he's done since I was a child, every sacrifice he's made, has been to keep me safe and protect me from being associated with him." She paused. "Did you know that, Jane?"

"Not until very recently. I've never been able to read him."

"I knew some of it. But I've had trouble understanding some of the things he's done lately because it hurt me." She sat up straight. "Okay. Now I have to get down to business and talk you into forgetting I've been such a bitch, and into doing the right thing." She moistened her lips. "And the right thing is letting me stay close to you and your brother until Caleb manages to take down that cult. I have medical training that will help, I can shoot, I do karate. I have an entire range of other skills and talents that you'd find useful." She paused. "And I have one other talent that you'd find of benefit if I find it necessary to call upon it."

"No." Jane instantly shook her head. "I saw what killing Santara did to you. I thought you were going to fall apart. I was grateful for my life, but I don't want you to ever have to do it again."

"I don't, either. It did something... strange to me." She stared her in the eye. "But I would do it to keep you or the boy safe. I *have* to stay close to you."

"Why?"

"Because Caleb will be close to you," she said simply. "You're the target, and he'll be waiting for them to attack you. If I'm there, they won't get the chance."

"All very dangerous reasons, Lisa."

"Good reasons. Shall I give you another one?" She took a deep breath. "I saved your life and changed my own forever when I used the blood talent on Santara. I never thought I'd ask you to repay me for what happened that day." She added softly, "But I have to give you another reason to make Caleb keep me here to take care of you. It's that important to me."

"And it's important to me that you stay alive," Jane said curtly. "I'd be crazy to let you take a chance like that. Caleb had the right idea. Go away and have him set up protection for you. Look, I don't know if Caleb's right about all this, but I'm sure he'll arrange enough security for me."

Lisa was silent. "You're saying no." She shook her head. "You can't do that. I told you, it's important." She got to her feet. "Please change your mind. I don't want to cause you any trouble. It would be so much easier if you'd help."

Jane didn't like the sound of that. "Easier? How?"

"If I can't stay with you, I'll have to go away and just keep an eye on you and Caleb from a distance. But that wouldn't be nearly as efficient." She tilted her head speculatively. "Yet I might be able to bypass you and go straight for those slimebags if I concentrate hard enough."

"You're bluffing. Caleb would never permit it."

"You're right, but he has a major disadvantage. He cares about me. Which means he would never hurt me. And I have a major advantage, I'll do whatever I have to do." She smiled. "And I could do this, if I had to, Jane. I'm not an expert hunter like Caleb who's capable of sending the bad guys straight to hell without batting an eye. But I've taken the time to learn how to listen and watch. Margaret Douglas taught me a lot during these last months on how to be animal- and woods-savvy. And I've always been people-savvy." She grimaced. "If I could only keep my mouth shut."

"That would be truly amazing and gratifying." But Jane was glad that Lisa hadn't kept quiet during these last minutes. She had been perfectly sincere, and what she had said had been fairly terrifying. "But you're on the wrong track. Think about it."

"No, you think about it. I've already made up my mind." She turned away. "Now I'll let you go back to bed while I go down and bunk beside the fire with Caleb." She'd started down the slope. "I'll see you in the morning."

"Wait. I'll get you a blanket."

"I won't need it. I've never had trouble regulating my body temperature. Guess it's just another part of the blood talent. I'll have to ask Caleb." She yawned. "Sleep well, Jane."

She doubted if she'd do that, Jane thought as she went back into her tent. It had been a disturbing night, and tomorrow probably wouldn't be any better.

"Jane..."

She stopped short, her glance going to Michael's sleeping bag. It would have been too much to hope for that he would stay asleep. "It's okay. Go back to sleep."

"I am," he said drowsily. "I just wanted you to know that Lisa always keeps her word . . . That's kind of . . . good."

Evidently on some level he had been very much aware of her conversation with Lisa. "Or kind of bad. It works both ways."

Michael didn't answer. He was back asleep.

But his words had only added to the worry and uncertainty that Jane knew would haunt her tonight.

Two hours later Caleb's phone vibrated in his pocket.

Palik.

He got up from the fire and moved several yards away to answer it.

"His name is Stefano Luca," Palik said when Caleb picked up his call. "He's been renting Villa Silvano north of Fiero Village for the last eight months. He appears to have a good deal of money, but no one knows where it comes from. Rumors are that he has investments in an automobile company in Milan. He doesn't go into town very often, and when he does it's usually to the tavern to talk and drink with the natives. The bartender says he's very quiet, but he's treated with respect by the others."

"You're certain it's him?" Caleb asked. "It doesn't seem logical he'd be this easy to find. He'd realize I'd be hunting him. Setting up only a few miles from the village and that cave where you just found three bodies? Very bold."

"I took the photo we got from the security cameras at Mantua and showed it to the bartender at the tavern as well as several of the merchants around the village. Definite ID. I'm on my way now to the villa he rents to check out his staff." He paused. "And see what else I might run across there."

"Take someone with you."

"I will. I've had my fill of risking my neck for one day. The bodies in that cave were enough to send a chill through me. I'm not like you. Blood has a tendency to turn my stomach. Particularly my own blood."

"I'd be interested to see what you're going to find at that villa, but I don't think it will be Stefano Luca. I believe that crucifix in the cave might have been the swan song for his introductory prelude. I'd judge he's ready to strike closer to the main selection now. I wouldn't be surprised if the residence was closed up."

"I'll still get in and check it out."

"Absolutely. And when you do, I want you to find some item of clothing belonging to Luca and send it to me."

"Right." He paused, bracing himself. "You haven't asked me about Haverty's report. He hasn't found your sister yet."

"I know. Lisa is here. She evidently decided that she didn't want an escort." He added curtly, "Not that the fact that she made it here on her own makes me feel any better about your competence in caring for her."

"Well, it makes me feel better." Palik gave a relieved sigh. "And I guarantee it will make Haverty feel better. Neither one of us wanted to face you. You'll need me to arrange guards for her?"

"Eventually. She's with me now. I'll let you know. Just concentrate on finding Luca and keep him away from Jane and this castle. Get back to me as soon as you have another report on him."

"Will do." Palik cut the connection.

Stefano Luca. Caleb had a name now. He slipped his phone in his jacket pocket, his gaze lifting to Jane's tent on the upper slope. A name and a face for the murdering son of a bitch. But he didn't know enough yet. If he'd been on his own, it would be no time until he had all the facts. But Luca had halted him in his tracks by his attacks on Jane. Caleb couldn't leave her exposed to him.

His gaze shifted across the fire to Lisa. She was sound asleep, and she'd said nothing but a brief good night before she had settled in.

But he imagined she'd had plenty to say to Jane when she had gone to see her. She would have been cautious because she didn't want to displease him, but he'd seen how upset she'd been when he'd told her what had been happening. He knew it would be no time at all until that upset translated into action.

That would be okay; he would take care of her and Jane and Michael. That was what he did. Hunt and protect. He just had to figure out the best way to do it...

———————◆———————

"Hi, Lisa." Two huge amber eyes were shining down at Lisa when she drowsily opened her own eyes. "It's time to get up. Remember me? Michael. It's really awesome that you came back."

"I'm glad someone thinks so." Lisa yawned and got up on one elbow to look at him. "Of course I remember you." Then she chuckled. "Just not like this. You were quite a bit younger the first time I met you. I vaguely recall almost a toddler..." She added, "Maybe not so vaguely. Because I recall you as being fairly awesome, too. And I probably remember you better than you do me, considering how young you were then."

"Age doesn't matter. I remember lots of things about you." He crossed his legs, studying her. "Are you going to dig with us? That would be cool."

"I hope so. I think it would be fun, too." She looked around the camp. It was barely light, but there was a stirring from all the tents in the area. "Where are Jane and Caleb? It might be up to them."

"Caleb came up to the tent to talk to Jane and told me to come down and wake you." He shrugged. "They're probably talking about you. But I think it's going to work out. Don't worry."

"I'll keep that in mind," she said gravely. "Thank you for reassuring me."

"You're welcome." He grinned. "I wanted to talk to you anyway.

Are you going to fix breakfast for us? We have a mess tent and a cook, but you'd do it much better. I remember the biscuits."

"What?" Her eyes widened. "The biscuits? You couldn't."

"Why not?" He frowned in puzzlement. "You were making biscuits over the campfire at the lake. You even let me make a few of them. I wasn't good at first, but I got better."

"Yes, you got better," she said softly. Memories of that dawn by the lake were flooding back to her. She'd been staying with Jane at that misty Loch Gaelkar in Scotland when Eve and Michael had joined them with the rest of the family. They had all been so close and loving, and Lisa had felt alone in comparison. She supposed that was why she had tried to prove her worth to them all by taking over the cooking. She recalled the firelight glowing on Michael's intent, round face as he carefully formed a biscuit into shape. So young... almost a baby... "You were almost as good as I was." She smiled ruefully. "Though I hate to admit it. I'd gone to a gourmet cooking school in Paris the summer before to learn how to bake."

He nodded. "We had a good time. So are you going to cook for us now? I'll help. I'll bet I can talk the cook at the mess tent into letting us use the kitchen for a while."

"I bet you could, too." The kid was bright, eager, and completely adorable. Who could resist him? "It wouldn't surprise me."

"Jane and Caleb would like it," he said coaxingly.

Why not? she thought recklessly. *Go for it.* She didn't have to prove herself to him as she did to Caleb and Jane. This boy was accepting her as he had when he was little more than a toddler. There was something infinitely comforting about that unquestioned approval. It wouldn't hurt to do him this small favor. "At the moment all I care about is whether you and I would like it." She made a face. "And for you to show me where I can get a quick shower and brush my teeth."

"Great!" He jumped to his feet and held out his hand to her. "I thought about that. There's a shower room next to the mess tent.

I'll take you there. While you're showering, I'll go talk to the cook and tell her what we want to do." He grabbed her duffel from the ground beside her. "We don't want her to get her feelings hurt. She's a really nice woman." He was pulling her down the hill. "And then I'll call Jane and tell her what we're doing and when you think that breakfast will be ready. Does that sound okay?"

"More than okay," she said slowly. With the speed of light, Michael had created a complete scenario that would give them the result he wanted. She could almost guarantee that the cook would be happy, that Jane would not worry, and that Caleb would at least be willing to put any decision regarding her on hold until after breakfast. And all the while keeping her in a cheerful, enthusiastic mood instead of the edgy wariness she'd felt when she first opened her eyes. She wasn't entirely certain why, but a tiny bit of her wariness was suddenly back. "And all for a few biscuits..."

Michael looked over his shoulder and met her eyes. "Biscuits are important." Then his face lit with a sunny smile. "But so are you, Lisa. I think we're going to have a very good time. Just enjoy it."

"I will, as long as we understand each other."

"We do." His hand tightened on her own as he turned and increased his pace. "We always did..."

CHAPTER

6

S tefano Luca," Jane repeated. A name for the monster who had
appeared like an ugly phantom in her life. "It seems...too easy.
He's a murderer yet he's certainly not trying to hide. It's as if he let
Palik find him."

"Maybe he did," Caleb said mockingly. "Perhaps he considers
Palik to be the goat to lead the tiger to the trap. We'll have to see
what kind of ingenious lure he'll construct for me."

"Or me."

His smile disappeared. "No, not you. Your part of this is over now
that Luca is sure he's caught my attention. Now it's just a question of
keeping you safe until I'm free to go after him."

"You must remember to tell him that," Jane said dryly. "Oh, that's
right, we have no idea where he's laying this trap." She met his eyes.
"That must be frustrating you. You're so accustomed to being able
to do whatever you please and letting the rest of us trail behind. But
I'm holding you to that promise about Michael. I don't care how
much you want to go after Luca."

"I'd never break that promise," he said. "Though I'd not expect
you to believe me. After all, I am who I am." He turned toward

the tent opening. "I just wanted to come up and tell you what was going on. You deserve to know, since I've managed to put you in the crosshairs of this Luca. I also called MacDuff this morning and arranged to put on those extra guards we discussed last night."

"You mean the ones to protect Michael and me when this Luca kills you? That idea sucks as much this morning as it did last night."

"I agree. I was in a weird mood last night, but I'm back to normal now." He thought about it. "No, maybe a little more on edge than usual. But I still want you protected if I happen to be busy killing Luca at an inconvenient time." He smiled. "And that mood did have its advantages. You were quite emotionally involved at the thought of my possible demise. You still are."

"Because you were being stupid. And I need you."

"Yes, you do," he said softly. "It's what I keep telling you. Someday you'll—"

Her phone rang.

"Michael." She picked up the call. "Hi. I was just going to come down and—"

"Lisa's going to make breakfast for us," he interrupted. "Remember when she used to cook for us when we were at Loch Gaelkar all those years ago? I was just a little kid then but those biscuits were so good. After I woke her this morning, I asked her if she'd cook them for us again today. But she said we have to wait until she's at least out of the shower. So could you and Caleb come down to the mess tent in about forty-five minutes?"

"I don't see why not. Everything okay?"

"Fantastic. It's going to be great having Lisa back. See you." He ended the call.

Jane looked at Caleb. "You heard. Breakfast in forty-five. It appears that Lisa is going full speed ahead to show how efficient she'd be." She stopped. "Or perhaps Michael had something to do with it. One can never tell."

"I'm sure that Lisa doesn't need any help," he said grimly. "She's definitely a self-starter. Would you care to tell me what you discussed last night? Or is it confidential?"

"Confidential? Lisa's too angry with me to consider me a confidante. It was all about how much she loves you. How I don't deserve to be the chosen one Luca is using as bait. How she has to stay and take care of you so the bad guys can't take you down."

Caleb muttered an oath. "I thought it was going that way last night before she went up to see you. God, I'm sorry. I'll call Palik and have him assign her guards right away and find a safe place to put her."

"That's what I told her would be the best course of action last night. Entirely reasonable." She shook her head. "But after tossing and turning for most of the night, I decided what's reasonable for most people wouldn't be reasonable for Lisa. She as much as told me that if she was sent away, she'd just disappear and go her own way. You know what that means. And she wasn't being difficult. She was telling me she had no choice." Her voice was tense. "I could see it. When you love someone, you have to do whatever is best for them no matter what anyone else thinks. She feels like that about you. She always has and always will. So we just have to make it work."

"And give in to what she wants?" He shook his head. "I can make her do what's best."

"No, you can't." She stared him in the eye. "And I'm not going to let you do what you think is best. Because being safe isn't always best in the long run. Not when it has consequences like Lisa running away and doing her own thing. You've made some crappy decisions lately, Caleb. You should never have sent her away instead of keeping her with you. I won't let you make another one. By all means, get Palik to arrange protection for her if you like. But she stays here with us where she wants to be. Get used to the idea."

He was silent, his gaze on her face. "It's a mistake."

"It can't be any worse than some of the others you've made."

Another silence. Then he turned away. "God knows that's the

truth," he said wearily. "Have it your own way. You might regret it." He left the tent.

She released the breath she hadn't realized she was holding. It was all very well to think about interfering between Caleb and Lisa, but their relationship was so complicated that to actually do it was a challenge. And he was right, she might regret it.

But not to do it would be worse. For months she had been hiding from Caleb, afraid to face the painful turmoil of the decision she had made in her own life. If she wasn't ready to face her own chaos, she should at least help to confront what Lisa was going through.

If Lisa would even let her get close enough to help, she thought ruefully as she turned away to dress. Oh, well, worry about that later. She had just confronted Caleb and it hadn't gone too badly. She'd simply have to take on one sibling at a time.

———◆———

TOWER HOUSE
ITALY

"Dimak Palik broke into Villa Silvano last night," Davron said as he strode into the library. "We let it happen as you told us to do, but I had trouble keeping Alberto from making a move." His lips indented sardonically. "Those kills at the cave have made Alberto much more aggressive. He wanted to go after Palik and his men and have his very own sacrifice. I think he's become a true believer."

"Nothing wrong with that," Luca said. "As long as he doesn't get in my way." He got to his feet and moved toward the French doors. "You let Palik see the bedroom?"

"Yes." He paused. "He took the photos you wanted. Caleb should be receiving them soon. Are you certain that it wasn't...too much?" He was hesitant. "It could be misinterpreted. I think Alberto was confused about it."

"Because Alberto is a fool." He added coldly, "As you are, Davron. I assure you that Jane MacGuire won't be confused and Seth Caleb will not misinterpret it. He'll understand exactly what I'm telling him." He looked out at the beautiful lake that stretched as far as the eye could see. He loved the sunlight on the lake far more than seeing its deep darkness at night. The darkness had strength, but the burning sunlight enveloped him and made him complete.

As Caleb's power had dark strength.

As Jane MacGuire would burn and light up the world to show everyone what Luca had created.

KENDRICK CASTLE

"You know, I don't really like digging in the dirt," Lisa said to Jane as she sat back on her heels and wiped her forehead. "I realize that it's supposed to be a learning experience, but I'm too impatient. Doesn't it bore you?"

"Sometimes." She smiled. "But there are always possibilities, and I've done quite a few digs. You just have to suspend the present and go back a few thousand years. Besides, I like being with Michael." She glanced at Michael, who was digging with a group of teenagers a few yards away. "And I don't believe he has to suspend the present, he just kind of glides past it." Her gaze shifted to Lisa. "But you don't have to dig with us if you're bored. I'm sure that Michael would be ecstatic if you went back to the kitchen and concocted another wonderful meal for dinner."

"It was good, wasn't it?" Then she shook her head. "I can't do it too often. Michael's too generous. He was feeling guilty about not feeding the rest of the volunteers. I can see myself running a glorified soup kitchen. Fun, but it would take me away from you and Michael, and that's why I'm here." She glanced away from Jane and stuck her spade in the ground. "And that would give Caleb an excuse to send me away again. I can't do that, not when you worked so hard to give me this chance. I don't know how you persuaded him to do it. Caleb doesn't change his mind."

Jane shrugged. "Yet you asked me to try. So perhaps he does."

"He said he told you it was a mistake."

"And I told him he'd made some of his own." She chuckled. "Thank heavens you weren't there to defend him to me again. It would never have worked out."

Lisa looked up at her. "I'm trying to say thank you."

"Drop it. It's done."

"Not exactly," Lisa said hesitantly. "I have to make something right. I thought it would be okay, but now I owe you. I'll have to clear it up."

Jane frowned. "Clear what up?"

"I was a little angry with you. I was thinking about doing something that wasn't quite...honorable." She added quickly, "Though I didn't do it. Caleb blew up at me and I couldn't convince him I was right." She moistened her lips. "I only wanted what was best for him. But he wasn't kind to me, Jane. It went on for months."

"What went on for months?" Jane asked. "And I can't imagine Caleb being furious with you for that long. He might be a bit stern, but he does adore you."

She lifted her chin. "I wouldn't give in. He wasn't being reasonable. After all, it was all your fault. Someone had to do something."

Jane sat back on her heels. "And now I'm in the middle of this?" She wiped her hands on her towel. "I think you're right, you might very well have something to clear up. What is all my fault?"

"When I asked about you, Caleb told me that you'd decided not to see him any longer." She shook her head, her eyes suddenly blazing. "I couldn't believe it. How stupid could you get? Caleb could have any woman he wanted and you walked away from him?"

Jane had suspected that this was the bone of contention from their phone conversation when she was at the tearoom. "That's none of your business, Lisa."

"Of course it's my business. For some reason he wants you, and you left him. You might have even hurt him. How could you do that?"

"You don't know that I did. As you said, Caleb has no problem finding women willing to play his games. It's not as if I'm special to him. I had no idea even where our relationship was going."

"Wherever he wanted it to go," Lisa said fiercely. "If he wanted you, that's where he could have taken it. But he wouldn't do it." Her lips tightened. "And he wouldn't let me do it. He wouldn't be reasonable."

"Wait a minute." She held up her hand. "What are you talking about? Do what?"

Silence. "What do you think?" she said. "The *persuasion*. He's much better at it than I am. He could make you want anything, do anything, that he chose. It would be easy for him."

Jane stared at her, shocked. "No, it wouldn't. Because it would be the last time."

Lisa shook her head. "I don't think so. As I said, he's much better than I am. I believe it's just a matter of concentration and repetition. But he wouldn't do it. He said that wasn't the way he wanted it to go." She looked her in the eye. "So I told him that I'd do it for him. It would be harder for me, but I could give him what he wanted."

"My God." Jane couldn't believe it. "That's incredibly *wrong*."

"It was for Caleb," she said simply. "He'd given me everything. I've never been able to give him anything. And after you were with him for a while, you'd see how lucky you were. I would have made sure you liked it. I didn't see why Caleb got so upset with me."

"Caleb's not the only one," Jane said grimly. She shook her head. "And I was so relieved when Caleb told me that you hadn't used the blood talent since that day you saved me. Yet now you pull this completely arrogant and selfish idea out of your hat? Have you used this . . . this *persuasion* before?"

Lisa didn't answer for a moment. "No, I really didn't like the idea. It didn't seem fair."

"Until it was for Caleb."

"What can I tell you? It was something that I could give him." She frowned. "And it was something that you should have given him yourself if you'd had sense. I thought about it, and the only reason you might have broken up with him was because you were afraid. Everyone has always been afraid of the things Caleb is able to do, but I didn't believe you were. So I decided it might be smart to just give you a push to get you over it." She frowned. "And it's not as if I actually did it. You didn't get hurt. I was the one who was punished."

"Oh, yes, you said he scolded you," Jane said caustically. "How terrible for you."

"It was more than that. It *was* terrible. Because I wouldn't promise I wouldn't do it. It didn't make sense to me." She paused. "He cut me off," she said jerkily. "From that day, he broke off all contact. Do you know what that did to me?"

Jane could imagine. For Lisa, losing Caleb would have been the cruelest punishment she could suffer. "Perhaps taught you a lesson?"

"He could have done anything else. He didn't have to hurt me like that. It went on for months, and I couldn't believe it was happening." She grimaced. "And the longer it went on, the angrier I got with you. You were to blame for it all. Why didn't you just do what he wanted you to do?"

"Because I have free will and I do what I please. But probably neither you nor Caleb would appreciate that concept. You're accustomed to reaching out and taking whatever you choose." She was trying to smother the rage searing through her. "And I don't appreciate being caught between the two of you. Go find someone else you can dangle like a puppet, Lisa."

Lisa shook her head. "He doesn't want anyone else. Besides, I gave him my word when he called a few days ago. I have to keep it now." She paused. "And I'd do it anyway, because I'm grateful that you talked him into letting me stay with you. That's why I had to be honest with you. Do you think it was easy for me? I knew you'd be angry. Caleb will probably be angry, too, if you tell him I let you know. He doesn't like me to interfere in his life."

"That makes two of us."

"But his life *is* my life," Lisa said simply. "I have no choice. It's been like that since I was a kid. He realizes that, too, when he's not angry."

"Well, I don't realize it." She took a deep breath. "Did he teach you that *persuasion* crap? I know he taught you the blood talent years ago for your protection."

"No, he just told me the basics and said that I'd have to learn the rest for myself. He said to be careful with it because it could be more dangerous than the blood talent." She shrugged. "I played with it a little, but as I said, I didn't like the idea, so I didn't try to actually learn it. But I knew enough to be able to do what I needed with you. That would be simple."

"I don't regard that as reassuring."

"You're really upset," Lisa said. "I guess I would be, too. That's why I never liked the idea. How can I make it up to you?"

"I'll think about it." She wanted to *shake* her. "It would have to be something very special to make up for that ugliness you were planning for me."

She frowned. "It wouldn't have been ugly. I told you, I'd have made sure you liked it."

"It would still have been ugly." She bit out, "And you will *never* think of doing it. Understand?"

"Of course. I promised Caleb."

"And now you will promise me."

She nodded. "I promise." She got to her feet. "And now I'd better go and dig with Michael and his friends. You won't want to be around me for a while. I don't want to make you any unhappier."

"That's very kind of you," Jane said carefully. "So considerate."

"It's the truth," she said quietly. "I like you. Since my sister died, I've never liked any woman as much as I do you. That's why I couldn't understand why you were being so idiotic. But I do want whatever is best for you."

"When you don't want to serve me up on a silver tray to your brother."

Lisa grinned. "I'm trying to keep that separate. Besides, I promised." She turned to go. "And I will make it up to you." She headed across the dig toward Michael. "See you later . . . "

Jane listened to Lisa laugh as she watched her slide down into the pit beside Michael and his friends. For her, evidently, the conversation was over and she'd moved on. Jane wished she could do the same. She was still feeling furious and indignant and a little helpless. She'd wanted to scream at Lisa all the time they'd been talking. The girl clearly didn't understand the concept of free will, or if she did, she couldn't connect it to Caleb . . . or Jane. She might very well have used that damn *persuasion* if Caleb hadn't stopped her.

And one of the irritations Jane was feeling was because she understood why. Right and wrong didn't exist for Lisa where Caleb was concerned. There was only safe or unsafe, happy or unhappy. She supposed she should be grateful that Lisa seemed to have a few ethical restrictions where everyone else on the planet was concerned.

Maybe. How did she know? The girl was unique and had her own code. Jane had to either jettison her or learn to read that code. She'd thought she'd come close at one time, but Lisa was much more complicated now.

Yet Jane genuinely liked her, dammit.

But what Lisa had almost done was totally wrong and incomprehensible. Would she have actually gone through with it? And could Jane run the risk that it might happen again?

"You're frowning," Caleb drawled from behind her. "It's not even noon and Lisa is nowhere in sight. Have you already banished her from your presence?"

"Her choice," she said curtly as she looked over her shoulder to see him standing a few yards away. "She's over there working with Michael."

"But that still doesn't explain the frown." He tilted his head, studying her face. "Something's wrong, but I'm not going to pursue it right now. I'm too pissed off myself and I don't need anything else to set me off."

"Heaven forbid. We wouldn't want anything to cause you any annoyance when you're always so even-tempered."

"And I'm too pissed off to have you sit there and take potshots at me." He reached down and pulled her to her feet. "I have something to show you. Come on, we're going to your tent where I won't have to be polite or civilized if I don't feel like it."

"I haven't finished for the day. Let me go tell Michael that I'll be—" It was too late. Caleb was already pulling her up the hill toward the tent. "Let go of me. If this is your idea of being polite, you must have been raised by wolves."

"No, I was the wolf." He dropped her wrist. "I was raised by wonderful, civilized parents for whom everyone in the neighborhood felt respect and a deep compassion. It just goes to show that you can never tell how a kid is going to turn out."

"Shut up, Caleb. I've had enough today." They had reached her tent, and she went inside. It was hot and stuffy in here, but she didn't bother to turn on the portable fan. They wouldn't be here that long. "Just show me what you want to show me. Palik? You said he was going to Villa Silvano and you were expecting something from him. How bad is it?"

"Not good."

She stiffened. "Deaths?"

"Two. It was the caretaker and his wife, a couple in their seventies.

No crucifixions, but still very bloody. They were propped up against the wall in the foyer with their arms outstretched, as if in greeting." He handed her his phone. "Touching, don't you think? Luca wanted to welcome me or whoever I sent to come calling. But he was sparing of the blood this time. He only used it to lead from the bodies in the foyer to the room he wanted to highlight."

Jane forced herself to look away from that elderly couple with their frozen expressions of stark terror. "Highlight? Which room was that? You said there were only two bodies."

"The master bedroom. As far as Luca was concerned, the butchery wasn't as important as the rollout of his plan this time. Though he left a note pinned on the man's chest that I'd be hearing from him soon." He nodded at the phone. "Take a look. He was very explicit about everything he was going to take from me...and you. You'll see that every one of the photos is labeled 'Mine.'"

"What do you—" She was staring down at a very familiar huge stone house where she had spent many weekends with Caleb. "This is your place in the Highlands."

He nodded. "He got some very good shots of it. The next picture is Fiero Castle in Italy. That's the place where the Ridondos moved when they decided to abandon the dark path and get away from the village." His lips twisted bitterly. "He might have thought of it as a treasured ancestral home, but God knows he'd be welcome to that one. I always hated it."

"It's magnificent."

"Yes. The Ridondos wanted to be sure to impress the villagers of Fiero with their palatial grandeur when they weren't being terrified by their skill in the black arts." He folded his arms across his chest. "There are two more of my houses, one in Geneva, Switzerland, the other in Paris, that he also evidently took a liking to. He must not have cared for the one in the Caribbean. Obviously he has no taste. That's one of my favorites."

"'Mine,'" she repeated as she flipped through those photos. "Very arrogant. And not bright or he'd know he couldn't take them away from you just by boasting he was going to do it."

"It amused me until I came to the next photos." His lips tightened. "Then I wasn't amused at all."

She glanced up at him and inhaled sharply. Not amused, indeed. She quickly brought up the next photo.

MINE.

It was the painting of Fiona MacDuff.

She brought up the next photo.

MINE.

It was a copy of the photo of her that he'd pinned to the wall at MacDuff's Run, and on the chest of the man on the crucifix in the cave at Fiero.

MINE.

Another photo of a painting Jane had done of a young boy on a street in Amsterdam. She inhaled sharply. "I did this painting two years ago. It won me the Euro Award for Excellence."

"I remember. It was compared to works of the Italian masters of the Renaissance. And it was sold to an anonymous collector right afterward. Don't stop there," Caleb said. "He didn't."

She went to the next photo.

MINE.

Another picture of her, this time a close-up on the lounge balcony at Mantua, smiling faintly, her eyes intent on her sketch pad.

MINE.

Another photo of her bending down to look at the waters of the bridge. It must have been taken from one of the second-floor windows of the house on the street behind her because he had caught a glimpse of the faint swelling of her breasts against her white shirt.

MINE.

A photo of her laughing, her head thrown back as she talked to one of the children at the ice cream shop down the street from the hotel.

MINE.

A photo of Jane sitting on her own balcony, drinking coffee and talking on the phone.

Her thumb moved more quickly.

MINE. MINE. MINE. MINE. MINE. MINE. MINE...

Jane couldn't believe it as she flipped through photo after photo. Every time of day and early evening there were pictures of her sitting, standing, walking. Some casual, some broaching on intimacy because she'd had no idea she'd been observed. A few were outright sensual as she raised her face to the sun with lips parted. Or the one where she was stretching, with her hands lifting her long red hair to cool the flesh of her nape.

"Good heavens," she murmured, stunned. "Incredible. How many are there?"

"Thirty. Forty. I didn't count after the first dozen or so. I was too pissed off. Each photo was blown up ten by twelve and mounted on the wall of the bedroom. There's one last long shot at the end that shows all the photos displayed from the king-size bed at the far end of the room." He paused. "Which Luca must have occupied while he was staying at the villa."

"That son of a bitch," Jane said between set teeth as she pulled up that final photo. "Was he trying to make me look like a spread from *Playboy*?"

"That was my first thought. But then I had another one that made me even more uneasy. Those photos were meant to catch the person you are. Even the more intimate ones were more sensual than sexy. He took his time with all of them. I told you when I came back from Mantua that he'd spent days getting those photos of you." He said harshly. "I didn't think they'd turn out to be...this."

She frowned, puzzled. "What?"

"They're almost a..." He shrugged. "He not only wants you, he wants to know you. Or maybe he thinks he does already."

"You're crazy," she said flatly.

"Probably. But that doesn't change the fact that sometimes lust isn't enough. One gets a hunger that can't be satisfied by the usual means." He bowed his head mockingly. "As I've learned from dire necessity. Which means Luca is going to be very, very disappointed that I won't give you up. Screw him."

"You don't have me. And I doubt if he's feeling anything for me that's in the least sensitive or cerebral. After all, he's a ruthless murderer."

"And I'm a hunter. Which some people might say comes down to the same thing." He snapped his fingers. "But that just proves your point, doesn't it? What could I be thinking?"

"I don't know. I never do." She looked at him. "But you're no Stefano Luca. Was this all that Palik sent?"

"No, he sent one more photo that I had trouble decoding. I had to think about it." He grimaced. "I was too involved with his first barrage of photos of you to pay proper attention to that one." He reached over and flicked the photo button. "It's a shot of the Royal Bank of Scotland in Edinburgh. Very substantial, very prosperous, but it's not my bank. I prefer Geneva and the Caymans. But I don't think that Luca made a mistake; I think he's indicating that whatever funds I have there are going to be taken from me." He shrugged. "Though we might hear more about it down the road."

"Royal Bank of Scotland," Jane repeated thoughtfully. Something was mentally stirring as she gazed down at the photo of the building. It wasn't her bank, either, but it was familiar, she'd been there recently...

Then it came to her.

She looked up to meet Caleb's eyes. "It's MacDuff's bank." She took the next step. "And the last time I was there was when I went with MacDuff and his men to deposit Cira's treasure after we found it at Loch Gaelkar. As far as l know, it's still there in a special vault."

"And it could very well stay there indefinitely," Caleb said. "Just the yearly interest on that treasure would pay MacDuff's bills and make several investments with millions left over. Interesting."

"But that's MacDuff's bank, MacDuff's treasure. Why would Luca send that photo to you?"

"Because in my profession, I've been known to wander off-track in a multitude of different fields in order to hunt down prey." He was looking at the bank speculatively. "Though I've never robbed a bank. But perhaps Luca believes there's always a first time. It seems that he might be including a service in his list of things he intends to acquire from me."

"Then we should warn MacDuff the bank might be a target."

He slowly shook his head. "I don't think so. It's better to wait until the threat becomes a reality. Particularly since depending on how you look at it, the threat might appear to be coming from me." He added dryly, "And my last encounter with MacDuff wasn't encouraging. I don't want him setting that inspector on me and getting in my way."

"He'd know you'd have nothing to do with it."

"Would he?" Caleb smiled recklessly. "I don't." He met her eyes. "And neither do you. I do whatever I have to do at any given moment. Tell MacDuff if you wish, but it just makes my handling of Luca more difficult. I don't like difficult, Jane. I tend to get frustrated, and that leads to me being more violent than usual. You've seen me like that before and you didn't like it."

He was right. She was remembering a time years ago when she'd asked him to help her hunt down an assassin in the mountains in Switzerland. He'd gotten impatient with her then and gone off on his own. She would never forget the moment when he'd come back up that trail carrying the killer bleeding and almost dead on his back to throw him down at her feet like some kind of barbarian tribute. His face had been lit with savagery as he'd met her eyes; there had been no regret and no mercy. "That was a long time ago."

"And you'd hoped I'd changed? I haven't changed. Oh, I have a certain code, but the wildness is still there." He smiled crookedly.

"I've tried to modify it when I'm around you. But that's pure self-defense, because I find the idea of losing you totally unacceptable. And it worked for a while, didn't it?"

"No, obviously not. We're not together any longer."

"Just because in the end I'm just the same, a throwback to those blackhearted Ridondo brothers who became the scourge of Fiero? We only have to work around it." He tapped the screen of his phone. "As we're doing now. So are you going to run to MacDuff with every bit of information?"

"He's my friend."

Caleb waited.

"What would you do if I said yes?" she asked.

"Nothing. But I wouldn't feel free to share information with you as I've been doing."

Jane wouldn't be able to bear being closed out.

And Caleb knew that.

"Okay," she said grudgingly. "But I want to know anything that happens that concerns MacDuff." She added, "And I reserve the right to change my mind if I find out you're going off on tangents."

"But tangents can be so intriguing. You see, we're already compromising beautifully."

"I mean it, Caleb." She couldn't get the memory of his savage expression as he'd thrown that assassin down at her feet out of her mind. "I walked away once. I'll walk away again."

"No, not again," he said quietly, "I couldn't take it twice."

She stiffened. "What would you do? Don't threaten me, Caleb. I've had enough of that from your sister this morning."

"Lisa." He nodded wryly. "That was why you were looking as if lightning bolts were about to strike when I came to get you." He paused. "How bad was it? She actually threatened you?"

"No." She shook her head in frustration. "She apologized. Though I'm still not sure that she wouldn't do the same thing again. Or maybe I guess I am, since I made her promise." She glared at him. "That damn *persuasion*. It didn't occur to you to tell me that even though she hadn't used the blood talent, she was playing around with it?"

"I knew it would upset you. She's very determined. I handled it."

"So she told me. Evidently not very well. I could tell you hurt her pretty badly."

"She wouldn't give up. She was new to the *persuasion*. I had to show her there were consequences for taking what you want." He smiled faintly. "Or what I wanted. It became a little confusing. It was much better I take care of it. I had to monitor that she wouldn't pay you a visit." He shook his head. "And you appear to be a little confused, too, Jane. You're furious and indignant with her and yet you're angry with me for being too hard on her. You can't have it both ways."

"I can have it any way I want it." She turned away and headed for the door. "I just wish I didn't have to deal with either one of you. I have enough to worry about with Michael."

"In this case, you only had to deal with the aftereffects. I made sure nothing she had in mind took place. Not from her." He added, "Not from me. I didn't break my promise."

Yet.

The word was unspoken, and she wanted to leave it like that; the air was too volatile between them at the moment. Even the dimness of this hot, stuffy tent seemed vaguely erotic. Her shirt was brushing against her taut nipples with every breath she took.

And she was aware Caleb knew it. He might be keeping his promise not to use anything but the natural sexual chemistry between them, but that was enough.

He was suddenly tense, catlike, muscles clenched, waiting for her to make the first move. As she had done so often in the past when that searing need had been too strong to resist, she thought. She remembered flying across the room to him and then her legs frantically clasping his hips as he lifted her and pulled her into—

Don't think of it.

But it was too late to tell herself that. The memory was too vivid. The movement. The plunge. The way he knew every way that pleased her, the frantic panic she felt that he might stop and leave her body. The way his fingers dug into her buttocks as he rubbed back and forth—

"Come on," he coaxed softly. "We need it. We have time. Michael won't be back up here for another hour or so, and Lisa is with him."

Michael. That thought jarred her into partial sanity. "Lisa," Jane repeated. "Yes, I'm certain that she'd keep an eye on him. After all, she goes to extreme lengths to fulfill family obligations." She threw open the door. "Let me know when you hear from Palik again."

She left him in the tent and escaped out into the sunlight.

<hr/>

Don't follow her.

Caleb's hands closed into fists at his sides and he stood very still in the tent where Jane had left him. Following her would be the wrong thing to do. He'd been able so far to crush down that temptation to reach out and take. He could still hold on and keep himself under control.

The *hell* he could. He was hurting. It was tearing him apart. He needed her. No one would expect anything else from him, he thought recklessly. He was the savage who had trained himself to have no regrets, and the code he had gathered for himself was flimsy at best. He was the shark in the darkness even for Jane. Why not?

Because it was Jane.

What difference did that make? He could make her feel anything he wanted her to feel. Only a little effort and he could have—

Don't follow her.

Think of something else.

He needed a hunt. He needed the thrill of the chase. He needed the feel of his heart pounding as he ran down the prey.

Stefano Luca.

He reached for his phone. Three minutes later MacDuff picked up his call. "I sent you a name and a face," he said curtly. "Hasn't Tovarth come up with anything? What the hell good are you, MacDuff?"

"Evidently considerably better than you, Caleb," MacDuff said sourly. "You're in a nasty mood. Might I point out that the only thing you've managed to send me are photos of blood and mayhem? Not that I'm surprised when I examine the source."

"Scotland Yard," Caleb said. "Tovarth. What did he find out about Stefano Luca?"

"That he's a very elusive son of a bitch. It was difficult for Tovarth to track him down. Luca doesn't have an extensive record for violence that he can find. Tovarth finally managed to trace him through the Art Thefts Division. The bastard does like his masterpieces, and he's very good at stealing them. He's been dancing around the world appropriating fine art from private owners and galleries for the past ten or twelve years. He's very selective and doesn't hit any country or area too often. Probably to avoid an intensive police search. And he's careful about whom his sales are targeted toward. The art just disappears into some wealthy collector's private stash. Judging by the canny way he's handling his career, I'd say he's probably a very rich man by now."

"The blood?" Caleb prompted.

"Not a visible signature in his early jobs. He wasn't shy about killing guards or anyone else who got in his way, but using the blood didn't appear until the last three jobs he did, in Munich, Istanbul, and Copenhagen." He added grimly, "And here at MacDuff's Run. But he also appears to be constantly evolving. The *Fiona* theft had another puzzling difference. It was valuable, but nothing like the multimillion-dollar masterpieces he'd stolen before. Hardly worth his time or effort. And the bloodletting was deliberate and excessive." He paused. "Almost as if it was a taunt. Which puts us back to square one, doesn't it?"

"So he likes his art," Caleb said. "What else did Tovarth find out? He wasn't hatched from an egg. Give me something personal. Was he born near Fiero?"

"No, Florence, Italy. His father worked as a janitor at the Uffizi Gallery, and his mother was a whore who deserted both of them when Luca was eight. Luca was very intelligent but showed signs of instability and psychosis from early childhood. His father was an alcoholic and often dragged him to work with him at the museums when his mother was doing tricks. Luca became obsessed with Renaissance art and history and spent every spare moment trailing through every museum in Florence. He became particularly interested in the Medici Palace. His teachers said he knew every fact available about the Medici family from the time he was a small child. When he was sixteen, his father was found at the bottom of a staircase at the gallery with a broken neck. Their flat had been ransacked for anything of value, and Luca had disappeared from Florence. Shortly afterward, the art thefts started."

"Any contacts? Friends?"

"No friends, just business acquaintances, and very few of them. He changed them after every few jobs and then they just disappeared from view. It makes one wonder how and where. Perhaps that psychosis was coming into violent play even during that period."

"A primary reason you might not have been able to find out much about his career," Caleb said. "You're right, he appears to be smart. But I don't know where he's going with this. He may be a bit psycho, but everything you've told me points only to an addictive dedication to Renaissance arts. I don't see any connection to cult activities. Was there any mention of it before that crucifix in the cave?"

"Not in Tovarth's report."

"Then this doesn't make sense to me. There have to be missing pieces. Cult members tend to be fanatics and driven by bloodlust. Luca displayed iron control most of his career, and any signs of bloodlust have only recently appeared on the scene." He frowned.

"If he does even have the bloodlust, then he was probably assuaging it by killing his criminal associates instead of guards or any other innocents. Much less likely to arouse a public outcry."

"*If* he has the bloodlust?" MacDuff asked. "It seems clear that he does."

"As I said, sometimes bloodlust dominates and can't be controlled. But he did control it until those last four thefts and the deaths in the cave. Either he had another outlet or the blood was just a setup for what happened at MacDuff's Run."

"Well, heaven forbid I argue. You should know about bloodlust."

"Yes, I should. And also about controlling it. Do you know anything else?"

"Tovarth's still working on it. I think he did a damn good job so far. How is Jane?"

"Stubborn. Worried more about Michael than herself. Handling it. Let me know if you find out anything more."

"You're supposed to be the one handling this. I don't want her involved. Do what I told you to do."

"Yes, my lord," he said sarcastically. "By all means, my lord." He cut the connection.

As if he could keep Jane out of it when Luca was zeroing in on her with every action he took, he thought in frustration. Did MacDuff think he wouldn't find a way to break free and go after the son of a bitch if he saw his way clear? And what MacDuff had just told him about Luca had given him an even stronger sense of urgency. He flipped open his phone again and glanced down at the wall of photos from the Villa Silvano. The care, the time, he had taken with each photo...It was clear Luca wasn't one of those bloodthirsty cult crazies Caleb had dealt with after his sister's death. He was intelligent and patient, and he had his own agenda that might not be what Caleb had first thought. Yes, he was almost certainly involved with a cult, and undoubtedly a bit psycho, but the reasons and motivations could be entirely different.

And different could prove even more deadly.

CHAPTER

7

"Are you still mad at me?" Lisa handed Jane a cup of coffee before dropping down beside her in front of the fire. "I was honest with you, and you like honesty. And I've been very good, haven't I? Didn't you enjoy your dinner?" She glanced across the fire where Michael was playing cards with Caleb. "And I fought off Michael inviting the entire camp up here. I told him you still needed to rest."

"I'm fine. I didn't need to rest."

"You were supposed to take it easy and you worked a full day. And I guarantee you would have needed it after we were run over by all of Michael's friends in the dig. He seems to know everyone and they're all his best buddies."

"That's Michael," Jane said simply.

"Yeah, that's Michael," Lisa said. "So are you still mad at me?"

Lord, she was persistent. "You sound like Michael. I had a similar discussion with him recently. But you're not ten and you shouldn't do things that require that degree of forgiveness."

"I agree and I've said I won't do it again." She was silent. "But I saw you go up to the tent with Caleb, and it worried me. After you came back I noticed he was watching you. He always watches you, but this was different." Her gaze was searching Jane's face. "He didn't want me to talk to you about it at all. Did you give him hell? He wasn't responsible."

"And you want to protect him from my wrath," Jane said dryly. "Very righteous wrath, by the way. But he knows that I leveled it at you and not him. I even said you'd apologized. Though I did throw in my frustration that I was involved with either one of you and wanted my life back."

"But that sounds like you've cooled down a little," Lisa said, relieved. "I can work with that. I'll just continue doing penance until I find something that will completely clear the slate. Is there anything I can do now? More coffee?"

Jane gazed at her eager expression and ruefully shook her head. "I can wait on myself, Lisa. The last thing I want is to have you hovering over me. You're right, it's been a long day and all I want is to stay here by the fire and relax and then get to bed. Why don't you go talk to Caleb and Michael?" She saw her start to frown and said quickly, "And I'm annoyed with what you were intending to do, but you're right, I've cooled down. As long as you don't even think about doing anything like that again, we can start over."

"Great!" Lisa's face lit with radiance. "A new beginning. I won't screw up, I promise." She jumped to her feet. "And I won't hover. But if you need anything, just tell me and I'll—"

"You're hovering."

"Yes." She grinned as she moved around the fire toward Caleb and Michael. "It's hard to dismiss my first plan of attack and go your way. Give me a little time to become accustomed to it." Then she was dropping down beside Michael and looking at his cards.

And Jane could relax and forget about them for a moment or two. She hadn't been lying when she'd told Lisa it had been a long day for her. She needed time to absorb all the information from Palik and MacDuff that Caleb had been shooting at her, as well as to fend off the emotional shocks she'd undergone today. If she could make peace with Lisa, it would eliminate some of that trauma.

Besides, she hated holding grudges, and clearing the decks would keep Lisa from launching an annoying all-out attack to get back in her good graces.

Forget about it. Just look into the red-blue flames of the fire and let it take her away.

He's always watching you.

But Caleb wasn't watching her now. He was smiling at Michael and listening to Lisa's chatter. It was nice to see him with his guard down and letting—

Her phone rang and she glanced down at it. Eve's ID.

Busted.

She'd have to tell her what had happened. She'd been planning on calling her anyway and it would be a relief not to have anything hidden from her.

"Hi, how did the inauguration go?"

"I really wouldn't know." It was a deep, male voice with just the hint of an accent. "Well, I hope, Jane. I'm afraid I arranged for one of my men with a technical background to hijack this number so that you'd take my call. I figured it was time for us to come together."

"Hijack?" She went still. "What do you mean? Who is this? Is this some kind of—"

"Stefano Luca," he interrupted. "And what I mean is that now that I've let you gather enough information about me to make you feel comfortable, it's necessary that we get to know each other. Did you like your photos? I worked very hard on them. Of course, I'm not a superb artist like you. I only play at photography."

She couldn't speak. She was frozen in shock. Luca?

"You didn't answer me. I want to hear your voice." He added softly, "I want to hear you say my name. I've been waiting for a long time."

Don't just sit here, she told herself dazedly. *Do something. Say something. Record the damn call so it can be traced.*

Her hand was shaking as she pressed the RECORD button. "Why should I speak to you? You're a bloodthirsty killer and a thief."

"True. But I'm also exceptionally clever and I'll find a way to make you overlook those other minor faults." He chuckled. "And you must not mind the blood since you took Seth Caleb as a lover. His presence in your life has always intrigued me. That's one of the reasons I decided to bring the blood into my plan for you. It's his specialty, and I had to show you that I can beat Caleb in his own arena."

"Caleb?" Panic seared through her. "You're insane. Why would you even think about that? We're no longer even together."

"Of course you are. I saw you at MacDuff's Run. I don't know what game the two of you are playing, but you're still lovers." He paused. "Until I change that dynamic. I'm a determined man, Jane. All my life I've decided on a course and then gone after it. I started out in the slums of Florence with a whore for a mother and a drunken janitor for a father who showed me all I didn't want to be. My mother was without class or intelligence, my father had no power and thought beating me would give it to him. They set me an excellent example, and after I got rid of them, I was on my way. The day my father obligingly fell down that staircase, I even made a list of my goals. Power. Wealth. Class. Intelligence. All very important, but I had far more goals than those on my list."

"Which you clearly failed to achieve. So instead you decided to go for being just a mindless killer."

Silence. "I'll ignore that, Jane. I understand I've taken you off-guard and you're upset. No, I've gained almost everything I put on that list. I went for wealth first, because that contributes to power. Thanks to the work of several Old Masters I liberated from unappreciative owners, I've almost fulfilled that ambition. Though not entirely. I wish to be fantastically wealthy, not just moderately comfortable. I deserve it. My plans require it. I was very bitter about having to give up those paintings. I would have preferred to keep them for myself, as I have a passion for art. That's one of the reasons you caught my attention all those years ago."

Her hand tightened on the phone. "*Years* ago?"

"Quite a few years actually," he said softly. "Do you believe in destiny? I do, Jane. Some people are destined for greatness and only need effort and determination to make that final push. I was lucky enough to recognize all the qualities of Cosimo de Medici, the great patron, in myself quite early, so I was ready to accept you when you came into my life."

"Cosimo de Medici? You must have been hallucinating. And I've certainly never met you before."

"Well, I guess it was more of an encounter. But I had the opportunity to see several of your sketches and even a few of your paintings at the time. You were just starting your career when we were all thrown together that summer in Atlanta, but I could see your brilliance, the technique, the passion. I'd just started to acquire those Old Masters that were going to make me my fortune, so I took your arrival in my life as a sign and decided to wait and watch you."

That summer in Atlanta? she thought in bewilderment. What he was saying made no sense. Or did it? Could she find something in those words that would help them find him? "I believe we make our own destinies by hard work and not by depending on signs." She paused. "And who was thrown together in Atlanta? As I said, encounter or not, I'm sure I've never seen you before."

"Because I chose to remain in the shadows. My business there with Kevin Jelak was finished, but he was surrounded by an interesting cast of characters and I wanted to see how it was going to play out. You were my principal interest, but Eve Duncan and Joe Quinn were involved, and then there was Seth Caleb. My client, Jelak, was particularly interested in him. Though he was a little afraid because Caleb had certain skills he was wary of going up against."

Her grip tightened on the phone as she finally realized what he was talking about. "Kevin Jelak!"

"Ah, I thought you'd remember that name. A very bloodthirsty serial killer who came very close to killing your Eve and Joe before Caleb stepped in."

"And Jelak was your 'client'?"

"As I said, I was just starting out. It took time and contacts to set up each theft, and I needed something on the side to keep me in funds. Dealing with those idiot cult members served to do that as well as anything. Jelak found me useful to run errands to his cult friends in Fiero."

"Kevin Jelak was a beast and a murderer. He killed Caleb's sister as well as several other innocent women. And you'd have to be just as much a beast to take his orders."

"I took no orders. I merely used him as he used me. But then as I watched you and thought about it, I suddenly realized why fate had sent me to take that menial job with him. It was really to bring me to you...and to Seth Caleb." He continued softly, "You with all that talent and skill I worship, and Seth Caleb with an even darker, more powerful talent, who was constantly revolving around you, never quite out of sight. Together I knew the two of you could give me what I want. Can't you see it?"

"I can see that you're a supreme egotist and a madman. You killed two children in that cave at Fiero. You should burn in hell for that alone. Do you think I should be flattered that you chose me for your sick fantasy? Besides being a murderer, you're a thief and know nothing about art."

Silence. "That was another insult. It stings because it comes from you, but I'm being patient because you haven't realized your place yet. Otherwise I'd have to punish you." He paused. "Shall I tell you what that place is?" His voice was suddenly intense, full of passion. "Think of the artists of the past, Michelangelo, Da Vinci, Botticelli, Raphael. They were nothing in themselves. They would have starved and never reached their potential without their patrons. The popes and noblemen who kept them fed and producing properly were the real creators. And in return it was the duty of the artist to give whatever was required to the patron. Personally, I believe the Medici family were the greatest patrons of their time, but I'll be far greater." He paused. "Yes, you should be flattered. Because no one knows you better than I do, and no one appreciates you more. I've been watching, studying everything about you since I decided that you were the one who was going to help me reach my own potential."

"And what is that?"

"I've told you what I require. To be the supreme patron, with enormous funds and a safe place to live to spend it where no government can touch me." He paused. "And perhaps you, a superb artist, a beautiful woman, to mentor and enjoy."

Shock kept her from speaking for an instant. The sheer egotistical arrogance that he was displaying was incredible. "Then you've already failed. There's no place that will be safe for you now that we know who you are and what you've done. And I'm supposed to believe all this nonsense you're muttering about being my so-called mentor? You're a liar. You shot at me, you almost killed me. You almost killed Michael. So much for your great plan."

"I had no intention of killing you. It was only the time to start teaching you. I only wanted you to feel pain and know it came from me. It's important you learn I'm the only one who can reward you or cause you agony. That's what the Medicis had to teach their artists—but look what glorious lives they led. That's why I was willing to risk you being injured more than I would have liked. I'm glad you survived with only a nasty memory and nothing permanent."

"Like a broken neck?"

"You had a seat belt."

"Or Michael dead? That bullet came close to him."

"I care nothing for your brother," he said impatiently. "Just as I cared nothing for those children in the cave. They don't matter. Why can't you understand? You had to learn who has the power over you. You're a significant part of my plan, and if the boy died, it would have only clarified that for you." He paused. "And I believe

I've done that, haven't I? That's why I called you. I decided that you have to get used to the idea. It will save me time later. I just wanted to touch base and tell you what's going to happen."

"Jane!" She suddenly realized Caleb was now kneeling beside her. His eyes were narrowed fiercely on her face, his expression grim. He held out his hand to take her phone, but she brushed him away.

"Nothing's going to happen to me or anyone I care about, Luca," she said hoarsely. "I don't believe anything you've said. It's all hogwash. Leave me alone."

"But that's not the plan, Jane. We have to be together or you'll ruin everything. I can't permit that. I've waited far too long to make it all come together. You have to be with me. Caleb has to be used and then discarded." He chuckled. "Don't worry, I'll take care of everything. It's all beginning to come together. Just think about me and your place in life. That's all you have to do at present. I'll get back to you." He cut the connection.

He was gone. She sat there stunned, staring down at her phone, trying to recover.

"Luca?" Caleb said grimly. He was swearing softly as he took the phone from her. "Michael suddenly froze and looked across the fire at you. When I saw your face, I knew it had to be bad, but I had no idea you were talking to Luca. Dammit, couldn't you have let me know?"

"Be quiet." She was shaking. "I was in shock. You're lucky I even remembered to record the call." She was still in shock. "It was the last thing I expected." She was trying desperately to keep her voice steady. "His message with those pictures said he was going to contact you later, but it said nothing about me. I thought I was only important enough to be the center of that *Playboy* spread."

"I told you I thought there was more to it than that. You recorded it?" His hand tightened on her phone as he stood up and strode several feet away. "I suppose you don't want to hear it again right now. Stay here." He called back across the fire to Lisa, who was staring at them with wide eyes. "Get her a cup of coffee and take care of everything. I'll be back in a minute."

"Right." Lisa scrambled to her feet and was at the coffeepot and grabbing a cup. "Michael, you put away the cards. I believe we're done for the night."

"I do, too." He was quickly putting the cards in boxes, his worried gaze on Jane. "It's okay now. He didn't want to hurt you this time, Jane. He was just so excited he couldn't wait any longer."

Shock on shock. Her eyes flew to his face. "You *heard* him?"

He shook his head. "Sort of. More felt him, I guess." He sat there watching as Lisa gave Jane the cup of coffee. "But it scared me until I found out what he wanted. You did make him angry that one time, but he wanted more to brag and show you how wonderful he was than to hurt you."

"Hush, Michael." Lisa squatted down beside Jane. "Caleb said I was to take care of her and I don't believe what you're talking about is going to make her feel any better." She grinned at Jane. "Though curiosity is killing me, I'll be noble and not ask questions." She glanced over her shoulder at Michael. "So we'll just sit here and let her gather herself together until Caleb comes back. Okay?"

"Okay," he said quietly. "But I have to tell Caleb right away, I promised to tell him everything and not try to put stuff in order from now on."

"I'm sure that's important," Lisa said. "Though he usually tries to get me to do the opposite." She looked back at Jane. "Drink the coffee. Do you want to get me in trouble?"

"I wouldn't think of it." Jane was beginning to get over that first shock and slowly put together the details of the conversation. Luca was madness. Lisa was real. Michael was real. Caleb was real. If she clung to reality, she'd be able to function again. She lifted the cup to her lips. "In this case Caleb could be right for once. Caffeine might be giving me the jolt I need."

"For once?" Caleb repeated dryly as he came back toward the

fire. "I'm sure that's difficult for you to admit." He jerked his thumb toward the tent. "Thanks, Lisa. Will you take Michael up to the tent and stay with him until Jane comes? I need to talk to her."

"As long as you realize what a sacrifice you're asking. I don't like to be left out of anything." She turned to Michael. "Come on, kid. They're insulting both of us, but we'll get our own back." As they started up the hill, she added, "At least I will, because I'll let you tell me everything you felt bound to tell my brother while we're waiting…"

Caleb's gaze was following them. "Michael felt he had to tell me something?"

Jane nodded. "You said he froze. I thought he actually heard the conversation. Maybe he did, but he said it was more like he felt it."

"And that could be even more valuable," he said quietly.

"I *hate* the idea," she said fiercely. "I don't want that poison to touch Michael. It's bad enough that I had to hear that vile son of a bitch. He's only a little boy."

"Who wants to help you. Let him do it." He paused. "Or he'll do it by himself."

She drew a deep breath. "I know he will. He made that clear to me." She grimaced. "In the nicest possible way. I just have trouble reconciling the boy with that other Michael that's tucked inside his head." She held out her hand for her phone. "And I don't want him involved with the nastiness that's Stefano Luca. Arrogant bastard."

"Determined bastard." He was looking into the fire. "Determined. Self-absorbed. Obsessed. Throw in the fact that he's undoubtedly a psychopath and you have a very ugly customer." His glance shifted to her face. "And extremely dangerous to you."

She shook her head. "Why? I was so upset that nothing was clear to me about what he was saying except that the major threat is still aimed at you." She looked down into the coffee in her cup. "You're the one who has to die. That always seems to be the main agenda, doesn't it? It's how you live your life."

"You really didn't listen if that's all you gathered. It appears that I'm not entirely to blame for the nightmare this time," he said mockingly. "Perhaps I should be insulted that I'm not on center stage. Very damaging to my ego. I'm not the cause, I'm only the impediment that stands in Luca's way." He paused. "It's all about you, Jane."

"You're crazy." She ran her hand through her hair. "No, *he's* crazy. He's actually been stalking me. When you said that you thought he had been watching me, I believed it had only been for a few days—and that blew my mind. But now he's saying he's been practically living in my shadow for years? What kind of creep is he? He was talking about Jelak, and that was the first time I'd even met you. At that time you didn't give a damn about me or Eve or Joe, all you wanted to do was use us to find Jelak who had killed your sister. Yet Luca was speaking as if we were all marionettes waiting for him to pull the strings. He has to be nuts."

Caleb shook his head. "That particular delusion would go right along with everything he said to you. His belief in his own destiny, his search for power, his right to take anything he wanted and not let anything stop him. Why wouldn't he think that his great destiny had rolled out the red carpet for him? And if he was stalking you, it was probably because he considered you the center that he could work his plans around."

Caleb's words contained a logic that she didn't want to accept. "It might not be true. He could just be trying to freak me out. Part of the game he's playing to get at you."

"For God's sake, wake *up*," he said harshly. All trace of mockery was gone from his expression as he fell to his knees beside her and grabbed her shoulders. "Listen to me. I'm having enough trouble coming to terms with this." He gave her a shake. "You're in this up to your eyebrows, and he has every intention of making you part of his master plan. How he does it will depend on what obstacles we put in his path. That thread of sheer egotism running through everything he said to you scares the hell out of me. He's not going to accept that he's to blame for anything. If he's destined to be this great patron to your artistic genius, then anything you do to stop it is going to infuriate him."

"That wouldn't be reasonable. You can't know that."

"I *do* know it. I'm a hunter. I listened to him and I know who he is now. I've seen it before." His eyes were blazing. "If anything goes wrong and I don't handle it right, he might decide that you've ruined everything, and he has to eliminate you. He wouldn't blame himself, he'd blame you, and he wouldn't let you live."

"Let me go." She was feeling as if she were enveloped in the flames that seemed to surround him. "If *you* don't handle it right? You just said it was all about me. Back off, Caleb."

His grip tightened for an instant and then he released her. "Sorry." He sat back on his heels. "But perhaps it's not quite all about you since Luca knows I'm your lover and wants to kill me. That would give me a vested interest."

"That's crazy, too. He said he saw us at MacDuff's Run, but there was nothing—"

"There was something," he said curtly. "It's always there and any- one who watched the two of us together as much as he obviously did would know it."

"Watched the two of us..." she whispered. "Maybe he wasn't lying about how long ago it started. He seemed to know everyone in my life. That mention of Eve and Jelak...He said he worked for Jelak. Is that possible?"

"Maybe. He wasn't a cult member, because there was no one named Luca among those cult members back then. And I guarantee I took care of all the active members after I killed Jelak. It could be what he said was true—that Jelak and the cult were just underworld contacts because he needed the money. It would explain why Luca would have made a connection with the cult when it definitely wasn't his main agenda. After Jelak's death, Luca might have still maintained that connection." Caleb's eyes were narrowed thoughtfully. "But he had to have been very smart not to draw attention to himself. And he's taught himself to be completely unobtrusive or I would have noticed him." He added through set teeth, "I *should* have noticed him. If he was watching you over the years, it had to be at a distance or I would have felt him. There's no way I wouldn't have been aware of the same presence constantly near you."

Jane shook her head. "But it's not as if you were always there. Luca was wrong. We had our own lives, we only came together fairly recently."

"He wasn't wrong. Just because we weren't having sex doesn't mean that I didn't know where you were, what you were doing, and who you were doing it with." His lips twisted. "Oh, yes, I was waiting in the shadows for my chance, too, and when you finally decided that maybe you could trust me enough to let me get closer, I went in for the kill."

"Don't talk like that." She shivered. "You sound as if I was prey you were hunting."

He shrugged. "Because that's how you always thought of me. The Hunter. I knew it even that first time you came to sleep with me. You were trying to overcome it, but I could feel it. But you liked the sex enough to let me keep coming back even if you didn't trust me to be what you wanted me to be." He met her eyes. "So in a way I've been stalking you far longer than Luca. He's very perceptive to have read me so accurately." He got to his feet with one lithe pantherlike movement. "But it won't do him any good that he's made you one of his pet projects on his precious list. I'll still bring him down. It just means that he's going to be more difficult than I thought. He's been thinking and plotting for a long time, and he believes he's ready to make his move. He would never have made that call to you if he wasn't." He reached down and pulled her to her feet. "And that means that he's going to make another move soon to emphasize everything he said tonight. I've got to be ready for him. Go on to bed and get some rest. I've got to call Palik and then Tovarth at Scotland Yard." He was swearing softly beneath his breath. "Luca knows too damn much about us. I've hardly broken the surface about what makes that bastard tick yet. The only way I'm going to be able to bring him down is to study and get to know everything about him. That way I can change and twist everything Luca believes he knows to suit myself. I should have been out there myself gathering information instead of depending on anyone else."

"Because that's what you do when you're on the hunt. That's how the *persuasion* works? Find out everything about the prey and then zero in on him," she said dully as she pulled away from him. "But you couldn't do that because you promised me that you'd stay and take care of Michael. I tied your hands."

"I tied my own hands. You had nothing to do with it. I'll find out all I need to know. It will just take longer. I'm just pissed off because the focus has changed and I didn't realize it was entirely on you."

"But it's not entirely on me," she said unevenly. "Evidently Luca only wants to keep me around to feed his ego and fuck. He wants to kill you. I'd say that tops it." She added with sudden fierceness, "And I'll tell you what else tops it. The fact that you actually had very little to do with this. You've convinced me that I was the one who caught Luca's attention and drew his fire. I was like you and MacDuff and thought that I was just a minor chess piece so that someone could get their hands on you. Because that's the way it's always been. We all accepted it." She stabbed her forefinger into his chest. "But that's not the way it is this time. None of this is your fault. And I'm not going to let anyone kill you just because that nut decided you were in his way. So stop trying to push me aside and send me off to bed, Caleb. I'll make my own decisions."

"Not this time, Jane."

"This time. Every time. It's my life and I have to live it. You heard what he said about Michael." Her hands clenched into fists at her sides. "He didn't care if he killed him. It didn't matter to him.

So I'm not only responsible if something happens to you, but I can't let him hurt Michael. And I can't be running to you all the time and asking you to please protect him. I'll have to handle it myself." She shook her head and said wearily, "I just have to figure how I'm going to do that. So call anyone you need to call to find out what Luca's Achilles' heel might be. I'll obediently go up to my tent and try to work out a way that no one will get killed because they have the misfortune to be close to me." She started up the hill. "No, not try, I'll do it. I won't let that son of a bitch do this to me."

"Stop shutting me out, Jane," Caleb called softly after her. "Even Luca could tell that there was only one way to do that."

By killing him, she thought as she reached the tent opening. And she could never let that happen. She drew a deep breath and then entered the tent.

"It took you long enough," Lisa said as she sat up from where she was lying on Jane's sleeping bag. "It didn't take Michael and me nearly that long to have our discussion and come to a decision what to do with Luca." She crossed her legs tailor-fashion. "I was for drawing and quartering, but Michael said that he wasn't allowed to do anything that violent. He brought up the ten-year-old thing again."

"But I told her I'd still think about it," Michael said with a grin. "And discuss it with Mom. She wouldn't have liked how ugly Luca was to you, Jane."

"Lisa shouldn't have even suggested that to you," Jane said. "And did you have to tell her what Luca said, Michael?"

He nodded. "She's my friend. She's Caleb's sister. She wanted to know."

"All very good reasons," Lisa said. "And it seems there would be no way that Luca would have chosen me to lure Caleb into a trap. But I never thought of you as a femme fatale even when Caleb wanted you. I guess you're beautiful, but you're too . . . wholesome."

"Be quiet, Lisa," she said wearily. "Luca is a nut job, and the principal things he finds attractive about me are my paintings.

Besides, I'm trying not to think of him right now. If you've found out everything you wanted to know from Michael, why don't you go to bed. Or maybe you'll be able to talk Caleb into discussing it all with you. He was on the telephone when I came up here and I'm sure he has plans brewing." She paused. "If I even let him put anything into motion. I have to clear my head first."

Lisa nodded. "That sounds like a good idea. He's probably so furious Luca thought he'd be easy to take down that he might even let me help in some way. Providing I can resist poking a little fun at him." She stood up, stretched, and then headed for the door. She paused a moment to look back at Jane. "Everything Luca said was bullshit," she said quietly. "You're far stronger and smarter than he is, and you'll get the better of him with no trouble at all. And if you need any help, I'm here for you." The next moment she was gone.

And Jane was feeling a rush of warmth as she gazed after her.

"I think it was okay that I told her what Luca was saying to you," Michael said. "She wants to help, Jane."

Jane nodded. "Everyone wants to help. But sometimes we can't let them. Sometimes we have to handle our own problems." She hesitated. "Did you understand everything he said, Michael?"

"I think I did. The feelings are just like words. It was pretty clear." He paused. "He wants to hurt you." He was silent. "And he didn't care if he hurt me."

"I was hoping you wouldn't have caught that. I wouldn't let that happen," she said quickly. "Don't be afraid."

"I'm not afraid." He came over to her and slid his arms around her waist, burying his head against her. "Except for you. He's one of the monsters, isn't he?"

It would be useless to deny it. "Right." She rocked him gently. "And you shouldn't have to deal with them at your age. I'm sorry that I've managed to bring him this close to you. I'll work something out." Her arms tightened fiercely. "He won't *touch* you."

"But you don't have to work anything out. We talked about this, there's a balance." He looked up at her, his eyes grave. "Where there's a monster, there's always someone who knows how to fight him. Caleb will know how."

"No!" She said it with more violence than she intended. She drew a deep breath. "I know you trust Caleb, but that would be what Luca would want. I've no idea what he'd do. I only know he wants to hurt Caleb more than he does me, and he's had time to plan for it. He could set a trap for him or something." She saw that Michael was beginning to frown and quickly smiled. "Hey, I think I'm insulted. I'm not exactly stupid. There have to be more ways than one to get rid of Luca, and I'll find all of them. Maybe I'm the one who's destined to bring down the monster."

Michael was not smiling. "Or maybe it's me . . ."

Shit.

"Sorry. You don't meet the age requirement." She gave him a quick kiss on the forehead and pushed him away from her. "Brush your teeth and get into your pajamas. I think I'll go outside and get a breath of air before I go to bed." She didn't wait for a reply before she was out of the tent. She caught a glimpse of Caleb and Lisa sitting before the fire as she moved into the shadows a few yards away from the tent.

The last thing she wanted was to go down there and join them. She could see Caleb talking on the phone, every muscle in his body tense. He was already readying for the hunt, she thought. And Lisa was sitting there quietly, but she was also intent, clearly ready to reach out and help Caleb.

To help Jane.

I'm here for you, she had said.

And what was worse, Michael's last words.

Or maybe it's me . . .

That had terrified her. Because she knew that no matter how she tried to control him, if he got it into his head that he was somehow meant to help her, there would be no stopping him.

Everyone was determined to jump into the flames to save her. But flames could burn everything in their path, and she couldn't let that happen. Life was so beautiful. None of these people she cared about should risk all that beauty for her. She closed her eyes and could feel the tears sting. So stop feeling and start thinking how to take the reins back in her own hands.

Michael, first...

Five minutes later, she took out her phone.

She didn't hesitate.

She quickly dialed Joe Quinn's number. "Joe, I need to talk to you. Are you with Eve?"

"No, she's working at her studio. I'm at the palace with the new president." He paused. "What's wrong? Should I get hold of Eve?"

"You tell me after I've finished. I'm leaving that entirely up to you."

"Why the hell didn't you call me before this?" Joe asked curtly when Jane finally fell silent. "It's been two damn days and you just decided to keep digging in that dirt and ignoring everything that had happened? When were you going to get around to telling us?"

"Soon." She had known Joe would be pissed off and added quickly, "I told Caleb after I regained consciousness that I had to tell you. I was just giving the police a little time to find out what had happened and maybe catch who had done it. Michael wasn't hurt, and Caleb was here. He promised to stay and watch over him."

"And that was all that was important," Joe said sarcastically. "It didn't occur to you that we might be concerned about you?"

"Of course it did. But I realize Michael has to be your first priority. As long as he was safe, I felt we all had time to take a breath and let the police give us an idea what happened before I dragged you back here the minute you got off that plane."

"So you took your breath and now you're calling me. It's about time." He paused. "And it means that Luca scared you. What's Caleb's take on him?"

"That he's crazy, but wily enough to be dangerous. Which makes Caleb very frustrated that he can't go after him."

"I can imagine. I'm beginning to feel the same way," Joe said grimly. "I'm going to be on the first flight out of here. I'll call you when I get in." He paused. "Eve?"

"I told you that it would be your decision. But I don't want her anywhere around me. You shouldn't be, either, Joe. Luca will try to use her because he knows that I care about her. I shouldn't have anyone near me he can use as a weapon. I didn't want to bring you into it, but I had no choice. I need you here to watch over Michael. I have to release Caleb from his promise because he's a target, too. Michael will be safe with you." She hesitated. "If Eve comes with you, you'll have to worry about watching out for her as well as Michael. She'd be safer there in Maldara, and that would make Michael safer."

"You've thought all this out," Joe said wryly. "But you haven't told me how to convince Eve."

"Just tell her Michael will be safer and so will you. It may be the only thing that will sway her." She paused, thinking. "And tell her that if she comes, it will only mean I'll have to go away somewhere to keep Luca from remembering how close I am to her."

"That might do it," Joe said grimly. "The last thing she'd want is to have you out there alone. But she'd know I'd never let that happen."

"And the last thing I'd want is to be responsible for anyone being hurt or killed because they were trying to help me. That's my worst nightmare." She was silent a moment and then said wearily, "Though this entire thing is a nightmare. It should never have happened to me. It doesn't make sense. I'm a damn good artist, but I'm not Raphael or Da Vinci. And I'm certainly not Helen of Troy or some glamorous model or movie star. There's nothing extraordinary about me. I don't know how to handle this nutcase fixating on me. All I can think of doing is keeping everyone else safe and away from me."

"Not the best plan," he said dryly. "I imagine Caleb will have something to say about it. I believe I'll have to call him after I talk to Eve."

"Caleb has already had something to say about it. But he's one of the people who could be hurt if I pay any attention to him. So talk to him if you like, but don't expect him to have any influence with me."

Joe sighed. "You're wrong. You are extraordinary. Extraordinarily stubborn. You haven't changed since the days when you were a kid running that slum neighborhood like a little general."

"That comes from spending my life bouncing from one foster home to another. If you didn't like it, you shouldn't have taken me home with you. I never promised you I'd change."

"Heaven forbid," he said. "I'll let you know as soon as I can if I've been able to talk Eve into staying put. You're right, she probably could be safer here now. I'll ask the president to keep watch on her while I'm gone. Bye, Jane."

She pressed DISCONNECT as he hung up.

Michael would be safe now. She had taken him from Caleb's protection, and she would try to stay away from him herself as much as possible. And no one was tougher, smarter, or more passionately defensive of his son than Joe.

But that was all she could do right now, she thought as she got to her feet. She needed sleep and rest before she'd be able to think of some plan to make Luca disappear into the sunset.

Plans.

Luca was full of plans and lists and ways to kill and maim and get his own way with everyone around him. Well, he'd had plenty of time. She was just getting started.

She glanced down the hill and saw Caleb and Lisa still awake and as intent as earlier. They were probably also forming a plan or two themselves. And now that she had turned Joe onto what was happening, his quick, keen mind would be going full steam ahead.

She was the only one without a clue what she was going to do to survive Luca.

But it would come, she thought tiredly as she went back into the tent. She was not a SEAL or FBI like Joe had been. Or a hunter like Caleb. But after talking to that ugly beast who had threatened both Michael and Caleb, there was no one with more motivation.

It would come...

MALDARA, AFRICA

"I'm going with you," Eve said flatly. "Stop trying to talk me out of it, Joe."

"I was just laying out the problems as Jane presented them to me," Joe said quietly. "And she was very clear that she doesn't want either of us there, but I was the lesser of two evils. She needs me for Michael."

"You're damn right she does," Eve said grimly. "And what am I? Chopped liver? I'm Michael's mother and I should be with him." Her lips tightened. "And Jane. This isn't only about Michael. The threat is really to Jane. I'm supposed to sit here in this steamy jungle, calmly working, as if they didn't exist? They're my family and I should be there. I don't know what Jane's thinking to believe I wouldn't come."

"Yes, you do. Because you'd be doing exactly what Jane's doing." He paused. "And you'd be right. Because you showing up will complicate things for Jane. If Luca knows everything about her, he'd realize how close you are to her. It would give him another target, another way to get to her. That's why she's trying to isolate herself."

"Like she's always done," Eve said. "Since the minute she came to us when she was just a kid, she's been trying to take care of us and everyone else she cared about. You'd think with all those foster homes she went through, she would have learned she should look out for herself, but it's just not her nature."

"And you're different?" He shook his head. "The reason you couldn't resist taking her in was that she was so much like you. And she feels the same way about you. But because she loves you too much, she knows you wouldn't strengthen her this time, you'd weaken her. She's doing the very best she can considering who she is." He paused. "There's another solution. Do you want me to bring Michael back here to you?"

"No way," she said instantly. "This country is still a tinderbox that could go up in flames if the new government doesn't strike a good balance. I'm a lot more optimistic now, but I won't risk Michael."

"Then will you trust me to take care of him?" He smiled. "Jane seems to believe I can do the job. And, because you're right, and Jane needs to be protected from that asshole whether she considers it a priority or not. Caleb and I will find a way to do it."

"I don't want you to go, either."

"Eve."

"I don't care if I'm being unreasonable." She was scowling at him. "I don't like any of this."

"I know." He paused. "But we both made a promise when Michael was born that we'd try never to be in a situation that would leave him without one of us to care for him."

He knew he didn't need to remind her of that promise, she thought in frustration. It had been one of the foundations of their lives for the short ten years of Michael's life. "And I'm not the one who has the training to keep him safe," she said. "You're backing me in a corner, Joe."

"So what are you going to do?"

She was gazing at him in exasperation. "You know what I'm going to do. I'm going to stay here and nag all of you to let me know what's happening while I sit and go crazy." She looked at the reconstruction of the skull of the little girl, Sada, on the dais in front of her. Sada had been about Michael's age when she had been butchered by soldiers in a village schoolhouse during the civil war that had devastated this country. The twenty-seven children who had died there one sunny morning had haunted Eve. That was why she had been so determined to finish the last few reconstructions she'd agreed to do for the parents and grandparents of the victims. "And I'm going to finish this reconstruction very, very soon because I'm not going to be able to sleep." She turned and went into his arms and held him tightly. Dear God, she loved him. "And if you see anything that starts to bother you, you've got to promise me you'll scoop up Michael and Jane and whisk them back to Atlanta and away from all that blood and turmoil. Okay?"

"Works for me." He kissed her. "I've made arrangements with Novak and his CIA team to give you extra security while I'm gone. If you feel uneasy, call our brand-new president and he'll bring you to the royal palace as his guest."

Her eyes narrowed accusingly. "You knew I'd stay."

"I'd never take you for granted, but I do know you, love." He turned toward the door. "I promise I'll keep Michael safe. And if I don't like the way things are working out, I might scoop you up, too, and take you all back to Atlanta. Home is sounding awfully good to me right now . . ."

CHAPTER

8

KENDRICK CASTLE

What are you doing down here so early?" Lisa asked as she walked toward the dig area where Jane was working. "You should have woken me. Did you have breakfast?"

"An hour ago. Michael and I were both up early and we grabbed something at the mess tent." She glanced at Michael working and joking with his friend Colin, a few yards away.

"I figured it would be a good idea for both of us to have something to occupy us. I wanted to get Michael's mind off that damn phone call and back into thinking about Roman soldiers instead. It seems to have done the trick."

"What about you?" Lisa asked. "I'm wondering what kind of night you had, if you were up and out early." Her gaze was on Jane's face. "Circles. Not so good?"

"I'm fine. I just had a lot to think about." She grimaced. "Not that it did any good. Though I actually tried to get to sleep." She glanced at Lisa. "Not like you and Caleb, who were obviously trying to hatch a plot to save the day the last time I saw you before I went to bed. Any luck?"

"No, Caleb was on the phone most of the night with Palik, Interpol, and that Scotland Yard inspector, but he had me calling a

few of his contacts in Copenhagen about the Luca thefts in that city."
She wrinkled her nose. "It's good that I could use Caleb's name or
they would have hung up on me for calling them in the middle of
the night."

"Why Copenhagen?"

"It was one of the cities where he started using the blood signature
after he took the paintings. Caleb was just following up and seeing
if there was anything else unusual about the thefts. When Caleb's on
the hunt, he makes sure he knows everything about the prey." She
shrugged. "I think Luca was just establishing a pattern. I couldn't see
anything different from his other thefts except that he cut the guard's
throat and used the blood."

"No photograph?"

"No photograph." She frowned. "Next time you decide to leave
the tent early, wake me. You shouldn't be down here without me
knowing. It might not be safe."

"There were other people down here digging. And the security
guards are always milling around by daybreak. I had no intention
of waking you to stand guard over me, Lisa. That was your idea,
not mine."

"It was a good idea. Besides, you made me look bad to Caleb. He
saw you go down and was keeping an eye on you until I woke."

"Ah, it's all about Caleb again."

"Only a little bit. The rest is you and Michael," Lisa said soberly.
"I want to do this right, Jane. Help me, okay? I can't be caught off-
guard as I was this morning. I think I'll have to get my own sleeping
bag and sleep in the tent so I'll know what you're doing."

"Lisa."

"You have to be safe. Not only for Caleb. I'm not going to let
that creep get away with raping or killing you. Nasty son of a bitch.
I promise I won't get in your way." She glanced at Michael. "And
maybe I can help you take care of Michael. We get along great."

"I've noticed." She started to dig again. "But that might not be necessary. I called Joe last night and he's on his way here now. He'll take charge of Michael and will probably want to be with him most of the time."

"So I've been officially discharged?" Caleb asked mockingly from behind her. "Shouldn't I have been the first to know?"

She turned to look at him. "Not officially until Joe actually gets here. I decided it would be better to keep Michael away from me...and you as much as possible. I won't have him be collateral damage if Luca tries to make good on his threats. He'll be safe with Joe."

"Yes, he will. And so will you. I'm not arguing," he said curtly. "I would have kept my word, but I'm relieved that you chose Joe to step up to the plate. I'm just surprised that you called him and told him what was happening. It would be like you to try to protect him, too."

She shook her head. "I told you from the beginning that I'd have to let Eve and Joe know if the police couldn't identify and catch those people who were shooting at us. But things have gone from bad to worse. They're Michael's parents, they have a right. I should have told them before this, but I became...involved."

"Understatement," he said grimly. "You're up to your neck."

"Hardly my fault."

"I didn't say it was. What about Eve?"

She shook her head. "Joe talked her out of coming. No doubt I'll be hearing from her."

Caleb nodded. "And when is Joe going to be here?"

"Four A.M. flight out of Jokan, Maldara. Eight hours in the air plus transport here from Heathrow. Sometime this evening."

"Good."

"You're very eager." She forced herself to smile. "I thought you would be. It means you're free to go on your hunt."

"You're damn right." His gaze was searching her face. "Is that why you did it? You wanted to unleash me so that I could go kill the bastard?"

"I just wanted you to stay alive," she said quietly. "And you'd more likely do that if you were free to strike first than if you had to wait for Luca to set a trap or go after you."

"Quite true. And I *will* strike first, Jane." He glanced at Lisa. "Keep an eye on them from now on, Lisa. I'll be leaving as soon as Joe Quinn gets here, but I have to make a few arrangements before I take off." He turned and headed toward the tent area.

Electricity was in his every step, Jane thought as she watched him move. She could almost feel the sparks flying. He hadn't even left the property, but he was already on the hunt.

And he could die on that hunt. She had done this. She could have kept him here with her, but she had chosen to let him go. She had thought it was safer for him, but what did she know? It was all guesswork.

And the only thing certain was that she was terrified she might have guessed wrong.

She forced herself to look away from him and turn to Lisa. "I suppose that means that I'll definitely be sharing my tent with you for the time being," Jane said. "Just don't think it's a permanent arrangement."

"I won't." Lisa was gazing wistfully after Caleb. "I've never wanted to go on a hunt, it's not my thing. Family history says they started because it was supposed to help assuage bloodlust in the Ridondos who were born with the blood talent, but I never had a bloodlust. I don't know why I'd want to go with Caleb now."

"No," Jane said firmly. "Forget it. Do as Caleb told you to do. Perhaps Michael and I need you after all."

Lisa smiled. "Are you trying to save me from myself?"

"Maybe. I know I don't want Luca to destroy or change anything about any of us. It would be a victory for him." She wiped her hands on her towel. "And I'm spending entirely too much time dwelling on the bastard. I've got to get on with my life." She started up the hill. "And playing in the dirt is losing its charm right now.

I'm going to go get my sketchbook and finish the sketches of the dig I promised to give Lady Kendrick. I meant to do it on the day I went to MacDuff's Run, when Luca erupted into my life. I have to get back on track." She saw that Lisa was starting to follow her and waved her back. "For Pete's sake, I'll only be a few minutes. Stay with Michael."

Lisa nodded. "Okay. Five minutes." She grinned. "Then I'll bring Michael up to look for you. I told you, I have to do this right."

Jane sighed. She had an idea Lisa's interpretation of "right" might be very wearing on the nerves. "Five minutes."

———————————

"Hey, time to quit." Lisa was squatting next to Jane. "The sun is going down and we have to get Michael his dinner."

"What?" Jane looked absently up from her sketch. "It can't be. I just started and—" She suddenly realized the sun was low on the horizon and the dig was almost deserted. The volunteers were still moving around the grounds, talking, laughing, but the workday had clearly come to an end. "I guess I wasn't paying any attention. We usually quit at least an hour before this. Why didn't you stop me?"

"Michael wouldn't let me." Lisa nodded at the boy sitting by himself a short distance away, staring at the setting sun. "He said it was important and to let you draw. He was very firm about it. I didn't dare dispute him. Those sketches of the dig must have been important to more than Lady Kendrick. Michael came over and looked over your shoulder while you were sketching an hour ago and then told me I shouldn't bother you."

Jane made a face. "I didn't notice him, either."

"You weren't noticing much of anything," Lisa said dryly. "Are you always that absorbed?"

"Yes. No. It depends. Usually not while I'm doing casual sketches. I can usually break away." She frowned as she looked down at the sketch she had been working on. "And I wasn't drawing the dig an hour ago. I'd finished those sketches by the middle of the afternoon. I just started playing around after that."

"It doesn't look like playing around to me," Lisa said as she gazed down at the pad. "The detail is incredible, but why a tower in the middle of a rainstorm?"

She shrugged. "How do I know?" She glanced at the towering round stone structure she'd drawn. The tower had a huge, tall, wooden door, and it was surrounded by elms that were being bombarded by ferocious winds, bending the trees almost to the ground. "I've never seen it before. Sometimes it just comes to me. Maybe I was hot sitting here at the dig and I wanted to cool off." She closed the sketchbook. "But it wasn't worth keeping Michael from his dinner. You shouldn't have paid any attention to him." She got to her feet and called, "Michael! Come and help me persuade Lisa to go with us to the mess tent and throw something together for dinner."

"You're through?" Michael jumped to his feet and ran over to her. "That's good, I'm hungry."

"Your own fault. You shouldn't have told Lisa not to stop me. It's not as if I wasn't finished with the drawings of the dig." She put her hand affectionately on his shoulder and started to lead him toward the mess tent. "I was just amusing myself."

"I didn't think you were amused. You looked..." He stopped and shrugged. "I thought that you should finish it. Did it turn out okay?"

"Great," Lisa said. "If you like rainstorms."

"I do. They're really cool. We get a lot of them in Georgia. But Mom won't let me sit on the porch when we do. She's always afraid about lightning striking me." He smiled at Jane. "Lady Kendrick will be happy that you finished those sketches. Are you going to give them to her tonight?"

"After I clean them up a little." She smiled back at him. "If it's not too late. It depends what time it is when your dad gets here and we get him settled."

"That won't take long. Dad knows all about camping, and this isn't even in the jungle. He learned lots when he was in the SEALs. Did you know the SEALs' nickname is Snake Eaters? But Dad said they didn't do that unless it was necessary."

"I'm sure that makes the snakes ecstatically happy," Jane remarked.

Michael nodded. "But I'm just saying that he's very fast and efficient when he's camping. If Mom was coming, he'd probably want her to be more comfortable and it might be different and take a little longer."

It was the first time he'd mentioned Eve since Jane had told him that morning that Joe was coming. He'd asked no questions and just said a casual, "Awesome. That will be great." And this mention of Eve was just as casual, but Jane felt she had to address it.

"It's better if she doesn't come this time, Michael. You know she wants to be here."

He nodded. "But Dad has to take care of her. We always have to be sure Mom is happy and safe." He shook his head soberly. "Sometimes that's hard to do, Jane."

"I can imagine. Well, he must have managed to pull it off this time." Her hand tightened on his shoulder. "Want to call her tonight?"

"That would be great." They had reached the common area, and he was staring inside the open doors of the mess tent. He glanced at Lisa. "I know you said we couldn't invite everyone at camp to dinner, but it's late and almost everyone has already eaten tonight. I only see about seven or eight people inside. Could we invite them?"

"I believe that would be entirely manageable," Lisa murmured. "Eight new friends are better than the forty-nine that you wanted to invite before." Her lips twitched as she glanced at Jane. "Maybe it was good that he insisted on letting you finish that sketch, Jane."

Joe had already arrived by the time they'd finished dinner and walked back up the hill toward the tent. He was standing beside the fire talking to Caleb, a frown on his face.

"Dad!" Michael started running as soon as he saw him. "You should have come to dinner. I was telling everybody about the Snake Eaters, and they really wanted to meet you." He flung himself into his arms. "Maybe tomorrow? I had Lisa invite them for breakfast, too."

"Yeah, maybe tomorrow." Joe hugged him and then held him close for a moment longer. "I'd rather have some time together now." He let him go, then turned to Jane and took her in his arms. "You okay?"

She nodded. "It's good to see you. I haven't heard from Eve yet."

"You will. She was a bit emotional and didn't want to release the full force of it on you." He gestured to Caleb. "He's been filling me in on the new info from Scotland Yard, which was practically nil. I have friends at the Yard. I'll see what I can scrounge up from them."

"Any help is appreciated," Caleb said.

Jane could sense the tension, the restlessness in Caleb, which was almost palpable. She looked away from him. "Do you need something to eat, Joe?"

He shook his head. "I had dinner on the plane." He looked over her head at Lisa in the background. "Hi, Lisa, I'm sure that will be a relief to you. I hear my son has been taking advantage of your good nature and driving you like a tyrant. I'll try to keep him under control." He smiled down at Michael. "Caleb arranged with Lady Kendrick to send up a tent for the two of us. I thought I'd put it next to Jane's. Would you like to help me set it up?"

"Sure." Michael was immediately excited. "I was worried about Jane getting lonely when she told me that I was going to be with you. But this would be like we're all in the same tent."

"Not quite," Lisa said. "I'm sure my presence won't be as appreciated as yours, but Jane has decided she can tolerate me taking your place for the time being." She looked hopefully at Caleb. "Unless..." He was shaking his head, and she shrugged. "I guess you're stuck with me. Need any more help with that tent? I don't eat snakes, but I spent a summer interning at Yellowstone with the National Park Service."

"That should definitely qualify you." Caleb was suddenly beside Lisa, his hands cupping her face. "You can do anything. I know, because I taught you." His face was suddenly alight with affection as he brushed his lips across her forehead. "I'm trusting you to take care of everyone. And take care of yourself, do you hear me?"

She buried herself against him in a bear hug. "Then you'd better make sure I don't have to go rescue you," she said thickly. "It would get in my way." She pulled away and turned to Michael. "You heard him, I can do anything." She was already halfway up the hill. "Let's go tackle that tent!"

Michael laughed and ran after her.

Caleb immediately whirled and turned toward Joe. All the gentleness had vanished from his expression. "I'm out of it?" His eyes were glittering with intensity as he stared directly at him. "The boy's under your care now?"

"Of course he is," Joe said. "Why else am I here?"

"I have to be sure. I can't take anything for granted. I made her a promise. I have to keep it." Caleb turned to Jane. "Have I kept it?"

She frowned in puzzlement. "You've kept it. You know this was all my choice."

"Good. Then I'll be in touch." He turned and strode down the hill away from them.

What the hell? Jane stood there watching him go. Then she was running after him. "Caleb!" She caught up with him before he reached the path leading to the main gate. She grabbed his arm and turned him to face her. "What was that all about? You're acting weird."

"And that's new for me?" he asked sarcastically. "I wanted to get away from here. I said what I had to say. I wasn't in the mood to be polite."

"And you weren't. I wouldn't want you to think that you'd failed. Are you angry? You said this was what you wanted."

"Would it bother you if I was angry?" He was smiling recklessly. "You're always saying I don't talk to you, that I don't tell you what I'm thinking, what's important to me. Well, I told you tonight that it was important to me that I kept my word to you. I had to make certain that you knew you'd reached out to me and I hadn't betrayed your trust as you always expect. After that, there wasn't anything else to say." He started to turn away. "I have to go."

"Wait." Her grasp tightened on his arm. "It's always about you. Did it occur to you that I might have something to say? I hate you doing this, and I hate that I'm letting you do it. It makes me feel guilty as hell." Her fingers dug into his arm as she said fiercely, "So you don't get killed and you come back. Do you understand?"

"I understand." His eyes were suddenly shimmering as he stared down at her. "What do I get if I do? I need an incentive."

"You get to stay alive and torment me. That seems to be your favorite sport." Her hand dropped away from him. "That should be enough."

"Not nearly." He took her hand, turned it palm up, and slowly lifted it to his lips. His tongue touched the veins at her wrist. He licked delicately and she inhaled sharply as heat shot through her. "But I'm encouraged by this touching display, and I believe I can get the rest of the way on my own." His lips covered the pulse point and he suddenly sucked, his teeth pressing without piercing.

She smothered a cry. Her spine arched as she felt the heat sear through her breasts and lower body.

Then the incredible sexual pressure was gone and his tongue gave a final stroke on her wrist that was almost loving. "I couldn't resist," he murmured. "You couldn't condemn me for committing a minor transgression when you were feeling so guilty?"

"Yes, I could." She had to take a deep breath to recover sanity. Once she did, she felt an overpowering sadness. "Because you never really understood that sex wasn't all I wanted from you. You were so good at it that you thought it would be enough." She took a step closer to him. "But you would never have dreamed of treating me as you did Lisa tonight. That was genuine, that meant something, because *she* means something to you. For an instant I actually envied her." She reached out and cupped his face as he had Lisa's earlier that night. "Goodbye, Caleb." She kissed him gently on the lips. "Take care. Good luck."

She turned and walked away.

"Jane!" She was suddenly jerked into his arms and he was kissing her. When he lifted his head, she could see his eyes glittering fiercely in the moonlight. "You want genuine," he asked roughly. "How is that for genuine? Open your damn eyes and see me." He kissed her again. "You're an idiot. I'd *die* for you. Is that genuine enough for you?"

Then she was watching him stride down the path toward the main gate.

She stood staring after him, dazed, bewildered. What had just happened? Something full of . . . wonder.

Then Caleb disappeared into the darkness.

He was gone.

She turned slowly and began to walk back up the hill toward their tents.

She still felt stunned. All the intensity and desperation and the wildness that was Caleb had been in those words. But she couldn't be sure whether he had meant them or if they had been born of frustration and anger.

I'd die for you. Is that genuine enough for you?

Either way, she knew that something important had just happened and she had to come to grips with it. Providing she could pull herself together to think about it. She wasn't doing too well at the moment.

Joe was sitting by the fire, drinking a cup of coffee, and glanced up as she approached. "You saw Caleb on his way?"

"You could say that." She poured herself coffee. "I had to see what was wrong with him. He was acting..." She shrugged. "I don't know. Strange. And no one is cooler than Caleb when he's on the hunt. But evidently not this hunt."

"You straightened him out?"

"Not really." She steadied her hand and took a sip of coffee. Then she changed the subject. "I thought you'd be supervising Lisa and Michael putting up the tent."

"I stayed out of it. They were having too good a time. It isn't the time for lessons. They're both stressed and needed an outlet. They're good for each other."

"Yes, but expect Lisa to be keeping an eye on Michael. You heard Caleb give her orders. She'll obey him to the letter."

"No problem." His warm smile lit his face. "Why should I object to having her fix an eagle eye on my two kids I love very much? It's all good."

"Yes, it's all good." She was silent, staring into the flames. And it was good having Joe here with them. His warm, easy ambience didn't hide the underlying alertness that was an integral part of his personality. Love and warmth and safety that had protected her since the day she had come to live with Eve and Joe. Yet the contrast between Joe and Caleb was patently obvious, and she felt a sharp jab of pain. Nothing safe about Caleb. Nothing clear or uncomplicated. "Thank you for doing this. I hope that this will all be over soon."

"If Caleb has his way, it will be," Joe said. "I'd judge the reason he's behaving a little 'strange' is that he's on edge about you being a target. And don't be ridiculous, you were right to call me. This is where I belong. We both know you should have phoned me when you first ended up in that hospital."

"Perhaps. The situation seemed...difficult. And Caleb was here."

She finished her coffee and got to her feet. "But as you say, I'm the target and I can't rely on him. I could have gotten him killed."

"Eve wouldn't approve of that attitude. She's been trying to wean you away from protecting everyone in your world for years." He stood up and brushed a kiss over her cheek. "And you don't try to pull that on me, Jane. Understand? You're just as much my kid as Michael, and I'm the one who will watch over you. I have certain privileges and I won't surrender them." He turned and started up the hill. "Now let's go make sure that Lisa is as good as she claims she is and see if I have a habitable tent."

"You will. Caleb is right about her being able to do anything." She followed him up the hill. "But I believe I'll duck into my tent and pack Michael up while you do your inspection. I did a few sketches for Lady Kendrick and I want to clean them up so I can give them to her in the morning."

And she didn't want to be around Michael or Lisa at the moment, she thought wearily. They were too full of energy and exuberance, and all she could feel right now was fear for Caleb and the sickening panic that she should be doing something to stop Luca. It was all very well for Joe to claim that she couldn't protect everyone in her world, but she'd never been able to make them see that she had no world without them.

Joe nodded understandingly. "I'll try to keep Lisa and Michael busy for a little while so that you can finish those sketches."

"It won't take long." She headed for her tent. "Good night, Joe."

"Good night." Before she reached the door of her tent, he called out: "Luca said he'd be talking to you again. Did he say when?"

Luca.

She felt a sudden ripple of tension. It wasn't that she had forgotten him; he seemed to always be with her since she had answered that call last night. "No, I'm not holding my breath. Probably whenever he wants to intimidate me." She went into her tent and stood there a moment in the dark before she lit the lantern. It was done. Michael was safe with his father. Not only was Caleb free to attack or defend himself, but she would have the same freedom. Luca thought she was helpless, some stupid bimbo he could manipulate to fill his precious list. But he was wrong as long as he couldn't touch the people she loved. Screw you, Luca.

She sat down on her camp chair and quickly finished the remaining work on the dig sketches. They weren't bad, she thought critically as she studied them. She had caught the mysticism of Kendrick Castle as well as brief glimpses of the young students actually digging, their expressions lit with enthusiasm and laughter. Who wouldn't want to come and play in the dirt as she and Michael had these past weeks? Lady Kendrick would be pleased. She started to close her sketchbook but instead impulsively flipped to that last sketch she'd been working on when Lisa had stopped her.

She felt a ripple of shock as she gazed at it. She didn't even remember starting the sketch. It had just...come. And Lisa was right, the detail was incredible. And powerful. The storm was whipping the branches of the trees and pounding against the stone of the tower. Yet the round tower looked as if it could withstand any storm and remain untouched...and waiting. She suddenly realized she was shivering. Waiting for what?

She was being ridiculous. She had been the one who had drawn this scene, and she knew she had never seen that tower before. She had merely loosed her imagination and created this sketch out of thin air because she'd had little sleep and been worried about Michael...and Caleb. She was tempted to tear it up, but then decided against it. The sketch was too good, and she might be able to work with it later.

Getting to her feet, she closed the sketchbook and put it on the camp chair. Just gather Michael's belongings as she'd told Joe she was going to do, she told herself. It must be almost time for Michael to get to bed.

I'd die for you.

Forget about those enigmatic words that might mean nothing at all.

But what if they did mean what she'd thought in that first moment he'd said them? Caleb had never lied to her, and they might be the answer she'd been searching for since the moment they'd come together. Search deeper and they might mean everything.

But put it aside because the hope and promise that had come out of darkness was too much right now. Take it slowly. Go to bed and get to sleep.

Forget about what Caleb might be doing, or weird sketches that came out of nowhere.

And, most particularly, forget about Stefano Luca.

———◆———

TOWER HOUSE

"They're all ready, sir," Davron said nervously. "Alberto asked if he could be the one to do it. He said he wanted to prove himself to you."

"I was planning on being in charge myself." Luca thought about it. He had enjoyed himself enormously the last time he'd shown these fools how powerful he could be. He remembered the rush, the sensual pleasure, the headiness of those moments. He'd thought the killings would merely be a means to an end, but there was no harm in enjoying the process as well as the result. He was beginning to understand the fascination Alberto felt at those blood fests. All those years ago back in Atlanta when he'd watched Jelak cover himself in blood as he'd murdered those women he chose as victims, he'd felt only curiosity. But now there was something...different. Yet he mustn't indulge himself if it was more intelligent to go another way. "But I might permit Alberto to show me how loyal he can be. I admit it would be a rather unusual sacrifice, and it might bring the others more firmly into line." He smiled slyly. "Unless you wish to do it, Davron? I haven't noticed you being of much value to me lately. Don't you want to prove yourself to me?"

"Not this way." Davron moistened his lips. "You know I'm not competent at that sort of thing. I wouldn't please you." He swallowed. "I thought you might want me to set up another theft for you, instead. That seems far more practical. I could do that."

"No, that phase is over. So you'd better study how to help me move on or I might have to leave you behind." He chuckled as he headed for the door. "And I'm certain Alberto will be eager to keep you company and make sure you won't be lonely."

Luca could feel Davron's fear as he slammed the door behind him. It was almost as exhilarating as the moist air blowing on his face as he strode across the garden. There was rain coming, and there would be lightning and excitement...and blood.

And this one's for you, Jane. Alberto and the others think it's for them, but the minute you see it, you'll know it's for you.

———◆———

MANTUA, ITALY

"You brought your plane this time," Palik said as he met Caleb at the steps of the Gulfstream G650. He grimaced. "That's serious stuff. I hope it doesn't mean I'm going to have the pleasure of your company for an extended time?"

"It means I don't leave until I get Luca, and I'll go where I have to go to do it." He was striding toward the tan Mercedes parked beside the hangar. "And you'll go wherever I tell you to go to lead me to him, and the quicker you move the sooner you get rid of me." He added dryly, "I'm sure that will give you the needed impetus to get the job done."

"It certainly helps," Palik murmured. "I don't care for trailing after you when you decide to take over the hunt. You tend to involve me in situations that aren't as safe as I'd like. I concentrate on being a devout coward at every possibility. It's bad enough you sent me up to the hills to retrieve those bloody bodies from that cave. Did I tell you that I felt as if someone was watching me?"

"Yes. But it didn't stop you from going to Villa Silvano later. So you must not be as devout a coward as you claim." He got into the driver's seat of the car and held out his hand for the keys. "So why am I here? When I called and asked where I should start, you told me to come to Mantua again. Why?"

Palik dropped the keys in his hand. "You told me to go after the second man, Luca's accomplice. The man who wasn't 'there' as far as that boy Michael was concerned. As far as we could tell, Luca was alone when he was stalking Jane MacGuire here in Mantua, but since he was accompanied at MacDuff's Run, and at the shooting at Kendrick Castle, I thought I should take a deeper look here."

"And?"

Palik smiled. "I think I found the bastard."

"Who?"

"Oh, that interested you." He leaned lazily back in his seat. "Suppose you drive me to the San Girano Hotel where I booked your reservations. I might even show you a photo or two of him."

"Palik."

"Just joking." He quickly straightened on the seat. "But you'll be pleased to know that kid was right about Luca not assigning his accomplice any importance. He didn't take the same precautions to mask his movements as he did his own." He added softly, "That could be a bonanza."

Caleb could see that. "You're very pleased with yourself. That probably means you've already started to discover a few benefits."

"More than a few. But I've decided you should buy me a fine gourmet dinner while I lay it out for you." He paused. "Luca didn't stay at the San Girano, but Davron did."

Caleb jumped on the name. "Davron?"

"Russell Davron." He tilted his head. "Dinner? I have more to tell you. You drive. It's only fifteen minutes from here. I'll call room service to have food ready so that they won't waste your time indulging my extremely well-earned bonus."

Davron. Caleb's hands tightened on the steering wheel. A lead at last. Evidently Palik had come through with something that might prove invaluable. He had taken a good deal of abuse from Caleb since he'd started this job, and he knew he didn't want the dinner so much as the sense of power that it gave him. So give him the respect he wanted. He deserved it. "Make that call to room service." He started the car. "But it better be worth it, Palik."

"My thought exactly," Palik said ruefully as he reached for his phone.

———◆———

"You didn't eat a bite," Palik said as he pushed his chair away from the room service dining table. "Vampires aren't supposed to eat." He added slyly, "Does that mean that all the rumors about you are true?"

"What do you think?"

"We've had a few meals together in the past, so I think I'm safe."

"Don't count on it. That remark isn't likely to endear you to me. I believe you were trying to push my buttons. For your information, I didn't eat because I'm too impatient to be hungry. If you don't start talking, that impatience is going to escalate. I'll only allow you to go so far, Palik."

He sighed. "It was enjoyable while it lasted. I admit I did get a little heady with power." He threw his napkin on the table. "Russell Davron." He reached in his pocket for his phone and threw it to Caleb. "It's dialed up to the photo that we got from the lobby lounge. Russell Davron registered the same day Jane MacGuire did. He insisted on a corner room that coincidentally was on the same floor and allowed him a perfect view of her when she was on her private balcony. He was never on that fourth-floor lounge balcony where Luca took those photos of her. Never made contact with her at any time during her stay. Never made contact with Luca, either." He paused. "But on the third night of his stay, the video cameras were inoperable in the hallway where his room was located. Only for a period of six hours, and then they resumed filming. The hotel thought it was a temporary glitch. So Luca would have been able to climb the emergency stairs to Davron's floor and take all the photos he wanted of Jane from his suite." He added, "Which, by the way, was this room. I thought you might want to look it over."

"Correct. And how did you know that he was Luca's contact if he was never videotaped with him?"

"We had videotapes of Luca from different shop security cameras as he moved around the city following Jane. We caught him twice at the same outdoor café as Davron. They weren't sitting together, but they were seen talking for a few minutes—and the conversation was not casual. Then we did another scan of hotel guests and came up with Davron."

"The name could be phony."

"Surprisingly, I don't believe it is. Davron isn't your usual gangster scumbag. I think he might be a front man for Luca's alter ego as an art thief. Luca wanted everything about Davron to be as genuine and checkable as he can make it appear." He added softly, "And he made it look like that to Interpol and practically everyone with whom he came in contact. No criminal record. He's an art dealer and antiquities expert who has a very respectable reputation all over the world with galleries and collectors."

"So how is it that he's fronting for a bastard like Luca?"

"Money. Laziness. Blackmail. Intimidation. Who knows? Maybe Luca has just managed to persuade him to go his way. Persuasion can be everything." He shrugged. "You've taught me that, Caleb."

"Have I?" Caleb asked absently. "Okay, so Davron was probably

the person who set up the thefts and then the reselling of the paintings. But somewhere along the way, he became willing to actually
assist and let Luca involve him in the murders he committed at the
museums. So he's not innocent, merely weak and cowardly. But that
might be enough to use to find Luca and bring him down. No one
could find out anything much about Luca's personal background.
What do we know about Davron's?"

"He's in his forties, grew up in Rome in a middle-class neighborhood. Mother was a dress designer, father worked as an art expert
for the Socci Museum where Davron was hired as an intern while
he was still at the university. After he graduated, he was hired by the
museum, worked his way up, gained respect, and eventually quit to
open his own art gallery. Evidently he didn't make enough money
or acquire enough prestige to suit him. Because it was about that
time that there was a theft at a museum in Venice that bore Luca's
stamp. Shortly after that, Davron began cutting down on his more
legitimate work."

"Because Luca owned him," Caleb said. "Personal. Give me
something personal that I can use."

"Davron's parents are dead now. But he has a longtime lover. Nicco
Barza. Barza's a male model in the couture house where Davron's
mother was employed, and they've been together for the last five
years." He shook his head. "Not really together. Barza is a man who's
ambitious, likes frequent changes of menu and nice gifts. At present
he's living in Rome and his bills are being paid by Julio Santo, a
crime boss who requires Barza to give him total attention."

"And is he getting it?"

Palik shook his head. "Davron has paid Barza several visits in the
last year. He must care something for him if he's willing to risk
getting chopped by Julio Santo."

"Or if he took the opportunity to leave Stefano Luca occasionally
and go back to his lover. Luca must not have been totally dominating
Davron's attention during that time." His lips twisted. "But Davron

showed guts trying to balance what he wanted against the two of them. When was the last time he saw Barza?"

"As far as I can trace, two months ago."

"Then Davron will be eager to see him again. I think we need to make a visit to Rome in the morning." He got to his feet. "And you need to find out what I need to know about Julio Santo and any men he has watching Nicco Barza."

Palik nodded. "I'm already on it." He stood up and headed for the door. "What time do we leave?"

"A few hours. I'll call you."

"Right. Get some sleep. Oh, I have something for you." He reached into his jacket pocket and pulled out a striped gray silk necktie. "You wanted something belonging to Luca from the Villa Silvano." He pitched the tie to Caleb and then stood at the door staring at him. "I did good, didn't I? You didn't expect this much. In fact, I was superb."

"You were superb," Caleb said. "I always expect that of you, Palik." He smiled faintly. "But perhaps you were a trifle extraordinary this time. Have you ever considered becoming a hunter?"

He shuddered. "Lord, no." He hurriedly closed the door behind him.

Caleb's smile vanished. He should lie down and rest, though he seldom slept much when he was on the hunt. He was always too charged. He could feel that electricity generating through him now as his mind went over all the options Palik had brought to light with his in-depth research of Davron. Let it go for now. By the time he reached Rome, he'd know which way was best.

His gaze wandered over this suite that Palik said Davron had also occupied. Palik had no doubt thought he might want to look around it for any clues, and he hadn't disillusioned him. But he'd known he wouldn't find anything of value in this hotel room. It had been too long since Davron had stayed here.

Instead he'd wanted to get the essence, the *feel* of the man. The scent and the presence lingered for many days, sometimes weeks, after someone left an enclosed area like a hotel room. The presence was the most important. Most of the time he could identify ingrained habits and memorize the essentials that drove the prey just from deciphering the presence he radiated.

And Stefano Luca had also been here for that one night. He stroked the silk tie Palik had thrown him. Then he set it aside.

Davron first. He closed his eyes and concentrated, eliminating the more recent spores until he reached a solid block at the appropriate time that Davron had been here. Four days . . .

He let it flow over him . . .

It took a relatively small time to get everything he needed from Davron. Then he concentrated on Luca, purposely ignoring the silk tie until he was finished with the room.

Nothing.

He tried again.

Nothing. But Palik had been certain Luca was here. Caleb should be able to sense him, identify everything about him.

Or maybe not. Luca's sole reason for being here had been to take those photos of Jane from the balcony. Caleb crossed the suite, pushed open the drapes, and went out on the balcony.

Overwhelming.

The presence and scent were all around Caleb, clinging to the drapes and to the wood that framed the glass panels on the French doors. Caleb didn't have the slightest doubt that it was Luca. He must have been out here almost all the time he'd been in the suite, staring at Jane's balcony. Caleb couldn't imagine that Jane had stayed out there on her balcony all that time, so he must have chosen to just stand there, watching, drinking in the closeness and the fact that she wasn't aware of his presence.

And that presence was stunningly overpowering and dark.

Yes, it was definitely Stefano Luca.

So come to me, bastard. He took the silk tie in both hands, shut his eyes, and concentrated, letting the darkness and the power flow over him, into him. *Come on, Luca. You can't escape me. I'm going to stay here a long time until I know everything about who you are, how you'll react. Until I am you.*

And then I'll be ready to come and get you . . .

CHAPTER

9

KENDRICK CASTLE

J ane." Lisa was shaking her. "For God's sake, wake up."

Jane opened her eyes sluggishly to see Lisa's face above her. Scared... She looked so scared. Why would she—

"Good, you're awake." Lisa's arms were around her and she was helping her to sit up. "Don't lie back down. It took me forever to wake you. You almost sent me around the bend." She drew a deep breath. "Now, are you okay? You were crying and whimpering like a baby, and when I tried to wake you up, you just lay there like an effigy on a tomb. Were you having a nightmare?"

"I don't think so. Or maybe I was. It's all a blur..." She ran a shaking hand through her hair. "I don't remember anything but a terrible horror and... sadness... an overwhelming sadness."

"I'd say that qualifies as a nightmare." Lisa opened a bottle of water and handed it to her. "And I'm glad that I was here instead of Michael." She made a face. "It might have scared him just like it did me."

"I'm sorry. But I'm fine now." It wasn't true; she was still feeling lethargic and numbingly heavy. She took a drink of water and glanced at her watch. "It's only a little after four. Why don't you try to go back to sleep?"

Lisa nodded. "I will. We both will. As soon as I tuck you in."

"Lisa."

"Shut up. I'm doing my job." She took the water bottle from Jane and pushed her back down in her sleeping bag. "But I don't see how you can be comfortable with all these sketches around you. Did you go to sleep working on them?"

"Sketches?" She raised herself on her elbow, watching Lisa as she gathered several drawings scattered on the floor around Jane's sleeping bag. "No, they were on the camp chair."

Lisa shook her head. "I don't recall a windstorm blowing through the tent last night, so you must not be remembering correctly." She finished picking up the loose sketches and opened the sketchbook. "Those dig sketches are still in here, it's these other four that were on the floor." She frowned. "The ones with the storm. But I don't remember you doing more than that one."

"I didn't." Jane frowned as she took the sketches from Lisa and started to flip through them. Then she stopped flipping, frozen, as she stared at the second sketch. "Dear God."

"What is it?" Lisa moved closer, trying to see.

"The tower," she said hoarsely. "Look at the tower. It's not the same as the first one I drew."

"No." Lisa leaned closer. "It's not." Her index finger traced the outline of the cross fastened on the massive door of the tower. "It's a crucifix. You drew this, Jane?"

"Of course I didn't." But she knew even as she spoke that it probably was her work. She recognized every stroke. The sketch had been drawn as if she had been walking toward the tower and was still a good distance away. "Perhaps. I don't see how I could—" She stiffened in horror. Because her eyes were narrowed in horror on the crucifix itself. She could barely make out what might be a figure nailed in agony on that crucifix.

Might. Maybe it wasn't what she feared it was, she thought frantically. She couldn't clearly make it out. It was a distant rendering, as if she was walking toward the tower.

But there were two more sketches. If she'd been walking toward it, wouldn't she have gotten closer?

She dropped the first sketch on the floor.

She flinched. The second sketch was nearer to the tower, the details of the crucifix more defined, and it had to be a figure writhing in agony on that cross though that figure was still only a shadowy blur.

"Jane, stop!" Lisa said, reaching out to grab her hand. "I don't like where this is going. It isn't good."

"No." Jane brushed her hand away. "But I can't tell . . . I can't see enough. I have to get closer."

She dropped the second sketch.

And she saw who was on the crucifix.

"Dear God." She bent double, her stomach cramping as the sketch slipped from her hand. "No. No. No."

"Shh." Lisa was there, holding her in her arms and rocking her. "I told you not—Never mind. I hate people who say *I told you so.* Oh, shit, you're crying." She pushed her away to look down at her and then was wiping Jane's cheeks with a tissue she'd pulled out of the box beside the sleeping bag. She thrust the tissue at Jane. "You'd better do it yourself. I never like anyone to see me this vulnerable except Caleb." She froze. "Caleb. Is it something about Caleb?"

Jane shook her head. "No." She had to get control of herself. "It's a little boy." Her voice broke, and she waited a moment before she could speak again. "It's a little boy that I drew on that cross."

"What?" Lisa snatched up the sketch and looked at the crucifix. "Damn," she whispered. "What the hell, Jane. Why?"

"How am I supposed to know? I didn't even know I was doing it." She closed her eyes. "It could be nothing, right? Just some sick, twisted reaction to Luca and the craziness that's going on around me. Maybe I've been so worried about Michael that I drew him on that . . ." Her eyes flew open. "No," she said fiercely. "I would never have done that. It can't be Michael. I can't even bear the thought.

I'd have had to be really insane, and I won't accept that." She held out her hand. "Give me the sketch. I have to look at the boy again. I don't believe he even looks like Michael."

"He doesn't," Lisa said as she reluctantly handed her back the sketch. "He appears to be a year or so younger and his hair is longer, thicker, and black. And you shaded his complexion to a darker tone. It's not Michael, Jane. You don't have to look at it again."

"Yes, I do." She braced herself and stared down at the sketch. She felt another wave of sickness. No, this child bore no resemblance to Michael, she had never seen him before. But it didn't change the fact that he was a child in pain; the agony of his body language was unmistakable. She thrust the sketch back at Lisa and said unsteadily, "You're right. It wasn't anxiety that was tricking me into drawing Michael. So I just have to assume I might be losing it."

"Or that it might be something else," Lisa said quietly. "It's not the first time that you woke from sleep and drew someone you'd never met before. That's how you met me all those years ago. I was in trouble and calling out."

"That was different," Jane said curtly. "You were Caleb's sister. Naturally I would have felt drawn to help you. It's not as if this happens to me all the time."

"No, not all the time. But everyone knew you were dreaming about Cira, MacDuff's ancestress, from the time you were seventeen. And lo and behold you found her treasure and saved MacDuff's family."

"There were other people on that hunt. Okay, sometimes I have weird dreams. But that's nothing. Stop speaking as if I have any special gifts. There's no way I'm psychic. I'm not like you or Caleb or Michael."

"No, of course not, your feet are firmly planted on the ground," she said gently. "Nothing in the least different about you, you're a realist to the core."

"That's right."

"Except sometimes you have dreams..."

"Everyone has dreams. I told you, I didn't have a nightmare tonight."

"No, it was closer to a heart attack," Lisa said dryly. "And then you went into a panic. Because you knew you were experiencing something that was scaring you to death. Stop denying it, Jane. Why are you doing that? You didn't hide away when you thought I needed someone to help me. You went after me and didn't stop until you had me safe."

"Because this time it's different. I don't know what's happening, dammit. That poor child..." She drew a shaky breath. "And I'm afraid it's already happened. It has to be Luca. That crucifix is his trademark. And if he's already done it, why didn't I get a chance to stop it?" Her hands clenched in frustration. "It doesn't make sense if there's any reason at all why I have those idiotic dreams. Why show me something terrible and not let me keep it from happening? With you, I could change things, I could *do* something."

"Is that all that's bothering you?" Lisa said, relieved. "Caleb will help bring him down. You won't have to do anything."

"Rely on Caleb, rely on you, rely on MacDuff and Scotland Yard? It goes on forever," Jane said wearily. "I remember Michael told me that he knew there were monsters out there. And it has to be a monster who would do something like this. I'm the one who drew this horror, so maybe it means I should do something about him." Her jaw clenched and her voice lowered to a whisper. "But if it does, then please don't make me go through this. Don't kill that child to show me. Don't make me wait until it's too late. Just let me go *after* him."

"You sound like Caleb." Lisa suddenly shivered. "And that's not good for me. I'm supposed to be taking care of you. I don't need you to get impatient and start thinking about stuff like that."

"Why not? You would."

"But that's me. You're the reasonable one, you're the one who keeps us steady."

"Then you'd better look for someone else to do that." She got to her feet and clumsily pulled on her terry robe. "Because I don't feel at all steady right now." She headed for the door. "And I need some air. Don't follow me, I don't want either a bodyguard or company. I'm just going outside for a few minutes." She didn't wait for Lisa to protest but left the tent.

She took a deep breath of the cool night air and then slowly let it out. Better. She was still shaking, but the coolness helped a little. She settled a few yards from the tent so that Lisa could see her. It might be the only way she could maintain these few moments of privacy.

"I want to sit beside you. Is that okay?" It was Michael. He was in his pajamas and barefoot and was already dropping down beside her and cuddling close. "I'm a little chilly. Dad and I put out the campfire before we went to bed, but you're nice and warm."

So much for privacy. She put her arm around him and drew him close. "You should have put on your robe and slippers."

"I wanted to get to you right away. I thought maybe you needed me." He nestled his head on her shoulder. "It's not okay right now, it's sad. But we can make the rest okay. I think *you* can make it okay, Jane."

"Can I?" She laid her cheek on his head. His chestnut hair was soft and slightly fragrant from his shampoo. Not like that other child's hair, which was black and plastered around his terrified face. She felt a wrenching pain as the comparison flooded her. She didn't know how Michael had sensed her disturbance, and she wasn't going to ask him. She only hoped that he hadn't been aware of that hideous moment when she'd seen that boy on the cross. "I'm sure you're right, though sometimes it's hard to see the light at the end of the tunnel. But we'll get there, Michael."

"That man doesn't want you to see any light," Michael said soberly. "He wants to frighten you. He thinks if he keeps you frightened, he'll make you weaker and you won't fight him. You can't let him see that you're frightened, Jane. It will only make him stronger." He frowned. "And he's getting stronger all the time. I think he might be ... changing. Getting darker ..."

And Michael was picking up entirely too much from that monster. Yet she was going to be forced to ask him. "How do you know that, Michael?"

"I believe he's thinking a lot about you, and it's connected to everything else around him. It's there whenever I feel anything about him."

"But Caleb told me that you said you could only feel him when he was near. Has that changed?" She nervously moistened her lips. "You didn't 'feel' anything about him tonight?"

He shook his head. "Only you. But I'm getting closer. Do you want me to try?"

"No!" she said adamantly, profoundly relieved. The last thing she wanted was to involve Michael in that hideous ugliness, even if it might confirm that that poor child was dead. "Forget it."

"I thought you'd say that," he said quietly. "It was bad for you tonight. That's why I wanted to try to make it better."

"And you did." She brushed a kiss on his forehead. "Just seeing you made it better." But she had a sudden thought. "You shouldn't be here. Your dad will be worried if he wakes and find you gone."

"No, he won't. I woke him and told him I had to go to you. He was fine with it. He only asked me if I wanted him to go with me. He said he'd be watching out for us."

"I imagine he will," Jane said. But Joe's reaction was what she might expect given Eve and Joe's relationship with Michael. Protective, but allowing him to have the space he needed because he was a very special child. She glanced at his tent next to Jane's. "I bet he can hear the sound of our voices from there, but he won't come out unless one of us calls." She straightened and pushed Michael gently away from her. "But that's no reason why we should keep him awake. You've done your duty and kept me company during a bad period. Now go back to bed. I'll see you in a few hours."

He hesitated. "You'll go back to sleep, too? It would make Lisa feel better."

"I'll go back to bed in a few minutes." She wouldn't promise about the sleep. She added ironically, "We wouldn't want Lisa to be upset, would we? She's such a gentle soul."

"Yes, she is," Michael said absently. "She just won't let you see it." He gave her a kiss on the cheek and jumped to his feet. "Like I said, it's sad and this part can't be made okay. But you can make the rest okay." He was running back to Joe's tent. "Just don't let him know you're afraid..."

He was gone.

And she didn't want to sit here and think about Luca or that tower or the fear of what that sketch of the little boy might mean. Maybe Michael was right about not showing fear. Maybe Luca could feed on it.

As he might have fed on the sight of that child on that bloody cross.

Please let it be a nightmare. Let that child be alive.

Or let her find a way to stop the monster before he could do anything like that again.

Yet she couldn't sit here and do nothing. She had to know so that she could act.

Her hand was shaking as she pulled her phone out of her pocket and dialed.

Caleb answered on the first ring. "What the hell's wrong?"

"I don't know. But I have to find out. Maybe it's nothing. It's not like any of the others."

"What isn't? Is Lisa there with you? Let me talk to her."

"No. I mean she's here, but I don't want the two of you having a conference about me. I just need you to do something for me and then call me back. I don't think I should even have you do it. But I have to know, Caleb."

"Then I'll make sure that you do, if you'll just tell me what's happening." He added harshly, "You're driving me crazy."

"I don't want to do that. I'm probably way ahead of you in that department." She drew a deep breath. "It was a dream and it scared me. When I woke, I found I'd drawn three sketches. But I'm only going to send you a photo of the last one, it's self-explanatory. I want you to see if you can find out if the tower exists and if it's happened yet. I'm going to go to my tent now and send you the photo. If you'll do this for me, let me know."

"Of course I'll do it," he said impatiently.

"No, see it first. I don't even have the right to ask this of you. And all I want is an answer to those questions, nothing else. I think perhaps the rest is meant to be in my court." She cut the connection.

Done.

She got to her feet and went into the tent. She waved Lisa aside as she started toward her. "Not now." She found the last tower sketch, took a photo of it, and texted it to Caleb. Then she took off her robe and lay down in her sleeping bag. "Now I'm going to try to sleep."

"Who?" Lisa asked.

"Who do you think?" She pulled her blanket around her. "I had to ask Caleb."

"Good." Lisa turned off the lantern and went back to bed. "I was hoping. It's what you should have done."

"No, it's not. I had no right to pile this on him, too. As I told him, I believe this one is meant for me." Her phone was ringing. "Caleb? Yes or no?"

"Of course you'll have your answers."

"Thank you." She hung up the phone.

So many emotions were bombarding her through the fear and sickness that had surrounded her since the moment she had seen those sketches. Just the fact that Caleb knew and had agreed to find that damn tower was giving her a sense of safety. Even if she could not accept anything else, it made her feel not quite so alone.

"You're wrong, you know," Lisa's voice came out of the darkness. "And Caleb won't let you run the show."

"Yes, he will. He'll have no choice. Go to sleep, Lisa."

"Okay, but as long as you're being foolish, it's good that I'm here to temper it." She yawned. "Where is Caleb, by the way?"

"I have no idea, I didn't ask him. I was a bit distracted."

"Never mind, he'll probably call me later..."

———◆———

MANTUA

He should probably call Lisa, Caleb thought as he set his phone on the coffee table. He could tell Jane was almost traumatized by the sketch she'd drawn, and he needed Lisa to tell him how deep that trauma had gone. If he couldn't get Jane to talk to him, he had to tap Lisa for information.

But perhaps not yet. Lisa was with Jane in that tent, and he needed to be able to question her without upsetting Jane. Wait and call her a little later. Get his mind on Jane's problem and not on the pain she was feeling.

He gazed down at the photo Jane had sent him and tried to remember anything similar that he'd seen in the years he'd lived in Italy, as a boy growing up and then later as a man on the hunt. He knew most of Italy and the surrounding countries very well. Yet nothing was occurring to him at the moment. He might have to wait and hope a location might pop into his head.

And it might not even be Italy or a neighboring country. He was only leaning in that direction because that cave near Fiero Village had already been used by Luca to kill Donzolo and his sons. There was no way he could be certain of anything.

Okay, then get help and avoid the possibility of having Jane draw an even more horrendous scene. Which might clarify matters but cause her more pain than what he sensed she was going through already. He picked up his phone again and dialed Palik.

"You're early," Palik said. "But I'll meet you in the lobby in—"

"I'm going to send you a photo," he interrupted. "Tell me if you know anything about the surroundings or the kid." He punched the button and sent the photo. "Anything at all."

An instant later Palik gave a low whistle. "Ugly. Very ugly."

"I don't want a commentary. I want information. What do you know?"

"Not a damn thing. The trees look vaguely familiar, but I can't be sure."

"Then be sure," Caleb said curtly. "Find out. Right away. Put as many men as you need to get me answers."

"Right away? I can't be 'superb' all the time, Caleb."

"This better be one of the times you are," Caleb said. "As you might note from the sketch, there's a certain urgency."

"Sketch," Palik repeated. "Jane MacGuire?"

"Yes. And she's not going to have to wait. I want that information."

"You'll get it. Shall I cancel Rome?"

"No, not unless you tell me that I can find that tower immediately. But I imagine you're going to have to turn your equally superb people loose to do that. I refuse to sit here and twiddle my thumbs. I'll go to Rome and see if I can cause maximum intimidation or damage." He paused and added harshly, "The way someone did to that kid on the crucifix."

"I'll meet you in the lobby," Palik said quietly. "Give me twenty minutes to start the search going for that tower."

"Twenty minutes," Caleb repeated. He cut the connection.

"I hear you had a bad night," Joe said, falling into step with Jane as they were walking toward the mess tent the next morning. "Do you want to talk about it?"

She shook her head. "Just a dream. You've been there before with me when I've been plagued by them. This one was particularly nasty, and it shook me. But there wasn't anything I could do about it." She shrugged. "I guess that was why I got upset."

"If you need me, I'm here."

She'd already involved Caleb; she couldn't bring Joe into it, too. "I know that." She squeezed his arm. "But you're doing enough just being here for Michael. I didn't want him near me right now."

"You made that clear."

"It's clearer than ever to me now. Like I said, it was a particularly nasty dream." She moistened her lips. "Did you hear anything from Caleb?"

He shook his head. "I assume you didn't, either. He just left last night. He said he'd be in touch, he didn't say when."

"I know. I just wondered if you'd spoken to him." They had reached the mess tent, and she stopped as Lisa and Michael went inside. "You go ahead with them. I'm going to go to the castle and give these sketches to Lady Kendrick."

"Couldn't it wait?"

"I'm not hungry and she's waited long enough. She was very considerate not to kick us out after that shooting."

"Or maybe grateful you didn't sue her," he said teasingly.

"Cynic." She grinned. "She's very nice." She waved and turned away. "See you later, Joe."

She probably should have waited until after breakfast, but she wanted to get those sketches into Lady Kendrick's hands.

Sketches.

Don't think about those other sketches that she'd deliberately left in the tent. She was only grateful that when she'd awoken this morning after a few hours' sleep, those sketches of the tower were exactly the same. She'd been half afraid she might have drawn another one. Or changed one.

But that might have been a good thing, she thought wearily. Maybe she wouldn't have shown the child on the crucifix at all.

Maybe it would have all been different and there would have been no dark-haired little boy in pain.

Or it could have all been imagination and she had panicked for no good reason. Other people had nightmares and it meant nothing.

But other people didn't make sketches of their nightmares without even being aware of it.

So it didn't matter if she thought it was different from the other times she'd experienced something similar to this. She had to see if there was any way she could keep the horror from happening. But first she had to—

Her phone was ringing.

No ID.

She stopped short on the path, staring at the screen. She didn't dare not answer it after that last call from Luca.

She punched the button. "Hello."

"How are you, Jane?" Luca asked. "I received my usual weather report on Kendrick Castle this morning and I was told you had a beautiful, sunny morning. It's been a bit stormy and gloomy here, but I'm looking forward to having you change all that when you get here. I remember in Mantua you seemed to light up the entire city."

Her hand tightened on her phone as she punched RECORD. Don't let him realize either the shock or the fear. "Because I thought I was alone. I had no idea you were snooping around like some weird pervert. Why are you calling me, Luca?"

"Because I had to hear the sound of your voice even if it says rude things. Of course, you'll be taught better when I have control of you. You might remember that every insult you speak now will receive a punishment when you're with me."

"Screw you."

"That's two." He chuckled. "You obviously don't believe me. But you will, Jane, I've been waiting a long time to start training you. I admit I've been looking forward to it. I'm willing to spend a long time schooling you."

"Threats? I'm not going to listen to this. I'm hanging up now."

"Actually, I didn't mean to threaten you. The words just came out because I'm accustomed to having everyone around me treat me with a good deal of subservience. Fear does that to people."

"Because you're a bully?"

"Partly. And partly because they're never sure what I'll do. I admit I have a tendency to be a little volatile, but that's my right. No, I called you because our other contact was just an introduction, not enough for you to truly get to know me...and what I'll do."

She stiffened. "What you'll do? I think I know that very well. I heard how you butchered a man and his sons in that cave."

"But that was the tip of the iceberg. It was only meant to exhibit power and push my agenda. It really had nothing to do with you...or us."

"There is no us," she said through gritted teeth. "What are you talking about?"

"I mean that any bloodbaths I inflict might be interesting and exciting but they're totally aside from anything connected with you. I realize I can only use people with whom you have a bond to further my dealings with you." He paused. "I must have frightened you if you sent for Joe Quinn to come to protect you. Do you feel safer now that he's there?"

She was silent. How had he known Joe was here? "I wasn't afraid of you. It was just time for Joe to come and pick up his son."

"After he and Eve Duncan had just gone back to Maldara?" he asked softly. "Don't lie to me. I told you I know everything about you. I'm glad he came, it shows that I had a significant effect on you. I'm not as happy that Caleb disappeared from the castle grounds last night. Did you send him after me, Jane?"

"No, I would never do that. And if you knew as much as you think you do about me, you'd realize that there's no reason for him to do it on my behalf. If he went after you, it was because you're a killer and he believes you had something to do with the murder of his sister Maria."

"That almost had the ring of truth," Luca said. "If I hadn't seen you together, I might believe you. I admit that I was a little concerned when I heard about your supposed breakup with him. It would have been most upsetting to my plans if that had been true. I need him to still have a passion for you. But I was sure I wasn't wrong, because you're not the only one I've been studying all these years. How could it be when Caleb has all those fascinating skills that could prove so valuable to me? It's difficult to know everything about a cipher like Caleb, but I do know the buttons to push to get him in a position for me to take him down."

"You know nothing about him."

"You're mistaken. I know a great deal about him. However, my plans for him are requiring me to be very careful. He can't die before he performs the functions to help complete my list."

"Absurd. You'll be disappointed. Caleb doesn't perform for anyone."

"I won't be disappointed. Everything is going splendidly on my end since I last spoke to you." He paused. "I had a perfectly exhilarating and different experience to enjoy last night. I kept wanting to share it with you. It was almost . . . erotic."

She felt sick. She could feel the tension grip her. Was he talking about the crucifixion of that child? Was this the moment he was going to tell her about it? "What do you mean?"

He was silent. "I don't believe I'm ready to share it with you yet. Perhaps later . . ." He added, "But not much later. I thought I'd enjoy this cat-and-mouse game with you. But I find I'm getting very impatient for us to start our own game. Good day, Jane. I don't have to tell you to think of me, do I?" He laughed. "Can you think of anything else?"

He cut the connection.

She was shaking as she thrust the phone back in her pocket. No, he didn't have to tell her to think of him. She wished she could forget him for even a moment. The only mercy connected to that conversation was that he had not mentioned that boy pinned to the door of that tower. She'd been waiting for him to do it, and it hadn't happened. Perhaps he was saving that particular horror to hit her with later. Which indicated that he didn't realize it would be no shock to her. He'd said he knew everything about her, but evidently he didn't know about the dreams that had haunted her all her adult life. Or maybe it meant that those sketches had been motivated purely by her imagination, and Luca had nothing to do with it.

She hoped with all her heart that was true. But that single sentence he'd spoken when he'd been telling her of his "different" experience had been full of darkness. Don't think of that right now, just be glad she couldn't be sure that he'd committed that horrible act.

Because heaven knows, there were plenty of other things to think about in that conversation.

It's rainy and windy here.

In her sketch, the trees had bent almost double with the force of the wind and rain.

And he'd known entirely too much about what was going on here at the castle.

She felt she had to go over every sentence he had spoken. She could give those sketches to Lady Kendrick later. Luca had wanted her to get to know him better? She was beginning to do so, and a few things had stood out stark and clear.

She was calling Joe as she turned around and started back toward the dig. "Set Lisa to watching Michael and meet me at the mess tent. I've just talked to Luca."

◆———◆

Joe's lips tightened as he finished listening to the recording of Luca's call. "Nasty. Was the first one that bad? No wonder you called me, Jane."

She made a face. "Don't insult me, Joe. I can take nasty, even when it's packaged by that scum. I originally called you because we both needed to keep Michael safe." She paused. "And I needed to get Caleb away from him...and from me. Luca was trying to give me bullshit about my being the reason he wanted to get rid of Caleb, but we both know I'm no femme fatale. It was ludicrous."

Joe shook his head. "Not so ludicrous. Those photos he took of you were almost obsessive. You do have your moments, Jane. I can see Luca wanting to remove the competition."

"I can't," she said flatly. "Not unless it served more than a single purpose. Caleb's take on Luca is that besides being a psycho, he's brilliant, complicated, and a complete egotist. He thinks he can have it all." She met Joe's eyes. "And he has some weird belief that he's destiny's favorite child and we're all just put on earth to help him reach his full potential. During this last call, he admitted that Caleb was important and had to function in more than one way on his list." She added quietly, "And I don't believe he was lying about his list. I can see him sitting there like a spider, ticking off every item."

"So can I."

"But if he needs Caleb, it might mean Luca is lying about how much he's accomplished in completing that list." She smiled bitterly. "Lisa told me once that Caleb is always the target; that's why she's wanted to protect him. I thought this time she might be wrong."

"Perhaps she is." He reached out and covered her hand on the table. "But there could be more than one target. I don't like Luca's concentration on you."

"And I don't like the fact that he seemed to know everything that's been going on at this encampment. The weather. And he knew that you'd come to be with me and that Caleb has disappeared. He didn't try to hide any of it. He didn't seem to care that I knew. It must be that damn egotism again." Her hand tightened on his. "But how did he know, Joe? I'm not liking the answer to that question. I told Caleb how safe Michael and I would be here. But now I'm not sure.

Did Luca manage to get someone into this camp? Is it one of the students?"

"I don't know, but I'll find out," he said grimly. "That was my first thought after I finished listening to that bastard. I'm going to go to the administration office at the castle and check out any new volunteers that have signed up." He added, "And while I'm at it, I'll bring Tovarth in to have the Yard start an in-depth background check on all the people who have been here since you and Michael came a month ago."

"That has to be close to a hundred people." She shook her head. "It will take too long. And who knows how many people Luca has managed to plant?" She braced herself and said, "You've got to take Michael away from here right away. It's not safe for him."

He went still. "I was afraid that might be where this was going."

"I was wrong. I thought if you were here, it would still be a secure place for Michael. But it's not going to work out because I'm still here and evidently they can get to me." She was nibbling at her lower lip. "Which means they can get to Michael. I can't allow that, Joe. I was terrified when that bullet almost hit him." She said urgently, "*You* can't allow it. Take him away from here and find him somewhere safe. Atlanta. Take him back to Atlanta."

"And leave you here?" he asked roughly. "You're not thinking straight. Do you believe I'd actually leave you here alone?"

"Alone? Lisa will be here." She added wryly, "There's no way I could get her to leave me after she promised Caleb. I'd have to find a way to get rid of her." Then she wearily shook her head. "No, you won't let me stay here now that we know it might be compromised. But you might do it if I promise to leave here myself tomorrow after you take Michael away. You could just disappear tonight and then arrange for Tovarth to assign someone to take Lisa and me to some kind of safe house for a while. You'd have Michael safe . . . and away from me."

"And the first thing Michael would do is try to get back to

you. He'd be as worried about you as I would be. Sorry, not good enough," he said gently. "I'm like Luca. I want it all. I'll take care of Michael and keep him safe. But you're my family, too, Jane. You're not going anywhere without me."

"I have to do it, Joe," she whispered. "It only makes sense."

"You heard me." He reached out and touched her cheek. "You want to leave? Maybe you're right that I should get you out of here. I was considering the option even before you started to panic."

"I'm not panicking. That's not how you taught me to handle emergencies." She smiled. "Assess the situation and then correct it."

"I didn't teach you that. You came to us knowing it. You probably learned it on the streets. But I did teach you to use good sense and pay attention to what I told you to do. So that's sort of the same thing."

"And you get your own way?"

"Exactly." He smiled. "So we don't run away from Kendrick Castle just yet. We think and we plan so that we can do this together. Now I'm going to the castle to find out who could be our mole. I might get lucky right away, and he'll be able to give us information on Luca. If not, I can start the process in motion for Tovarth to follow up on. Then we spend the night here and we exit tomorrow morning after I decide where it's safest to take the two of you." He held up his hand as she started to protest. "I'm open to suggestion, but not an argument. We'll work it out together."

"You should pay attention to me, Joe."

"Nah." Joe grinned as he got to his feet. "Eve would say you're just trying to run the family to suit yourself again. I can't allow you to do that, Jane. You mean too much to us." He turned away. "Now go back to Lisa and keep an eye on Michael for me while I spend a few hours at the castle. Like I said, maybe I'll get lucky."

And maybe he wouldn't, Jane thought as she watched him leave the mess tent. He'd spend time digging and questioning like the brilliant detective he was and then he'd come back and they'd sit around the fire and discuss it, and he'd try to convince her to do what he wanted her to do. She knew he wasn't going to listen to her unless she said the words he wanted to hear.

And no matter what Joe said or how much she loved him and wanted to please him, she knew she wasn't going to be able to say those words.

———◆———

ROME
14 CALLE DANTE

"What else can I expect from this Nicco Barza?" Caleb asked as he jumped out of the speedboat onto the dock and gazed at the luxurious two-story apartment at the end of a row of other equally impressive units beside the Tiber River. They had all been renovated from the eighteenth-century palace of a nobleman, and every detail was impeccable. "Other than that, judging by his apartment, he must charge Julio Santo exorbitantly for his services."

"I was going to fill you in on the flight down here," Palik said sourly. "But you insisted on me making all those calls to try to locate that damn tower. And now you're pushing me to tell you everything at the last minute?"

"Because those calls were important," Caleb said. "Not that you found out anything. Besides, I knew you wouldn't let me go in after Barza blind. Is this really the last minute?"

"Very close. I tried to tell you that Santo was scheduled to take his Nicco to Paris for a long weekend before he went off with his wife and kids to visit her parents in Capri. Barza is supposed to be picked up at midnight and driven to a private airport to board Santo's jet. It's nine forty now, dammit."

"Plenty of time." Caleb was checking out the exterior of the apartment. Two elegant balconies, and there was a skylight. But skylights tended to be very messy and noisy . . . "Tell me about Barza. Will he present any problems?"

"Probably not for you." Palik thought about it. "But maybe you should be a bit careful. Because Barza's a popular male model, he'd probably keep himself very fit anyway, but he also works out at the gym for several hours every day and he's strong as a horse. That's what Santo finds attractive about him. Santo has a normal heterosexual wife-and-family situation, but he wants it all. He not only swings both ways, but he likes to play rough, and Barza can give him what he needs. Santo thinks it's titillating to have his own sexual punching bag to play with, and Nicco Barza evidently makes sure he's in shape to give him what he wants. In return, Barza appears well taken care of and seems content enough." Palik shrugged. "Though the word is, if he doesn't perform to Santo's satisfaction, the rough play can become extremely painful for him."

"Not all that content if he's still occasionally willing to take a risk with Davron. I'll have to explore it. How many guards did Santo assign to assure that his Nicco walks the line and doesn't go wandering?"

"Two. One at the front entrance. One at the speedboat Santo gave him down at the pier." He paused and then said reluctantly, "I suppose I could help with the man at the pier. Though that's not my job, and you really should have let me arrange to bring in someone more qualified."

"I appreciate the offer, no matter how grudging," Caleb murmured. "You'll be relieved that I agree with you. You're not qualified. Stay and wait here at our boat."

"Thank God." Palik waved his hand. "I'll think good thoughts and be ready to whisk you away."

"Do that." Caleb was already moving across the garden toward Barza's apartment building. There were lights on in the back of the apartment. It was still early; perhaps Barza was packing for his trip to Paris . . .

Then Caleb was scaling the balcony using the trellis and stones for purchase, his hands and feet moving, digging. A moment later he jumped down on the balcony and headed for the glass doors.

Yes. Soon. He could feel his heart beating hard, the blood coursing through his veins. The hunt was on.

Prey. Just ahead, inside those doors. And Palik had said it might not be easy prey. So much better that way.

The balcony doors were unlocked, and he silently opened them.

He froze. Darkness. Complete darkness. From the boat dock he'd seen a light gleaming from the back of the apartment, but now there was no glimmer from under any of the doors leading from this central living area.

And he could sense someone standing there in the darkness, waiting.

Oh, Barza, you are going to be a pleasure. He faded to the side of the door so that he blended into the darkness while his eyes became accustomed to it. In seconds he could make out Barza's outline across the room near the door. Tall, lean, athletic, powerful shoulders. And he was pointing a gun at the balcony door Caleb had just entered. Interesting...

"Why didn't you try to shoot me, Barza?" he asked as he dropped to the floor. "You had a chance."

"You son of a bitch, I *will* shoot you." The voice was deep and fierce as the gun swung toward the place Caleb had previously stood. "Tell Santo I won't take any more. He has to come himself. Now get out of here."

"I'm afraid I can't do that." Let's see, Barza's gun was in his right hand, but Caleb must be careful to keep him alive. "Though you're welcome to try to rid yourself of me if you like. I think I'd like that." He was moving lightning-fast through the darkness as he spoke. Then he hit the man in a low tackle, striking his right wrist with a karate chop and sending the gun flying from his grip.

Pain.

Barza's arm was around Caleb's neck and he was squeezing it. Then his fist lashed out and struck Caleb's cheek. More pain. Strong. Very strong. Caleb couldn't allow it to continue.

"I was wrong. I appreciate it, but I don't like it." Caleb grabbed Barza's arm. His hand closed on the wrist as he put intense pressure on the veins.

Barza screamed! His arm dropped away from Caleb's neck.

"Shh, you don't really want to give that guard at the front door a reason to come running up here." Caleb's other hand pressed against Barza's mouth. "That would only make everything difficult. I'm trying to keep you alive."

"Let—go—of my wrist," Barza gasped. "It's...exploding. And I think I'm bleeding."

"Oh, you are. And I have to stop and heal it or you'll die. Now I'm going to put you to sleep for the next several minutes while I keep that from happening." He put his fingers on Barza's carotid artery and exerted pressure. "Then we'll have a chat..."

———◆———

"Who...are you?"

Caleb turned away from looking out the window to see that Barza's eyes were open again. "Back with me?" He strolled toward the bed where he'd placed the man before he'd started to work on him. "I thought it would be another five minutes or so. I was told you were strong. It appears you also have endurance."

"Of course I do. I could have put you down if you hadn't used something to burn me." His gaze was on his bandaged arm. "What did you do to me? I couldn't see in the dark, but it burned like hell..."

"I caused a little damage to a few arteries." He dropped down in the chair beside the bed. "Nothing that I couldn't repair. But I've heard it does have that sensation."

"How did you do it?" Barza was glaring at him. "Some kind of acid? Was it supposed to make me more compliant? I should have shot you when I got the chance."

"It was a slim chance. I'm very fast." He was studying him objectively. Nicco Barza was undoubtedly one of the most attractive men he had ever seen. Olive skin, dark hair, Greek god features, and that strong, lean body. Nothing effeminate about him, pure male warrior stock. "No acid. That would have damaged you."

Barza stiffened. "And Santo wouldn't have liked that, would he? Did he want more movies for his collection?"

"This isn't about that scumbag Santo. He's merely an impediment or an impetus, I haven't decided which yet."

Barza's eyes suddenly narrowed. "Who are you?" he asked again.

"Seth Caleb." He leaned back in his chair. "My turn. Why didn't you shoot? Why did you just try to scare me off?"

"Because I knew what Santo would do to me if I spoiled his little plan. If I'd shot you, it would mean I'd gotten the better of him, and he doesn't permit that. He lets me win sometimes, but I can't ever totally beat him." He met Caleb's eyes. "You'd know that if you worked for him. So either you're a liar or you came here for something else."

"The latter, but I'm still interested in Santo's nasty little plan. I might be able to use it. Tell me about it."

"Screw you." Barza's muscles were readying, getting prepared to spring. "I'm through with this stupidity. You caught me off-guard before but I'll—"

He groaned. He was bent double on the bed with pain. He gasped. "My heart..."

"Only a twinge," Caleb said. "But the pain will get worse if you don't cooperate. I don't need to touch you to cause you pain. I'd hardly leave you untied if I couldn't be certain that I could control you."

"Control—" Barza choked. "You—do work for—"

"I work for no one but myself. But I'm capable of making you suffer extreme agony or killing you without anyone knowing I did it. However, I don't want to do either to you at this time. If you tell me what I want to know, you won't be hurt."

"I don't believe—" He gasped in agony, clutching at his chest.

"Have a little faith." Caleb shrugged. "Or not. But the clock is ticking and I need answers. Don't disappoint me. I'm telling you the truth. What did you think Santo's man was going to do to you?"

Barza was silent.

Caleb nudged him a bit.

He groaned in agony and then gasped, "What the hell do I care?" He took a deep breath. "Rape. Photos. Movies. Santo likes control. Six months ago, he sent two of his men to pay me a surprise visit. They came in through the balcony like you did. They tied me up and took turns raping me and taking movies of each other doing it. Santo visited me the next night and made me sit there and watch the movies. He laughed and said if I wasn't a good boy, he'd release them on YouTube. Do you know what that would do to my career? The only job I'd be able to get would be as a porn star. Damn his soul to hell. I have a chance of making it big in Paris or Milan if I can break with that son of a bitch."

"Perhaps you should have done that long before this."

"Do you think I wouldn't have if I could?" he asked fiercely. "Look, I grew up on the streets, trying to dodge the pedophiles and dirtbags who taught me that all I have to make it out of the gutter is a photo-genic face and a good body. I found out the first weekend I spent with him that Santo likes to hurt me. I had to learn to survive him." His eyes blazed. "And I will survive him. And I'll survive you, too."

"You might do it," Caleb said thoughtfully. "With a little help. I really don't like what I'm hearing about Santo, but that's beside the point. You're obviously a very practical fellow and you realize that sometimes a deal has to be struck to make survival possible."

"Deal?" Barza's voice was suddenly wary. "What kind of deal?"

"The kind that led me to come to you tonight. I give you freedom from Santo." He paused. "You give me Russell Davron."

"What?" His eyes widened. It was obviously a complete surprise. "Davron? What do you mean?"

"I want to know where he is. I might want you to trap him or get information from him." He raised a brow. "Unless you're too fond of him to consider it. You've been seeing him behind Santo's back. That's taking a big risk."

"I like him. He was always good to me when we were sleeping together. And he's too involved with that creep Luca to make any demands on me. For me it's a way of getting back at Santo without getting either one of us killed." He shrugged. "And when I leave, he always gives me money to stash away for a rainy day. Santo is one big rainy day."

"Then you shouldn't object to having Santo disappear from your life."

Barza was silent. "Maybe this is a trick," he said suspiciously. "Maybe Santo sent you."

"Then Santo would have to know about Davron. Does he?"

"No. I was careful." He was silent again. "You could really get me away from Santo?"

"Are you saying that you're willing to deal?"

He frowned. "Is there a chance you might have to kill Davron?"

"Maybe. Not likely unless he's set on protecting Stefano Luca. But I can't promise. Would that make a difference?"

"It might." He was nibbling on his lower lip. "What would you give me?"

"Tonight I'd send someone very reliable to have those movies that they made of you retrieved. I'd also help you escape. I'd make sure Santo didn't immediately go after you." He looked him in the eye and added softly, "And someday soon when I find it convenient, I'll make certain that Santo no longer walks this earth." He paused. "It's a very good deal, Barza."

"Yes, it is." He swallowed. "Will you try not to kill Davron?"

"I will try."

"Then I'll do it." He dazedly shook his head. "What the hell am I doing?"

"You made a deal. I don't allow reneging on deals, Barza." He checked his watch. "It's almost eleven, we'd better get moving. I want to get you out of here before your escort shows up tonight."

"Tonight?" Barza repeated, startled.

"I can't risk Santo taking you to Paris and wasting my time. Start packing." He got to his feet. "I want to leave in twenty minutes."

Barza moved tentatively, and when he didn't feel pain, he got off the bed. "Was all that stuff you did some kind of trick?" he asked belligerently. "Some way to get my attention?"

"No trick," Caleb said. "Do you want another demonstration?"

"No," Barza said quickly as he took a step back. "I believe you." He started to open drawers and throw garments into a suitcase he dragged out of the closet. "But you have to admit, it's weird. And I'm taking a big risk going along with you. I still don't know how we're going to get out of the apartment building. Santo would rather kill me than lose anything he owns. Those goons know what he'd do to them if they—"

"Stop talking. You're beginning to annoy me. Just answer questions. What's the name of the guard at the front door?"

"Ron Franco."

"And the man at the pier?"

"Adolfo Gilata."

"Either of them in charge?"

"Franco."

"Did they know about your rape?"

"Of course they did. Norris, one of the scum who raped me, is a buddy of Franco's. And I'm sure Santo told them to ignore it if I caused an uproar when it was happening," he said grimly. "And I did. It was good that there were two of them or I'd have killed the bastards. Just as I would have taken you down if you weren't—"

"Are you ready?" Caleb was moving toward the front door. "I'm going to go down and talk to Franco. You wait on the landing until I tell you to come running."

"Talk to him? Are you nuts? You're not supposed to be here. You'll get both of us—"

Caleb shut him out as he ran the rest of the way down the steps. He stopped at the foot of the staircase, concentrating on the man behind that door and letting the information flow into him. *Franco. Weapons: Gun in holster beneath jacket. Switchblade in right-hand pocket of jacket. Okay, now character and motivations: Scumbag. Full of his own importance. Afraid of Santo. Hates this job of watching his bitch. He wasn't even allowed into the Barza rape, but had to stand here listening while they had their fun. He could move up in the organization if Santo would give him a chance doing something else. But Santo's fucking was always getting in his way.*

Caleb was ready. All he had to do now was build a scenario from what he'd just learned. He focused and then made the first mental adjustments inside Franco. Nothing too complicated. Recognition. Guilt. Acceptance. Recognition and acknowledgment that Caleb was really Norris, who had committed the first rape. Guilt that Franco was the one who must be confused and must have done something wrong. Last and most important, acceptance that everything Caleb said was truth.

"Franco!" he shouted as he ran toward the front entrance. "It's Norris. Where the hell were you?" He threw open the door. "Santo is going to kill us both."

Franco whirled on him. Confusion and then recognition. "What are you doing here, Norris? I didn't see you come in."

"Of course you didn't," Caleb said impatiently. "Santo told me to come in the balcony like we did last time. He wanted Barza to know it could happen anytime he wanted it to happen before he took him off to Paris, where it might be easier for Barza to get away." He scowled. "But you were supposed to be there, too, dammit. You gave Santo enough hints that you wanted in on screwing Barza the next time it happened. But when I came over that balcony tonight, you weren't there and neither was Barza." He added menacingly, "Did you and Gilata double-cross Santo? Did you take Barza's money to help him escape? You should have known it wouldn't work. I'm not going to let you pull me into this mess and get me in trouble."

Franco's eyes widened. "Barza's gone?"

"As if you didn't know." His gaze narrowed on his face. "Maybe you didn't. I think you're smarter than that. Then it must have been Gilata. We didn't go easy on Barza, and he must have been desperate not to have it happen again. Gilata would have no trouble squeezing a fat bribe out of him to let him go." He stared Franco in the eyes and increased the concentration. "You realize that's true because you know him best."

"Yes, I know that's true. No one knows Gilata better than I do." He began to curse beneath his breath. "He's not going to get away with this. I'm in charge, and Santo will hold me responsible."

"Yes, he will. But maybe you can save yourself. I saw Gilata down at the pier when I came up the balcony. He probably smuggled Barza out of the apartment, took his cash, and then went back on duty to keep anyone from suspecting him. Does that make sense to you?"

"Of course. And he'd hope that I'd get the blame." His face was flushed. "Dirty, sneaky asshole." He whirled and started across the garden, still glaring at Gilata standing on the pier. "I'm going to kill the son of a bitch."

"That's up to you," Caleb murmured. "I'm sure he deserves it."

He stood there watching until Franco reached the pier. Gilata evidently could read his body language and was straightening warily. Time to go. It might get both noisy and violent at any moment.

He turned and called up the stairs, "Get down here, Barza. It's safe now."

"Safe?" Barza was running down the steps. "It was crazy. I couldn't tell what was happening."

"You didn't have to know. I just needed Franco to think he knew what was going on and to accept everything I suggested. That went off quite well." He was pulling him out the door and then toward the docks. "My friend Palik is waiting in that speedboat and we'll get you out of here right away. If all continues to go well, Gilata and Franco will soon try to kill each other, and I don't want you seen. It doesn't really matter who succeeds. Santo will no doubt be so frustrated, he'll get rid of the survivor afterward." His lips turned upward. "Though it would be amusing if the survivor was Franco and he tried to talk his way out of having let you go missing *and* killing Gilata."

"Amusing?" Barza shook his head. "Insane. The entire fucking gibberish was insane."

"Not insane. Not gibberish. It has a name and a purpose as ancient as that fancy palatial apartment where I found you." He had reached the speedboat and nudged Barza toward it. "Some call it the *persuasion*..."

CHAPTER

10

J ane tried to gasp, but there was no air!

She couldn't breathe!

What was happening...

Pain...

Her lungs were on fire...

She was coughing, trying to stop that searing congestion—

Not right. Something was wrong.

She opened her eyes and immediately closed them again as the stinging smoke struck them.

Smoke?

She forced herself to open her eyes again and saw the haze of smoke in the tent.

Something had to be on fire!

Michael! No, Michael was with Joe. He'd be okay.

Lisa...She had to get Lisa out of the tent.

She grabbed her shoes, jeans, and shirt from the camp chair. Then she was crawling across the tent toward Lisa's sleeping bag. She shook her hard. "Get up." Her voice was a croak. "Fire."

Lisa opened her eyes and then started coughing as soon as she took a deep breath. "What are you doing?"

"I'm saving you. Get the hell up." She got to her knees and then her feet. She tried to take shallow breaths to keep from inhaling that stinging smoke. "Get out of here. Hurry. I have to go check on Joe and Michael..."

"I am hurrying. I'll go...with you." Lisa was staggering to her feet and grabbing her clothes. "But I don't see any fire in here, just smoke..."

Neither did Jane, and once she was outside for a brief instant even the smoke seemed less dense. "No fire? Then I don't know what that—"

And then she saw the fire.

The entire lower tent city was in flames! Dozens and dozens of the volunteers' tents were blazing. And the fire was creeping closer to the mess tent and the showers.

Screams!

Jane saw one of the students run out of a tent enveloped in flames. Dear God, even her hair was on fire!

"I've got to go help." She was throwing on her clothes and shoes. "Wake up Joe and Michael, Lisa..."

"I'm awake." Michael was standing outside Joe's tent with Joe just behind him. His eyes were wide with horror as he gazed down at the blazing tents. "What happened? Why, Jane?"

"We don't know how it started. That's not important now. We've just got to get those people out of there. Stay with your dad, Michael. Call the fire department, Lisa." Then she was running down the hill.

———◆———

"Jane, stop, dammit!" Joe shouted after her as he ran out of the tent. "Get back here!"

But Jane had already disappeared into the smoke. Another teenage boy ran out of a tent, screaming.

"I think that's Colin, Dad. He's my friend." Michael's voice was anguished. "They're all my friends." He was frantically throwing on his clothes. "I need to be there."

"No, you don't. The last thing we need is another kid down there in that bonfire." Joe was already grabbing his jacket and thrusting his feet into shoes. "But I do need to be down there, Michael." His voice was urgent. "Listen, you know I'm in the volunteer fire department back home at the lake. Maybe I can organize a water brigade down there at the creek and help put out the fires. Trust me, okay?" He whirled on Lisa and said fiercely, "You said you wanted to keep Jane and Michael safe? Well, do it, dammit. I'll go down and find Jane and send one of Tovarth's men up here to guard you and Michael. But you call the fire department and then you keep Michael up here and out of danger. *Promise* me."

"I promise." Lisa's gaze was on the flames that were leaping upward from the tents to the ancient oaks beside the path. "Get out of here, Joe. Michael and I will be fine." She reached for her phone. "I'll keep him safe."

Joe gave a last glance at Michael as he started down the hill. "You'll stay with her? It's important, Michael."

"Dad...Jane's there, too." Michael's gaze was on the horror of flames and screams. "I should go—"

"Trust me," Joe said again. "Tell me you'll stay with Lisa."

"I'll...stay."

"Good boy." Joe motioned to Tovarth's guard as he passed him to go back up the hill to Lisa and Michael. Then he broke into a full run as he raced down into the smoke.

The scene was pure chaos.

Flames. Smoke. Screams. Moans. The smell of burnt flesh.

He covered his mouth and nose with his shirt and ran toward the mess tent. Buckets. The mess tent should have the buckets he needed and hopefully a hose as well. Maybe tablecloths that he could soak in the brook...

"Joe!" He looked over his shoulder to see Jane kneeling beside a woman who was moaning with pain. "I think there are at least two more burn victims. Where is it safe to take them to get them away from the flames?"

"In the woods across the brook," he said curtly. "The fire is jumping from one tent to another. Get everyone over there, away from the tent area. I have to get some kind of equipment from the mess tent to get buckets to—"

It was too late. The mess tent was now in flames!

"Shit!" Joe's hands clenched into fists as he turned away. "Okay, we're screwed as far as a water brigade goes. I'll help you herd everyone across the brook." He carefully picked up the woman Jane had been tending. "I'll take her across now. You follow as quickly as you—"

But Jane was already on her feet, running through the smoke, shouting, and gathering survivors in her wake. "The brook! Get across the brook. Stop running and help each other, dammit."

It jarred them enough to make them start toward the brook, and then they were doing as Jane asked and helping each other. By the time Joe was back among them assisting the other burn and smoke victims, all signs of the panic had disappeared. Between them he and Jane managed to get the burn victims and the rest of the shocked and dazed survivors to the comparative safety of the woods.

"Where are those firemen?" Jane wiped the smoke from her face with her shirtsleeve. "They should be here by now, Joe."

"Soon. It hasn't been that long," Joe said. "It only seems like a hundred years."

"Tell that to those burn victims. They need to get to a hospital." But at least now that the first panic was over, they were being cared for as well as they could by the other volunteers. One of the teachers even held a first-aid certificate and was ordering the other volunteers like a top sergeant. "Should we call again to—"

"Shit!" Joe's gaze was fixed on the castle. "We didn't need this."

Fire!

They could see the glow of flames through the deep-set windows of the first floor of the castle. And smoke was pouring from beneath the massive oak door.

"No, we didn't," Jane said. "And neither did Lady Kendrick. I was hoping the sparks wouldn't jump from the tents to the castle. She doesn't need to lose any more than she has already." She suddenly tensed. "But where is she? I don't see anyone on the grounds outside the castle. I saw her secretary, Nigel, running up here to help at the tents when I first arrived. She probably sent her staff to do whatever they could."

"Because she thought the fire wouldn't reach the castle, either," Joe said grimly. "It appears that we were all mistaken. I've got to go check on her. She's not a young woman. Even a small amount of smoke might damage her lungs." He was already running out of the trees toward the castle. "You'll be okay?"

"I've got plenty of help. Just get her out of there." Jane watched him until he reached the edge of the forest and then turned back to the others to see what else she could do for them. Had she heard a siren? Lord, she hoped so. It was sad enough what had happened to all these bright young people that she had grown to respect and like. Now she had to face the possibility that the kind, tough lady who had only wanted to keep her home and heritage intact could have died tonight.

She could only hope Joe got there in time.

———◆———

"I should have gone," Michael whispered. He hadn't taken his gaze from that smoke-filled inferno at the tents since Joe had run down there several minutes ago. "I need to help, Lisa."

"I know how you feel." Lisa pressed the DISCONNECT button on her phone and turned back to him. "But the fire department should be down there any minute. When I finally got through to them, the operator said that the fire had already been reported." She put her hand comfortingly on his shoulder. "And between your dad and Jane down there, they should be able to take care of everything until the fire trucks get there. Of course they'd be better off if we helped. Because we're truly awesome." She made a face. "But we both made promises and we have to keep them. Is your dad really a volunteer fireman?"

"Yes, he says everyone should be prepared to protect their homes. But he won't let me do that, either. I have to wait until I'm sixteen."

"That sounds like Joe." She could see a new outbreak of flames to the left of the tents. Was that the castle? She had to get Michael away from standing here watching this destruction. "Why don't we throw on some more clothes and then straighten up the tents?" She motioned to Harold Albert, the policeman whom Joe had sent up to guard them, to come and help. He'd been standing transfixed, staring at the fire with the same horror as Lisa and Michael. "Will you go into my tent and start getting it ready for visitors, Harold?" As the policeman nodded and quickly hurried to obey her orders, she turned back to Michael. "We might need to temporarily share accommodations with some of your friends. Don't you think that's a good idea?"

He nodded jerkily. "And maybe call Jane and tell her to bring them up here right away." He ducked into his tent and was quickly finishing dressing. "Colin was hurting. I could *feel* his pain. Will you phone her and ask, Lisa?"

"I'm already doing it." She tried twice and made no connection. "There's a problem. It's probably the fire. Or maybe she's too busy helping Colin and the others. I'll call later." She was throwing on her own clothes. "You start straightening your tent and getting it ready for visitors."

"Okay." But he had come back outside and was staring at the flames. "The castle is on fire. Do you suppose Lady Kendrick is okay?"

"I'm certain she is," Lisa said. "Jane says she's very smart and tough. And everyone would make sure that she knew what was happening on her own property." She tilted her head sideways. "I think I hear the sirens of the fire engines. I told you everything was going to be all right."

Michael's gaze never left the castle. "Maybe..." He was suddenly tensing up. "It's not all right. *She's* not all right. She can't breathe and there's darkness. She's trying to get out the door, but it's locked..."

Lisa stiffened. It could be only imagination, but this was Michael and she wasn't about to shrug it off. "Are we talking about Lady Kendrick or Jane?"

"Lady Kendrick. Jane is still safe...no darkness." He moistened his lips. "But there's so much darkness and it's all around..." His gaze flew in panic to her face. "It's all around *you*, Lisa."

She shook her head. "I'm fine, Michael."

"No, you aren't. It's close. Too close." He suddenly dived toward her and rammed her, knocking her off-balance. "Down!"

Pain.

A stabbing pain in the flesh of her shoulder.

She instinctively pulled Michael down to the ground and rolled on top of him. "Don't move. I have to—"

"They don't want to hurt me." He was trying to get out from underneath her. "It's you they'll hurt, Lisa. Run!" He stopped, his gaze on someone beyond and above her. "It's too late. He's here..."

Another stabbing pain, this one in the nape of Lisa's neck.

And then, nothingness...

———◆———

Thank God the fire trucks were here at last, Jane thought as she watched the flashing red lights of the vehicles wheeling through the gates followed by two ambulances.

At last? Joe was right, maybe it only seemed a hundred years.

Should she make one more pass to check those still-burning tents? She was sure everyone was out of that inferno now, but it wouldn't hurt to verify. There had been so much smoke...

Her phone was ringing. Lisa. She'd heard it before, but she'd been too busy to answer.

"Sorry, Lisa. It was crazy down here. But thank God there aren't any deaths so far. Now that the EMTs are here, we'll get the patients to—"

"I hate to interrupt, Jane, but I'm really in a bit of a hurry," Luca said. "I'm sure your friend Lisa would have been interested but I understand she's a bit indisposed at the moment. Do you suppose it's all the smoke?"

She went still. His meaning was unmistakable and chilling. "Hello, Luca. Smoke? Then I assume you're to blame for all this ugliness and pain? Could I hope that you're somewhere on the property so that you feel some of it yourself? Though I'd rather you'd burn in hell."

"You could hope, but you'd be disappointed. I'm not on the property. Though I'm close enough to still get a whiff of that smoke every now and then. It hurts the lungs, doesn't it? Poor Michael is coughing every now and then."

Chill iced through her. "Michael? You're lying."

"Do you want me to let you hear him?" Silence. "Oh, he's being shy. Do you want me to make him talk to you? I assure you I can do it. But I didn't want to hurt the poor lad."

"No, don't make him talk to me." It could be a lie, but she couldn't take the chance of stressing Michael if it was true. But Luca had mentioned Lisa and Lisa had been with Michael. "You said that Lisa was indisposed. Do you mean she's—" She stopped. "Did you hurt her?"

"You almost said 'dead,'" he said. "Actually, it was very close. I was tempted to leave it up to Alberto, and he's a trifle bloodthirsty.

After all, he does believe he deserves a reward since I did trust him and a few of his friends to take care of bringing me your brother. But I told him to try to keep her alive and evidently she survived him. Of course, he'd just killed that rather useless guard who was supposed to protect them. Perhaps he'd had his fill of gore for the time being." He chuckled. "No, Alberto never has enough, he has an amazing capacity. But I believe he did leave her alive. Perhaps he was having problems with your brother and was in a hurry to get your Michael to me."

"I don't believe you."

"You don't want to believe me," he corrected softly. "But you're beginning to do it, aren't you?" He added, "So I'd better tell you what you need to do so that I can cross this off my list. I've only allowed a certain number of hours to get this done tonight and I'm behind schedule. Neither one of us would want you to get it wrong. I'm sending you a photo of a child right now, and I want you to think of Michael while you're looking at it. Because it *will* be Michael if you don't obey me. You've brought it to my attention how soft and weak you are where children are concerned, and I decided to take advantage of it. Though I don't really want your brother. He might be a decent enough tool to use against you, but that would be a petty way to start our relationship. I'm more interested in showing you that I'm the only one in your life who can give or take away on a large scale. That's much more satisfying."

"And egotistical."

"Nothing wrong with ego. So I'll let Michael go, if you take his place. When you decide to take my proposition, just run down to the parking lot outside the main gates and get into the blue Volvo. Drive out, press the button on the phone you find on the front seat, and I'll give you further directions. I'd suggest you don't tell anyone we had this conversation because they'll try to persuade you to do things their way. And you should know exactly what that's going to mean. If you don't come, I'll kill him. If you come and bring anyone with you, I'll kill them and still kill Michael. If you come and give me exactly what I wish, I'll let your brother go free." He added, "What could be more fair? You've never been helpless. I'm sure that you have enough confidence to believe you can find a way to escape or kill me. The only way to lose is to do nothing and let me kill the poor boy."

"Don't *do* it, Jane." It was Michael's voice in the background, fierce, hoarse, desperate. Unmistakable. She felt sick to her stomach. True. It was all true.

"Ah, the brave lad speaks," Luca said. "Now you have a decision to make for all of us. I hope it's the right one." He paused. "Look at the photo, Jane."

She pressed the button. It was the photo she'd known she'd see. The pain-racked little boy on the crucifix. It was good that Luca would think this was the first time she'd seen this image, because her shock and horror silenced her for an instant. There was no doubt that was the face of the dark-haired child she'd dreaded to see. Not her sketch, an actual photo taken by this monster of that child twisting in agony.

And that was true, too. No nightmare. Somewhere out there, this tragic victim was being used as a pawn. "Is . . . he alive?" She could barely get the words out. "Who . . . is he? Did you kill him?"

"Perhaps he might not be dead yet. The child was totally un-important to me, I only used him to demonstrate what fate Michael could expect if you don't cooperate. Should we take him down and put your Michael up on that crucifix instead? Because that's what you're choosing. And you don't have many hours to make up your mind. As I said, I'm a bit behind schedule."

"Choice? You'd kill Michael anyway."

"No, I wouldn't. That would be foolish. You're suspicious and would never sacrifice yourself unless you could be certain it would allow your brother to live. I fully intend to let you see him go free before you take the final step toward me. I've worked it all out. I'm hanging up now. I have to make final preparations and you have to see if your friend Lisa survived Alberto. We both have to get busy, don't we? There's a deadline."

He pressed DISCONNECT.

Dear God. She closed her eyes for a moment as the waves of terror hit her. Michael!

Deadline.

Her lids flew open and then she was running past the burning tents, crossing the bridge over the creek, and tearing up the hill toward their tent area where she'd left Lisa and Michael.

Then she saw Lisa lying crumpled in a heap on the ground. Still, so still.

She fell to her knees beside her. Unconscious. But no blood. No, that wasn't true, there was a thin rivulet of blood issuing from a tiny mark on the side of her neck. Her hands grasped Lisa's shoulders. "Wake up." She shook her desperately. "He said you were all right. Tell me he wasn't lying."

No answer.

"Lisa! Talk to me."

Lisa's eyes slowly opened. "Dizzy . . . Stop yelling . . . at me, Jane . . ."

Relief poured through Jane. "It looks like you might have a mark made by a dart on your neck. Are you hurt anywhere else?"

"Don't think so—But Michael said I was the one . . . they wanted to hurt." Her eyes widened in shock. "Michael!" She was struggling to sit up. "Where's Michael?"

"Sit still. I'll find him." Jane was already dialing her phone to get hold of Joe. "You're in no shape to be staggering around searching."

Then Joe came on the line and he was speaking quickly. "It's okay, Jane. The door was jammed shut and Lady Kendrick was unconscious, but I got her out in time. The EMT thinks she'll be fine."

"That's good." Lord, she was glad something was going well during this nightmare that had erupted out of nowhere. She said curtly, "But that wasn't why I called. You have to come back up to my tent right away, Joe. Bring a medic if you can. Lisa's hurt and needs you." She cut the connection and turned back to Lisa. "I'm going to leave you now. Don't move around until you find out what chemical they used to put you out." She squeezed her friend's hand and jumped to her feet. "There's nothing you can do now. But it's going to be okay. Joe will be here soon." She turned away. "I've got to get my jacket out of my tent. I'll be right back."

She ducked into her tent and almost stumbled over the body of the guard Luca had told her Alberto had killed. His throat had been cut, and he was staring sightlessly at the ceiling. No time for horror or sadness at this butchery. Just accept that so far everything Luca had said was true—and hope what he'd said about Michael was also true and act accordingly. She threw on her jacket, took her .38 revolver from her backpack, and thrust it into her pocket. Then she was outside the tent again.

Lisa's eyes were narrowed on her face. "You didn't tell Joe about Michael."

"Because I'm going to find him now myself. I told you that, Lisa. I'll make sure he's all right." She'd already started running back down the hill. "Don't worry, we'll get him back."

"Jane, you're being—" Lisa broke off and then shouted after her, "Come back. Stay here. I don't *like* this!"

Neither did Jane. But she ignored Lisa as she tore down the path and headed for the front gate. Because Luca had been right: If she hesitated, if she listened to arguments, it might be too late for Michael. It was up to her to get him back, because she was the target. She could do it, but only if she was careful and didn't let Luca play her.

The front gates were right ahead and wide open, and the entrance driveway before them was filled with ambulances and fire trucks. There was no question that anyone would pay attention or try to stop her as she pushed her way through the crowds of patients, firemen, and EMTs. She could even see the blue Volvo parked by the edge of the road where Luca had told her it would be. It must have been so easy for Alberto and his men to get Michael out of the castle grounds without being noticed during that first panic after the fire started, she thought bitterly. Just light those fires that would endanger all those innocent students and volunteers and cause panic, pain, and fear.

Damn him to hell.

———◆———

"I'm a mile north of the castle," Jane said as she punched the button on the burner phone that she'd found on the seat of the Volvo. "Tell me where I'm to go."

"Turn on the GPS. It will lead you right to me. However, I do have to tell you that the car is bugged, and if you try to transmit a message to anyone then Michael will go to the great beyond. But may I say how delighted I am that you've proved my judgment of your intelligence correct?"

"No, I want you to put Michael on the phone again so that I'll know he's still alive."

He made a clucking sound. "But I gave you my word."

Then Michael's troubled voice. "You shouldn't do this, Jane. He's really a bad person. Is Lisa okay?"

"She's going to be fine. And I know what I'm doing. He hasn't hurt you?"

"Only a little."

"A very little." Luca's voice was back on the line. "But that could change. He's beginning to annoy me. Kids are so stupid. He doesn't seem to realize how much danger he's in."

And he had never met anyone like Michael, and it probably disturbed him that he couldn't intimidate the boy. "He's not in any danger. Because we made a deal and you're going to keep it." She was looking at the GPS. "You're not far. Lake Cairnes. A boat?"

"Helicopter. Much more efficient. We have a good distance to travel once you join me."

"Where?"

"Now, if I told you that, your brother would hear and I'd have to kill him. See how careful I'm being to keep him alive?"

"Just keep on doing that." She cut the connection.

A helicopter. And once she boarded it, she'd have a difficult time knowing where she was going or how to escape. Much more difficult than if a vehicle or boat was involved.

Well, she couldn't worry about that now. Her first priority was to find a way to make sure that Michael would get free.

And stay free...

Look.

Plan.

Not much time...

———

KENDRICK CASTLE

"Don't you dare make me go to that hospital, Joe," Lisa said fiercely as the EMTs were trying to put her into the ambulance. "I need to go with you. It was *my* fault. I was supposed to look out for both of them and I screwed up. Caleb's going to strangle me. You should want to do it, too."

"None of us were expecting those sons of bitches to try to burn up the entire encampment," Joe said grimly. "When you see a major disaster, you think first about saving everyone involved. In the confusion you sometimes lose sight of the ones who are most important to you. In all the noise and trauma, it was natural that you wouldn't be aware of anyone on the attack."

"Michael was aware. He said they wanted to hurt me, not him."

"Yes, you told me. But Michael didn't realize that in time, either.

And I sent that guard up there to watch over you, but he was killed trying to do it. So stop blaming yourself." Joe was trying to hold on to his patience. "Look, I'm not blaming you. But Michael is gone and I have to find him. I've spent the last hour searching for him, and neither he nor Jane is on the property. If you want to help, just let me get you off to the hospital to make certain that whatever chemical was on that dart isn't going to have a delayed poisonous effect on you."

"Jane knew what happened to Michael. She said she was going to find him." She waved her hand as he opened his lips. "Okay, I'll go to the damn hospital. But she *knew*, Joe. Find Jane and you'll find Michael."

He wasn't about to mention that one of the firemen had already told him that a woman of Jane's description had driven away from the castle shortly after the time Jane had called him. Lisa would never have given up and let them take her to be tested. "Don't worry, I won't stop until I find both of them."

He slammed the door of the ambulance.

She knew, Joe.

And if Jane knew, it meant Luca's deadly plan was in motion and he might already have both Michael and Jane.

And that possibility was scaring the hell out of Joe.

———◆———

LAKE CAIRNES
WALES

Jane punched in Luca's number the moment she got off the main road and caught sight of the large gray-and-black helicopter.

It was sitting on a plateau that extended about three miles along the bank of the lake. The moonlight was bright enough to reveal the copter clearly, but otherwise the plateau appeared deserted.

No Michael.

"I'm almost there," she said when Luca picked up. "I see the helicopter and I'm stopping the car now. But I'm not going to get out until I see you bring Michael toward me."

"How very demanding of you." Luca stepped out of the shadow of the aircraft. "Do you have any idea how vulnerable you are, Jane?" He snapped his fingers, and someone shoved Michael out of the darkness behind Luca. "How vulnerable *he* is?"

Michael seemed all right, Jane decided, relieved. But he did look as small and as vulnerable as Luca had said. "I have to make sure you haven't hurt him." She got out of the car. "Michael, come toward me."

"By all means, take him," Luca said sourly. "He's been a complete little ass. I almost gave him to Alberto to enjoy a dozen times in the last couple of hours."

"Alberto?" she repeated as she watched Michael run toward her. "I want to see this Alberto and whoever else you have there." She pulled her gun out of her jacket pocket and pointed it at Luca. "I need to be certain that you don't have anyone hiding in the trees ready to grab Michael again after you've supposedly let him go."

"Why don't you shoot me and find out," he said softly. "Because you're very smart and know that I'd be prepared for you to be armed." He nodded over his shoulder. "Come out into the light, Alberto. You'll notice that AK-47 he's holding is aimed at your Michael, Jane. I'm sure Joe Quinn has told you what a gun like that can do to the body of a child. Even if you aimed at me and pressed the trigger, Alberto would get off a round that would still kill your brother." He smiled. "And Alberto regards me as his spiritual leader and naturally would instantly avenge any shot aimed at me. You can't imagine how much he's developed since I showed him the pleasures of power." He tilted his head. "Correction. You can imagine. I sent you that photo."

"That was *his* work? It was hideous." Michael had reached her;

she motioned him to one side so that she could still cover Luca. "As you are. Is there anyone else there?"

"Just Davron." He motioned, and a man came slowly out of the shadows. "I designated this as a personal pleasure trip, but how could I forget to include him when he was so impressed with the painting of your ancestress, *Fiona*." His smile was fading. "I've been very patient, but I'm beginning to become annoyed by you. You're showing a distinct lack of respect."

Her hand tightened on the gun. "Michael, have you seen anyone except these three men since you were brought here?"

"No." Michael took a step closer to her. "That's all. No one else. And I was watching and listening." He whispered, "I know what you're going to do. Please don't do it. Think of something else and we can do it together."

"Not this time, Michael."

Because Luca was already shouting from the plateau. "You can see I didn't hurt that kid. But that doesn't mean I won't. Throw your gun down and I'll let him go. You know you've lost, Jane. Two minutes."

"Just let me say goodbye. I doubt if you'll let me see him again." She tossed her gun beneath the oak tree next to her. Then she was reaching down, her arms sliding around Michael in a fierce hug. "I'm slipping my phone into your back pocket," she whispered low and fast in his ear. "Call your dad as soon as you get out of rifle range and then give him my phone as soon as you see him. Run as fast as you can back to the main road. About a mile down that road, I saw lights burning in a cabin nestled about halfway up the hill. Go there and tell the people who live there that you need help. Promise me you'll do it, Michael."

"I promise, but I don't—"

"Hush." She hugged him again. "I love you. You'll be fine."

"He's getting angry, Jane. And I shouldn't leave you to . . ." His grip around her neck was anguished. "This isn't *right*. You shouldn't do it. I won't let him—"

"Go!" She tore his arms from around her neck. "Don't look back. I'll distract him. Run!"

And he was running, thank God. Tearing down the path toward the main road. Michael was incredibly smart and more woods-savvy than they dreamed. Now that he was free, he had every chance to reach Joe.

She straightened and stood in the middle of the path so that she'd block any shot at Michael from the plateau.

There was no shot.

But only a moment later she felt a brutal hand on her shoulder that spun her around to face Luca. His lips were curled and his eyes glittering with rage. "I told you I don't permit a lack of respect." His hand lashed out, backhanding her with all his strength.

Pain!

Her jaw was hot, burning.

She staggered backward and fell to the ground.

Dizzy. She was vaguely aware he was bending over her. "I intended to let him go...maybe." His voice was harsh. "But you interfered and tried to take control. Only I can give or take away. That's what this lesson was all about. And you spoiled it."

She shook her head to clear it. "Then choose someone else for your lessons. And leave me and my family out of it."

She could feel the waves of rage he was emitting as he looked down at her. Then they were suddenly gone and he was smiling. He reached down and pulled her to her feet. "I forgive you. After all, I did choose you for a reason. That doesn't mean I won't continue to punish you until you learn, but this was only the initial skirmish." He pushed her toward the helicopter. "And now we'd better get out of here before that brat sends up an alarm of some sort. Alberto says your brother was trouble from the moment he took him."

"It runs in the family. So this might not be worth your while." She was still dizzy, weaving back and forth and having trouble staying on her feet. She felt a chill as she gazed at the helicopter. But Michael was free, and if she boarded that helicopter Luca wouldn't be going after him. "You might keep that in mind, Luca."

"Oh, I will," Luca said as he opened the door of the helicopter for her. "And when I do think about it, I'll have Alberto describe to you what he wanted me to let him do to your brother. One must always be ready for future eventualities. Your Michael might be free now." He jumped in the pilot's seat of the helicopter and started the rotors. "But, as they say in that city where your dear brother was born, tomorrow is another day, Jane."

———◆———

MACALLEN CABIN
WALES

"Okay, Michael?" Joe asked huskily as he rushed into the small bed-room where Rod MacAllen had just led him. He enfolded his son in a giant hug, closing his eyes with relief. Then he pushed him back to look at his face. He touched the cut on his son's lower lip. "Maybe not so okay," he said grimly. "Who did this? Luca?"

Michael shook his head. "Luca called him Alberto. He's the one who hurt Lisa. Jane said she's all right?"

"She will be." His gaze was raking over Michael's face and body. "Anything else but the bloody lip?"

"He hit me in the stomach when I was trying to get away from him at the castle." He drew back as Joe reached out to examine him. "But Mr. MacAllen said that it was only bruised when he looked at it. It kinda made him mad and that's why he called the police instead of waiting for you to get here. I told him he should wait for you, Dad."

"I'm glad he didn't." He turned to the burly, gray-bearded man who was hovering, frowning suspiciously at him from the doorway. "Thank you for taking care of my son. I can't tell you how much I appreciate it."

"You should take better care of him," MacAllen said bluntly. "Not let him run around knocking on strangers' doors in the middle of the night." He shrugged. "Maybe I shouldn't have called the police, but you can never tell in this day and age who might be the bad guy."

"That's absolutely true."

"But the lad evidently doesn't think you're anyone to worry about." He turned and headed toward the door. "I'll give the bobbies a cup of tea and then send them on their way."

"He's a nice man, Dad." Michael watched as Rod MacAllen left the cabin. "But at first he thought I was just some crazy kid and didn't pay any attention when I told him about the fire, and the helicopter, and Jane. He thought I was just making up stories." His gaze shifted back to Joe. "But you believed me when I called you and told you about the helicopter, didn't you?"

"I always believe you, Michael."

His eyes were searching Joe's face. "But it was too late, wasn't it?" he whispered. "By the time you tried to get to Jane, the helicopter was gone?"

Joe nodded. "They must have taken off right after you ran away."

Michael shook his head. "Not right after." He was silent. "Jane told me not to look back, but I did anyway." Another silence. "He hit her. *Hard.* Then she was lying there on the ground and he was looking down at her and smiling." His hands were clenched into fists. "I wanted to turn around and run back to her. But I didn't do it, because I promised her. But I should have done it, Dad. I was *wrong.*"

"No, you were right." Joe could see the pain and torment the boy was feeling. He was experiencing the same thing Michael was going through. All the frustration and worry and rage. Only his anger was more deadly, and he wanted to reach out and *crush.* "And Jane was right. If you'd gone back, she'd have had to fight for you. She would have probably been hurt much more than what Luca did tonight. We'd never want that to happen."

"No, but he did hurt her. And I *hate* it." He drew a deep, shuddering breath. "It wouldn't have happened if it wasn't for me. I have to get her away from him."

"That's my job, Michael."

"No, it's not," Michael said fiercely. "Not this time. Go ahead. You do your job. But I *have* to help her. I told her I would."

Shit. Joe was gazing at Michael's expression with exasperation. Usually his son was reasonable and respectful, and he paid attention to rules from either him or Eve. That was not going to be the case today. Michael's expression was stormy and determined. There was no way he was going to be talked out of searching for Jane. Okay, accept it, and draw away from the argument. Find a way around it.

If he could manage to do it.

"Suppose we try to mount a partnership. But there are a few things we'll have to do immediately. We have to call your mom and let her know that Jane's in trouble." He paused. "And it might be a good idea if we tell Caleb right away what happened to her."

"He'll be angry."

"Absolutely." He added, "And I've been debating whether or not I should mention that you saw Luca hit Jane. He might get a bit upset."

Michael shook his head. "I told him I'd always tell him the truth. Not mentioning is like telling a lie."

"Yes, it is, but I know how I felt. It was like a kick in the gut to think of Jane being hurt."

"I know," Michael said hoarsely. "Me too." He moistened his lips. "But we'll be able to bring her back. There are ways I can help. You always try to keep me away from everything, but you can't do that this time. I have to be part of it." He was talking fast, his eyes fixed pleadingly on Joe's face. "Luca would be hard for me, but maybe not Davron or Alberto? But you'd have to let me get close . . ."

Joe tensed. "What are you talking about, Michael?"

"You know." Michael stared him in the eye. "You've always

known. I can *do* stuff. You and Mom might not like me to do it, but what if those men try to hurt Jane? That Alberto is really bad, Dad. Tonight every now and then I'd pick up one of his thoughts and it was...ugly. So much pain. And I'm not the only one he wanted to hurt. There was something about another boy. He was wishing I was more like Tomas so that Luca would give me to him. He didn't see what difference it would make to him since we were both just kids." He paused, thinking about it. "But if he thinks I'm just like this other kid, that might make it easier."

Joe felt his stomach lurch.

A little dark-haired boy twisting in pain on that cross.

"*Another* boy? How old?"

"I don't know. Younger than me." Michael's gaze was on Joe's face. "You know something about him, don't you?" he asked softly.

"I might." But he wasn't about to share that knowledge with Michael. The boy had already gone through enough horror for one night. "Enough to know that I don't want this Alberto to start comparing the two of you."

"Why not?"

"Because you *are* a kid," Joe said roughly. "And I'm not going to let you do anything you'll regret because you're feeling guilty. I'm the one who was responsible for both of you. Anything that happened is at my door. That's still the way it is. So get anything else out of your head."

Michael was looking soberly at him. "I don't think I can. I think you'll have to let me help you, Dad." Then he suddenly shrugged. "But I can try to do as you like. I don't want to make you and Mom unhappy."

It was clear that Michael wasn't going to give him anything more than that tentative promise. It was going to be a fight. Joe could see it coming. The smart thing would just be to accept what he'd been given and work behind the scenes for a final victory. "Good. I don't believe your Mom would approve of you planning on going after a creep like Alberto for any reason. It would make her very unhappy."

Michael nodded gravely. "But she would understand if it was because of Jane. She wouldn't like it, but she'd realize that we have to get her back."

"But not if she had to risk you to pull it off. Understanding doesn't mean giving approval. She'd tell you to go another way. And that's what we'll do." Joe held out his hand. "Come on, let's go back to the castle and see if the medics have released Lisa from the hospital yet. I know she wanted to see you. Then we can get busy finding Jane."

"We can do that now." Michael jumped off the bed and pulled Jane's phone out of his pocket. "She told me to give her phone to you when I saw you. I was curious so after I got here I looked to see why. She must have palmed her camera while she was talking to Luca. She took photos of Alberto, Davron, and Luca and the helicopter. There was moonlight, but the photos are still kind of dark. Maybe you can get someone to brighten them up?"

"Maybe I can," he murmured. It was like Jane to grab any opportunity she could to get an advantage. He just hoped she'd managed to give him something he could use. "We'll see what Scotland Yard will say about them."

"They all like you at Scotland Yard. They'll work hard to help us find her." Michael was hurrying across the room toward the door. "Maybe you can call them once we're on the road? I only have to thank Mr. MacAllen and say goodbye and I'll be ready to go..."

Michael was more than ready now, Joe thought. He was almost frantically eager to go after Jane. Joe knew that no matter how often he told the boy he was not to blame for drawing Jane into Luca's trap, he'd still feel guilty.

And so would he, Joe thought wearily. It stung that there was no way to deny that Luca had been clever enough to trick them. He'd have to dismiss the memory and go after Luca with every weapon at his disposal. He just hoped that Jane wasn't going to have to pay for it.

Though according to Michael she already had begun to do that, he thought bitterly.

He hit her. Hard . . .

———◆———

MANTUA

"He *hit* her." Caleb repeated Joe's words. He could feel the blinding rage tear through him. The blood was pounding; he felt as if he couldn't breathe. Smother it. It would do no good right now. Save it for when he was on the hunt. But he *was* on the hunt, he thought. He had been on the hunt since the instant Quinn had told him about Jane. "How could you let him do that? You said that you'd keep them safe. I trusted you."

"I know you did," Joe said curtly. "I screwed up. You're an idiot if you think I did it on purpose. I could have lost them both. But Jane saw that I didn't lose Michael and that probably pissed off Luca. So stop fuming and let's find a way to make sure the asshole doesn't make her suffer more because everything didn't go quite his way. Unless you'd rather just indulge yourself by going on the attack at me."

"Tempting," Caleb said harshly. "What can you say that would convince me that I can't do both?"

"Not a damn thing except that Jane wouldn't forgive you if you went after me. That would make a difference to you. And somewhere deep in that twisted psyche of yours, I think you might actually like and trust me. Now, shall we get down to business? Jane managed to smuggle out a few photos with Michael. I'm going to send them to you." Caleb heard a faint ping. "We have Luca, Davron, and this Alberto who Michael says is more vicious than smart. I don't know if their photos will help. I was more interested in the helicopter.

Evidently from where Jane was standing she was only able to get the first two numbers. I just turned it over to Tovarth, and he's trying to trace it or get a location."

"It's a Bell 407. Not a new model, perhaps six years old." Caleb was looking at the photo. "I'll get Palik on it right away. Anything else?"

"One thing." He paused. "It might not be useful. But I think the name of the boy Jane was drawing is Tomas and that he was connected in some way to this Alberto."

"How do you know?"

He hesitated. "Michael told me. He said he . . . caught something."

"And you were waffling about telling me because it meant admitting that Michael is psychic?" Caleb asked fiercely. "It's time to forget about that crap. I don't care if it makes you uncomfortable not to pretend that Michael's just like any other kid. He is what he is. Just as I was when I was his age. You just do what you have to do to survive it. And I'll use anything Michael can do or tell me to get Jane back. Just as I'll use everything I have. You want him safe? I'll keep him safe. But I won't take a chance on sacrificing Jane to do it."

"*You* won't take a chance?" Joe repeated with soft menace. "Did I ask you to do that, you son of a bitch. I don't care what kind of hell you went through when you were Michael's age. He's my son and I'll do whatever I can to help him get through this with as few scars as possible. He's feeling so guilty about Jane that I'm just trying to keep him from doing something crazy that will get him killed. Now I'm going to hang up because I have to call Eve and tell her that I don't know what the hell is happening to Jane this minute, much less what Luca will be doing to her in the future. Do you realize what that's going to do to Eve? So I don't want to hear from you again until you can give me something else to tell her. You're this great master hunter? Well, go prove it. I need a location and then I'll be on my way to join you. I don't care if I get that information from you or Tovarth."

Caleb was silent. Even through his own fury and frustration he could sense Quinn's pain. He knew how much Quinn loved Jane and could hear how this was tearing him apart. But Caleb's own pain was so intense that he was barely able to process anything else. "You'll get it from me," he said unevenly. "And soon."

He cut the connection.

He stood there for a moment while the waves of rage swept over him. How was he supposed to function when he was having trouble even thinking? Bullshit. It was a hunt. Think about the hunt. Don't think about Jane. She must not exist until the last moment when he moved in to take her away from Luca. Otherwise she'd get in the way.

He was punching in the transfer of the photos Jane had taken to Palik's phone as he strode back into the suite where he'd left both him and Nicco Barza. "Pull up the photos I just sent you, Palik. There's a helicopter in that photo and I don't know if it was a rental or if Luca owns it. It was used by Stefano Luca in Wales last night, but I think it's likely he'll be heading in this direction. He appears to know the area and has cult members on hand at his beck and call. Find that helicopter and trace it to Luca." He turned to Barza. "Davron was with Luca last night, so Luca must be keeping him trailing at his heels. Call Davron and arrange a meeting for tomorrow."

Barza shook his head. "It's not that easy. He might not call me back right away. I told you that he's afraid of Luca."

"Not acceptable," Caleb said softly, his eyes flickering in his taut face. "Make it easy. Say the right words to make him come to you. Promise him anything."

Barza frowned. "You're pushing me too hard. And I might not want to go through with—" Then he broke off as he met Caleb's eyes. He inhaled sharply. "What the hell's the hurry?"

"Don't ask, just do it, Barza," Palik said quickly. "Believe me, you don't want to go there with him right now." He was now looking critically at the photo. "This is damn bad quality. It looks as if whoever took it was on crack. Don't blame me if I can't trace that helicopter right away."

"Oh, I'll blame you," Caleb said. "Count on it."

Palik raised his gaze. "I was afraid of that," he said quietly. "I knew when you walked back in here that the stakes had been upped." He paused. "Jane MacGuire?"

Caleb didn't answer. "Find the helicopter. And pay attention to anything you hear about a child, Tomas, who might have something to do with Luca or the cult."

"Anything else?" Palik asked. "What are you going to be doing while Barza and I do your work for you?"

"Luca gave me a list of all the things he's going to take away from me. I'm going to take a look at a few of them in the vicinity and see if he's already started to take possession." He headed for the door. "It would be like the arrogance of the asshole to think he could get away with it right under my nose."

"Not if he knew you," Palik said.

"But he doesn't," Caleb said as he opened the door. "He only thinks he does, and that could be a fatal mistake..."

CHAPTER

11

Another lake...

Jane had seen at least three lakes as the helicopter had begun its descent, though there might have been more. But no villages, no houses that she could see. Still, she *knew* these hills; she'd painted those lakes when she came here earlier in the year. The rest of the trip from Wales in Luca's helicopter had been a complete puzzle, but she'd recognized the lake country of Italy when it had come into view almost twenty minutes ago. She leaned forward so that she could see anything else. She needed to locate a distinctive marker so that she could find her way out of these hills when she managed to escape.

"Curious?" Luca's smile was catlike. "Of course you are. You've been sitting there, not saying a word during the entire trip. If you were any other woman, I'd think you were frozen, terrified. Not you. You're studying everything, hoping to escape. Go ahead, it amuses me. But you're not going to get away, Jane. I'll make certain that every one of my people knows what will happen to them if you manage to wander away from me." He glanced over his shoulder at the two men in the backseat. "Isn't that right, Alberto? You went to a good deal of trouble to bring her to me. What would you do to someone who made all your fine effort a total waste?"

"Whatever you want me to do." Alberto shrugged. "But you shouldn't bother with anyone who was that foolish. You should give her to me instead. She's the one who's the troublemaker. I could break her for you in no time. She's only a stupid woman."

Luca threw back his head and laughed. "Do you hear that, Jane? Alberto doesn't tolerate troublemakers, and he doesn't appreciate your uniqueness. I think I need to explain you to him." He was no longer looking at Alberto, but at Jane. "Or let you demonstrate that uniqueness. There's no way she's in any way stupid. She's an artist, Alberto. She looks deeper, sees more than other people. For instance, I'd wager that she knows exactly who we all are and our capabilities just from being with us this short time. Isn't that right, Jane?"

What game was he playing? "There's not much to know," she said coldly. "You're all fairly shallow."

"But I won't have anyone believe I'd select anything less than quality goods." His hand reached out and closed on her thigh. "So you'll show Alberto and Davron how exceptional you'll be when properly trained."

She looked down at his hand. She could feel its warmth through the material of her slacks. She *hated* him touching her. Don't fight it. Not yet. She had to explore every avenue to find what would work and what would not. She had to find the key to escaping this place. "Why would you want to impress them? They're nothing to you."

"You're wrong. Every ruler must have subjects. Why else did I waste all those years and effort making Alberto and his blood-thirsty friends accept me in that capacity?" His hand tightened with bruising force on her thigh. She inhaled sharply at the pain but somehow managed to keep her face without expression. He added softly, "Now show them I chose well. I think Davron first. I do hope you won't hurt his feelings. I told you how fascinated he was with Fiona's portrait."

She forced herself to look at Russell Davron. "Weak. Not

particularly evil, unless not fighting against it is evil in itself. He's afraid of you and he'd like to be you. But only because of the power you wield. He probably thinks he's much more intelligent and has a better eye for art." She tilted her head appraisingly. "I also think he might be a little vain and lazy, but I can't see anything else. However, you just tolerate him, and I believe you've already made a decision about him. He won't like that decision."

Davron tried to laugh. "Ridiculous."

Luca ignored him. "Now Alberto."

Jane's gaze shifted to Alberto. "He is a giant, isn't he? He's not afraid of you. He reminds me of one of those statues on Easter Island. Brutal, crude, primitive." She paused. "Evil? Yes, maybe as evil as you are. You like that about him. You're very intelligent and don't permit yourself to give vent very often to that totally black soul of yours. But as long as you have this Alberto under control, you have the best of both worlds. He might be your alter ego." Her glance shifted to Luca's face. "Is he?"

"Perhaps." His gaze was narrowed on her face. "But you'd better hope that I keep that ego firmly at bay." He was suddenly smiling recklessly. "You've done very well with them. Now it's my turn. I have to caution you to be very careful. I wouldn't want you to hurt my feelings. I might lash out and damage you."

"Then I'd do better not to speak at all. Everything I think about you tends to be obscene."

"But that's not your choice. I want my turn with that scathing tongue. Give it to me." His fingers were digging in and out on the soft flesh of her thigh. "Who knows? I might not punish you."

He was already punishing her. Ignore it. It appeared she wasn't the only one who was curious and wanted to explore the boundaries. She turned to look at him. "You have every intention of punishing me. You've been looking forward to it. It's just a question of what form it will take. You won't choose something ordinary. You'll want to prove something to me."

"How very clever of you. I do have a few ideas that might suffice. Now tell me what you see when you look at me."

"Blood."

His lips tightened. "What else? That was too easy. I've already shown you that side of me. I won't be cheated."

"I suppose you'd be considered quite handsome if anyone was able to ignore the coldness. You're well spoken and appear educated, which is amazing if you weren't lying to me about your parentage and background."

"I wasn't." His voice was suddenly reverberating with intensity. "But I didn't look upon them as my real parents. I was only a small child when I began to groom myself to be the man I knew I was to become. From the moment I looked at that portrait of Cosimo de Medici at the museum, I realized my true destiny. I knew then I'd have to start to educate myself."

Probe a little more. Every bit of knowledge might prove valuable. "To emulate the Medicis? You were reaching a little too high, weren't you?"

"No, the Medicis were a banking family who started out with money, but they still had to fight to become the kingmakers and art patrons they intended to be. But they knew they'd be able to do it." He smiled. "There's even a family portrait of the Medicis that they commissioned that showed them not as a business banking family, but in the robes of the Magi. That's how they saw themselves." He gave a half shrug. "Even though they sometimes used poison and murder to accomplish their aims. That was when I realized that I might have to cheat and steal and do whatever was necessary to reach my goals, too. Ambition and drive can take you anywhere you want to go, but you must have direction. The Medicis gave me that direction."

"It's too bad you couldn't channel all that drive into something more positive than thievery and murder." Her gaze was still searching his face. "You try to keep from showing it, but there's something...missing. You're...unfinished. And, in spite of all your plots and ambitions, it's frustrating you." She shook her head. "Interesting. If I thought I could bear all the darkness inside you, I might even like to paint you. But I'm no masochist."

"Yet you must have painted Caleb," he said mockingly. "I'm sure he's as dark as I am."

She shook her head. "I've sketched Caleb, but I've never done a painting." She paused. "And he's nothing like you. There's nothing missing. Sometimes there's too much."

"But I'm glad that you've never done a painting of him. I want to be the first," he said. "It's already on my list. You're going to be a great artist and I should reap the benefit of being immortalized."

"I'm not a masochist," she repeated.

"You *will* do it." He banked the helicopter. "We're almost there. Right over the next hill, you'll see Fiero."

"Fiero?" Her gaze flew to his face. "That's where you're taking me?"

"Not at once. That would be a little obvious. Just a brief passing glimpse. You should see it, since it's Seth Caleb's family home. He's never taken you there, has he?"

"No, he hasn't lived there since he was a teenager. It doesn't have the most pleasant memories for him." She was staring at the huge stone castle as it came into view. "Renaissance-gloomy and ostentatious. Why did you want me to see it?"

"Because I want to tell him you've seen it and I was the one who showed it to you. Talk about darkness? It's bred in Seth Caleb. He knows everything that's ever happened here. And in the beginning of his family history, there was nothing that wasn't dark. It will make him...uneasy that I brought you there. I like the idea of being able to do that. I told you that Caleb was very important to my plans." He was now flying away from Fiero and over the hills, and he didn't speak again for another thirty minutes. "Fiero fascinates me, but I can wait. I've waited a long time already for it. Several years ago, I had a much smaller place built in preparation for this visit. I can't tell you how I've been anticipating having you here to see it. It's very luxurious, well hidden, tucked among the lakes. And you'll notice that I've arranged for more than enough sentries on the property to keep you from leaving me. We should be there in another few minutes. You'll see it soon..."

She was already seeing it.

She lost her breath, freezing.

A round stone tower.

The trees bordering either side of the walk.

The huge oak door.

No crucifix.

But there was something dark that might be blood staining that door.

Luca was smiling maliciously as he watched her face. "That's right, I showed you that photo with the boy. How foolish of me to think that you might not recognize that door. But aren't you happy that your Michael is safe with his father instead of here with us? You should be grateful to me."

"Who...was that...boy?"

"Presently." The helicopter was descending. "Tell me you're grateful that your Michael isn't nailed on that door."

"Of course I'm grateful," she said fiercely. "But to God, not you. Is that other boy alive?"

"Such a soft heart." He turned off the rotors and jumped out of the helicopter. "Come along and see for yourself. You too, Alberto. I know you're eager." Luca had already reached the door of the tower. "You see, not too much blood on the door." He opened the door for her. "But then he was a small child."

He was moving across the foyer to a door opposite the main entrance. He threw it open. "And the boy's name is Tomas. Go in and look him over, Alberto."

Alberto pushed past Jane into the room and strode over to the bed against the wall where a dark-haired young woman was hovering over a little boy.

Jane *knew* that little boy. She had sketched him, agonized over his agony.

And the child was looking at Alberto and screaming!

The woman was crying hysterically, standing in front of the boy to protect him.

Jane instinctively started to move forward to help her.

"No!" Luca's hand grasped her arm. "Wait."

Alberto struck the woman and she fell to the floor. His hands grasped her throat and pulled her to her feet, firing questions at her as she struggled to answer him.

"Enough," Luca told him. "You need her to care for the boy."

Alberto's face was twisted as he stared at Luca over his shoulder. "Rosa said he'll be well enough whenever I'm ready," Alberto said. "When can I finish it?"

"When I say," Luca said. "Go away. I'll call you when I need you."

"You should have let me finish." Alberto was glowering at him. "He belongs to me. You said I could *have* him."

"Get out. You forget yourself."

Alberto turned on his heel and strode out of the room.

"Introductions are in order." Luca turned to Jane and gestured to the weeping boy in the bed. "Tomas." He nodded at the woman. "And his mother, Rosa. Did you enjoy the show? It was even more dramatic than I thought it would be. Alberto really should have had more control over his wife."

Jane tore her arm from his grasp and the next instant was helping the woman to her feet. "He was choking her, dammit. Show? Are you going to tell me what's going on here?"

"I've only been waiting for you to ask." He glanced at the boy's mother. "Stop crying and get out of here."

"Please don't tell Alberto to hurt him, sir." Her voice broke. "Not again."

"But you told him yourself your son was well enough," he said mockingly.

"Please..." she repeated. "I only told him what he wanted to hear. If I hadn't told him Tomas was better, he would have killed me."

Jane couldn't stand it. Luca was enjoying this too much. "Your son won't be hurt," she told the woman. "Just go sit over there in the corner and be quiet."

The woman hesitated and then scurried over and curled up against the far wall.

"You might not be able to keep that promise, Jane," Luca said. "But at least she's not wailing."

"You didn't answer me. What's going on here?"

"Why, Alberto has found his true calling in the cult. I believe he must have been very bored before I came back here and helped him and his fellow cult members to release their inner demons. They only needed a Grand Master to lead them. At times I have to keep him from being overenthusiastic." He smiled. "He even came up with the idea of offering his son as a sacrifice on his own. He thought it would give him more prestige."

She stared at him in horror. "In your eyes?"

He shrugged. "He wanted to impress me. But he also has ambitions to take over as Grand Master if I decide to step away from the cult. Since I have no intention of staying active when I complete my final plans, I decided to let him have his day. Of course, I knew it would increase my own influence with the cult to sanction it. It takes boldness to use a child to make that kind of statement. Prestige is everything. And, if I decide to return to the cult for any reason, Alberto would be grateful enough to give me anything I wanted...as long as he could get rid of me quickly."

She was staring at him in disbelief. "And his mother let that son of a bitch do that to her son?"

"As you saw, she had objections, but Alberto can be convincing."

She felt dazed. "You're all beasts." She moved over to the bed. "How old is he? Seven? Eight?" Tomas had stopped crying but was still staring up at her with desperation. Then she was looking down at the child's bandaged hands and wrists and felt sick. "Will he be able to use his hands again?"

"Perhaps with decent surgery. I told them to be careful with the wrist piercings and to tie his lower body securely to the cross so that his weight wouldn't pull and cause additional trauma. I even had him given antibiotics and sewn up afterward by one of the cult members who worked at a hospital in Venice. I gave the boy every chance to survive." He paused. "That's providing I decide not to let Alberto finish the job. When I made him take Tomas down after only a few hours, he was very upset, as you saw." He shrugged. "But I already had what I needed. All I wanted was to send you that photo as a message so that you'd get the comparison to your Michael I was looking for."

She stared at him in disbelief. "You're saying this was all for me? You put this child on a crucifix because you wanted to hurt *me*?"

He smiled. "I thought it might not be wise to take Michael if I decided a trade was in order. I knew I might have to treat you with a certain delicacy in the beginning. I was afraid your feeling for him might just get in the way of your lessons. So I had to have a powerful alternative for demonstration purposes." He added softly, "Tell me, is the punishment extraordinary enough? Have I proved anything to you by it?"

She was looking down at those bloody bandages. "You've proved that you're a demon from hell." She leaned forward and gazed down into the boy's enormous dark eyes. "Does he speak English?"

"Yes. It was helpful for me to have Alberto know it, and I had his family taught as well."

"I'm sorry this happened to you, Tomas," she whispered. "I promise I'll do everything I can to make it up to you."

"Why? You didn't...hurt me." His voice was shaking, but he wasn't sobbing any longer. "It was him. It was my father. It's always him. And I don't know why." Tears were running down his cheeks again. "I never know why. What did I do?"

What could she tell him? That he had been born within this hideous circle where the weak were devoured by the strong? "You did nothing," she said hoarsely. "Your father is an evil man who should have been on that crucifix instead of you. But you mustn't think about him, it will only make you more frightened and unhappy. Just sleep and get well."

He shook his head. "He'll come back."

"No, he won't." She raised her eyes to meet Luca's across the room. "I'll find a way to keep him away from you. Now close your eyes and go to sleep. Try to dream about things that make you happy. Trust me."

"Dream?" His lids were already closing. "But all I see is their faces and the blood . . ."

Jane drew a deep breath and turned away from the boy to his mother. "Watch him," she said curtly. "I'll be back to take a look at those wounds." She moved across the room to Luca. "Get me out of here. We need to talk," she said through clenched teeth. "You've had your fun. Did you enjoy it?"

"Exceedingly." He was smiling. "I'm still enjoying it. Even the drama Alberto provided added its own bit of thrill. You reacted just as I thought you would. All the pathos and sympathy, all the horror and strength. It was quite touching. I was complimenting myself that I'd called it so accurately."

"I told you that I knew you'd punish me." She had to keep her voice steady. "But I admit I didn't expect this. Torturing a little boy just to stage a way to threaten and control me."

"You should have expected it. I'll do anything to make certain I always win." His voice was almost gentle as he added, "Haven't you realized yet that I've managed to eliminate any feelings that I find inconvenient? Actually, I regard this interview with Tomas as a complete success." He opened the door for her. "But it's time I showed you your apartment now. It's just down the hall."

"Not a dungeon?"

"Of course not. I'll be occupying it with you whenever I choose, so that would be foolish. I always appreciate the very best."

She could tell that by the rich furnishings and carpets of the hall. She was finding out a lot about Luca. That last exchange alone had revealed that he was more sociopath than psychopath. Though the two disorders shared many elements, Luca's control and ability to handle the cult set him apart. It was necessary that she keep that fact in mind as well as everything else about him going forward. "And the reason you believe bringing me to Tomas is a success is that you think you can use him."

"Oh, I know I can use him."

"You're right, I don't want you to let Alberto see him again. I want to go back and look at his wounds and make sure they're healing." She paused. "And I want you to start thinking about what price you're going to demand to let that little boy go."

He chuckled. "What a delight you are, Jane. So bold...I have no problem with the first two demands. It falls into line with teaching you that I'm the giver and taker of all things—as a true patron should be regarded. But the last one requires thought."

She made a rude sound. "You're lying. If you've been making plans as long as you say you have, you'd have another list ready."

"But the question is: Do I want to bargain or take? Now that I have you secure, I have a choice. Both are interesting in their own way." He had stopped before an ornately carved oak door. "What are you offering?"

"You're talking about sex." She met his eyes. "You want to rape me? A man like you would think of that first. It involves cruelty, pain, and domination and you'd believe that would give you some kind of advantage. It wouldn't. Go ahead. I won't fight you. Sex is nothing compared with saving a child. It wouldn't take me long to forget it ever happened. Because you're *nothing* to me."

His smile faded. "Now, that annoyed me. I assure you that I'd make sure you'd remember every minute I was with you. But I'll let it go for now. I have other business to attend to that has to do with Seth Caleb." He opened her door. "You look quite dreadful and still smell of smoke. You'll find a complete wardrobe in the closet. Change for dinner at seven on the veranda. Make certain you're exceptionally beautiful. I want all my men to see what a prize you are. Again, prestige is everything. You're free to roam wherever you wish in the tower. You'll be watched, of course. I'll always know where you are. And if you cause me trouble, I'll send Alberto to pay another visit to his dear son." He was walking away from her. "I do hope you'll enjoy my preparations for you. You'll see that I put a lot of thought into establishing you comfortably into your new life."

And she could see what he meant when she entered the suite. It was enormous and the décor rich and lush, from the king-size bed to the tufted satin couch at its foot. The portrait of Fiona occupied the primary position on the east wall. Jane stopped short as she caught sight of a small painting on the south wall. Good heavens, was that a Da Vinci? She thought she recognized the technique but not the work itself. If it was a Da Vinci, it was probably an original. Her gaze shifted to the north wall, which was composed entirely of windows. A canvas and easel were set up in front of it to take advantage of the sunlight pouring into the suite.

Of course there was a canvas, she thought bitterly. Her talent as an artist was the prime value he'd indicated she had for him. He wanted to have his private gallery and had chosen her to fill it to his specifications. But she still found herself walking over to examine the paints and canvas he'd chosen. Her work was often her salvation. And it wouldn't mean anything she created belonged to him just because it was painted here.

She stood there in front of the canvas. Top quality. Paints, the same. The view of the verdant hills outside the window was a scenic marvel. Once she started painting, she could get lost in them and soar away from all the ugliness that surrounded this tower. It would be so easy . . .

No, it would not be easy at all.

I have business to attend to that has to do with Seth Caleb.

And those words had frightened her almost as much as what she was going to have to face with Luca. Because of what she'd done when she'd traded herself for Michael, she'd put Caleb squarely in danger. She hadn't allowed herself to think of anything but Michael when she'd gone after him, but Luca had made it clear that he'd use Caleb if he could.

And Caleb would never allow himself to be used unless he chose. All his life, he had been used by everyone around him; Luca would just be one more. But this was different, because he'd let himself be used for her. She *knew* it. He might be a mystery to her in many ways, but she knew that Caleb would always be there for her when she needed him. It was strange that out of all the uncertainty that had torn her apart during these last months, this single truth was so clear to her now.

I'd die for you.

Those words that had so shocked her and filled her with a sense of profound wonder.

"*I thought you must be afraid of him,*" Lisa had said. "*Everyone's always afraid of him.*"

"*The Hunter.*" Caleb's sardonic words. "*That's how you always thought of me. I knew it even that first time you came to sleep with me. You were trying to overcome it, but I could feel it.*"

She hoped it wasn't true, but perhaps he'd been right, because she'd been so confused and bewildered about what she was feeling for him during that time. That bewilderment was gone now, lost in the fear for him and the knowledge that no matter the danger, he would always choose to reach out to her.

But she had no right to force him to make that choice. The mere idea was agonizingly painful. She was the one who had made the decision to save Michael. Now she had to get herself out of this nightmare and not pull anyone else into it with her.

So stop dreaming of paints and emerald-green hills and get to work trying to find a way out of here. She turned away from the blank canvas and headed for the bathroom to wash away some of the smoke and filth before she went back to Tomas. It was time to examine that little boy's wounds and try to heal them. Tomas had been caught in the middle of this horror, and she had to find a way to get him out of here before he ended up on that crucifix again.

She shuddered at the thought. She could almost see that hideous photo of Tomas on the crucifix before her eyes. The solution seemed simple: Save the innocent, keep Caleb out of this, and try to live through it herself.

Yeah, piece of cake.

———————

"I'm coming back," Eve said hoarsely. "No arguments. You wouldn't have a leg to stand on, Joe. There's no reason now why I shouldn't be with you. That bastard *has* her."

"I'm not arguing. I'll take all the help I can get. I told you how Michael is feeling. He needs you. I need you, too. We're both feeling as guilty as hell." He added grimly, "Though I'm the only one who has any right. I shouldn't have run into the castle when the fire broke out there."

"And then Lady Kendrick might have died," Eve said.

"She was fine after I got her out. She's a tough old bird."

"But you couldn't have known that. So quit blaming yourself. It's pure instinct. You'll always be the one who goes after the old or helpless."

"And leaves his own family to be gathered up by the Lucas of the world," he said bitterly.

"Shut up, Joe. I'm not listening. I'm sure you heard enough of that bullshit from Caleb."

"I did. More than enough. And I took it for the most part. All that mattered was getting him over that first rage so that he'd start thinking again and find me some way to get to her."

"And he'll do it. He won't stop, Joe. Now let me get off this phone and throw some things into a suitcase. I have to get to you right away. I need you, too." Her voice was unsteady. "And I don't want to be alone out here in this blasted jungle. All I can think about is the Jane we first knew when she was as young as Michael. So fragile and yet brave as a lion..."

She had ended the call.

Joe's hand tightened on the phone. That call had been just as difficult as he'd told Caleb it would be, he thought wearily. But Eve was coming and they'd be together and somehow they'd make everything right.

"Mom was scared for Jane?" Michael asked from behind him at the tent entrance. "Did you tell her how that Luca hit her?"

"I didn't go into that particular detail." Joe turned to face him. "She was upset enough, and I didn't think she needed to have that on her mind on the long trip here. It might be a good idea if you don't mention it, either."

Michael nodded. "I won't. Not unless she asks me." He met Joe's eyes. "But I bet you told Caleb. You'd want him to know."

"Yes, I wanted him to know. Sometimes arousing an emotional response in Caleb can be...valuable." His lips twisted. "I'm surprised you weren't eavesdropping on my conversation with him, too." He tilted his head. "Or did you?"

"No, I thought you wouldn't like it when you were probably talking about how to catch Luca. You always try to keep me away from stuff like that." He added quietly, "Even if you're wrong."

"Michael."

Michael went on quickly, "But could I call Caleb and talk to him? I don't think he'd feel the same way. He might think I could be valuable, too. Sometimes I know stuff or *feel* things. I wouldn't get in your way, Dad."

"I realize you'd try not to do it. And you *are* valuable, Michael," he said gently. "It's not a good idea for you to contact Caleb. I imagine he's going to be very busy. You can always come to me and I'll listen and we'll talk about it."

"I know you will." He was frowning. "But you worry a lot because you know Mom will worry. Caleb won't worry, he'll just go do what he has to do."

"Which isn't always a desirable course of action," Joe said dryly. "I'd prefer that Caleb worry a little more."

"He worries about Jane. That's all that counts." He was studying Joe's face. "Is that the only reason you don't want me to call him?"

"It's a very good reason. I think your Mom is scared enough about what's happening to Jane. She almost lost you, too. She'd be a lot happier if you weren't involved in this at all." He paused. "Or at least at a good distance away from the action. Caleb will never be that in a hundred years."

Michael nodded slowly. "I thought that was it. I was trying to do what I promised you, but I hoped maybe I could talk to Caleb sometimes if I needed to do it." He turned away. "But it's okay. I'll work it out."

Those last words were sending up red flares for Joe. "I don't want you to work it out. I want you to come to me if you see any problem. I'll always be here for you. Why would you have to go to Caleb?"

"Maybe I won't." He was gazing soberly at him over his shoulder. "You're so smart and you understand everything, Dad. It's just that Caleb seems to think the same way I do most of the time. And he doesn't let anything get in the way. That kinda helps sometimes." Before Joe could reply, he changed the subject. "Lisa just got back from the hospital and she's going down to the tents to help with the cleanup. A lot of the volunteers lost their belongings in that fire. May I go with her?"

Joe was just as content to have this conversation that was going nowhere end. "That seems like a good idea. It appears as if the entire camp is in total chaos. I have to call Tovarth at Scotland Yard, and then I'll be down to help. Try to get Lisa not to overdo it until I get there."

"She says she's okay. See you..."

Joe watched Michael leave the tent before he reached for his phone again.

He seems to think the same way I do most of the time.

Of course Michael and Caleb would think alike, he thought in frustration. Both had gifts that were unique and could be more troubling than rewarding. And because they'd been forced to confront every imaginable trauma connected with those gifts, they'd developed ways of coping that puzzled even the people who loved them. For an instant he felt a flash of sympathy for Jane, who'd had to deal with a much more mature and complicated Seth Caleb these last years. At least Michael had known only love and honesty in his short life.

Regardless, the man and the boy were clearly feeling a bond that might cause Joe problems down the road.

All he could do was keep an eye out for possible repercussions.

———◆———

TOWER HOUSE

"I told you to be ready at seven."

Jane stiffened as she looked up from dressing Tomas's wounds to see Luca standing in the doorway. "I'm not done here. I'll be with you when I'm finished."

"Wrong. You are done here." He strolled over to the bed and looked down at the little boy. "Isn't she, Tomas? You don't want her to get in trouble with your father, do you?"

"No." Tomas's eyes widened in terror. "Don't tell him to do bad things to her. I didn't ask her to stay." His gaze flew to Jane's face. "Go away. He'll hurt you, too."

"Does it make you feel like a big man to frighten a little child?" Jane asked Luca as she got to her feet. She smiled down at Tomas. "I'll see you tomorrow morning. Take those pills I found in the drawer and gave to your mama. They should make you sleep."

"Don't come back." His voice was frantic. "You were nice to me. I don't want them to—Don't come back."

"I'll be here tomorrow," Jane repeated. "Your beast of a father won't touch me." She glanced at Luca. "Because this other beast who pulls his strings won't let him. We'll come to an agreement and everything will be okay. Won't it, Luca?"

"If we come to an agreement." He added softly, "And if you don't disobey when I give you orders. I don't see why Tomas should get upset again."

"Neither do I." She strode out of the room and down the hall. "He's gone through enough."

"But you appear to be a comfort to him in his time of need. He was looking at you as if you were an angel from heaven." He added mockingly, "Are you going to be able to save him from me, Jane?"

"I'll try. Someone has to do something. His mother is so frightened that she can barely function. She wants to help her son, but she let that atrocity happen to him. I lay the blame for that at your door, too."

"Of course you do. And I accept it. No, I welcome it. The man who wields the power is always to blame. It's a sign of that power."

She shook her head in disbelief. "You're incredible." She increased her pace. "It will take thirty minutes for me to shower and dress. I'll meet you on the veranda."

"Take your time," Luca said. "You'll be punished regardless. You disobeyed and you can't expect me to overlook it again. But now you'll realize that Tomas will know you're not exempt and it will frighten him. I believe that will cause fewer incidents. You're incredibly soft where children are concerned, Jane. First Michael, and now this youngster who is a complete stranger to you. Why?"

"Other than sheer decency? Children are innocent, and the innocent shouldn't suffer at the hands of people like you. There should be some special hell to send you to keep them safe."

"Innocent?" He tilted his head. "But didn't Ernest Hemingway say something about everything that was truly wicked starting from innocence? Doesn't that mean that poor, gentle Tomas will turn into his father as time passes?"

"No." They had reached the door of her suite and she threw it open. "It means that what you did to Tomas was sickening. And that I hope I find a way to pay you in kind."

He chuckled. "And in the meantime, I'll have the child to use as a weapon against you. You do have such a delightful frankness. I'm really so glad that you're completely unable to hide what you feel." He turned away. "But you must remember you have to be magnificent tonight. You have to be everything I want you to be. It's essential to my plans..."

The dining room on the veranda was faultlessly elegant and resembled any fine restaurant Jane had visited in Paris or London. The veranda was at the rear of the building and overlooked a lake that had been invisible from the tower entrance. The sunset view mirrored in the water was splendid. There were several tables covered in the finest linen, and she could see at least four waiters in attendance.

But only one of those tables had anyone seated at it.

Luca stood up and inclined his head as he saw her coming toward him. "You did very well." His gaze went slowly over her, from the top of her shining red hair, to the curve of her breasts revealed by the low neck of the peacock-blue taffeta gown. "Quite splendid with your hair. Even breathtaking." After he seated her he motioned to the hovering waiter, who quickly disappeared. "I thought that blue would be wonderful on you. You look like a princess."

"It's not my thing at all. But I couldn't find anything simpler or less formal." She met his eyes across the table. "And I was afraid that you would be an asshole and insist that I change if I showed up in slacks. I'm hungry and it wasn't worthwhile to make an issue of it."

"I'm glad you're hungry. I've already ordered dinner, and you'll find it absolutely superb. I brought the chef from a hotel in Rome. He's a master at his craft."

"Well, it must not take much effort since it looks like he has very little to do." She glanced around the empty dining room. "Are you usually his only guest?"

"Yes. For the time being, but that will change when I leave this place for a more permanent residence."

"The magnificent city-state you create in some extradition-free heaven?"

"Exactly. I'm considering either the South Seas or Russia." He watched the waiter pour her wine. "And I'm not appreciating your sarcasm, Jane. It will be as close to heaven as a man can get."

"Will it?" She glanced around the empty tables of the dining room. "It seems very boring to me. There's no life. You've worked so hard to reach what you think is perfection but it's like a barely begun sketch that will never be a painting. Unfinished."

"You said that before." He quirked his lips. "It will be finished. It just takes money. I've come so far and I'm getting close. You'll get me even closer." He stared directly into her eyes. "Perhaps it will happen tonight."

She was suddenly wary. There was a reckless excitement in his face. "What do you mean?"

"What I said." He lifted his glass and finished his wine. "You with your talk of painting and unfinished work. You don't know anything. I'll have whatever I want. By the way, did you see the Da Vinci in your suite? I thought only you would properly appreciate it."

"Because you stole it? I didn't recognize it. Where did you get it? From a private collector?"

"Yes. Who stole it from another collector. Who stole it from a Nazi general who stole it from a Jewish banker. And so forth. But I'm the one who has it in the end. I'll always be the one who wins in the end." He gestured to the three waiters who were parading toward them carrying silver trays. "Now be quiet and eat the dinner I've provided you. You might need your strength later."

"Is that supposed to intimidate me?"

"Just a warning. You'll know it when I want to intimidate you." He smiled. "Now I only want to keep you fit and healthy so that you'll maintain those stunning good looks that I require of you."

"Screw you."

"Oh, that will come also. But not quite yet. That also has to be just right, and will happen after we've settled at our final palace. I've been planning for years exactly how we'll come together." He motioned to the first waiter to remove the lid from his tray. "Now, try this artichoke salad and we'll proceed from there..."

FIERO CASTLE

The castle was still deserted.

Caleb was swearing beneath his breath as he moved out of the woods toward the gardens. He'd thought Fiero might be one of the places Luca would choose as a base. He'd seen no guards on the way here, but he'd hoped that he'd see some sign of occupancy at the castle itself.

Nothing.

Son of a bitch!

Check it out. Make sure.

He moved quickly through the rose gardens toward the front

entrance, his gaze narrowed on the windows and balconies of the upper floors. Shuttered. The entire property appeared neglected and totally without life. It wasn't quite as bad as it looked, Caleb knew. He'd arranged minimum maintenance for the castle and gardens after his parents had died. As far as he was concerned, the place could have been burned to the ground, but his sisters Maria and Lisa had been left as much of the property as his parents could arrange and Caleb had to protect their inheritance. It was a bittersweet duty when he knew that if his mother and father had been able to fight the complicated clauses of the Ridondo trusts, he would have received nothing at all from the estate. Which would have been fine with him—all he'd ever wanted was to be free of the place.

He stopped at the front door. Should he go inside? Was it worthwhile? He'd hoped Luca wouldn't be able to resist the castle: This was Caleb's family home, and its macabre history should have appealed to Luca and the cult he'd acquired. Why hadn't he done it?

And why the hell was Caleb hesitating? There might be nothing in that damn house except memories—but maybe Luca had left something behind when he'd chosen this place. Some random clue that might lead him to Jane. Doubtful, but Caleb was here and he wouldn't lose any opportunity.

He turned off the security alarm, unlocked the door. He threw it open and entered the grand foyer. Grand in every sense, he thought cynically. His parents might have tried to abandon the memory of their notorious ancestors as they'd abandoned Caleb, but they'd kept all the treasures their black sheep forbears had gathered over the centuries. The crystal chandelier from Venice, the finest crafted woodwork in the cabinets and the curving staircase. The magnificent onyx-and-malachite-trimmed full-length mirror facing Caleb had been created by the Russian artist who had designed the Malachite Room at the Hermitage. The foyer was only dimly lit by the fading light streaming through the windows, and his reflection appeared dark and menacing as he moved from the door toward the mirror. Very fitting, he thought sardonically. Hadn't he always been the shadow-figure that haunted these hallowed halls?

But this wasn't about him or the past. This was about Luca and Jane. Which room to start the search for—

And then his phone rang.

CHAPTER

12

W hat are you doing?" Jane was frowning as she watched Luca punch in a number on his phone. It was the second time he'd placed a call since they'd finished dinner and she could see he was annoyed. "Who are you calling?" Her gaze flew to his face. "Alberto?"

"Would I spoil a fine dinner by bringing him into the picture?" He leaned back in his chair and motioned for Davron—who'd just come into the dining room—to set the computer he was carrying in front of her. "No, as you can see, I had our friend Davron bring dessert." He added, "For both of us. If I can get the bastard to answer. I can't believe he ignored that first call. I've had that tablet set up for Skype so that he can get a clear picture of you. I'll do the talking, but I guarantee he won't want to look at me."

She tensed. "He?"

But Luca was now speaking into the phone. "It's about time you answered, Caleb. I'd almost think you didn't want to talk to me. I was going to hang up, and I know that would have upset you. You'd have missed the chance to see how well I'm treating Jane. Just press 'accept.'"

She inhaled sharply as her gaze flew to the screen in front of her. "Caleb? More games, Luca?"

Then she saw Caleb on the screen. He was standing in a dimly lit interior, and she was vaguely aware that there was some kind of reflective mirror behind him. "Hello, Jane. She looks well enough, Luca," Caleb said noncommittally. "A little overdressed for her usual taste, but I'm sure she told you that. I'm surprised you called so soon. I expected you to let everyone stew for a while before you came forward with any ransom demands. That would be what I'd do. Well, let's hear them."

"So cool," Luca said. "But you're always cool, aren't you? Except about Jane. Then you're white-hot. You can't pretend with me. I've watched the two of you for too long."

"I don't pretend. I've always found it a bore. Sex is sex and it's always white-hot at the time. I found her exceptional. I'm sure you will, too. Now give me your demand so I'll know if I want to comply." He shook his head. "Incidentally, those ridiculous photos of all my houses won't be included for consideration in any demands. She's only a woman after all."

For an instant Jane could see a ripple of unease on Luca's face. He said quickly, "A woman you've been obsessed with for a number of years. Don't think I'll be fooled by this charade."

"I don't really care if you are or not." Caleb's tone was totally indifferent, and so was his expression. "It entirely depends if I believe she's worth what you're asking. As for me being obsessed with her for years, we've only been sexually involved for a relatively short time. Before that there were countless other women to amuse me. What makes you think she was different?"

"I believe you're protesting a little too much," Luca said harshly. "I think she *is* different for you."

"Why? Because she's different for you?" Caleb's voice was silky smooth. "You've already said that she was the one you chose years ago as the woman you felt might be suitable to come with you when you flew off to set up your Medici-inspired kingdom. Perhaps you're the one who became obsessed and thought that she was the key to everything *you* wanted. Then when I happened along into her life, you took it as a sign that you'd been right and she could bring my services to you, too." He chuckled. "But you didn't take into account that I already could take whatever I wanted. I have everything that you've been fighting to get all these years, and I stopped letting anyone else control me long ago. Did you think I'd let a woman have that power? Or you, Luca, just because you imagine you have something I want?"

"Imagine?" Jane could see that Luca was trying to stifle his rage. "I *know* it."

"Do you?" Caleb shrugged. "I think you saw what you wanted to see. You might have had a better chance six months ago when I was still sleeping with her. Though our affair was dwindling anyway. I'm sure you know that she was becoming temperamental and broke with me months ago. I thought I'd give her a chance to change her mind, but I can only tolerate that for so long before I move on."

"Do you hear that, Jane?" Luca turned on her. His cheeks were flushed with anger. "He was through with you. Of course I don't believe a word of it. I'm sure you don't, either."

"Why not?" She had no idea what Caleb was trying to do, but she had seen him manipulate situations before. She remembered he'd told her that he'd study and find the best way to change Luca's perception of them. If there was a chance of throwing Luca off-guard and giving Caleb an edge, she had to play along. "You're wrong, Luca. It makes sense. I never knew what he was thinking anyway. It seemed ridiculous that he didn't accept our breakup right away when I'd realized from the beginning I was only a ship that passed in the night to him." She shrugged. "I guess I damaged his ego. He can be very stubborn."

"No, I'm *not* wrong," Luca said through set teeth. "I wouldn't make a mistake like that. I've studied you both. I know you're of value to him."

"Am I? It doesn't seem as if I am." She stared him in the eye.

"Why don't you tell him what you want and we'll see? You told me earlier that this might be the night when everything finally comes together for you. I think you're wrong and your wonderful plan might be coming apart at the seams."

"Are you mocking me?" he asked. "I warned you, Jane."

"Tell him what you want," she repeated.

"Do you hear her, Caleb," Luca said. "She wants to know her worth to you."

"So do I. Or what you perceive to be her worth. You're taking long enough," Caleb said. "What's the price?"

He was silent. "Cira's treasure."

Caleb threw back his head and laughed. "No. Hell, no. I admit I wondered if you'd be fool enough to ask for that. That photo of the Bank of Scotland where the treasure is kept stood out among all your other dream fantasies."

"They weren't fantasies. I'll have them *all*." His cheeks flushed. "It will just take time. But I need Cira's treasure first. That would give me the same kind of start the Medicis had when they were able to rule popes and kings of their era. That will be the linchpin."

"A treasure estimated at over a billion dollars would be quite a linchpin," Caleb said dryly. "And the odds against the ability to acquire it would be astronomical. Why would I even try?"

"Because you might be the only one who could do it. You're known to be very arrogant, Caleb. But you have certain unique talents that might make it possible, and the challenge would excite you. That's why I chose you." He moved behind Jane and put his hand on her throat. "Together with the lure that Jane brings to the table. I would hate to kill her, but if she isn't as valuable to my plans as I thought, I would do it." He stroked her throat. "You've half convinced me that she didn't please you as much as I thought she had. Which means that she might not be the woman I believed her to be. I find that troubling."

"That's your problem." Caleb's voice was totally indifferent as he shrugged. "But I've no desire to see you kill her. She did please me for a while. Choose something else and we might come to terms."

"But that would ruin my plans." Luca's other hand rose to completely encircle Jane's throat. "I don't think I could permit that to happen. No, I believe it has to be the treasure or nothing. Though I can see it's a high price to pay if you found her as irritating as I have since I took possession of her." His hands tightened on her throat. "Do you know she told me that she wouldn't mind at all if I raped her? She said it wouldn't matter as long as it saved a life. I believe she actually meant it. Of course, I regard that as my own personal challenge. But I have plenty of time. We'll work it out." His hands opened and he slid them down beneath her gown to cup her breasts. She inhaled sharply and forced herself not to move. Anything she did would aggravate the situation. She was almost sure now that Caleb's tactic was to take away her value as a weapon for Luca. It just might work if he could pull it off. "See how meek she's becoming?" Luca was rubbing her breasts slowly, sensuously. "How content she seems to be here with me?" He bent down to lick the lobe of her ear. "You wouldn't go even if I said you could leave, would you, Jane?"

Tomas. The threat was velvet-soft but she knew it was there. "You know I wouldn't," she said, through set teeth.

"See, I told you," Luca said as he released her breasts and slid his hands out of her gown. "So it's over to you, Caleb. Your decision."

"The decision is made. You're asking too much," Caleb said flatly. "For too little. She wasn't worth it toward the end." He shrugged and then was silent a moment, thinking. "But the idea of the treasure *is* rather intriguing," he murmured. "You're right, I'm probably the only one who would be able to do it. That kind of payday is almost irresistible even for me. I'll consider it and let you know. However, if I decide to go along with it, it will be my rules, my conditions."

"Of course." Luca's hand moved to the switch on the Skype. "Now one more thing..."

Caleb's face was suddenly filling the screen in a close-up that revealed every nuance of expression, even down to the pulse beat in his temple. His expression was completely without any emotion except perhaps annoyance and impatience. Even that pulse beat was absolutely steady. "What?" Then he understood and smiled mockingly into the camera. "Oh, you were trying to catch me in a moment of weakness? How absurd of you, Luca. It wouldn't be for Jane MacGuire." He looked directly into the camera. "She's nothing to me. Satisfied?"

"I had to see that for myself. I admit I hoped to catch you off-guard." Luca forced a smile. "Of course, there might be more weakness than you permit to show. I do know that even if you're getting bored with her, you'd still be tempted with the chance to prove you can do the impossible. I believe that might prove irresistible to you, even if she's not. I'll expect to hear from you."

He pressed DISCONNECT.

All trace of smoothness instantly vanished from Luca's contorted face. "Son of a *bitch*! I think he meant it."

Jane's shocked gaze was on his face. It was livid with rage. Caleb had managed to push some major buttons. It was clear he'd done exactly what he'd intended to do: change the perception and deprive Luca of a weapon. Luca's ego hadn't permitted him to believe he was wrong at first, but now he was doubting and it was making him furious. "It's your own fault," she said. "If you'd told me you were depending on Caleb to give you something that outrageous, I could have told you that your chances were going to be zilch. I'm not anything to him."

"Then why aren't you?" He grabbed her arm and jerked her from her chair. "You could have been, if you'd put out a little effort instead of tossing everything I've worked for away. I *wasn't* wrong. I know he enjoyed you once. I watched the two of you." He was pulling her out of the dining room and up the staircase. "Now you might have spoiled everything."

"What a pity. Did you ever consider blaming yourself for completely misreading our relationship? And probably every one of those items on your wonderful list. You should go back and start over and—"

He slapped her and she fell to the steps.

Pain.

Dizziness.

"Shut up!" His eyes were glittering with rage as he stared down at her. He pulled her to her feet again and pushed her the rest of the way up the stairs and down the hall. He opened the door and shoved her inside. "Get out of my sight. I can't stand to look at you right now. I had it all planned and you've made everything difficult. It's not my fault. It would have worked if you'd been everything I thought you were." His lips curled. "Maybe I can still make it work. But now I have to wait for him to make the next move." He took a step closer, and she instinctively braced to defend herself. She wouldn't let him hit her again. His eyes were blazing into her own. "I'm tempted to send you to Alberto and his friends to teach you a lesson tonight, but I can't do that, either. Because there's a possibility Caleb might still want you and they would definitely damage you."

Alberto. Fear iced through her. What had she been thinking? She wouldn't be the only one "damaged" if she fought Luca while he was in this mood. "You won't send Alberto to hurt Tomas? I did everything you wanted tonight. Tomas shouldn't be—"

His fist lashed out, punching her in the stomach.

She lost her breath and bent double as the pain washed over her. She fell to her knees, clutching her stomach, struggling to get her breath.

Don't fight him. Don't fight him.

"That's how I like you," he said viciously. "On your knees." He kicked her in the ribs. "I told you that the punishment would always come." He kicked her again. "No, Tomas won't be punished tonight. He might die and then I'd lose a weapon against you." He kicked her viciously one more time. "Though you may already have lost me Seth Caleb."

He turned and slammed the door behind him.

She couldn't move for a moment. The brutality had come so swiftly and painfully that she was still in shock. All that civilized smoothness had been transformed into ugly savagery in the space of seconds. Then she slowly forced herself up from her knees and toward the bathroom. She washed her face in cold water and stood before the vanity mirror assessing the damage. Her taffeta gown was ripped, and she had a bruise on her cheek. Besides that blow to the stomach, he'd kicked her three times, but she didn't think she had more than bruises. It could have been worse.

She left the bathroom and dropped down to sit on the silk padded bench at the foot of the bed. It took her a moment to let her head stop whirling as she went over what had just happened. Only one sentence stood out clearly.

You might already have lost me Seth Caleb.

Yes, it could have been much worse. Caleb had been very clever to gain instant dominance over Luca by making him believe he no longer wanted her. It robbed Luca of any power if he couldn't offer Caleb anything that would tempt him to go for the theft of the treasure. He had no weapon to wield, and that was enormously important. Caleb had put himself in a position of strength.

And thrown Luca into frustration and rage. Luca must have totally believed his precious plans were foolproof. The egotistical bastard had concocted this grand scheme since childhood, and convinced himself that because of his brilliance every aspect would fall into place. Tonight Caleb had yanked that confidence away from him, and it had blown his mind.

And she should have helped him more, she thought wearily. She'd been so angry about being used as some kind of sexual pawn that all she'd been able to do was keep her temper and her mouth shut. Which had only lasted until she'd been exposed to Luca's tantrum.

If she'd been able to keep her composure, she might have avoided these bruises.

No, probably not. Luca had enjoyed hurting her to release his frustration. But she should attempt not to do it again. Just try to find a way out of this tower and save that poor kid down the hall.

And let Caleb handle Luca for the time being. He'd managed to manipulate him very well tonight. He'd obviously gauged every emotion and response Luca had displayed and turned it against him. He was so icy cool and indifferent that he almost convinced her. But then Caleb was able to be exactly who and what he wanted to be most of the time. Master of all he surveyed and so damn controlled...

———◆———

Control.

Caleb stood with fists clenched, staring straight ahead into the Venetian mirror.

Keep his blood pumping smoothly so that he could breathe.

Blood flow was always the secret to keeping his expression exactly the way he needed no matter what he was feeling. But it could be traumatic, even dangerous, in situations such as the one he'd just gone through. It had an effect on his blood pressure and heart. Even though Luca could no longer see him, Caleb had to exit carefully out of the rage that he'd been holding back since he'd answered that call. He'd felt as if he was going to explode with every passing second... Two more breaths and he could release it.

Done!

The release.

Hatred.

Fury.

Frustration.

Aching pity.

Fear.

Swirling around him, attacking him, becoming him.

He whirled and his knotted fist crashed into the mirror!

It splintered and then shattered.

Then his eyes closed and he stood there, panting.

Okay, now don't move; let everything come together. It was done. Change of perception complete. He'd rolled the dice and chosen how to handle Luca based on what he'd learned from his study of him in that hotel room. It could have gone either way—and that still held true. To eliminate Jane's value to Luca was dangerous, but to let her remain a weapon in his hands could make both of them helpless. Don't think about what Jane might be going through now. Don't think of anything but the next step in the hunt.

Five minutes later, he was ready. He turned and left the castle and was striding back through the garden. He punched in Joe Quinn's number. "I just talked to Luca," he said curtly. "I saw Jane on Skype and she's not been hurt yet."

"Yet?" Joe swore beneath his breath. "That's not very promising."

"We take what we can get. I'm doing what I can. I'll get her away from the crazy son of a bitch, I just have to find a way to finesse it. I've managed to make him think what he's taken for granted about me is wrong, and it's caught him off-guard. I was even able to ease in the initial insertion for *persuasion.* Now I just have to keep him off-balance. That's going to be damn difficult with a subject like him. But if he doesn't know what to expect, I'll be able to control him." He added thoughtfully, "He's in a hurry, though, or he wouldn't have called me this soon. If I can put everything in motion right away, he won't have the time to get impatient or angry with Jane. That's essential. He's into power, and if he thinks he's going to get what he wants, there won't be an explosion."

"And what does he want?"

Caleb was silent. "I don't think I'll tell you yet."

"Why the hell not?"

"It might make you an accessory. I'll have to decide if I want to do that. All you need to know is that Luca will get what he wants from me. And that means there won't be any repercussions on Jane."

"Damn you, that isn't all I need to know. I need to know everything."

"Maybe later. Now I'm going to send you a photo I took while I was talking to Luca on Skype." He punched the button. "Jane was sitting on a porch or veranda when I saw her. She had her back to a lake and there was a motorboat and some kind of dock to her left. The dock had an ornate decorative railing that looked like some I've seen at gondola stands in Venice."

"The lake?

"Don't ask me which one. There are over fifteen hundred lakes in Italy and most of them are in the north. But I'd know it if I saw it again. It was one of the lakes in the lake region."

"How can you be sure?"

"I grew up in the lake country. At Fiero, I saw a lake anytime I looked out a window. And no, it wasn't the lake at Fiero. I'm certain because that's where I am right now. I'm sending a photo to Palik as well and the two of you can see who finds it first. I might be too busy to look for it myself."

"Doing what?"

"Supplying Luca with what he wants. The planning might get very intricate."

"And Jane couldn't give you any other hint where he has her?"

"Jane wasn't really talking. Luca was being difficult." The memory of Luca's hands on her breasts, his tongue on her ear, was causing the tension to start again. Block it. Extract only what was important. "You might say he dominated the conversation. I did get an impression she won't be of great help when we try to get her away from him."

"I don't believe that," Joe said flatly.

"Believe it. He's using someone against her. She told him that nothing that happened to her was important if it meant saving a life and that she wouldn't leave. Now that Michael's safe, I don't think just a threat against you or Eve would cause that reaction. The danger would have to be more immediate."

"Who?"

"I don't know. Maybe that boy Tomas? As I told you, she couldn't really talk. But it will all come together."

"I'm glad you're so confident."

"I have to be confident. She's going to be fine. Call me as soon as you find anything resembling that dock." He pressed SEND. Then he cut the connection.

The next minute he was dialing Palik. "I'm sending you a photo of a dock I want you to locate," he said when Palik answered. "Then I want you to get me a complete architectural diagram of the Royal Bank of Scotland in Edinburgh."

<hr/>

KENDRICK CASTLE

"Hey, what are you doing just lolling around in here, Michael?" Lisa came into his tent and strode brusquely to where he was sitting on his sleeping bag. "You offered to help and the job's not done yet." She grinned as she held out her hand to pull him to his feet. "And I absolutely refuse to do it without you, so don't think you're going to get out of it."

He didn't move. "You know I wouldn't do that," he said quietly. "I was going to come and help later, but I needed time to think first. I thought I'd have time before you came to get me like Dad told you to do."

Her smile vanished as she studied his sober face. No, more than sober—abstracted and terribly intense, and it made her uneasy. "How did you know your dad told me to come and rouse you from your lair?" she said lightly. "Maybe I like your company."

He nodded. "You like me. But it was almost time for him to leave for the airport to pick up Mom and he didn't want me to go with him. He'll want to talk to her without me around so that he can tell her what Caleb told him." He paused. "Just like he took you aside down by the brook and told you."

"And how did you know he did that?" Her gaze was narrowed on his face. "Have you been eavesdropping, Michael?"

"Yes. There are other ways to do it, but that would be intruding. Dad and Mom would get nervous. It was better if I just wandered down there and listened."

"But not particularly honorable. Joe told me that he'd already updated you with the news from Caleb—that Jane is still safe and Caleb is working on a plan. Why did you have to sneak around and—"

"Because Dad never really tells me everything," Michael interrupted. "He protects me. I told him I couldn't let him do it this time. I can help, Lisa. But he has to tell me stuff." He gazed up into her eyes. "You have to tell me stuff."

"Why should I bother when you're so good at eavesdropping?" she said dryly. "You heard it all, didn't you?"

"But some of it I didn't understand. I could tell something happened before that I don't know about—" he said in frustration. "I can *feel* it, Lisa. That's why I had to come up here and think about it."

"Think about what?"

"The reason Jane wasn't willing to leave Luca. I know why. It keeps repeating over and over." He whispered, "It's Tomas. She won't leave that kid, Tomas. Remember I told you all about that boy that Alberto kept thinking about when he took me?"

"I remember," she said slowly. "You said Alberto was thinking about how he'd like to hurt you as he had Tomas. Now you think that Jane wants to protect this boy?"

"She's Jane," Michael said simply. "Of course she does."

"You can't be certain."

"I'm almost sure. I keep *seeing* him now."

Her eyes widened. "What?"

"Since Dad brought me back to camp, I've been concentrating, trying to bring Tomas closer. It was the only way I could help since Dad was shutting me out."

"Your dad was doing what he thought best," she said absently. But she was too interested in what Michael had just told her to defend him any more than that. "Seeing him? Woo-woo stuff? You actually saw him? His face?"

Michael nodded. "A couple of times, but that was when he was asleep. Most of the time, it's just a sort of strong impression. But I need to get deeper, get closer. He keeps drawing away because he's so scared."

She shivered. "Yeah, I can imagine how he would be."

"More than imagine." Michael's gaze was searching her face. "I think you know why he would be. You're shutting me out, too, Lisa. *Tell* me."

"And be the bad guy? You're ten, Michael. Your mom and dad would not be happy that I exposed you to that kind of ugliness."

"You're not my mom or dad. It's important that I know things. I think Jane would tell me. She's beginning to understand that, Lisa."

"Well, she didn't tell you this," Lisa said crossly. "And now you're cornering me and I'll be in deep trouble. Though I don't really know why. I hated having anything kept from me by grown-ups when I was your age because I knew I was every bit as smart as they were." She grimaced ruefully. "And you might even be smarter than me."

"Tell me, Lisa."

"There was a reason why Jane didn't want you to know about that boy, Michael," she said gently. "She might understand you, but she wouldn't want you to see anything that might hurt you. None of us do. Leave it alone, will you?"

He slowly shook his head. "I can't do that." He leaned forward, his entire body tense. "Look, don't you think there could be a reason why I sometimes know stuff? What if it's because it could help me find Jane? Or maybe it's because it might help this Tomas."

She gazed at him helplessly. "You're tough, kid." She sighed resignedly. "I'm probably going to regret this. Stay here. I'll be right back." She left the tent and came back with Jane's sketchbook. She handed it to him. "The last sketch is probably the one you'll want to see." She shook her head. "No, correction, no one would ever want to see that sketch. But it's the one Jane drew a couple of nights ago that tells the story. Just glance at it and then give it back to me. Don't dwell on it."

But Michael was looking at all the sketches, taking that journey through those trees toward the tower as Jane and Lisa had done that night of Jane's nightmare. Then he reached the final sketch and he stopped in shock.

Lisa inhaled sharply. She had made such a big mistake. She took an instinctive step forward as she saw his face. It was pale, his lips tight with pain. "Give me the sketches back. This was a lousy idea. I shouldn't have let you talk me into it."

"No, it was a good idea." His voice was hoarse, his eyes never lifting from the figure of the boy on the crucifix. "It did what I needed. It's pulling me deeper. So much pain..."

"Stop *looking* at them, Michael."

"Not yet. He's bringing me closer." His finger gently touched the curve of Tomas's cheek in the sketch. "He was scared and he really hurt. And he didn't know why..."

"Michael, I want you to—"

"Shh." He closed his eyes. "Just a minute more..."

What the hell? What difference did one more minute mean? She'd probably already done her worst and left him traumatized, she thought gloomily. She dropped down beside him, crossed her legs tailor-fashion, and gave him his minute.

Which turned out to be four minutes. Then he opened his

eyes and took a deep breath. He smiled at her and said, "It's okay, Lisa. You didn't do anything bad." He closed the sketchbook. "And I didn't, either. Because I found out that I was right, and Jane would never leave that boy on the crucifix. She's kind of bound to him...It happened when she drew these sketches." He handed the sketches to her. "You can have these back now. I won't need them any longer."

He still looked strained, but the pain appeared to be gone from his expression, she realized with relief. And he had even given her that fleeting smile. "Why won't you need them?"

"I think if I work at it, I'll be able to reach him. Maybe even talk to him."

"Really?" She frowned. "But then why can't you reach out to Jane? That would be much better."

He shrugged. "Yeah, but she's grown up and I think that makes a difference. Kids accept stuff that grown-ups don't. It just kind of slips in. I could reach out to Mom and Dad, but Jane isn't my real sister. It would probably get in the way."

"Then you should try to *make* it work."

Michael sighed. "I'll do my best. I don't even know much of what I'm doing yet, Lisa." He suddenly chuckled. "And you know even less. So stop nagging me."

"Well, I thought suggestions might not do any harm. As long as I was getting myself in hot water, I decided this should be done right." She tilted her head. "Okay, you can't reach out, but if you're near them could you make contact then? Sort of mind-meld or something like that?"

"I think mind-meld is *Star Trek*," he said solemnly. "But I've gotten close to that without trying with some people, so I don't see why not."

"Close?" She leaned forward. Her eyes were bright with curiosity. "Why didn't you do it?"

"It would have been an intrusion," he said quietly. "And if I didn't do it right, I might have scared someone. I didn't want to do that."

"You're a nicer person than I am." She grinned. "I don't think I could have resisted experimenting. I always want to dig down deep and see what I can turn up."

"You're nicer than you think you are," he said. "You're just... different."

She nodded. "And so are you. I guess I always knew it. I just didn't realize how different." She grimaced. "But that's okay, it's interesting. Just don't let me do anything to screw you up. I was pretty scared when you were looking at those sketches."

"I know." He got to his feet and headed for the door. "I'm ready to go down to the tents and help with the cleanup now. It was bad that so many of those people were hurt and lost their stuff. I hate it for them."

"And I hate the person who did it," Lisa said. "Because it had to be the same person who hurt that little kid, Tomas." She hesitated. "I'm going to have to call Caleb and tell him that you think the reason Jane won't make any moves is because she's definitely afraid for Tomas." She made a face. "And I should tell your parents I showed you those sketches. I'm not looking forward to it."

"I'll do it." Michael smiled mischievously at her over his shoulder. "I'll say you couldn't help yourself. I'll just tell them I mind-melded you into doing it."

———◆———

"My God," Eve murmured as she gazed in horror at the burnt-out tents and blackened earth. She was remembering her last visits to see Michael and Jane here at Kendrick Castle. That bright, clean encampment with its cheerful instructors and joking students was as far from this scene as night from day. "I can't imagine anyone doing this to innocent students, Joe. How many injured?"

"Three burn victims. Two that will require additional treatment for the next few months. One released yesterday." Joe was helping her up the rutted path. "Only one death. Lady Kendrick's secretary, Nigel Montad, was found in the garden outside the room at the castle where I discovered her." His lips tightened grimly. "He was bludgeoned to death. The police believe he was trying to help her get out of the castle. Evidently Alberto had orders to create as much turmoil as he could and decided killing Lady Kendrick would do it."

"And they killed her secretary? Poor man."

"In more ways than one," Joe said grimly. "I found proof that Montad had opened the gates for Alberto and his men that night. The police later found Montad's wife and daughter at his home in town. Both dead. They'd been held hostage for a number of days, but were killed anyway when Montad completed his assignment of letting those bastards on the property."

"He must have been torn apart by having to make that decision."

Joe nodded. "But I guess everything could have been worse. There could have been more deaths. And though the students and volunteers lost most of their camping gear and personal possessions, they're working together to clean up the mess here at the tents. Most of them are going to stay for at least another couple of weeks to help."

Eve glanced at the castle with its bank of burnt-out windows. "Lady Kendrick?"

"The fire didn't spread past the first two rooms. She had to spend one night in the hospital, but she's home now." He shook his head. "She was pretty much in shock when she found out that her secretary had been the one who opened the gates for Luca's men. She liked and trusted him."

"Another blow that will be difficult for her to bear." She shook her head sadly. "She's lost so much. Jane said she was working hard just to keep her head above water."

"She's a survivor. She'll just pick herself up and start over. She'll have help. And she could have been—"

"Mom!" Michael was running across the tent encampment toward her. Then he was launching himself into her arms.

She caught him and gave him a giant hug. "Hi." She had to clear her throat to keep back the tears as she brushed his hair back from his face. "I leave you guys for a few days and come back to this?"

"Not our fault." His arms were tightening around her neck. "But now that you're here, you could stick around and keep us in line."

"I just might do that. I hear you've been getting all kinds of weird ideas in your head about you being to blame for what happened to Jane." She shook her head. "Not true, Michael."

"If you say so." He took a step back and his arms dropped from around her. "But now I have to go help Lisa. She's making barbecue for everyone helping with the cleanup. I'll see you later, Mom. Do you want me to bring you and Dad some food when I come up to go to bed?"

She shook her head. "We grabbed a bite at the airport. Your dad needed to fill me in on what was going on anyway."

"I thought he would." He gave her cheek a quick kiss. "See you later." He was gone, running toward Lisa at the barbecue grill.

Eve looked after him, frowning. "There's something different…"

Joe nodded. "And it's more obvious the longer you're with him. I guess we should have expected it. He's getting older, and all that's happened to him lately has jump-started the process. I suppose it's a natural reaction."

"You're saying that he's just growing up?" She shook her head firmly. "I don't want to hear it. He's still a kid. Is it wrong for me to try to hold on to this special time for him? Sometimes I think he was born older than the rest of us. There should be a way for us to put that in reverse and give back a little of the joy other kids take for granted."

"If anyone could, I'd bet on you." He chuckled. "I think we've done a great job of giving Michael a good life considering the circumstances. I know you have." His smile faded. "But we can't change those circumstances, and it might be time to adjust to it. You said last year when I was wounded that Michael was a great help to you in several, shall we say, unusual ways." He paused. "Do you think he might have already moved on and left us behind? That wouldn't be good, Eve."

"But he stepped right back into being the old Michael the minute he knew you were safe," she said quickly.

"Because he knew that's what you wanted, and he loves you. But I've been thinking that perhaps it's more dangerous to hold him back than to accept and offer help." He linked his hand with hers and added quietly, "I realize this is difficult for you, and I'll go along with whatever you decide. I just want you to think about it."

"You know I will," she said unsteadily. "How could I not? But the idea scares me, Joe. It would be almost like letting my little boy go."

"Or bringing him closer to you by helping him break through that portal all kids have to navigate."

"But not all kids have to deal with what Michael does." She added wryly, "I get your point, though. You're a very smart man, Joe."

"Yep, but it's still your decision. I'd just as soon you put it off until we get Jane back." He paused. "But I'm not sure Michael will." He lifted her hand and pressed a kiss on her palm. "I have to call Tovarth and check on that helicopter and make a few other calls. Why don't you make yourself a cup of coffee and try to get some rest? I bet you didn't get any sleep on that plane."

"Not a wink. All I could think about was Jane." She made a shooing motion. "Go get to work. I'll see you later."

He gave her another kiss and turned away. "Try to stop worrying. That news wasn't all bad. Caleb seems to be getting a handle on the situation, but the bastard isn't sharing. I'll not put up with it for long..."

She watched him pull out his phone as he walked down to the

campfire at the bottom of the hill. She envied him having something to do. Everyone here in this encampment was bustling, moving, trying to pull resurrection from the disaster. That's what Eve wanted, too. Only she had no idea how to stop the disaster that had swept Jane away.

It would come. She and Joe would find a way to make it happen.

But first she had to do as she promised Joe and think about the puzzle that was Michael.

9:40 P.M.

"Mom?" Michael whispered from the doorway of the tent. "I didn't mean to wake you. I just wanted to tell you that I was back."

"You didn't wake me." She turned on the lantern beside the bedroll. "I was just lying here, thinking. I still have to shower and get ready for bed." She tilted her head. "You look much cleaner than you did when I first got here. I take it the fire didn't get the shower tent?"

"It did, but that was the first thing we got working again. Lady Kendrick insisted." He grinned. "She said she didn't want to be rude, but we all stank from working at the tents and had to have a shower every night."

"Well, let me take a test sniff." She held out her arms to him. "Come here."

He ran across the tent and plopped down beside her on the bedroll and cuddled close. "I smell real good. Lisa gave me some of the shower gel she invented when she was working at a flower farm in Nice. It's just kind of fresh, not perfumy."

"You smell just right." She inhaled not only Lisa's soap but all the wonderful scents of childhood that clung to his hair and skin. "I'll have to thank Lisa for her efforts. How did the barbecue go?"

"Great. Lisa is always great." He hesitated. "But she's a little worried about you being mad at her."

Her brows rose as she looked down at him. "Mad? Why?"

"Because I talked her into doing something she thought you wouldn't want her to do." He added quickly, "It wasn't her fault, Mom. I had to know and I wasn't sure I could you get you to tell me."

"Maybe because I'd think it's something that would hurt you to know," she said quietly. "And, yes, that would make me mad at her. It's my job to keep you from any harm or pain."

He nodded gravely. "Just as it's my job to keep you and Dad and Jane from harm. Because we're a family and that's what families do. You've always told me that, Mom. But you're not letting me do my job now when Jane needs me. So I'll have to do it on my own . . . unless you'll help me."

He was looking up at her, and she was suddenly aware that his stare was more adult than any he'd ever given her. Adult and curiously sad.

Do you think he might have already moved on and left us behind?

The words Joe had spoken returned to frighten her. She had an idea that there would be no going back this time to please or comfort her.

"It won't be so different," he said softly, as if reading her mind. "How could it be? It's just you and Dad letting me help when I can."

Yes, how could it be different when they had love and family? But it already felt a little different and she was having to blink back tears. "With a little help from your friends. Just what did you talk Lisa into doing for you?"

"Showing me the sketch Jane did of the boy on the crucifix."

She inhaled sharply and instinctively pulled him closer into her arms to shelter him. "Yes, I definitely disapprove of her doing that. Your dad only told me about it, but I took a look at those sketches when I first got here. It was a terrible thing for anyone to see. It must have hurt you. Why, Michael?"

"Because I can reach him, and it might help Jane." He added simply, "And it didn't matter if it hurt me. What they did to him hurt him much worse. I have to do this, Mom."

He had made up his mind. She could see it. And she could also see that from now on he might make other decisions that might frighten her. But she wasn't going to let him move on and leave her behind. "Yes, you may have to do it." She had to clear her throat. "But your dad and I will always be with you whatever you do. We just have to figure out how we're going to adjust to this minor revolution. Still, there's a pecking order in every family and we're still at the top rung. That won't be different, because we can't bear not to keep you safe. Understand?"

He grinned. "Top rung."

She nodded and gave him a hug. Then she forced herself to let him go. "Now I'm going to go out to the campfire to tell your dad we've had a discussion and there will probably be more to come." She got to her feet. "Then I'm going to go down to the shower tent and take my own shower. You'll probably be asleep by the time I get back."

"Maybe."

She looked back over her shoulder, and her eyes narrowed on his face. His expression was thoughtful, and she realized she had no idea what he had meant when he'd said he could "reach" Tomas. Well, she had no intention of asking that question or delving into any other things that were reputed to go bump in the night. That would wait until she accepted and came to terms with these new qualities her son was showing her. Right now she wanted to go to Joe and just have him hold her and rock her and tell her that they would find Jane.

And not lose their son while they were doing it.

CHAPTER
13

TOWER HOUSE

The sun was just coming up over the lake when Jane carefully let herself into Tomas's sickroom. Luca might have said he wouldn't punish Tomas, but he'd been too angry for her to trust him. Understatement, she thought bitterly: Luca could never be trusted.

But the young boy appeared to be all right and sleeping peacefully. Rosa, his mother, was curled up on the floor beside the bed and sat up as she saw Jane. The woman had probably not been able to bring herself to leave her son since that horror, Jane thought. She motioned her to be silent and then nodded at the door.

Rosa jumped to her feet but hesitated and then came toward Jane. "Thank you," she whispered. "I wish I was brave like you, but I'm too afraid. If you can save my son..." She shook her head, her eyes filling with tears. "No, that's too much to ask. If you could just keep them from hurting him like that again..."

Then she was scurrying out of the room.

Even though Jane pitied her, she was glad to see her go. She didn't want to be reminded how helpless the woman had been to keep her son's torture from happening. Had Tomas called out for help when those beasts had taken him to that crucifix? Had he been bewildered when no one came?

I don't know why.

The memory of his words was excruciatingly painful. She quickly moved a chair closer to his bed, sat down, and opened the sketchbook she'd brought with her. She'd meant to sketch the view of the lake from his window in case she had an opportunity to smuggle out a message in some way. But she found herself drawing Tomas lying there asleep instead. Her pencil flew over the page. Show the peace instead of the pain. Show the hope instead of the despair.

"What . . . are you . . . doing?"

Tomas had opened his eyes and was looking at her.

She smiled at him. "I'm sketching a picture of you." She held up the sketch to show him. "I wanted you to see how much better you are today than yesterday. It's black and white so you can't see how much your color has improved, but now that your eyes are open I can show how they seem to sparkle." She started to sketch again. "You were sleeping very soundly. Did you sleep well all night?"

"I . . . think so. But I had strange dreams." He was looking around the room. "Where's my mama?"

"She needed to take a little break. Don't worry. She'll be back soon."

"I'm not worried," he said dully. "I wish she'd never come back. I was hoping she'd run away."

She went still. "Why?"

"She wants to help and she can't. And when she tries, he hurts her, too." His lips were quivering. "Could you tell her to run away? She won't listen to me."

"I don't believe she'd listen to me, either," Jane said gently. "So we'll just have to make it as easy for her as we can. Then maybe someday we can all run away together."

"He won't let us."

She smiled. "The purpose of running away is to run away from whoever is hurting you. That means your father and Luca and anyone else who gets in our way. Whether they allow us or not."

He shook his head. "It cannot happen."

"It can happen. I'll make it happen." She reached out and carefully touched his hand. "*We'll* make it happen. And your part will be to keep on getting stronger and better so that you'll be ready when we get the chance. Then when I tell you it's time, we'll leave this tower behind us."

"And take Mama?"

"Yes, but maybe not talk to her about it. Then your father won't have any reason to be angry with her if she makes a mistake and tells him. Remember, we're going to try to make it easier for her."

He nodded. "And she would be scared." He frowned. "I think I would have been scared, too. But he said that I shouldn't, that he'd take care of me."

"He?" Jane repeated, frowning, puzzled. "Your father? What are you talking about?"

"I don't know. Not my father. I'm all confused." He moistened his lips. "I told you I had kind of strange dreams. It was all bleary. I just remember my arms kept hurting and that I felt as if someone was there with me, but I couldn't see him. But it didn't matter because he was there and I wasn't alone anymore. And then my arms stopped hurting and that was good, wasn't it? It wasn't like the other nightmares I've had since they..." He looked down at his bandaged wrists. "Different. And I still felt okay even after he went away. The last thing he said was that all I had to do was get well, just like you told me."

"I'm glad you had encouragement from someone besides me." Jane smiled gently. "Even if it was from the realm of dreamland."

"I'd rather have you," Tomas said. "Dreams aren't real, and I think he was just a kid, like me. That means that he wouldn't be able to do anything to help me anyway, would he? Even if it wasn't just a dream."

A kid? Jane stiffened as a thought leaped immediately to her mind. "Did this dream kid have a name?" she asked lightly.

He shook his head. "I told you, it was as if he wasn't really there. Why?"

"No reason. I was just curious. You're right, it was kind of a strange dream," Jane said. "I'm glad that your pain went away, but I don't believe we should rely on a dream having the same good effect next time. I'd rather depend on you doing something to help us get out of here while you're very wide-awake." Her gaze went to the window. "Have you lived here on this lake for a long time?"

He nodded. "Maybe for two...three...years," he said vaguely. "Before that we lived in our village that's a long way from here. We had to leave there one night and come here because Master Luca told us to do it. He told my father it was the time of the gathering and they should come together in a new place."

"Do you think you could find that village again if you tried?"

He frowned. "Maybe. I don't know. I work in the fields with my mama and that's near the road my father uses when Master Luca sends him for supplies."

"Good. Do you think you could draw me a map or maybe take me for a walk around the lake after you get back on your feet?"

He nodded. "I don't think I could draw anything, but I could tell you and you could draw it."

His poor mangled wrists. She'd spoken without thinking. "Of course you couldn't draw." She added fiercely, "But you *will* be able to use your hands, Tomas. I promise you."

"You shouldn't make promises you can't keep," Luca said from the doorway. "I thought I taught you last night that I'm the only one in control."

She stiffened warily as she turned to look at him. "You taught me what a bully you can be. It's not the same thing."

"It was a lesson learned. Only the first of many." He strolled toward her. "And you're lucky that it didn't go worse for both you and the boy. I was very angry with you." He reached out and touched her bruised cheek. "That's a reminder that you should always be very careful to do exactly what I want."

"Bullshit."

He laughed and turned to Tomas, whose eyes had widened apprehensively. "You must tell your new friend that you don't want her hurt as you were hurt, and she must be polite. If I was in the same mood as I was last night, both you and she would already have paid for that discourtesy." He turned back to Jane. "But I'm feeling much more positive this morning, so I'll forgive you. What are you doing here so early? Had a few aches and pains to keep you awake? Not that I mind you spending time with the boy. The closer you get, the more power I'll have over you." He took her sketchbook from her and looked at the Tomas drawing critically. "Very good. At least you're doing something to fulfill one of the purposes for which I brought you here. But he's not really a worthy subject now. You should have been here to sketch him on the cross. It had much more drama."

"I'm sure it did." She smothered the angry reply that was on her tongue. It wasn't safe for Tomas, and she would learn nothing from pouncing on Luca at every remark. He held all the cards—and the principal one was this pitiful child with those bandaged wrists. "But I'll pass, that kind of drama would give me nightmares." His remarks in front of the child were the stuff of nightmares. Totally callous, and every word must remind Tomas of what he'd gone through. She had to get Luca away from the boy. She took her sketchbook back from Luca and walked over to the window. "Would you rather I sketched the lake? It's pretty enough, I suppose. Though I've painted a few more beautiful when I was here in the lake country before. Lake Como is fantastic."

"If you like." He followed her across the room as she'd intended. "Or you might paint my special garden down there on the bank of the lake." He pointed to a wrought-iron fence with an ornate gate. "That would please me more. It has much more meaning to me."

"Why?"

"It's a poison garden. Almost all the plants contain the ingredients for poisons that are completely deadly. I created it to honor the poison garden the Medicis planted in Padua." He chuckled. "They evidently found it necessary to have an abundant supply constantly on hand. Now, there's a subject that has true drama and power. Sometimes I take a leisurely stroll through it in the evening. I can't wait to take you with me and see if it inspires you."

"I believe I'll pass."

"I might not permit you to do that." He was no longer smiling. "You'll do as I wish, when I wish." Then he suddenly shrugged. "It's not worth arguing about now. I don't care. You might not be here that long."

Jane tensed, her gaze flying to his face. He was still looking out the window and the strong sunlight revealed the excitement in his expression. Oh, yes, his mood had definitely changed from that brutality-charged period after he'd hung up from Caleb. "Why wouldn't I? Why are you feeling more positive?"

"The situation might have changed." He looked at her, his eyes glittering. "I'm almost sure it has. Because I received a call from Caleb this morning. It was a very brief call, but promising. He said he'd been thinking about Cira's treasure, and the possibilities were beginning to intrigue him. He said he'd get back to me with terms after he did research and made his decision." The excitement was growing by the second in his expression. "I think I've *got* him. He called me back in less than eight hours. That must mean something. Seth Caleb has always been so sure he can do anything he sets out to do. I dangled a prize in front of him that anyone on earth would be excited about. I knew he wouldn't be able to resist trying to reach out and grab that treasure."

Jane tried not to let him see her surprise. She had not expected that quick a response from Caleb, either, and had no idea what it meant. She just knew she had to maintain and reinforce the attitude toward Caleb she had shown Luca last night. "And he told you that he hadn't made a decision yet," she reminded him. "He's just holding out a carrot. Why don't you change your demand to something more reasonable?"

"Shut up!" His hand closed with brutal force on her arm, his eyes blazing. "I won't hear that negative trash from you. I don't *want* anything else. Cira's treasure was always the endgame, from the time I heard that you'd helped MacDuff find it. You're nothing in comparison. I can find another artist, that's what a patron does. You and your work only exist because I permit it. But I *need* the kind of fortune that treasure will bring me." His eyes were blazing down at her. "And I'll get it. I can make this work. I just have to be careful with Seth Caleb." He turned on his heel and headed for the door. "And not let you ruin it for me!"

She watched the door close behind him, absently rubbing the bruise already forming on her arm. Luca's volatility appeared to be increasing with every passing minute, and a good deal of the poison he was spewing appeared to be aimed at her. Which was perfectly natural. He'd been bound to be disillusioned to realize the woman he'd studied for years and thought he knew would prove to be so troublesome. Add the knowledge that he must be nearly convinced that she was worthless to him in the role he'd cast her for—to serve as a weapon against Caleb—and it must be a double blow to him.

"He was angry." Tomas's eyes were big in his pale face. "Did he hurt you?"

"No." She pulled her hand away from the bruise and strode back to the bed. She smiled down at him. "He's a bully and bullies can't hurt you unless you let them. Not on the inside. You just close your eyes, think good thoughts, and push it away. Maybe a little on the outside, but that goes away after a while."

"Sometimes it's more than a little." Tomas's voice was low, a mere wisp of sound. "My father is a bully, isn't he? Mama says he's my father and whatever he does is right, but then why does she cry?"

He looked bewildered and so fragile it was breaking her heart. And how could she tell him how to understand the kind of punishment that he'd undergone from Alberto, or the fear that had driven his mother. "She's confused and frightened. And she's so wrong, Tomas. Nothing he did to you was right, but she might be afraid that it would be worse for you if both of you fought him." She took him in her arms and held him close for a long moment. He clung to her desperately. It was almost like holding Michael, so warm and soft and endearing, but he was smaller and thinner than her brother. And Michael had never had to suffer the torture this boy had undergone. Then she gave Tomas a quick hug and said huskily, "And there are times a bully can turn into a monster and you have to fight monsters. There's no other choice but fight or run." She smiled with an effort. "You're a little young for fighting monsters, though, so that's why we have to run." But she had to try to keep his mind busy and not let him dwell on the monsters waiting in the shadows. She sat down again in her chair and opened her sketchbook. "We'll start with having you tell me all about your village and anything else that you remember about this tower and all the lakes and roads and secret places that you boys like to explore..."

FIERO CASTLE

"I've sent you the security and architectural plans," Palik said when Caleb picked up his call. "You should be getting them any minute." He paused. "Tell me that you're not going to use them to do what I think you're going to do. That could mean big trouble for me."

Caleb ignored the question. "The plans are up to date?"

"Of course. Aren't they always?" Palik added gloomily, "Which means you are going to do it."

"I'll need personnel files of bank employees including background and psychological testing they underwent for the job. Plus the guard scheduling setup for at least the next two weeks."

"Two weeks?"

"With the emphasis on the next seven days. I'd like to have it even sooner. I hate leaving Jane with that bastard any longer than necessary. But if I go after the treasure, it will be intricate as hell, and I just don't know how quickly I'll be able to work it." He added harshly, "I might not have to do it at all, if you can track Luca down and get me a location. What do you know about the helicopter?"

"None with that description at any of the private airfields in north Italy. He must own the helicopter and have his own pad. I've sent men to scour the lake country asking everyone in the area if they've seen a copter of that description and when and where."

"And did you locate the boy, Tomas?"

"Do you realize how many boys are named Tomas in Italy?" He added quickly, "But I've traced an Alberto Nazaro who used to live in a village near the village of Fiero. A few years ago he packed up his wife and son, Tomas, and moved out almost overnight. No forwarding address. And that same year, several other families also moved away. Same circumstances."

"It sounds as if Luca was staging a gathering of the cult brethren." Caleb swore beneath his breath. "They couldn't have been members of the original cult, but they might have been a splinter group who went into hiding when they heard I was going after Maria's killers. Luca must have taken them under his wing and kept contact after Jelak was killed."

"That makes sense," Palik said. "And, because the families drifted away one by one and there were no actual indications of a new cult forming in this area, it didn't send up any red flags to Donzolo when I hired him to watch for signs."

"Until Luca decided to set loose the hounds," Caleb said grimly. "And Alberto's son is named Tomas?"

"The neighbors weren't sure, but that's what they thought. He was only a little kid, and Alberto never let him play with the other children in the neighborhood."

"That's close enough for me," Caleb said. "But all those families couldn't have just disappeared. Someone must know where they are. They've got to be somewhere here in the lake country. Find them."

"Here? You're still in Italy? That's good, I was afraid you were already in Edinburgh casing the bank for yourself. The longer I can keep you away from there, the better."

"I've told you how to do that. Now I need to talk to Barza. Is he there?"

"Yes, dreading the minute you were going to ask for him. I'll give him my phone."

The next minute Nicco Barza came on the line. "I don't know where Davron is," he said quickly. "I can't help it. It's not my fault. He's scared and he won't talk about it. He said that Luca is crazier than ever since he brought all those freaks in that cult together and it wouldn't take much to make him snap."

"But Davron's talking to you now?"

"He's talking to me. I told you that we were good together. I think it's a relief for him to talk to someone who's not under Luca's thumb. But if I put pressure on him, he might panic and stop taking my calls." He paused. "Besides, I don't want to pressure him. He was good to me. I don't want to get him killed, Caleb."

"I need that information. We made a deal." But he was thinking quickly, weighing options. "But you might be right about him panicking. Okay, I'll go along with you for the time being. It might be just as well for you to omit the pressure and be the sympathetic listener. But you'd better nudge him diplomatically to let you know everything happening there, particularly with Jane MacGuire. I want him to feel as if he can run to you to bare his soul if Luca puts the screws on him."

"Would you help Davron if he did?"

"No, I don't give a damn about Davron. He was with Luca when Jane was taken. That means he's high on my list." He paused. "But I'd let you broker a deal with him that might save his neck if he can give me what I need. That's as far as I'll go."

Barza was silent. "Even if he proves to be a good source of information? Davron said something about Jane MacGuire when I talked to him the last time. He said he didn't know how long she was going to last. Luca is...he gets impatient. He hurts her. She keeps making him angry."

Caleb went still. Eliminate the chill. Smother the rage. "Did he say anything else?"

"No, but you said you wanted to know anything he said about her. I thought I should tell you."

"Yes, you should," he said hoarsely. "Let me talk to Palik again."

"I heard what Barza said," Palik said warily when he came back on the line. "I take it this is going to change our schedule."

"I'm going to be ready to move in five days max. I want the info in thirty-six hours."

"Shit!"

"My feelings exactly," Caleb said. "But if I can manage to pull a plan together that will satisfy that son of a bitch, you can get your ass in gear and get me what I need."

He cut the connection.

———◆———

TOWER HOUSE
THREE DAYS LATER

"Come on!" Luca threw open the door of Tomas's sickroom and strode toward where Jane was sitting by the bed. "Leave the brat. You have to go with me."

Jane stiffened. "Why?" Luca's entire being seemed electrified, his eyes wild. Her first thought was for Tomas. "I won't go anywhere until you—"

"You'll go where I tell you." He grabbed her wrist and jerked her to her feet. "I don't know why Caleb wants to talk to you, but he said the deal is a go and I'm not wasting time listening to you right now."

Caleb. This wasn't about Tomas, she realized with relief. The boy was safe for the time being. She was looking over her shoulder as Luca pulled her from the room and trying to indicate that reassurance to Tomas. She didn't know if she succeeded because Luca was now dragging her down the long hall. "Where are we going?"

"My study." He threw open a door and pushed her inside. "Go sit down and we'll see what Caleb has to say."

The computer was on the desk in front of her as she sat down before it.

Caleb.

She had been expecting to see his face on Skype, but it didn't keep her from feeling a jolt of pure relief at the sight of him. All the tension of the last three days was flowing out of her. He was alive. He was well. Nothing else seemed important. Why had it ever been important?

Try not to let Luca see what this moment meant to her. She kept her voice steady. "Hello, Caleb. Here we are again. We've got to stop meeting this way."

"Actually, I regarded it as necessary this time, Jane," he said without expression. "I had to make sure you were up to giving me what I wanted."

"I did what you told me to do. I brought her," Luca said impatiently. "Now stop yammering and tell me how we're going to do this."

"I'm the one who's going to do it," Caleb said. "Your only involvement will be to furnish what you need to transport the treasure out of Scotland...after I've permitted you to collect your share of the spoils."

"Share?" Luca repeated. "*All*, Caleb."

"Not likely. I might be doing this as a challenge, but I want a size-able fee for my trouble. Not too much. Only a third of the treasure." He paused. "And I'll also take the Judas coins."

"The hell you will." Luca was swearing beneath his breath. "The coins Judas was given to betray Christ? They're priceless."

"And they'll be very hard to dispose of in the usual way. You know that there are arguments going on whether or not they're the authentic coins. All kinds of religious and antiquity experts will be fighting over them and trying to dispute their validity when MacDuff lets them be examined. Much better to take a bigger share of the rest of the treasure and let me have the coins. I'll sit on them for a decade or so and then quietly sell them to a private collector." He added, "What are you arguing about? It's a good deal. In three days, I'll deliver Cira's treasure into your waiting hands." He smiled recklessly. "Except for my small tokens to prove that I was the only one in the whole damn world who could pull it off."

"Arrogant bastard." Luca's lips twisted. "I might not have to give you anything. You were very eager for me to get Jane in here today. A few threats, a little torture, and I could write my own terms."

"Are we back to that again?" Caleb shook his head mockingly. "You're a slow learner, Luca. I don't let women dictate anything in my life but the usual pleasure." His glance shifted back to Jane. "Sorry, but you always knew that was true. That's why you sent me away. I want you to know that I thought you were magnificent. Sometimes I came very close."

"I'm touched," she said dryly. "Then may I ask why you had Luca drag me in here? You said it was necessary."

"I had to see you. I expected Luca to do a certain amount of damage, but if it was too much it might ruin my plans." His gaze was scanning her face. "Bad bruise on your jaw. It's healing but it should still be visible for the next several days. That might be enough. Anything else?"

"Ruining your plans," Luca repeated. "What do you mean?"

"I'll get to you in a minute." Caleb's gaze was still on her face. "Anything else?"

"A few more bruises here and there. Like most bullies Luca likes to beat up on women."

"Nothing visible?"

What on earth was he up to? It was obvious from Luca's frown that he was puzzled, too.

"Not unless I stripped down to my birthday suit," she said. "Nothing visible."

"I don't believe that would be necessary." His glance went to Luca. "I admit I thought there would be more signs of mistreatment. Then I would have had to figure a way to strike a balance. But I think you've got that balance right now, and that means you'll have to keep your hands off her until you turn her over to me tomorrow, Luca. You might get carried away and go too far. MacDuff has a temper and you could spoil everything."

"MacDuff? What's all this about? Why should I care if he has a temper?" Luca added coldly, "And stop trying to give me orders. I'm in charge here. And I have no intention of turning Jane over to you tomorrow."

"But you will," Caleb said softly. "Because she's not a weapon you can use with me, but MacDuff is a different matter. He might be a tough bastard, but he has a weakness for Jane. You've researched him enough to know that's true. He regards her as a close friend, and she was responsible for him finding Cira's treasure. He's grateful enough to do almost anything for her . . . if handled correctly."

Luca went still. "Ransom?"

"No, you've made your statements too bloody for him to trust you in a ransom situation. He won't go that route." He smiled. "But MacDuff is a true Scot and we can play on that side of his character. He's descended from a long line of Highland raiders, and he sometimes has problems being as civilized as his august title calls for. He was in 45 Commando Royal Marines, where he won a whole chestful of medals. When he was younger, he brought home an Olympic gold for archery. And he spent decades traveling and searching for that family treasure until he found it. All of this means he gets easily bored these days, and if I offer him something to liven up the situation, I can see him stepping up to the plate."

"And just what are you offering him?" Luca asked.

He smiled. "I'm going to let him help me rob the Bank of Scotland."

Luca's eyes widened in shock. "What?"

"Well, not actually letting him rob it. A little sleight of hand makes the world go 'round. I'll let him think I have a plan to go after you that would not only let him keep you from robbing the bank of his treasure, but also give him the infinite satisfaction of killing you. I assure you, that combination will bring him running."

"That's crazy," Luca said. "It would never work."

"On the contrary, I'd never try it if I wasn't sure I could pull it off." Caleb smiled mockingly. "You think *you've* researched MacDuff? It's nothing to what I've done over the years, and you'll admit that I have qualifications you don't possess. I know exactly what I have to do to make him jump when I snap my fingers. As for arranging the rest, all it takes is blending the elements carefully and making them come together. I can handle breaking into the bank and taking care of the guards on duty myself. If I have advance info, I'll be able to convince them to do anything I want them to do. The problem was always going to be getting access to the vaults and the passwords and codes for the Cira treasure. But MacDuff owns the treasure; if anyone knows the passwords and codes at that bank, it would be him. Once I get him in the vault area and take him down, I'll have our key to getting everything we want."

"You'd kill him?"

"Probably. And blame it on the guards. But I'll have to think about it. There might be an even better way to frame it out."

Luca's eyes narrowed suspiciously. "And why would Jane be necessary?"

He shrugged. "You haven't been listening. She's the goad to make sure MacDuff's motivated to go after you. I show him poor Jane whom you've obviously mistreated and I was forced to rescue. That's why the bruises are necessary. But remember that too much could be counterproductive. He mustn't get too angry and decide to tell me to take a hike. He knows I'm valuable, but he might still get so furious he could call a team of his old marine buddies and try to go after you on his own." He paused. "And I also have to get him down to those vaults, and I can use Jane to do it. MacDuff knows how stubborn Jane can be. It would be natural for him to believe she'd want to go with me to the vaults to make sure you were caught and punished for everything you've done to her. Since he's never fully trusted me, I really doubt if MacDuff would be able to resist going along to protect her." He added, "Besides, I have a personal reason why I want her down there in those vaults. Jane's studied the history of the treasure over the years and could recognize the Judas coins if MacDuff gets stubborn about giving them to me. I might be able to manipulate him, but he's one of those subjects who could prove exceptionally difficult if I tried *persuasion*. It would save time if she was with me in that vault." He smiled into Luca's eyes and added softly, "Because I won't leave those vaults with the treasure you think will make you the great patron you deserve to be until I get my share of the booty."

Luca was silent, but Jane could see that his cheeks were flushed and the excitement was beginning to flicker in his expression. "It might...be possible." He was breathing hard. "You might be able to pull it off. I always knew that *persuasion* talent could make the difference from the moment I heard you possessed it. But it's totally wasted on you. I could rule the world if I had it."

"Sad that your destiny didn't accommodate you in that way," Caleb said caustically. "But then I don't believe the Medicis had it, either, so you're still playing in their ballpark. Though I've heard they had many deadly talents you might have admired. Do you believe they would have tried to steal my Judas coins?"

"Why not?" His lips curled. "When you're probably a Judas yourself. But I can deal with betrayal. One must just make allowances and adjustments and monitor the situation to prevent losing control."

He was actually becoming convinced, Jane realized dazedly. Caleb had played on everything from Luca's ego to the obsessive belief in destiny that had guided his life since childhood. Then he had blended it with that powerful *persuasion* and made Luca believe his plans for the robbery could work. He had even skillfully woven in that thread about her presence in the bank being necessary to make the plan come together. She had never fully realized how powerful his *persuasion* could be. Hell, *she* almost believed it. But that didn't mean she wasn't thrown into complete confusion about what to do about it. Tomas. She hadn't the slightest doubt he'd be one of the "adjustments" Luca would make. That meant she had to just follow her instincts about how to handle the situation and try to protect him. As well as reinforce Caleb's play in her own way by forcing Luca to react as he always did when she defied him.

"You've forgotten one thing, Caleb." Jane leaned forward to stare at him in the monitor. "You're right about MacDuff being my very close friend. You and Luca may think nothing of betrayal, but I do. I won't betray him, and I won't let you kill him. The world doesn't revolve around you. Other people are important. MacDuff is important. There's no way I'd let you use me like that." She shook her head. "I won't do it."

"I was afraid of that." Caleb sighed and looked at Luca. "As I said, she's very stubborn. But perhaps you have a way to overcome it? As I've told you, no excessive force, of course. But it's a pity to scratch the plan. If you decide to go forward with it, call me back."

He cut the connection.

"Bitch!"

Luca's hand lashed out, struck the side of Jane's head with a blow that knocked her off her chair to the floor. He grabbed her hair and lifted her head to glare down into her face. His features were twisted, his eyes blazing. "You'll do whatever I tell you to do!" He slapped her again. "Do you hear me? I won't let you do this to me. Do you think you have any say in this? I won't let you stand in the way of me getting what I've wanted all my life." He bent closer and hissed: "You do anything Caleb tells you to do or I'll let Alberto do whatever *he* wants to Tomas. That wouldn't be pretty. He's very frustrated, and your pampering of the boy has been stoking the flames."

She'd known that threat would be made, but it still terrified her. Ignore it and try to get as much as she could from him. "But if I do it, you won't let him be hurt? Let him go now. I'll do anything you say as long as you'll let Tomas and his mother leave here."

"You're bargaining? No bargains. Do you think I don't know how stupidly soft you are about children? As long as I have that boy, all you'll be thinking about is how to keep me from nailing him to a cross. Tomas stays here at Tower House until I get that treasure. Then I might take you back here and let you 'bargain' over whether I kill him or we take him with us when I turn the cult over to Alberto. I can't tell you how much I'm beginning to enjoy this." He dragged her to her feet. "Now get out of here and let me call Caleb back and tell him that you won't be a problem to him." He said fiercely, "*Say* it."

"I won't be a problem." She pulled her wrist away. "But whatever happens, don't blame Tomas."

"You believe that Caleb might cheat me? I told you, I won't let that happen. Do you think I'd let you go if I wasn't sure I'd get you back? It will be me who decides if and when I dispose of you. I'll be in complete control of this entire operation." He shook his head. "Just as I'm in control of you. And Caleb may get a few shocks before this is over if he tries to get the best of me." He was dialing the phone. "I'll tell him you'll be leaving here tomorrow morning. I'll arrange to have you dropped off at Caleb's old family estate of Fiero. You did say he had no liking for it? I think forcing it down his throat will set the mood for our future relationship."

He was very pleased with himself, Jane thought as she left the study and walked unsteadily down the hall. Pleased and excited and certain that everything would be going his way. It was what she had intended him to feel. The violence he'd just visited on her was only an expression of the exhilaration he was feeling that he was growing closer and closer to a major goal in life. She'd known letting that brutality and power loose within him would seal the deal Caleb had offered him. But she hoped Caleb had a plan to rob Luca of that damn confidence. Luca had been right: All she could think of at this moment was Tomas on that crucifix. Well, there was nothing she could do right now but trust Caleb, go along with Luca, and still try to keep Tomas safe.

She stopped and drew a deep breath before she started brusquely toward her bedroom. She had to put a cold compress below her right ear where Luca's fist had struck, straighten her clothes, and put her tousled hair in order before she could go back to Tomas. He'd been frightened when Luca had rushed her out of his sickroom, and he didn't need to see her like this.

It was going to be difficult enough to explain why she was going to desert him tomorrow and leave him once more to the monsters.

———◆———

"I'll come back, Tomas," Jane said urgently. "I promise you. I just can't stay right now."

"It's all right if you can't come back." Tomas's eyes were glittering with tears. "I knew Master Luca would take you away. He takes everything away. Except my father, he always leaves my father here with me."

And that was the most terrifying power that Luca possessed over Tomas. "I *will* come back," she said fiercely. "Believe me. But you've got to help, you've got to eat and heal and get stronger. You have to be ready. Will you do that for me?"

He nodded unsteadily. "Whatever you say. I'll be ready if you come back."

If. He was still uncertain—and how could she expect him to trust her, trust anyone? She didn't even know when she'd be able to return or if it would be safer to find a way to send someone else to take him from this hellhole. Tomas was so alone. He wouldn't understand . . .

He was there and I wasn't alone anymore.

But that had only been a dream, and Tomas had not mentioned it again after the one time. Yet it had been Michael she had first thought of in that moment.

Michael's eyes glittering with tears in the woods that night. *"We'll do it together, Jane."*

Maybe it had only been a dream, but what if it wasn't?

"I can do stuff other people can't do?"

What if Michael had reached out somehow to Tomas? They needed a miracle right now, and she'd take one any way she could get it. It was time she did a little reaching out of her own.

She leaned forward and said softly, "It's good that you'll try to trust me, but that doesn't mean that you'll be alone when I'm gone." She paused. "Have you had any more dreams since the one you told me about, Tomas?"

He hesitated and then slowly nodded. "Many times. But I'm not supposed to talk about it to anyone. He said that it was very hard for him and he might not be able to come back if I did. But you're different, aren't you? You have to be part of the dream, because I can feel you're with him whenever he comes to me."

"I am?" She hesitated, and then she went for it. "Then maybe I am different. Who are you dreaming about, Tomas? You didn't know when I talked to you before. Do you know now? What's his name?"

He frowned, puzzled. "Why do you ask? You know his name is Michael."

She was silent and then drew a deep breath. "Yes, I guess I did know," she said. "And Michael helps you and makes the pain go away. What else?"

He nodded. "He talks to me and asks me questions. Like you do. He says he's my friend. But I've never had a friend, and he's probably just a dream."

"Sometimes a dream can be wonderful. Listen to him. There are bad monsters in the world, but there are also boys like Michael who can be your friend and other people who will help you. Will you remember that, Tomas?" She bent closer, brushed a kiss on his forehead, and whispered, "Listen to him and be strong. If you do, then all the loneliness will go away..."

———◆———

FIERO CASTLE
NEXT DAY

The castle looked even bigger and more impressive than it had when she'd first seen it from the helicopter, Jane thought as she gazed out the window of the Mercedes that Davron was driving.

But she didn't see any sign of Caleb, and that was making her nervous. There was no telling if Luca might have decided to switch the meeting site at the last minute. Or, worse, had plotted a way to trap Caleb. She hadn't thought he would because he'd obviously been getting such malicious pleasure out of sending her to Fiero when she'd left this morning. It wasn't likely that he'd give up the vindictiveness he'd felt when Caleb had been firing out all those orders at him. She glanced at Davron. "Where's Caleb?"

"He's supposed to be here. Luca told me I wasn't to leave you until he showed." Davron looked at her, his hands tightening on the steering wheel. He added harshly, "And when he does come, make him help you run away. It's the only way you're going to live through this."

She stared at him in shock. It was the first thing he'd said since he'd started the long drive from Tower House. She'd spent the first hour blindfolded before Davron had taken the cloth from her eyes, but he'd still not spoken to her until this moment. "I think you know I can't do that. You saw what he did to that child."

He nodded. "I saw it all. I couldn't turn my eyes away or Luca would have been angry. But it made me sick."

"Then call the police and tell them what's happening there." She added urgently, "Save Tomas."

He shook his head. "I can't do it. He'd have them hunt me down and kill me. I'd be the one on that crucifix. But you can run. Forget the kid."

"I told you that I can't—"

"There's Caleb coming out of the house." He screeched to a stop at the start of the curving driveway. "Get out. Now!"

She opened the door and grabbed her duffel. "Davron, come in and we'll talk about—"

He almost pushed her out of the car. "No! Shut the door! Luca told me not to get near Caleb. I have to get out of here."

She slammed the door and watched as he stomped on the accelerator and took off down the driveway.

"Jane."

She turned to see Caleb coming toward her.

"It was Davron. I thought I might be able to—" She broke off as she saw his face. Her eyes widened. "Caleb?"

"Be quiet." His hands were cupping her face and he was looking down at her. His index finger was touching her lips with the most exquisite gentleness and then moving to brush over her cheek. "Just be quiet. I don't care about Davron," he said hoarsely. "All I want to know is that you're here and safe. I'll worry about everything else later." Then his fingers were tangling in her hair and he was kissing her.

He felt so *good*. So strong and alive. Her arms slipped around him. Why had she ever doubted that he was everything she wanted? Because he would also cause her endless problems and complications? Because he would never be easy? Screw the problems. She could handle anything as long as she had him, as long as she had *this*.

But then he was pushing her away and looking down at her face again, this time searchingly. "Are you okay? What were you saying about Davron? Did he hurt you?"

He was the hunter again. She took a deep breath and stepped back. "No, I think he was trying to help me." She ran her shaking hand through her hair. "But he did it at the last minute and didn't give me any solutions. Then you came out of the castle and he only wanted to get away from here." She grimaced. "Luca had evidently given him a warning to stay away from you."

"It's just as well. Davron was one of the ones who took you. I might have struck first and asked questions later." He reached out and touched the swelling below her ear. "This is new." His lips tightened. "Yesterday...My fault."

"You told him not to do it."

"But I knew very well he might." He looked away from the bruise and took her duffel. "Come on. Let's get out of here. My car is parked on the side lawn. We can be in Mantua in a few hours."

"No, we can't," she said quietly. "We have to stay here tonight. Luca gave me orders."

"What?" Caleb froze. His gaze flew to her face. "Orders?"

"I made the mistake of telling him how you hated this place. That's why he arranged for you to pick me up here. He didn't like it that you were taking the control out of his hands and wanted to assert his authority." She shrugged. "He evidently decided to start with Fiero. The last thing he told me when he put me in Davron's car this morning was that we were to stay here until tomorrow and then go on to Edinburgh."

"Too bad. Screw him." He was smiling recklessly. "I have you now and I'm getting you out of here. Let him come and try to enforce those orders. I'll be glad to see him."

She could see that he would. She couldn't remember a time she had seen him like this. He was on fire. "We have to stay. I'm not going anywhere." She turned and headed toward the front door. "It's necessary. We'll leave tomorrow."

"Now." He didn't move. "I want you away from here. Don't fight me." He paused. "I could take you."

"Yes, you probably could," she said. "But then I might not ever forgive you." She gazed at him steadily. "And I know that would make a difference to you. I realize you want to keep me safe, but I'm not the only one who's important."

"You are to me," he said fiercely. "That little boy Lisa told me about? I'll go back and get him. After I have you safe. I'll take care of everything else later."

"And it might be too late. Do you think Luca isn't having this place watched? You'd take me away from here and then somewhere along the way, I'd get a phone call from Luca." She met his eyes. "And it would break my heart." She held out her hand to him. "So come with me into this monstrosity of a castle and we'll play the bastard's game. We'll let him think he's succeeded in making you suffer, and Tomas will be safe for at least another night." She smiled. "And if we work at it, maybe we'll manage to turn all that viciousness against Luca."

He was gazing at the hand she was extending to him. She could still feel the explosiveness just beneath the surface. For a moment, she thought that he'd ignore that silent plea.

Then he was moving toward her and his hand grasped her own. "Have it your way." He pulled her into the foyer. "It seems you will anyway." He turned on the foyer chandelier. "Luca would be very disappointed if he knew that no suffering is involved. I was over that long before the time I slammed that front door behind me."

"Were you?" She was looking around the magnificent foyer. "This furniture is fantastic." She went to the mirror and touched the shattered surface. "Pity. I would have thought this would have been repaired."

"I broke it only recently." He smiled crookedly. "I've been a bit preoccupied and haven't had time to have a craftsman called in to do the work."

She turned to look at him. "*You* broke it? How?"

His lips twisted. "I was a bit upset after I hung up on that first night I talked to you. I put my fist through it."

"What?" She moved toward him. "Were you hurt? Why would you do something stupid like that?"

"Why are you surprised? I just did what was expected," he said mockingly. "It's what I do. I break things."

She was looking at his hands and picked up his right fist. "It's bruised but it seems to be healing. Did it bleed?"

"I don't remember. I wasn't paying any attention to it." He was studying her expression curiously. "I suppose it did, but my body usually has an automatic heal response to any blood flow."

"But you might have paid attention if you'd cut an artery?" she said crossly. "Stupid."

"You're upset about it." His lips turned up at the corners. "Do you want to kiss it and make it better?"

"No way." She took her duffel from him. "Now tell me where I can go to shower and change. I had to wear a blindfold for part of the way here and I felt as if I was smothering. And is there anything we can eat in this place?"

"Bread and cheese. Wine." He gestured to the grand staircase. "The bedroom wing is on the second floor. Choose any room you want. There are dozens. They're only cleaned every two weeks, so you might have to contend with a little dust." He turned and opened the door. "You'll be safe here. I'll lock the door behind me, and anyone trying to enter will show up on my phone."

She stopped on the stairs and looked down at him. "Where are you going?"

"You said that you were sure the place was watched. I'm going into the woods to see if you're right. If it is, they're new arrivals. I bunked out there last night."

"You slept out there in the woods instead of one of those bedrooms you offered me?" She added dryly, "But Luca was wrong, and this place doesn't bother you at all?" She started up the stairs. "I think you're lying. We might have to do something about that . . ."

"Jane."

She looked back down at him.

"You're . . . different." His eyes were narrowed on her face. "Why? I've never seen you like this. Did Luca frighten you that much?" He paused. "Did he hurt you?"

She wasn't about to answer that last question. "Yes, he did frighten me," she said. "And I am different. But I'm not going to talk about it right now. You're on the edge and I don't want you to get any more volatile. Later, Caleb."

"But we *will* talk about it." His lips were tight. "I'll wait, but I have to know everything he did to you, Jane."

"So that you can kill him? I thought that was already on your agenda anyway."

"It is. And there are all kinds and degrees of pain before that happens." His gaze was holding her own. "But that's not what I'm talking about. I have to know so that I can try to make it right for you."

She shook her head, puzzled. "I don't know what you mean."

"It doesn't matter. Not right now." He opened the door. "Call me if you need me."

The door closed behind him. She heard the lock turn.

She hesitated an instant, gazing after Caleb. She wanted to go after him. She could sense the savagery that was driving him, and it was partly her fault. But there was no question that he would have gone on the hunt anyway—he'd wanted an excuse to get her out of here to safety. And her following him would only add to his distraction and danger.

She turned and started back up the stairs. She could not help him out there in those woods, but sometimes a hunt did not always take place in the wild . . .

CHAPTER

14

J ane was sitting on the third step of the grand staircase waiting for him when she heard Caleb unlock the door almost two hours later.

"It took you long enough," she said as he swung open the door and came into the foyer. "Was I right? Did you run across any of Luca's men? And if you did, are they still alive?"

"There wasn't anyone in the woods, but I saw signs that they'd been there earlier. But there were two men in a speedboat on the lake in back of the property." He shut the door. "And they are still alive because it would have taken me another hour or so to dispose of them. I didn't want to leave you that long." He frowned. "Why are you sitting on the steps? You could have gone into the sitting room and been more comfortable."

She shook her head. "I decided that I didn't like this place any more than you do. It's all wonderful furniture and splendid tapestries and ostentation, but it's . . . cold. And the only thing I was interested in about the place was you, and I couldn't *feel* you here." She shrugged. "After I finished dressing I went through all those bedrooms on the second floor, but I didn't find any sign of you. Which one of them was yours when you were here?"

"None of them." He smiled sardonically. "And, no, they didn't keep me in the dungeon. I had a suite on the third floor where I didn't have to be around my family. It was better for all of us."

"Was it? I don't think Lisa would agree."

"Then she'd be wrong. She was always defending me and getting into trouble. The less she saw of me, the easier it was for her."

"Or maybe it was more difficult because it made her feel helpless. I know what my reaction would have been if I'd been here. I wouldn't have been able to take wandering around all those splendid, ornate rooms on the second floor when I knew what it meant. It meant that you would never be there." Her glance shifted to the broken mirror. "So I came down here to sit and look at that mirror. Because I knew I'd *feel* you here. It's part of the man you are."

He smiled mockingly. "You mean all the violence and the ugliness?"

"No ugliness. Violence, yes. Pain, yes. *Your* pain. No one said you don't make mistakes, and it hurts you as much as or more than it does people around you." She met his eyes. "But you would have found a way to fix the mirror. You were already planning on it. Like you tried to fix Lisa by sending her away from you."

"I told you that you were mistaken about her."

She slowly shook her head. "You didn't convince me. But I admit I'm interested in what you were going to do to make *me* right."

His smile faded. "We have to talk."

"Soon." She got to her feet. "You promised me bread, cheese, and wine. Is there a scullery where I can find it?"

"No, there's a very modern kitchen. My mother and father wouldn't tolerate anything that reminded them of the Ridondo brothers who built this castle unless it increased their status." He moved down the hall. "The wine is good because the maintenance people also harvest grapes from the vineyards and I allow them to take the profits as long as they leave several bottles on the property. The cheese is decent, but the bread may be completely stale depending on when the maids baked it for the workers." He opened the door and threw it open. "I told you we should leave here."

"And you know why we can't. So stop growling and we'll make the best of this." She smiled at him over her shoulder. "You're so worried about keeping me safe. Stop it. You're never worried about yourself."

"I can't lose you again." He looked her in the eye. "I won't do it."

"No, you won't." She was no longer smiling. "Because you've already figured out a way to keep us together. Now we just have to figure out how to do it so no one gets hurt but Luca." Her lips tightened. "I have no problem with Luca being hurt." She shivered. "If you could have seen what he did to Tomas."

"And what did he do to you?" Caleb asked.

She ignored him as she opened the bread box. "The rolls look a little stale, but not too bad." She opened the refrigerator door. "The cheese looks good anyway..." She took it out of the refrigerator and looked for a cheese board. "How much of the plan you told Luca have you been able to initiate so far?"

"Only the research. I had to make certain I had you free first. I'll contact MacDuff when I get you safely to MacDuff's Run."

She shook her head. "Safely? There you go again, Caleb. You can't take me to the Run and leave me there. You have to do what you told Luca you'd do and use me in the robbery. Otherwise he'll realize that it could be a trap. You know that as well as I do."

He was silent. "I'll find a way to do it." Then as she continued to stare at him, he said harshly, "What the hell do you want me to do?"

"What you promised him. Whatever will keep Tomas alive and give us a chance to get Luca." She cut into the cheese. "You're a hunter. That shouldn't be so hard for you."

"Everything about this is hard for me," he said between his teeth. "And it's particularly hard to have you not letting me know what that son of a bitch did to you when it was probably all my fault."

She looked up and then inhaled sharply as she saw his expression. "I'm sorry," she said quietly. "I thought I could wait a while. I could see how angry you were and I didn't want to stoke the flames. I'd forgotten that in this house you were told you were to blame for everything." She threw her knife on the cheese board. "So I believe we'll delay this snack for a while." She took his hand and was pulling him back toward the door. "You want to talk, we'll talk. But not here, Caleb." She was half running down the hall toward the staircase. "I want to see that third-floor suite that was better for everyone. Will you take me there?"

"You seem to be taking me," he said dryly as they started up the staircase. "Though I don't know why you're doing it. Why won't you believe me when I tell you that I was never the victim Lisa told you I was?" He smiled sardonically. "Everyone knows I'm a throwback to the first Ridondos. Really, Jane. Do you think I couldn't get the best of a little parental harassment?"

"I believe you could, but you chose not to do it. All your life you've had to make choices. And you were reckless and bitter and had all that power. It's no wonder some of those choices weren't exactly wonderful." They'd reached the third floor, and she whirled to face him. "But some of them *were* wonderful. You saved Eve. You saved Joe. You saved Michael. You saved Lisa. You saved me. And there were so many other people you saved that we probably don't even know about because you never wanted us to know it. That means something, and I'm not going to let you say it doesn't. Now, where is that suite?"

He gestured down the hall. "By all means step into my parlor, but you'll be disappointed. As I said, no dungeons at Fiero."

"I won't be disappointed." She threw open the door and switched on the lights. "You're never disappointed if you can accomplish a purpose." She glanced around the room. "It's what I expected." It was a large room, and the furniture was as rich and well crafted as in all the other bedrooms: the velvet drapes, the large bed, the oak desk. The only difference was that the décor was spare and clean-lined, the colors dark blue and gray, and there were no paintings or tapestries. "You wouldn't have left anything of yours behind that you cared about. When you walked out that door, you wanted it to be forever."

"Very perceptive. But it was no loss when there was nothing here that I ever wanted to keep. May we go now?"

"Not yet." She turned to face him. "Because no matter how hard you try, you can't leave everything behind. You remember this room and everything that happened at Fiero."

"Not really. I'm excellent at blocking." His eyes were narrowed on her face. "Why the hell did you bring me here, Jane?"

"Because I'm not as good at blocking as you. If I have a bad memory, I have to put something in its place. And when you said that about you being to blame if Luca had hurt me, I kind of exploded." She smiled unsteadily. "Because it reminded me how Lisa said that you were always held to blame when things went wrong. And I couldn't have that happen to you again."

"That was a long time ago. And, after all, it's not as if I'm Michael, Jane."

"No, Michael never had that happen to him. I hope he never does." She took a deep breath. "Now be quiet and let me get this out. You are *not* responsible for anything that happened to me and you never will be. You want to know what happened to me at Tower House? I'll tell you everything. Those few new bruises? I have them because I chose to make certain that Luca went along with your plan. Defying him always increases the ego factor and makes him more likely to do what I don't want him to do. Rape? You probably thought of that first, because Luca told you what I said to him. I meant every word. Rape is terrible, but what happened to that child is worse. I couldn't risk him losing his life if it meant I could stop it. But there was no rape. Luca was so angry with me that he didn't want to look at me after you got through telling him how worthless

I was to you. Though he did threaten to throw me to Alberto and his friends. But it turned out he was afraid they'd damage or kill me and spoil his chances if you changed your mind about me. You told me that you'd learn everything about him and his reactions and you did. So that part of your manipulations worked on him, too."

"That close?" Caleb asked hoarsely. "No wonder you were frightened. It's a wonder I didn't get you killed."

"Stop it." She grabbed his arms. "None of this was your fault. I never thought that for a moment."

"Then you're deaf and blind," he said harshly. "Luca reacted just the way I played him. I could have gone down another path, but I chose that one because the percentages were higher it would work."

"And it did work." She shook him. "Did you think I didn't realize what you were doing? You'd studied him and you were able to gain the upper hand. You made the smart choice."

"And left you there to take the punishment." His eyes were glittering down at her. "Don't lie to me. I know he hurt you."

"I'll never lie to you. He did hurt me. Do you want to see the bruises? But that was *nothing*. I'm here with you and I'll forget it." She released her grasp on his arms. "And I'd appreciate it if you'd forget it, too. Because that's not what I intended when I brought you here." She went to the switch and turned off the light. It was still twilight, and a dim golden haze suddenly pervaded the room. "I don't want to think of Luca or your damn family or anything else but what I want you to do to me." She came back to stand before him with hands clenched. "You said you thought I'd changed. You're right. And, yes, it's partly Luca's fault because it was only when I was terrified of what he might do to you that I found out what was happening with me. I hadn't realized before that I'd always been afraid of you."

"I don't know why it came as a surprise." He smiled ironically. "I always knew that."

"Well, I didn't. Even when Lisa told me that was the only reason she could think of why I would leave you, I denied it." She shook her head. "And you probably think it's the reason everyone else is afraid of you. Because you're the Hunter, the big, bad Ridondo throwback everybody dreaded. Bullshit. It's because I was afraid to trust myself." She took a step closer. "When I came to you, I didn't really know what I was doing. You had me so dizzy that I couldn't sort out what I was feeling except for the sex and the fact that there was something *there* that I couldn't let go."

"Well, you did let go, didn't you? I did everything I could to give you what everyone calls normal and it didn't work. You still left me." His lips tightened. "But I can't let *you* go. I'll just have to try something else."

"Go ahead. Feel free. It might be interesting. I'm not afraid of anything you'd do to me. I can hold my own with you, Caleb." She made a face. "Though why bother to get inventive? You're not going to have that much trouble with me. As I said, I didn't really know what I was doing before. All I could see was that it wasn't going to be what Eve and Joe gave to each other. It kind of scared me, because I knew how good and wonderful they'd always been together. I didn't realize until lately that we weren't Eve and Joe and what we give to each other should be totally unique. But it also didn't help that you were intimidating me because you were so damn complicated, and I knew that life was never going to be easy with you. So I blamed you and ran away. Just like everyone else." She reached out and punched her finger at his chest. "But that's over, I'm done running, and I can handle anything that comes along with you. Because I'm just as strong, and I have a few complications myself."

He went still. "Just what are you saying, Jane?"

"Quite a lot. I can't blame you if you can't make heads or tails of it. And it's only the beginning, and I'll require you to listen to much more in the future. Not now." She stepped back and began to unbutton her blouse. "It's time to make some new memories in this damn room. I told you I wasn't good at blocking." Her blouse and bra dropped to the floor. "I just have to tell you one more thing." She stepped closer and laid her head on his chest. She could hear his heartbeat beneath her ear. "Now I know what that something was that I didn't want to let go. I want to say it. My choice. Because I'm not even sure you'll believe it. I screwed up and it may take a while for me to work this out. Don't think that you have to make any commitment." She said quietly, "I love you, Seth Caleb. I will always love you, and I'll trust you, and be there for you."

She could feel him stiffening against her, and then his arms slid around her. "That's very generous," he said hoarsely. His hands were moving over her naked back. "In more ways than one. And how kind that you spare me the commitment. But then you know how selfish I can be." His lips were hovering over the pulse in her throat. "Some would say that's a lack of the trust you promised, but who am I to question?"

"I told you that I wasn't sure you'd believe me." His mouth wasn't touching her, but she could feel his breath and it was causing the blood to riot through every vein. Her nipples felt engorged, on fire . . . "I don't care. I had to say it. Because when I was so terrified that Luca might kill you if you came after me, I realized that I might never get a chance to say those words." She backed away from him, shedding the rest of her clothes. "Now undress and come here. I *need* you."

"So demanding . . . In a moment. I want to look at you. You're all gold and flame in this light." He touched her red hair. "I feel as if you could burn me."

"Caleb."

"Would you like to burn me?" He bent his head and his tongue touched her nipple. "Like this . . ."

Sensation jagged through her! Heat that was not heat but pure eroticism.

She arched upward with a cry.

She was throbbing, and every nerve and muscle was suddenly

erotically alive and aching. "What the hell?" she gasped when she could finally breathe.

"You said you could hold your own and to go ahead. You thought it might be interesting." His smile was almost teasing. "Is it interesting, Jane?" Then he was no longer smiling. "Never mind. Tell me later." He was stripping with lightning speed. "I can't wait to play any games. It's been too long…"

Then she was beneath him on the floor and he was moving her legs, his hand seeking, finding. "Everything. Give me everything. I want *all* of you." He was staring down at her, his eyes wild. Then he plunged inside her.

Deep.

She cried out, her nails biting into his shoulders.

She could feel the heaviness, the heat, the textures, the force that was taking her breath. But it wasn't enough. "More. I want—"

"Then that's what I'll give you." He was lifting her legs, spreading them, rotating inside her. "Like this? Anything you want. I want you to feel everything." His palms were lifting her buttocks as he pulled her into each thrust. "Is this what you want?" His chest was heaving with every breath. "Tell me."

"You know that—" She couldn't speak; all she could do was feel.

"Tell me."

Deeper.

Stronger.

The feel of him…

His eyes staring into her own while he pounded into her body. "I want the words, Jane."

For some reason it was important to him. So give him what he wanted. "*This* is what I want. *You're* what I want."

"Then take me."

His hips drew back, and he thrust still deeper.

Wildness.

Fast.

Heat.

Madness.

Caleb...

She was crying, screaming, trying to get closer when there was no closer.

"Now?" Caleb asked thickly. "Now, Jane?"

She couldn't answer, all she could do was move, and move and move, while wave after wave of feeling was breaking over her.

She still couldn't speak for a moment even after Caleb shifted off her body and drew her into his arms. She finally managed to draw a deep breath. "I'd say that was as close to everything as I've ever felt." She laid her head on his shoulder. "It was very—"

"Shh." His lips brushed her temple. "Just rest for a minute. We both know that was just the opening act. I was in too much of a hurry because it had been too long. I promise I'll make it right for you if you'll give me the chance."

She laughed. "Oh, I'll give you the chance." Even though she had just left him, she could feel her nipples hardening, breasts tautening. Incredible that it was happening so soon. No, not really. Sex had always been hot for them, but now it seemed even more intense. "And I don't feel like resting right now." She pushed him down and was moving on top of him. "So let's see what I can do to encourage you to bring up the curtain on Act Two right now..."

———

He was lifting her, carrying her to the bed across the room...

She buried her face against his chest. She loved the feel of her lips against his warm skin. She brushed them back and forth and then opened them to taste him. She could feel his heart leap and the familiar stiffening. Yes, that was what she wanted...

"No." His lips were brushing her temple. "Not now. Later. You're too tired. I was too rough on you the last time."

"No, you weren't," she whispered. "It was..." She lost track of what she was going to say. It seemed too much effort to speak right now. "Maybe I was too rough on *you*."

He chuckled. "That definitely wasn't the way it was. If you think so, then you do have to rest. I couldn't get enough of you and I kept taking."

And she had kept giving. Every movement, every touch, had not been enough for her, either. All those times, every one different and passionate and only leading to the next coming together. Building until that last explosion had been almost too much to bear.

How many times? she thought dazedly. She didn't know. She only remembered reaching out to him again and again. She yawned as she cuddled closer to him while he slid into bed next to her. "That was... fantastic."

"Yes, it was fantastic, and so are you." His hand was gently stroking her cheek. Then it moved down to stroke her breasts and belly. "I love the feel of you like this. It always filled me with a kind of wonder." He'd moved her and was rubbing, massaging, stroking her from shoulders to her buttocks as if she were a cat. "Every muscle relaxed, your skin silky and warm and glowing, and knowing that what I did made it happen. Do you know how much I missed it?"

Caleb seldom revealed any hint of vulnerability, and she was so touched that she had to treat it lightly. "Well, if you keep doing that I won't remain relaxed for long. You're much too good at it."

His hand paused, then moved back to her throat. "Perish the thought. Just when I was making an attempt to change my image by being considerate." His tone was back to its usual mockery. "And I'm glad I pleased you. It must have been because I felt you'd freed all my inhibitions by saying that I had no commitments where you were concerned. What do you think?"

She was thinking that she'd made a mistake and wanted to hear that gentle note in his voice again. "I think for some reason it bothered you a little."

"Maybe."

She chuckled. "I don't know why. It was just important you didn't feel bound to me. I'm not accustomed to making confessions like that, but I knew I had to be fair. You had to know it was my choice. I didn't want you to owe me anything."

"You made that clear."

And for some reason he hadn't liked it. She changed the subject. "I think I'm hungry."

"You've worked up an appetite." He added lazily, "I could take you to Mantua for dinner. Just give me a couple hours to get rid of those men in the speedboat and we'll be out of here."

She shook her head. "Nice try. But I told you why I wouldn't risk it. Not until morning. As soon as I get my breath, I'll go down and tackle that cheese. Or maybe we could take a nap first."

He was silent. "You do that." He got out of bed and began dressing. "I'll go out and take a look around and make sure Luca's men don't have anything more dangerous in mind than keeping an eye on the place."

She raised herself on one elbow to look at him. Even in the darkness she could see how charged the muscles of his body were. And he'd mentioned getting rid of those men only a moment before. "I don't want you to leave."

"And I don't want you to stay here and let Luca dictate to you. It scares the shit out of me that he has that kind of power over you. Did you think I didn't know I have to go after the kid?" His words came like bullets. "I would have left one of those men alive and forced him to take me back to Luca. It would have been over. But it seems you don't trust me to even do what I do best." He added harshly, "So neither of us is going to get what we want. I'll see you later."

He was gone.

And she sat up and immediately swung her feet to the floor. There had been so much emotion in those last words that they frightened her. At least he'd said that he knew he wasn't going to get what he wanted, but that acceptance might be only temporary and there was no way she could relax while Caleb was in this reckless mood.

The next moment she was throwing on her clothes and striding out of the room.

Find him.

The lake.

He'd said Luca's men were on the lake . . .

She saw the speedboat in the middle of the lake from the time that she left the castle and walked around the back toward the pier. Two men, dark jackets, and she couldn't identify either one of them from this distance. Alberto? No, she doubted Luca would have trusted him to handle any dealings with Caleb. He was too willing to—

"You shouldn't be out here." Caleb stepped out of the line of trees growing along the bank.

"Neither should you." She jammed her hands in her jacket pockets. "Luca might not like you wandering around the property instead of being held prisoner in the castle."

"Screw him."

"That's what I thought you'd say." She smiled. "So I decided to come and take a stroll with you, since you told me you weren't going to launch an attack on those bastards in the speedboat." She paused. "Unless you've changed your mind?"

He didn't answer for a moment. "It might have occurred to me I had nothing better to do."

"You could make sure I don't starve to death. Do you think I like trekking after you when I could be eating?"

He was silent. Then he smiled. "Nag. Nag. Nag. For a woman who forgets to eat most of the time when she's working, you're not coming off with any great degree of authenticity."

"Baby steps. I don't have to make you believe me. All I have to do is get you out of this mood and on our way back to the castle. It beats having you go after those men and end up throwing one of them down at my feet as you've done in the past."

"Only it would be at Luca's feet."

"Whatever." She held out her hand to him. "If you want to act the caveman, provide me with food you've foraged in that super modern kitchen. I believe that would give you something better to do if you're really looking."

"Oh, I was really looking." He took her hand and started back toward the castle. "And being a caveman chef doesn't nearly provide the impetus I need to replace my first plan of action." He smiled. "But you did remind me of another one that would do it. Since I'll have to spend a little time refining it, I might as well devote myself to feeding you while I'm doing it." He lifted her hand to his lips and kissed her palm. "For instance, one of the most valuable things I learned in my caveman days is that the best way to turn stale bread into a delicacy is to butter and toast it."

◆━━━◆

"You're right, it smells wonderful." Jane watched him take the grilled cheese sandwiches out of the skillet and set them on the kitchen bar. "You can't call it a complicated process, but it works." She grinned. "Not that I wouldn't have thought of it myself. And preparation was a snap."

"True. But then you wouldn't have been able to keep me busy cooking it for you." He poured wine into her goblet. "And we both know that was the point of the exercise. Sit down and eat."

"I will." She sat down on the stool and cut into her sandwich. "And it's not as if I didn't help. You had me trimming crusts, and you even sent me running to get you that wine."

"I like to see you move." He poured his own wine and then leaned back against the cabinet. "I used to watch you and think how alive you were even when you were just sitting painting. Every tiny movement was tense and full of stored energy waiting to break free. I found it was much more gratifying being able to command it to happen." He took a sip of wine. "Besides, I thought I deserved something to compensate for giving in so easily."

"I can see how being able to order me about would have pleased you." She'd stopped in the middle of taking a bite to stare at him. "But I never knew you watched me."

"Why would you? You probably would have thought it was creepy." He smiled. "And I wasn't going to tell you. You'd already taken too much from me. I have very good survival skills."

"I don't know what you mean. I didn't take anything from you."

"Didn't you? Remember when Luca told you that you were the center I was revolving around? He was right. I knew I had to have you, and I was very careful not to scare you away. From the beginning, I realized that I'd never be what you wanted. You wanted a man like Joe Quinn or your lover Trevor, who was one of the ultimate good guys. When I finally did get you to come to me, I gave you what you wanted from me and no more."

"You're talking as if I was some kind of threat to you. How did you know what I wanted?" She put her fork down. "If you'd talked to me, you might have found out. And why are you telling me this now? Am I suddenly less of a threat?"

"No, you'll always be a threat, because I'll always be waiting for the penny to drop and you to walk away." He smiled. "But perhaps by that time I'll have gotten to know all your secrets and I'll be able to attack from another direction."

"Ridiculous. You didn't listen to me. I'm not going to walk away."

"No, you won't." He finished his wine and set the glass on the bar. "As I said, I'll find ways to make you want to stay." He looked at her sandwich. "Are you going to finish that? You said you were hungry."

"I've had enough."

"Good." He was around the bar and taking her hand. "Then let's get out of here." He was whisking her out of the kitchen and down the hall. "There was something I wanted to do before we left here, and I don't know how long it will take." They were in the foyer, and he suddenly stopped and turned to face her. His eyes were glinting with mischief. "But we're not going back to that suite upstairs. In spite of your bleeding heart, that was never me. None of this house was me, but you thought this foyer came closer." He was unbuttoning her blouse. "And it certainly suits you better. Persian carpets, glittering mirrors, and crystal chandeliers...Just the setting for you, Jane."

"You're crazy." She couldn't help but laugh. "It's not me at all. I'd hate to live in a place like this." Then she stopped laughing and inhaled sharply as he touched her breast. "You know me better than that."

"You'll find it suits you tonight." His head bent and his tongue touched the hollow of her throat. "Tonight will be different. With your permission..."

He was undressing her quickly, then she was down on the carpet and felt the soft wool beneath her body. "Look up at the chandelier," he whispered. "While I look at you."

"Do you think I can wait? I don't give a damn about that chandelier. I want you to—" She gasped and her eyes flew to meet his own. His hand was pressing gently on the bruise on her abdomen. "What are you—"

"Shh. I won't hurt you. I saw those damn bruises when we were upstairs. I just want to make sure there's not going to be any more pain from them. Just be still and I'll increase the blood flow. It will help to heal them."

"You don't have to do this. I'd almost forgotten about them."

"I hadn't." His fingers were moving, finding another bruise, pressing gently—and all hint of pain disappeared. "Look up at the chandelier. All that glitter and shine." His hands were moving swiftly and this time she felt only warmth and tingling sensation. The crystal shards of the chandelier above her were blurring into a haze of beauty and yet she seemed to feel them on her body, in her body. No, that was Caleb's hands, she realized dazedly. So deep, so fast. He was looking down at her. "See, I told you that I'd never hurt you. That's over, now we come to the good part."

"And what is that?"

He paused. "The part where you lose any lingering memory of how you got them."

She stared at him in shock. "No."

"I was afraid of that." He moved his finger to trace the shape of her lips. "I was tempted just to do it. I don't want you to remember the moment that son of a bitch hurt you."

"You can't destroy any of my experiences just because they were bad. You don't have the right."

He smiled. "Quite true. However, that's seldom interfered with anything I've done in the past. But since it's you, I guess I'll just have to make do with trying to blast them into oblivion." He bent down and kissed her lingeringly. "Would that be okay?"

"It depends on what you mean by blast." She could scarcely breathe. It was difficult to speak. Her body felt full, ready, and she was acutely conscious of everything around her. The crystal chandelier, the Persian carpet rubbing against her, the broken mirror reflecting their naked bodies.

And Caleb ... wonderful Caleb ...

"It has to be demonstrated, not explained," he whispered.

He plunged deep!

Heat.

Fullness.

Her entire body alive and taking every bit of him.

She arched, and her fingernails dug frantically into his shoulders.

"Good." He rubbed slowly, sensuously against her. "Much better than an explanation." He started to move. "And it will go on and on and on. And then we'll dream a little, and visit a few wonderful places, and you won't remember what Luca did at all. It will fade away and all you'll remember is what you felt tonight..."

The sensation was so intense that she could feel the tears running down her cheeks as she gasped with pleasure. It was like nothing she'd ever felt before, and she could only take and take and take...

And then it changed and there were clouds and valleys and running down a mountain path with Caleb holding her hand. The wind on her cheeks and the exquisite beauty of a rainbow on the horizon. She had to paint it...

"Not now," Caleb murmured. "Paint it later. The Louvre Museum, you always loved it. Look at all the other paintings..."

And the paintings were suddenly there before her, filling her with the same awe and beauty as the first time she'd seen them. Paintings. Color. Depth and meaning. And that beautiful architecture that was Paris. Then Florence and more paintings, and then the statue of David, and the excitement she had felt the first time she had seen it. And city after city whirling around her...Books she'd read and treasured. Friends she'd treasured even more. Suddenly the lake cottage and Eve and Joe sitting on the swing on the porch and smiling at her. Then the smell of heather beside Loch Gaelkar where they'd found Cira's treasure. Caleb again, over her, in her, part of it all, past, present. View after view. Vision after vision. Experience after experience, all beautiful, all meaningful. Taking her breath and then whirling her away again. She mustn't let it stop. It was all too wonderful and she must hold on to it. And she did hold on to it, and it went on and on and on. But it was becoming slower now and she was afraid that she was losing it...

"No, it's time to go to sleep. You're tired. Let it go." Caleb's lips were brushing her closed lids. "It's not as if you can't have it back whenever you want it. It will always be there. You won't even have to ask me. I'll know..."

But it was so beautiful that she didn't want to let it go. She was sure that there was another adventure right around the corner, a wonderful memory to cherish, a view that she had never seen, a feeling that she hadn't explored, and he could give it all to her. "Maybe in a little while..."

He chuckled. "Now. You've had too much to deal with for the last few days. You need to rest." He pulled her into his arms, her cheek resting in the hollow of his shoulder. "You took to this with an enthusiasm I didn't expect. You always insisted you were the complete realist. You've been fighting me for a long time to keep me from using any hint of *persuasion* on you."

"Because I didn't understand. I didn't trust you. It's different now. I know you would never do anything that would hurt me." She rubbed her cheek against him. "And the *persuasion* is just another part of you...a beautiful part."

"Not always beautiful."

"No. I imagine it could be terrible." She paused. "But you'd never do that unless it was to someone like Luca. It wouldn't be your fault."

"It would be entirely my fault. My choice. It always has been."

"I don't want to think about that right now. I'm right and you're wrong, and we'll leave it at that."

"Aren't you afraid that I used the *persuasion* to make you think you're right?" he asked mockingly.

"No, absolutely not." She yawned. "And I really am getting sleepy so at least you're not wrong about that. So I'll take a nap if you're determined not to..." She nestled closer. "But you'll keep holding me? I'll at least have that to..."

"I'll keep holding you." His arms tightened. "I won't let you go."

———◆———

She was asleep.

She looked so trusting when she was sleeping, Caleb thought as he gently pushed back the hair at her temple. And these days she trusted him even when she was fully awake and not under the influence of the *persuasion*.

Or at least she thought she did. She had been through so much during this time after she'd been taken by Luca that she believed she'd had a breakthrough in understanding who and what Caleb could be in her life.

A very optimistic breakthrough, he thought cynically. All the wariness and confusion gone, enveloped in the warmth and faith she usually reserved for her family. She wasn't looking at him clearly and didn't really know anything more about him than the opinions and judgments she'd already formed. Even the bright side of *persuasion* she'd found so wonderful had a dark side that he hadn't let her see. If it went on too long, it had addictive properties that made it difficult to bring the subject back to reality. But he would always protect her from that pitfall and let her see only the good, never the bad.

As he protected her from the darkness inside himself, which she was now refusing to admit was present. How long would he have before she found out that she had made a mistake? It didn't matter, he thought impatiently. It would come when it came. He would enjoy it as long as he had it, and then work to turn the situation around when it turned bitter. That was the way it had been since the moment they had come together. It would not be any different.

But he would miss this glowing warmth, this feeling of welcome and total trust when she'd nestled closer to him a few moments ago. Well, that was now, live it, savor it. His arms tightened around her. They still had a few hours before they had to leave. He would lie here and allow himself to drift off with that memory before reality intruded again. After all, he'd promised not to let her go . . .

6:40 A.M.

"Wake up," Caleb whispered. He was handing Jane her clothes. "We're getting out of here. Hurry."

She scrambled to sit up. She was still a little bleary, though she felt brimming with energy. "I'm glad that you're going to allow me time to put on some clothes." He was already dressed and looked as wide-awake as she felt. "How long have you been awake?"

"An hour or so. I was only waiting until it got light enough for Luca's goons to see us leave." He watched her dress and then was heading for the door. "Come on. Luca's had his way and now it's our turn. Let's get going."

"I'm coming." She had to almost run to keep up with him. "You're lucky I'm feeling so energetic. I'd think I'd be more tired after that—" She glanced at him. "Or should I? Is that usually an aftereffect of the *persuasion*?"

"Only when I leave a post-suggestion. I didn't think you'd mind." He glanced at her. "Do you?"

"No. I was a little too much out of it to have a discussion about pros and cons of anything. I might if you hadn't told me about it. It's good that I know the possibility is there though."

"Yes, it is." They'd reached the car, and he was opening the passenger door for her. "I wouldn't want you to hesitate in taking something you want because you thought you couldn't trust me." He was running around to the driver's seat. "I'll avoid that at all costs."

Ten minutes later, they'd left the estate and were driving down the road toward Mantua.

She gave a glance behind her at the castle. "Luca didn't entirely get his own way."

"Yes, he did. He kept me from taking you somewhere safe."

"But he wanted you to hate being there." She grinned. "You might have been pissed off about not getting your own way, but I guarantee you didn't hate every minute you were there."

"No, I did not." He smiled. "I accomplished a couple of things I wanted to do, and we made a few steps in the right direction. But that doesn't mean I wouldn't have wanted to do those things in Mantua. I want you safe."

"I believe I get the picture," she said dryly. "But that doesn't mean that—"

Her phone was ringing.

She stiffened as she saw the blank ID. She answered the phone and put it on speaker. "Luca?"

"You left early. Weren't you entertaining enough to keep Caleb amused? Or was he too edgy to bother with you?"

"I told you he didn't like the place. And he hated the idea that I wouldn't leave because you'd forbidden it. But he went along with it." She paused. "Is Tomas all right?"

"As far as I know. I've had no need to have interaction with him. You would have known if I had." He asked, "Is Caleb listening?"

"Yes."

"Good. I hope you didn't have too dreadful a night, Caleb." His voice was brimming with malice. "I can see why you wouldn't want to spend much time there. It must have been upsetting to be forced to remember how everyone there recognized you as the freak you are. It's no wonder they threw you out of the place when you were only a boy. I wouldn't have been quite so callous if you hadn't needed me to give you another reminder." His tone hardened. "First lesson. I'm always in control. I had to show you that if you need Jane, you have to go through me. Now you'll be allowed to go to Edinburgh and set up the plans to get Cira's treasure. I've arranged for you to stay at an estate out of the city where I can have my men keep an eye on you to make certain you won't do anything foolish. I'll be in contact with you again once you've arrived and can tell me exactly when I'll get the treasure. Don't take too long. I do get impatient." He cut the connection.

"Son of a bitch," Caleb murmured. "He's a smug bastard."

"You've known that from the very beginning. Egotist all the way."

"And he's sure he has you in his pocket," Caleb said bitterly. "Nothing could be more clear."

"Because he does," she said quietly. "That's why we have to get that child away from him. Nothing else will work unless we make that happen. Now tell me you know how we can do it."

"I'm working on it. We might be able to use Davron. You said before he left you yesterday that you thought he was a possibility."

She shook her head. "But he was too frightened. He said that what Luca did to Tomas made him sick, but he didn't stop it when it was going on. And he didn't try to stop Luca from hurting me. I don't believe he has the courage to go against Luca no matter what he does."

"It depends if he has the right person to keep whittling away at him."

Her eyes flew to his face. "You?"

He shook his head. "I don't whittle. I tend toward using a machete. But I have someone in contact with Davron who might be able to do it. All I'd need from him is the location. That wouldn't be too dangerous a risk."

"Dangerous? Luca nailed a child on a crucifix. I'd think Davron would consider anything to do with him as dangerous." She was nibbling at her lower lip. "And whittle sounds too slow. We need to get Tomas out of there right away. If Luca gets impatient, he'll kill Tomas just to show me who's in control."

"I'll be on the alert. I know him now. I'll be able to tell if he's wavering."

"How? You pull all this mysterious crap out of a hat and I don't know how you do it. Or how I can help." Her voice was suddenly urgent. "The blood talent, the *persuasion*... Tell me how they work."

He suddenly chuckled. "When you're dealing with 'mysterious crap,' it's kind of difficult to describe."

"Then give me the CliffsNotes. I have to know what to expect when someone out there is trying to kill you."

"CliffsNotes." He tilted his head consideringly. "That concept would amuse Lisa." He shrugged. "Two principal talents. The blood talent with which you've become familiar through the years. You know what it can do. It has almost no limitations and can be used on anyone as long as they're within a certain distance of me. The *persuasion* does have limitations, but very few. Changing subjects' emotional and mental perceptions feels completely natural to them. Almost everyone is susceptible to it in some degree. But there are always those rare individuals who are not."

"You were able to influence Luca. That means he must be susceptible?"

He shook his head. "He's one of the rare ones, probably because of that ego and psychotic belief in himself. I was only able to influence him because I'd done that in-depth study on him and could immerse myself. I *know* the bastard."

She shivered. "But he also knows you. He's been studying everything about you for years."

"But that also means he's likely to be overconfident." He added grimly, "And I'm never overconfident. You can trust me to always know what I'm doing."

"I *do* trust you. I just wish that Davron wasn't the only arrow to our bow."

"He's not. Just the one you'd find less troubling." Caleb paused. "I promised I'd turn the hunt for Luca and Tower House over to Joe as soon as I knew it was safe for you."

She went still. "Joe?"

He nodded. "I'm going to call him as soon as we board the plane."

She had a sudden vision of that bloodstained door at Tower House. "I don't want him to go after Luca."

"You're not going to be able to stop him. Even if he didn't realize what you'd been through, Luca put Michael in danger. Joe won't allow anyone to do that without making sure that person is never around to do it again." He shrugged. "But if we can get the timing right, Luca might no longer be at Tower House if we can lure the bastard into a trap using Cira's treasure as bait."

"And that's another thing. I meant what I said when I told you I didn't like involving MacDuff."

"And I'm ignoring it. You can't have everything, Jane. I have to use MacDuff if I'm going to get rid of Luca in the quickest, most efficient way possible. While Luca's alive, he's a threat to you," he added, "and to Joe and everyone else you care about."

Caleb. She felt a chill. Luca hated and envied Caleb more than anyone else. He was the one Luca would attack first. No, not the first; he'd choose a more helpless target.

"Even if we could get him to come here and managed to draw him into a trap, he'd leave orders to kill Tomas whenever he gives the word."

"Then Joe will have to make an adjustment and see that either Luca is dead or Tomas is no longer there to act as victim. I can help him with the first option." He looked at her. "However, you've got to ask yourself: If Luca somehow managed to escape me, and he told you to come back to him or he'd kill the boy, what would you do?"

"You know what I'd have to do."

"Yes, I do, and so does Joe. So he'll go after Tomas and take him out of the equation. No matter where Luca is at the time." He shook his head. "You should have let me go after those guards last night. Joe might not have had to become involved."

"Or one of them might have managed to call Luca before you had time to put them down. I know you said all you needed was a location, but I don't like the word 'might,' Caleb."

"I realize you don't, and I'll do everything I can to erase it from the situation," he said quietly. "But it does exist without—"

"A location," she finished for him in frustration. "I tried and tried to find out where Tower House was located while I was there, but it looked like just any other pretty lake in the area. I even asked Tomas to help me draw the village where the workers lived to see if there was anything different about it."

"And?"

"He's a little boy. I had to push and prod." She shrugged. "He said there was a road his father used when Luca sent him for supplies. And the fields where they all worked were near a small waterfall where his mama let him swim at the end of the day. That was no help. Do you know how many waterfalls I ran across while I was painting in the lake area?"

"A lot. But it still might help. Anything else?"

She shook her head. "As I said, I had to prod. Maybe if I'd had a little more time with him."

"You had far too much time with him for me," Caleb said grimly. "We'll give the info to Joe and see what he comes up with. Right now I'm only interested in getting you on that plane and on our way to Edinburgh."

———◆———

Caleb phoned Joe as soon as he took off and got the Gulfstream to cruising altitude. "I've got Jane," he said curtly. "She's not in bad shape. We're on our way to Edinburgh. I'm going to let you and Eve talk to her because I knew you wouldn't be able to concentrate on anything else until you did. I'll talk to you later." He handed Jane his phone. "Let me answer the questions. All they'll want to know right now is that you're well and that they're going to get you back." He smiled. "And they'll want to hear your voice. That's important."

"Yes, it is." She lifted the phone and spoke into it. "Hi, Joe. I'm fine. Just a few bruises. How are you?"

"Other than wondering why you'd do such a dumb thing as playing Luca's game when you should have come to me? We're all fine here."

"It seemed the only thing to do at the time. Is Eve there?"

"Where do you think I'd be?" Eve asked. "When can we see you?"

"Soon." It was so good to hear her voice. Suddenly the looming problems seemed to fade and everything was clearer and easier to handle. Just as it had been since the first day she'd met Eve on the streets of Atlanta all those years ago. "It's not over, but we'll work until we bring Luca down. It appears Luca isn't the mastermind that he thinks he is." She added lightly, "If he was, I wouldn't have thought that Caleb would have been able to talk him into releasing me. Though that *persuasion* is magic. He played him brilliantly."

"And I'll be grateful to him for the rest of my life," Eve said soberly. "And when is soon, Jane? It's not only me and Joe. Michael needs to see you. He's been frantic since you've been gone."

"I don't believe 'frantic' is the right word," Jane said slowly. "He might be worried, but I don't believe he's ever stopped thinking or planning." She added, "And I want to talk to Michael, too." Then she saw that Caleb was holding out his hand for the phone. "But not right now. I think Caleb wants to talk to Joe again. Bye, Eve." She handed his phone back to Caleb. "They wanted to know when they'll see us."

"See *you*," Caleb corrected. "I think that we might be a little busy to plan on immediate reunions." He looked her directly in the eye. "Because the minute we get off the plane, we're hopping a helicopter and I'm taking you directly to see MacDuff." Then he spoke into the phone. "Joe, do you remember I told you that I couldn't decide whether to tell you what I was planning because it might make you an accessory?" He was smiling recklessly. "I decided to hell with it. I'll worry about breaking you out of jail later if it comes down to it. So I'll tell you exactly what's on the agenda so far and what you need to do if you want to keep Jane from running back to that son of a bitch."

CHAPTER

15

It might work," Joe said slowly to Eve after Caleb had hung up. "It's absolutely bizarre and shouldn't have a chance, but it's Caleb and he could pull it all together." He shook his head ruefully. "Hell, he managed to get Jane away from Luca."

"Yes, he did that," Eve said. "And at the moment I'm just grateful that Jane is on her way here and not still with that beast who tortures helpless children." She grimaced. "That makes it difficult for me to consider the ramifications for you if we become involved with aiding and abetting a bank robbery." Her gaze was on his face. "But you're already considering it, aren't you? You're going to go for it."

"Well, it's not as if Caleb needs me for the bank robbery itself. But Jane won't be free of that bastard until we get that child away from Luca. All I have to do is find where they're keeping him." His lips twisted. "And, if I stumble over Luca while I'm doing it, all the better."

"You never stumble. And you're mad as hell with Luca. So am I." She met his eyes. "What if Caleb decides he does need your help to rob that bank?"

He grinned. "Well, Caleb promised to break me out of jail. But you might have to take care of Michael on your own until he does it."

"No problem." She went into his arms and held him tightly. "I just had to be certain we're on the same page. Actually, I might prefer the bank to having you wander around all those cult weirdos. I don't suppose I get to go with you?" She shook her head impatiently. "I know. I know. One of us always has to be there for Michael." She gave him a quick kiss and then pushed him away. "Go ahead and make your arrangements. I have to go talk to him."

He nodded. "You're going to tell him about Jane."

She shook her head. "I'm going to tell him everything. He's told us we have to trust him and that he has to help. If we ignore him now, he might try to do something on his own. I can't have that, Joe. It's too dangerous." She shrugged. "So I'm going to trust him and so are you. That way we have a chance that Michael might not try to smuggle himself onto your flight to Mantua."

He nodded wryly. "I hear you."

"Let's hope Michael hears me." She turned and left the tent and started down the hill toward where Michael and Lisa were working. She hadn't gone more than a few yards before Michael came out of one of the tents and stood watching her. A brilliant smile lit his face. "Jane's safe?"

She should have known Michael would know the minute he saw her. "Not entirely. That's what I need to talk to you about. But Caleb has her and she's not with Luca."

"Then she's safe. We can handle the rest. Wait here. I'll go get Lisa. She'll want to know about Caleb. He hasn't called her lately." He disappeared back into the tent and a minute later he was pulling Lisa toward Eve. "Now you can tell us both. It's not as if she's not family."

Lisa blinked. "It seems I've been adopted. That's a little pushy, Michael. I'm not everyone's cup of tea." Then she said to Eve, "But that doesn't matter. He said you've heard from Caleb?"

Eve nodded and sat down at the picnic table a few yards away. "Just now, they're on their way to Edinburgh. But there are still problems." She took a deep breath. *Smother the doubts and second thoughts. Go for it.* She dived into the explanation. When she'd finished, she looked at Michael. "And that's all your dad and I know about the situation. You wanted us to trust you and that's what we're doing. You said that you wanted to help, and Jane apparently thinks you're already doing something. Are you? Have you been able to contact Tomas again?"

He nodded slowly. "But I haven't been able to find out much from him. He was very unhappy and scared and pushed me away yesterday. But that might have been because Jane wasn't there any longer. I'll try again today and tell him Jane is safe. That might make a difference." He paused. "Dad's going to try to find him? Maybe I should go with him. If I was closer to Tomas, it might—"

"But you don't know that," she interrupted. "And you being there might make your dad worry, and that would get in his way. You can see how that could happen."

He nodded, still troubled.

"Wouldn't it be better for you to just concentrate harder with Tomas to get the info your dad needs?" Eve asked. "The minute you find out where Tomas is located, we'll call him."

He hesitated. Then he nodded. "I guess that would be okay. Or I might be able to do something with Luca..."

Eve let out the breath she'd been holding. "Stick with Tomas. Now go up and say goodbye to your dad. He'll be leaving soon."

"Right." He got to his feet and started trotting up the hill.

"You handled that very well." Lisa was watching him leave. "I thought for a moment you'd lost him."

"So did I." Eve got to her feet. "And it only worked because he allowed me to do it. He was probably thinking that I might insist on going along, too, and he's very protective."

"And you knew it."

"I know my son. But I'm having to learn more every day." She raised a brow as she studied Lisa. "You were very quiet. I was beginning to wonder if Joe was going to have to worry about you tagging along."

"Why?" Lisa threw back her head and laughed. "I admit that I've been a little bored and the idea intrigued me. But Caleb is on his way to Edinburgh, and robbing a bank sounds much more exciting."

———

MACDUFF'S RUN

MacDuff was waiting in the courtyard when the helicopter landed. He opened the passenger door and pulled Jane out of her seat and into his arms. "You're well?" He pushed her back, his gaze raking her face. He gently touched the bruise on her cheek. "I mean as well as you can be. Considering that Caleb allowed this to happen."

"Stop it." Jane broke away from his embrace and then backed away from him. "I'm not going to put up with this any longer," she said fiercely. "Everything that happened to me was my doing and Caleb still managed to get me away from Luca." She looked him in the eye. "I'm grateful. If you're happy I'm alive and here, you should be grateful to him, too." She paused and then added pointedly, "And show it."

"Wicked dilemma," Caleb murmured.

"Indeed." MacDuff grimaced. His gaze was suddenly searching her face. "Something's . . . different. You were always defensive of him, but I believe I sense a certain tigerish protectiveness now." He shrugged. "I suppose I'm grateful for the act of saving you, if not the consequences he allowed to be inflicted. But since he's told me that he has a favor to ask, I might enjoy watching him beg enough to admit he didn't do too badly in that extrication." He was leading them toward the house. "Of course, I could have done better. Come in and have a drink in the study and I'll tell you how." He glanced with catlike malice over his shoulder. "After you tell me how much you want that favor and what you're willing to do to get it."

"Anything," Caleb said. "Do you want me on my knees?"

"Oh, that would be delightful. I'd almost give anything to see that." MacDuff opened the doors to the study. "But I have an idea that you still intend to rob me of the satisfaction. So come in and sit down and tell me how you're going to cheat me of it…"

"Amazing." MacDuff leaned back in his chair after Caleb had finished outlining what he wanted from him. His expression had gone from incredulity, to amusement, to intense curiosity. "And totally outrageous. Did you actually think that I'd do this?"

"Could you do it?" Caleb asked. "I told Luca that you'd know all the pass codes and security measures. Do you?"

"I…might."

"I believe you do. You'd want to know everything about the security arrangements for your treasure. It took you a long time to find it, and you wouldn't risk losing it. That's why you keep it here in Scotland—so that you can keep an eye on it." He paused and said softly, "And that's why you no longer have that treasure in the Royal Bank of Scotland, but in another location they offered you a few years ago."

MacDuff's expression didn't change. "I beg your pardon?"

"The Royal Bank of Scotland was already one of the safest banks in the United Kingdom, but they wanted to go a step beyond for their best customers. So they built a new, incredibly high-tech facility to protect certain key accounts."

"Indeed?" MacDuff had not stiffened, but Jane could see his sudden alertness. "Just what do you mean?"

"North Atlantic Loan and Trust," Caleb said softly. "A small establishment at the edge of Edinburgh that appears to only be an ordinary neighborhood bank. But if you go behind the scenes it becomes very interesting."

"How interesting?"

"It possesses one of the most secure vaults in the world, custom-made by Bossert and Sons of Switzerland. Although this creation is actually the product of Bossert's youngest daughter, Emily, the family's one true genius."

"I've never been fond of nepotism."

"Evidently you accepted it this time. Perhaps because she'd developed this masterpiece. I won't go into details at the moment because you're very familiar with every facet. I'll just reel off a few of the main accomplishments. Absolutely foolproof vault programming of the biometric info on two of the bank's senior officers to open the first vault doors. Very hard to keep up-to-date and accurate, but she found a way. Then, on the second door, scanners of those officers' handprints that concentrate not only on the prints but also on an instant DNA analysis based on trace amounts of skin perspiration."

"Impressive. If it works."

"It works. And of course there's also the retinal scan on the final vault door that's also totally unique. But you're also aware of that, MacDuff." He paused. "Have I caught your attention?"

MacDuff was silent a moment. "As you said, interesting. I'd be more interested to know how you came to know about that particular establishment." His expression hardened. "And whether I'm going to have to pull Cira's treasure out of that supposedly foolproof financial institution that I was positively assured no one even knew existed outside of the top echelon."

"No, it's safe enough. Everything they told you was true. It has wonderful security that absolutely can't be breached in the usual manner. You couldn't be in better hands. I wouldn't have even known about it if I hadn't had to gather all that information about the Royal Bank of Scotland." He shrugged. "I ran into a few anomalies that I had to look into when Palik gave me what I asked. It took me a little while to tap those Bossert executives in Switzerland for additional info and then put it all together. Then a little while longer to verify that your treasure was no longer in that bank. I guarantee no one else will notice or be able to use the information. I also promise that Luca won't know those vaults exist until the last minute before we're ready to spring the trap."

"How comforting," MacDuff said dryly. "Then I'd only have to worry about you robbing me."

Caleb smiled. "That's right. Unless you'd care to help."

"You ask a lot." His gaze was narrowed on Caleb's face. "If you know all those details about those vaults, you have to know exactly how much you need me."

"I know exactly how much I need you. Is this the time I fall to my knees?"

"Not yet. I might want to savor it. Not only do I have to worry about your extremely intrusive interference in my affairs, you also want me to keep an eye on some scum stealing it from me instead? Yes, Cira's treasure is mine, but those vaults contain billions more than that treasure. Setting you loose down there would be dangerous as hell. I'd be putting the bank's assets at risk, and the police would not be understanding. I'd say that makes the entire idea a bit ridiculous, wouldn't you?"

"Yes, but you might do it anyway." Caleb was smiling. "Because everything I told Luca about you was true. It would amuse you to help me go after Luca. You're angry that the bastard stole from you and murdered that guard who had spent most of his life working for your family. You'd hate the idea of anyone abusing or killing a child." He nodded at Jane. "And you'd also hate the idea that Luca had hurt your friend who'd helped you find that treasure."

MacDuff's gaze shifted immediately to Jane. "No, I wouldn't like that at all. How bad was it?"

"I told you, only a few nasty bruises. It could have been much worse." She leaned forward. "And you're not to do this for me,

MacDuff. I told Caleb I didn't want that. Let him find another way to get Luca that doesn't involve you. Luca is a wild card. There's no telling what he might decide to do, and I don't want you hurt. And what about your reputation? You're respected, practically a folk hero, in this country. Robbing a bank isn't exactly what's expected of the lord of MacDuff's Run."

"Quite right." Then he suddenly smiled. "But it's a new world and I'm only an earl. Have you noticed how not even the royals are doing what's expected of them these days? Though I don't believe any of them has robbed a bank." He thought about it. "Though in his wilder days, the idea might have intrigued Prince Harry."

Jane's eyes widened. "MacDuff!"

"It's all right, Jane. You've tried to save me from myself, but I find that Caleb knows me very well indeed." His eyes shifted back to Caleb. "Now I have to make certain I know *him* before I take the chance. Will you promise I will lose nothing if I do this, Caleb? Can I trust you?"

"You will lose nothing." Caleb smiled faintly. "Except a few days of boredom. And you've never trusted me, so you'll have to make up your own mind about that."

"That's not good enough this time. The stakes are too high." His gaze still held Caleb's. "Jane, you answer for him. Can I trust him?"

She was startled at the question but answered instinctively. "You can trust him."

MacDuff's gaze never left Caleb's. "How much can I trust him?"

"He gave you his word. You can trust him with your life." She added, "If you're crazy enough to do this, MacDuff."

"It seems I am." He looked away from Caleb to smile at Jane. "Because I realize that Caleb can accomplish amazing things if he chooses, and it's clear you believe he'd never betray me. Besides, I'm going to enjoy keeping Caleb on tenterhooks, never knowing if I'll back out at the last minute." He got to his feet. "So go ahead and make your plans, Caleb. When is this madness supposed to take place?"

"Tomorrow night."

"What? You did cut it close. And what would you have done if I'd said no?"

"You've just said you might still say no." He shrugged. "Worried about it then. I need this to be over for Jane."

"You're impossible." He shook his head. "It might be a bit too quick. But I do admit it does increase the entertainment factor. Just keep me informed of what you need and when you want to make the move. Will you be staying here?"

"No, we'll be going back to Edinburgh," Caleb said. "I have to make the advance contacts with the guards at the bank." He shrugged. "And we're waiting to hear from Luca. I'm sure he's been keeping an eye on us since we arrived here."

"Bastard," MacDuff muttered. "Keep him away from Jane. I'd rather she stay here."

"So would I," Caleb said as he opened the door for Jane. "But that won't happen. The next time we see you will be tomorrow night at the North Atlantic Loan and Trust. I'll be in touch about when and where you meet us to go into the bank, MacDuff."

The next moment his hand was on Jane's elbow, nudging her toward the helicopter. "Mission accomplished," he told her. "Though I'm not sure he would have gone for it if you hadn't been there trying to talk him *out* of it. It just reminded him what a good friend you are, and why he should go after Luca for hurting you."

"And is that the way you planned it?"

"No, you had a right to tell him your opinion." He paused. "But I thought it might have that effect on MacDuff. If I'd been wrong, I would have just had to find another way to convince him."

He opened the passenger door of the helicopter for her. "But then you took care of that, too. He believed every word you were saying when he asked you if he could trust me. Even I was convinced."

"Why shouldn't he believe it? It was the truth." She slipped into the seat. "Though he caught me off-guard. It's really annoying that I have to run interference between the two of you. You'll have to do something to work that out."

"I'll keep it in mind." His lips indented at the corners. "But you have to realize that the conflict seems perfectly reasonable from MacDuff's viewpoint."

"Because you're usually difficult. And expect no one to trust you." She waved her hand impatiently. "You should expect it. You deserve trust. You've never done anything to MacDuff to show him anything else."

"If you say so." He went around and got in the pilot's seat. "At any rate, he's accepting your word for it. And that means we can—"

Jane's phone was ringing.

No ID.

"And here we go," Caleb said. "Even sooner than I thought. I'd be glad to take it, Jane. I'm definitely in a mood to talk to Luca."

"No, I'll talk to him. He's a bully and likes the idea of intimidation. Let him take it out on me. It keeps him from looking around for another target, like Tomas." She drew a deep breath and answered the call. "Hello, Luca."

"You've been busy," Luca said. "I have a report that you've been talking to MacDuff. I can't tell you how happy I am that you're being so cooperative. How is MacDuff? Was Caleb able to persuade him to his way of thinking?"

"MacDuff agreed to do it. It wasn't that difficult. He reacted just as Caleb thought he would. He thinks he's going to be able to either kill you or put you behind bars. He doesn't realize that if it suits Caleb, he'll have no compunction about killing him after we're down in the vaults."

"And you didn't tell him?"

"You know I didn't. I *hated* sitting there and listening to Caleb talk him into doing it. But I knew there wasn't any doubt that you'd kill

Tomas if I did anything to make you lose that damn treasure." She added wearily, "And I hoped I might persuade Caleb to let MacDuff live if he doesn't give him too much trouble in the bank."

"I doubt it. It would be much more efficient to kill him, and Caleb is very, very efficient. Though you have my permission to offer him any lure you think would please him to do it. By all means, keep Caleb content and working hard and fast to get that treasure for me any way it can be done."

"Your *permission?*"

"You're offended? Yes, everything depends on my permission. You have to remember that you're just on loan to Caleb. By the way, your new address is Twenty-Four North Thorn Way in Edinburgh. I hope the two of you will both be very happy there. I'll be keeping a close eye on you and expect a report from Caleb as soon as he finalizes the plans for tomorrow night." He paused. "Otherwise, I'm afraid you'll be hearing from Tomas, Jane."

"Caleb will call you," she said coldly. "Is that all?"

"For the time being." He suddenly burst out, "I'm really finding you a trifle boring, and your insolence is unbearable. I'm beginning to wonder why I thought you might be suitable for my purpose. You've given me nothing but trouble since this began. I'll have to consider how you should be punished for wasting my time." He cut the connection.

"I believe I might be on Luca's discard list. What a pity," she said bitterly as she turned to Caleb. "I didn't handle him very well. I could tell he was seething with impatience. I should have shown him more panic and pain. He likes pain. I was so angry and frustrated it was all I could do just to keep myself from screaming at him. I'll be more careful the next time."

"I told you I'd talk to him." He started the helicopter and it lifted off. "His reaction was . . . extreme. But you did everything you should have. You verified that Luca has men watching us and assured him that MacDuff is on board to help me get what he wants.

And he wouldn't have believed you if you'd been any more docile. He knows you too well after Tower House." He was silent for a moment, thinking, before he added slowly, "No, it wasn't you, it was something else Luca has on his mind. Something else is going on with him. I could *feel* it." Then he shook his head. "Don't worry about it now. Let me think about it. Relax and I'll have you back in Edinburgh in no time."

"To that house on North Thorn Way that Luca so kindly set up for us?" she asked sarcastically.

"No, I've already got a house there that suits me better. It will have no bugs for him to listen to what we say and no easy access for any of his men to pay us visits." He grimaced. "Though I'm already regretting the latter. I'm going to really need an outlet in the next couple of days."

Her eyes widened. "Caleb."

"You're worried about the boy if I don't toe the line? It will be okay. Luca might be feeling a little heady with power after he managed to have his way about making me stay at Fiero. But he's not fool enough to believe he can keep me on a leash." He added, "As far as he knows, I care nothing for the child and only gave in because you were upset and asked me to. He believes he has you under control, but he won't think that you'll be able to sway me for very long. I was very careful about changing his perception of me. He accepts it totally. It would be against everything he's certain he knows about me now, everything I've made him believe, and it would make him suspicious if I change anything."

She could see it, but it still frightened her. "Luca's not stable, Caleb."

"But he can see he's almost at the finish line. And he'll do anything to cross it and get what he wants."

She nodded. "Even give me *permission* to 'keep you happy.' That was one of the times I almost lost my temper. It was pretty clear where he was going. As I said, I might be on his discard list." She paused. "But you'll be careful with him? You won't let him—No, of course you wouldn't. I was just scared for a moment."

"And remembered to whom you were talking?" he asked cynically.

"No, I *forgot* to whom I was talking. You would never do anything that would hurt either me or Tomas. You'd find a way to keep us safe." She looked out the window as MacDuff's Run faded into the distance. Everything seemed to be moving at lightning speed now, and she could feel the fear gripping her. "But that's not enough, Caleb. MacDuff is right, you might be moving too fast because you want this over. I won't have anything happen to you, do you hear?"

"Oh, yes, I hear you loud and clear. I have no intention of letting anything bad happen to me." He smiled mockingly. "Haven't you noticed that only occurs to other people around me? Everyone else can see it. It's all in the genes."

"Bullshit." But she could see he wasn't going to promise her to slow the pace. She could sense the reckless tension beneath that smile. She could tell he was in full hunter mode. "I won't lose you, Caleb."

His smile ebbed and then disappeared. "No, you won't," he said quietly. "I'll always be there. But it's time that I started moving, and I can't let you stop me. Things are changing, and we have to adapt." He paused. "And I guarantee you're not going to like how I'm going to handle Luca when I call him back today."

She stiffened. "Why not?"

"Because you'd consider it going into hyper speed." He changed the subject. "Didn't Eve say that she wanted you to talk to Michael? Why don't you call him now?"

"So that I'll stop nagging you to tell me what you meant?"

He nodded. "Exactly."

She was not going to get anything more out of him. At least that recklessness had lessened, if it hadn't entirely vanished. She took her phone out of her pocket and started punching in the number.

Michael picked up after only one ring. His words tumbled out. "Hi,

Jane. I was going to call you, but Mom said you might be busy with Lord MacDuff and to let you call me. You're okay, aren't you? I was worried about you. I told you that you shouldn't do that. We should have been together. You shouldn't have been alone with—"

"I remember you said that," she interceded to try to stem the flow. "But it seemed the best thing to do at the time. And I'm okay." She paused before she added, "And I don't think you let the fact that I left you behind keep you from trailing after me, did it? You were contacting Tomas?"

"It was the only way I could think to do it. I wasn't sure I could reach you. It was so far away. I'd only been able to reach Mom, and then later Dad, a couple of times when they weren't right there with me. But I guess a kid is kind of... open." She could tell he was trying to work it out for himself. "It was hard at first but then Tomas got easier and easier. On that last night before you went away, I didn't even have to wait until he went to sleep. If I concentrated, I could be there with him, seeing what he saw. It was pretty cool."

"I can see how it would be. How is he, Michael?"

"Sad. Scared. He pushed me away after you left him, but I've been concentrating and talking to him and he's better now. And I'm learning all the time about how to do stuff. I didn't try before because I knew Mom and Dad didn't want me to do it. But it's... exciting, Jane."

"And pretty cool," she repeated. "But I think that your mom and dad would prefer you focus on finding us a way to save Tomas while you do it. It's important that your dad get Tomas out of there as soon as possible."

"I know that." His voice was troubled. "I had Tomas get up and walk across the room with his mama this morning and he almost fell down. His legs are really weak, and his balance is off because his arms are all swollen and hurting. It was bad what they did to him."

"Yes." And it was bad that Michael was having to face that torture. "But we'll get him well and strong again."

"I know we will." He was silent. "But we mustn't let those people ever do it again. Tell Caleb that, will you?"

"I don't believe I'll have to tell Caleb. But you're doing your part just helping to get Tomas stronger, and it will help if you let us know what's going on with him." She paused. "I'm sorry you have to see all this, Michael. It's terrible, and I know it hurts you. You're being very brave. I'm proud of you."

"It hurts *him*. Tell Caleb."

"Okay, I'll tell him. I'll let you go now. I'll be in touch. I love you."

"Bye, Jane. I'm glad we have you back."

Caleb was gazing quizzically at her as she ended the call. "He's having a difficult time?"

"Yes, and I hate it for him. He shouldn't have to face this. But he won't stop because he might be able to help."

"And what did he ask you to tell me?"

"He told me once he believed there were monsters, but that he thought there were also people who could fight them. Now Tomas is showing Michael what agony a monster can cause every time he's with him."

"And his message for me?" He held up his hand. "Never mind. I can imagine. Michael and I both have a very simple and direct mind-set. You can tell him I understood."

She shook her head. "I'll try my best not to do that. He's facing enough ugliness at Tower House trying to help that boy survive without discussing when and how to eliminate monsters."

———◆———

TOWER HOUSE

Luca received a call from Caleb at 5:40 that afternoon. He snatched up the phone, punched ACCESS, and shouted, "What the fuck do you think you're doing, Caleb?"

"As you can see, I'm humbly obeying your instructions to Jane that I should phone you," Caleb said. "Enjoy it. It won't happen again."

"Where *are* you?" Luca hissed. "You're not at the Thorn Way house as I instructed. And I've been calling both of you for the past two hours."

"What a waste of time. Though Jane would have answered, but I told her that I wouldn't permit it. I was bored with playing your game. That night at Fiero was enough for me, and I wouldn't have let you get away with it except that I discovered it had dividends. Actually, that little egotistical indulgence of yours backfired. I found I still had a few lingering feelings for Jane, so I gave her what she wanted when she asked me to stay. In fact, she was so entertaining and convincing that night, I decided to keep her with me after all. So you'll have to find another artist to play your patron games with, Luca." He paused. "But that also means I'll have to change the arrangements we have for Cira's treasure."

"What the *hell* do you mean?" Luca grated through set teeth.

"Just a small adjustment. Jane wants Tomas released and I'm not in the mood to refuse her. She didn't trust that you'd see your way clear to letting him go after you have your hands on the treasure, so it will have to be at the time I deliver."

"Are you insane?" He added viciously, "I'll send you his *head*! I'll chop him into pieces!"

"No, that wouldn't do at all. You're not talking to Jane; threats won't work with me. It's the time for choices, Luca. Jane told you that today I'd made sure I could use MacDuff to go after the treasure. That's the last piece in the puzzle as far as I'm concerned. Now you have to decide if you still want your share." He added mockingly, "And I have to decide if I want to take it all for myself. I'm tempted, because you tried to use me and that pisses me off. If I let you keep it, it has to be on my terms. You'll do a trade for the boy at the time of delivery of the treasure. You'll permit Jane to call and talk to Tomas anytime she wishes before then so that she can verify he's alive and well. Agreed?"

"Bullshit!"

"Then you'll get zilch. I know you'll probably kill the boy sooner or later anyway if you don't take my offer. So does Jane or she wouldn't have come to me and asked me to make him part of the deal."

"She'll call me back and tell me not to listen to you." He spat out the words. "She'll *beg* me not to kill that kid."

"No, I won't let her. She knew when she asked me to interfere that I'd be in charge. Besides, she doesn't beg, though she might make an exception and beg me to kill you if you actually do something foolish and hurt Tomas." He added softly, "She wouldn't have to plead long or hard. On some subjects, I'm putty in her hands."

Luca felt as if he were choking with rage. "You can't *do* this to me."

"You should have known I wouldn't stay under anyone's thumb for very long. After all that studying and research you claim you did on me, didn't you learn anything? I don't know why you're complaining. Well, I guess I do, you hate to lose. But it's only a slight adjustment. And then I grab Cira's treasure and do whatever I choose to make this work for both of us. Shouldn't you just agree so that we can get down to the business of taking that treasure away from MacDuff?"

"You're bluffing."

"Am I? You'll have to judge for yourself. Think about it. You've always assured me that you know everything there is to know about me. Maybe you were right and there is a touch of obsessiveness in my relationship with Jane. Do you want to take the chance? Tomorrow night I could make you an enormously rich man. I can give you everything you've ever wanted. Hell, with your share you could build your own city-state that would dazzle the world. You could be greater than the Medicis ever dreamed of being. You only have to arrange to get your treasure out of Scotland and then give Jane what she wants." He paused and then added, "I've gone to a great deal of trouble and money to set this up, but if you won't give me what I want, I can walk away and do it later on my own. Can you say the same?"

The bastard knew he couldn't, Luca thought furiously. He'd always realized Caleb was a unique asset that couldn't be substituted. *Everything you've ever wanted...Dazzle the world...* He could see it gleaming in the distance, beckoning him. "Perhaps we could discuss it," he forced himself to say.

"Not good enough. Commit."

"She can have Tomas," he said stiltedly. "Whatever you want. He doesn't matter."

"Excellent. I'm glad you're being reasonable."

Malicious asshole. Luca struggled to hold on to his temper.

Dazzle the world. I can dazzle the world.

"It will still happen tomorrow night?"

"That's what I said. Three thirty A.M. I'll make the final selection I need from the guards tonight and set them up. But I'll need to know where to deliver your share of the treasure. Have you made the arrangements yet? It should be outside the city. After we leave the bank, I don't want to be anywhere near it in case something goes wrong."

"Do you think I'm an idiot? I arranged all of that eight months ago when I knew I was ready to get you to go after the treasure. It's a house in the Highlands with a landing field that will allow me to ship that treasure out within an hour of receiving it from you."

"Now I do feel very taken for granted," Caleb said derisively. "Yes, I'd say that's far enough to give us wriggle room. Would you care to give me the exact location?"

"Hell, no. I'll tell you that when you're on your way to put it in my hands." He paused. "And when the men I have watching you tell me that you've left the bank with the treasure, and I'm sure you're not trying to trick me." He didn't bother to try to keep the rage from his voice. "You keep changing the rules and you just think I'll put up with it? You believe because I let you dangle that treasure in front of me that you can persuade me into giving you anything you want? I might give you that useless boy, but I'm still in control of everything else and I won't be cheated. Here's what's going to happen the minute you leave that bank. There will be a van waiting outside in which you'll put the treasure, then you and Jane will get in and drive to the private airport outside the city that's keyed into the GPS. Any deviation and I kill the child. When you arrive at the airport, there will be one of my men there to meet you. You will open the chests and show him that what you've brought is the genuine article. If the treasure passes inspection, only then can you board the plane and be given the flight plan that will take you to the delivery site. I don't have to tell you that I won't tolerate any type of trickery. I want that treasure, but I won't hesitate to blow it and you out of the sky if I think that you're trying to make a fool of me."

"Now, why would I try to do something as useless as that would be?" Caleb murmured. "Good enough. And I'll be just as careful about my arrangements for delivery. You won't get your hands on your share of the treasure until you bring Tomas out to the plane for the trade. Though I realize an honorable man like you would never think of a double cross." He cut the connection.

"Condescending son of a bitch!" Luca's hand clenched on his phone. He was panting, shaking. He'd barely been able to finish the call after he'd had to give Caleb that humiliating victory. Then he was swearing vehemently as he threw his phone down on the desk with all his force. "I'm going to *kill* him."

Davron tensed warily. "You've always said he'd have to die. It wouldn't be safe to leave him alive. What did he do now?"

"He treated me as if I was *nothing*. He as much as told me he could do anything he wanted and I'd be helpless." He was trying to get control of himself. It was only another two days and he could dispose of Seth Caleb. Then he would be on his way to gaining everything he had been working toward all these years. But he wanted it to happen *now*. He needed to do something, anything, to soothe that stinging blow to his pride. "And that bitch is doing whatever he wants her to do. I told her that I owned her, that was how it had to be. Yet she didn't even answer my call. She went running to him because she thinks that he can force me to do anything he wants me to do." He could feel the rage tearing through him again as he jumped to his feet and headed toward the door. "None of this was my fault. I knew I was right about her trying to sabotage all my plans. Well, she won't succeed. Neither of them will get away with this. Everything is going to go just as it was meant to. I'll show them both that in the end I'm the one who will always win. Go and tell them to get the helicopter ready, Davron. We're leaving right away." His lips were drawn back in a feral grimace. "I have to have enough time to prepare a surprise for them."

EDINBURGH

"You're right, I didn't like anything about that call," Jane said tightly after Caleb hung up. "It scared the hell out of me. Hyper speed? Luca could have exploded any moment and decided to go and kill Tomas."

"But he didn't," Caleb said. "I was betting on him going after the prize he'd been fighting for all his life and not letting himself blow it on a temper tantrum."

"Because you'd studied the prey," Jane said dryly. "And you were willing to trust yourself as a good hunter should."

"And braced myself to change course if you panicked and went on the attack, and I had to take a step back." His gaze was studying her face. "But I didn't have to do that. You were gritting your teeth, but you didn't panic. You went along with me all the way. Why?"

"Because I trusted the hunter, too," she said quietly. "Though I can't say I didn't have a few bad moments. I was terribly afraid. I'm still shaking. Why did you insist on the trade to get Tomas?"

"No choice. I had to get him out of there. We weren't having any luck finding the tower and we don't have much time left. The obvious answer would be to eliminate the need to find it. If Luca was forced to move the boy here, we'd have a better chance to track him. In the meantime, we can tell Joe to try to locate the house Luca rented in the Highlands."

"You might have told him that before he flew off to Mantua," she said ruefully.

"He'll tell me that, too." He shrugged. "I couldn't do anything else. I told you, no choice. I was playing the situation by pure instinct because I had a bad feeling while you were talking to Luca earlier today. That combination of egomania and the drive to fulfill his so-called destiny was bringing him to the edge. He was starting to blame you, and he always blamed me. It wasn't going to take long for him to decide to do something that would show everyone he was in complete control." He paused. "Clearly, killing the boy would be one way to do that. Even if he had to convince himself it was the smart thing to do. I was trying to watch closely, and today I could tell something had changed with him. I caught something in his tone that disturbed me. I have an idea that Luca is getting impatient and ready to tie up all the loose ends and maybe change course..."

And one of those loose ends would be Tomas and any deadly promises Luca had made to Alberto about his son. She shivered. "Then by all means let's get Joe back here right away. I'll call Eve and tell her. What are you going to do?"

"Make a few calls. Maybe talk to Barza and see what he can find out from Davron about Luca. Davron is probably getting some very bad vibes right now." He smiled faintly. "Then I'll go over the records for those guards I'll need to use to help us in the vaults tomorrow night."

"May I help?"

"Why?" He was gazing at her curiously. "I think you realize that not all *persuasions* are as pleasant as the ones I gave you at Fiero. And since the first minute we met you've always stayed as far away from my so-called talents as you could get. You wouldn't let them touch you."

"I've decided that was a mistake," she said bluntly. "Lisa once said that the reason I broke up with you was that I might be afraid. I'm not afraid, but ignorance breeds fear. All that stuff you can do is a part of you and I should know every part of you."

He gave her a half smile. "Not *every* part of me."

"Yes, I should. But I'll start with just this part. I'd like to see how you manage to change perceptions, and this seems a good time. Those bank guards are innocent, and you might trick them, but you wouldn't deliberately hurt them."

"Such faith," he said lightly.

"Yes, I told you I trust you." She smiled. "Someday you'll believe me."

He lifted his shoulder in a half shrug. "I believe that you believe it now. It's very interesting, but enormous pressure. I'm afraid that when I disappoint you, the fall will be all the worse."

"If you disappoint me, then we'll talk about it. And there will be no fall. There will just be adjustments as there always are when two people come together." She asked again, "May I help you?"

His expression was enigmatic as he stared at her. "Maybe." He was already pulling out his phone to call Barza. "We'll see a little later..."

"I'll call Joe," Eve told Jane. "He's not going to be pleased that Caleb is going to change the game plan, Jane."

"What can I say? Caleb had a feeling and went with it. You know his instincts are usually sound. He wanted to get Tomas out of there." She hesitated and then asked, "Is Michael there? Could I talk to him?"

The next moment Michael was on the phone. "You're scared for Tomas? He's fine right now, Jane."

"And we want to keep him that way. Caleb wouldn't have forced Luca to move him if he hadn't thought there was a possibility he might be in trouble soon. Your dad is going to try to track them to the house in the Highlands where Luca is taking him, but you might be able to help. You said you could see what Tomas saw. It's important that you pay particular attention now so that you'll remember everything about the trip and where they're keeping him. Can you do that for us?"

"Of course I can." He paused. "They're going to try to hurt him again? I can't let them do that, Jane. I promised him that if he did what I said, I'd take care of him."

"And you will be. That's what I'm saying. That's what we're all trying to do."

"But I *promised* him." Michael's voice was hoarse. "He's just a little guy, and he wouldn't understand if I broke my word. I couldn't do it. I'm just telling you that I can't let it happen."

Just a little guy. But Michael was only a couple of years older. And yet he was trying desperately to shoulder the responsibility of saving the boy, and she was the one who had just added to the burden. This loss of childhood for Michael was what Eve and Joe had been struggling to prevent all these years, she realized helplessly. "Remember, whatever happens, it's not your fault."

"Yes, it is. I told you, I made a promise." Then he was silent for a moment. "You're worried about me. You shouldn't be. This is what I should be doing. But I'm only learning, and that makes it harder. Maybe later I'll be—" He broke off and then said quickly, "I have to get back to him. Something's happening and Tomas is worried about his mother."

Then he was gone, and Eve was back on the line. "I know

what you're feeling, Jane." Her voice was shaking. "I've been seeing Michael being pulled deeper and deeper toward that poor child. He's been monitoring him constantly and I have no idea where it's going to take him. The only thing I've been doing is watching and waiting and trying to be there for him. That's all he'll let me do right now." She drew a deep breath. "But I won't stand by if I see it getting completely out of control. I'll find a way to stop it."

"Tomas is relying so much on Michael. I only hope you can do it."

"I *will* do it, even if it means I have to make a choice. I won't lose my son." She added huskily, "Now let me make that call to Joe so that we can start the wheels turning to bring him here at warp speed to find that house in the Highlands. Maybe between the two of us we'll be able to do the job ourselves and make sure that I don't have to make that choice."

CHAPTER

16

Have you decided to let me help you?" Jane came into Caleb's study and closed the door. "It's not as if you'd let me do anything that would get me tossed into jail. I just want to be—"

"Part of it," he finished for her. "But anything you do for me from now on will make you an accessory to bank robbery. That's why I tried to keep Joe out of it." He smiled crookedly. "Until I managed to suppress my more altruistic impulses and decided to let him take his chances."

"Bullshit." She sat down in a chair across the desk from him. "You're still trying to keep him away from the robbery. That's why you sent him hunting for Tomas and Tower House." She smiled at him. "But you're being ridiculous about me being involved when you're going to be taking me down in that vault with you tomorrow night." She added, "And I know very well you'd make certain that no one will be able to connect me with whatever happens down there. Right?"

He nodded slowly. "Never."

"Then let me know this part of you, too. How are we going to choose those guards?"

His smile deepened. "My, you are eager to join the dark side." He tossed a pile of folder-enclosed reports on the desk in front of her. "The first order of business is to decide what qualities are needed to furnish the effect I need. Then choose the type of personality and background to provide those qualities when I persuade them it's necessary."

She tapped the reports. "Do you always have to go through all this?"

"No, rarely. I usually wing it. But this is a special case involving other people to whom I've made promises. Like you, Jane."

"And MacDuff." She took the reports and glanced through them. "So what do you need from these men?"

"One should be younger, efficient, kind and respectful to older people, willing to accept guidance."

"Michael would say you wanted a Boy Scout."

"That's not too far off. The other should be older, accustomed to being in charge, smart, ready to go the extra step even if he's never done it before."

"A Boy Scout and an Eagle Scout?"

"Not an Eagle Scout. Add authority, and you forgot the maturity."

She looked down at the dozen or so folders before her. "You have quite a few reports here. Do you have any preferences?"

"No, I'd just started." He leaned back in his chair, his eyes narrowed on her face. "But it's been a long day, I think I'll just let you choose. Whoever you decide, I'll go with."

She grinned. "Responsibility. You mean, unless I choose someone you don't think would cut it."

He shook his head. "No second choices. I trust you."

She met his eyes. "That's what I told you," she said softly. "But you wouldn't believe me."

"But you're a much more trustworthy person than I am. You asked for it, now do it," he said. "Get to work, Jane. I don't have all night."

She laughed. "You're impossible." She started to go through the reports. After the third psychological test and appraisal she forgot all about him, trying to gauge the family background of the applicants against the actual testing scores. Family was always so important...

Two hours later, she pushed the other reports aside and tossed him two folders. "There you are. And it will be your fault if you can't persuade them to do what you want them to do. They were much more likely than any of the others." She nodded at the first folder. "James Smythe. He had a great attendance record through school, which means he likes to play by the rules. He came from a low-income family, and he obviously tried to help support them judging by the number of part-time jobs he held while he was growing up. His employers all gave him great recommendations when he left their employ. After he graduated from school, he joined the army and became an MP. But he still arranged to send his pay home to his mother, who was in a nursing home for two of those years he was in the service. When he got out, he was given this job at the bank. He's been working here for the last year."

"You did find a Boy Scout," Caleb said, amused. "I'm surprised you chose him to run a risk that might ruin his image."

"I thought about it. But then I realized we could work at making his life a lot easier once this was over, and we'll just add him to the list of people whom you're going to be sure aren't going to be connected to this." She beamed at him. "You'll just have to work harder, Caleb."

"And I suppose that goes for your other choice?"

"He could probably take care of himself, but it's not fair to play favorites. Donal Campbell. Forty-six, has worked for bank security for six years and before that with Edgewood Security in London. He was a lieutenant in the army, decorated for bravery in Iraq, well educated, divorced, has a child, Emma, whom he adores; he takes on extra security jobs to send her to a great school in London."

"And we wouldn't want her school to miss any paychecks?"

"No, but you wouldn't do that," she said. "Unless you decide to choose someone else."

He shook his head. "I told you, no second choices. Smythe and Campbell are our guards. I'll live with the additional burden of charity you've thrown into the mix." He got to his feet and grabbed the two folders. "Well, now that you've done your part, I've got to go and do mine."

"What?" She straightened, startled. "Where are you going?"

"I told you I didn't have all night for you to choose. Now I have to go to their homes and do an advance programming of both subjects. I want everything to go off with no problems."

"May I go with you?"

"There wouldn't be anything for you to do." He was moving toward the door. "I promise I won't hurt them, Jane."

"But will they hurt you? You might startle them, and they might react. Maybe I should be there to help."

"And protect me?" he asked solemnly. "I think I can handle it."

"I realize you can. But I also know that you might be at a disadvantage that I put you under when I chose those particular men. So I should be there to distract them."

"You would be a distraction, but to me, Jane."

And a distraction was always dangerous. "When will you be back?"

"It should take no more than twenty minutes per subject plus travel time between the two residences." He glanced at the addresses. "They're near here. Perhaps three hours."

"That seems a long time." She gave him a searching look. "What aren't you telling me?"

He was silent.

"Caleb."

He sighed. "I should have known I couldn't slip it by you. It would have been much easier if I didn't have to be so damn careful about using the *persuasion* around you. I have to make one more stop and visit Angus Wilson."

"Who's Angus Wilson?"

"The third subject I decided I had to have in that bank tomorrow night."

"Another guard?" She frowned. "I don't remember a report on an Angus Wilson."

"Not a guard. Wilson is the branch manager of the bank. And you didn't see a report because there was no choice. He was one of the two officials who is being biometrically monitored to permit opening the vaults. I had to have him, regardless of how difficult he was going to prove to be."

"And you think he's going to be difficult. Why?"

"I told you that some people are resistant to *persuasion* of any kind. Very few. But I believe Wilson might be one of them. On that first day I received Palik's lists, I went over Wilson's life history and all the usual tests. There were several small signs in the overall package that indicated he might be one of those few. I've seen those signs before and they sent up red flares. He was put in charge of MacDuff's treasure for a reason. Besides being completely honest, his entire record shows a mental block where any sort of applied influence is concerned."

"But you're not sure?"

"I will be after I go to see him tonight. I hope I'm wrong."

"But why do you need him? Couldn't you find a way to get him transferred for a few days?"

He shook his head. "He's stubborn, and he'd immediately go on the alert. He knows how valuable he'd be to anyone who wanted to go after the treasure. He has all the codes to MacDuff's vaults memorized, and his DNA is keyed in to the handprint ID system— and we also need him because his vision scan unlocks the final process on the Cira vault through iris identification. In short, we need either his cooperation or his eyes."

She shuddered. "And you're thinking he'll not be willing to give us either. What will you do?"

"First, find out if I'm going to have a problem. Perhaps I'm wrong about him." He met her eyes. "And, if I'm not, there are always ways of handling it. Just not pleasant ones."

She shook her head vehemently. "Wilson is an innocent man."

"So is your Tomas innocent. Luca is on the edge. If he thinks this robbery is going to fall apart, he'll kill the boy without another thought. Do you want to choose between him and Wilson, or should I?"

"Neither," she whispered. "We have to find another way."

"And I'll try." His lips twisted. "But don't worry, I wouldn't make you choose. I'm uniquely suited through birth and years of experience to accept any guilt that comes my way. This would just be one more." He opened the door. "Go to bed. I'll wake you when I come back and tell you if we have a problem."

"Caleb."

He glanced back at her.

"You said Angus Wilson was one of the two officials who had to be present to open the vaults. Who is the other one?"

"Who do you think? MacDuff would never totally give up access into those vaults."

She drew a breath of relief. "Then we don't have to worry about that."

"Don't we?" he asked cynically. "MacDuff is a complicated man, and there's no telling what he's feeling about me at any given minute. That treasure means everything to him. I'd almost rather trust Angus Wilson."

Jane watched the door swing closed behind him. For a while earlier tonight, she'd felt more optimistic at the thought of them working together for a common purpose. Caleb had appeared to accept that she could be part of his life and not just teetering on the border. But that was before Angus Wilson had appeared on the horizon. Any help she'd given Caleb with the guards was nothing in comparison with what he'd face if he had to make that decision with

Wilson. As a hunter, he might be accustomed to that sort of trauma, but it was poison to the soul, and she couldn't allow him to shoulder it alone. If she could find a way to—

Her phone was ringing.

Michael.

"It's late for you. Is everything okay?" she said as soon as she picked up. "You said that Tomas was worried about his mother when you hung up before. She wasn't hurt?"

"No, or I would have called you right back. She was just upset because his father had just told her she couldn't go with Tomas." He paused. "They put Tomas on the helicopter an hour ago and he was so scared, Jane. But you said it was a good thing that he was going, that maybe Dad and I would be able to find him." He repeated in a whisper, "But he was so scared. He's never been on any kind of airplane or helicopter. They just put him in the back with the luggage and other stuff and there was no one there to tell him what was happening."

"You were there, Michael. I'm sure he must have felt that, and it would have made him feel better."

"Not at first. I couldn't get through to him. I kept trying and trying, but he didn't know if he was going to die or be hurt like he was before. But when he finally went to sleep, I was able to explain that this was a good thing, and I wouldn't let anything bad happen to him." He added wearily, "But by the time I got through it, he had me scared, too. I thought it would be all right if I just took a couple of minutes away from him to talk to you and tell you what was happening." He stopped and then said, "And for you to tell me that what I was saying was the truth. We're going to be able to help him, aren't we?"

"Yes, we will. You've already started to do it. You've let us know that Luca is on the move, and you've made Tomas feel better about it than if you weren't there for him. Who else is on the helicopter?"

"Luca, Davron, Alberto, and a man named Pietro that Tomas hadn't seen before."

"See? More information. And Caleb and I are getting our own information, too. I'll call your mom and tell her what you've said. She'll let your dad know there's a good reason for him to get back here to find that house in the Highlands."

"I would have talked to her myself, but she worries about me. I thought you could tell her how okay I sounded to you."

"Very okay." For a kid going through something no child should have to experience. "I'll tell her you're doing great. Now, why don't you try to take a nap while Tomas is taking his? You'll need the rest. It's a long flight and I know you're going to stay with Tomas all the way. Can you do that?"

"I think so, and maybe I can keep Tomas asleep longer if I concentrate harder. This helicopter bounces and hurts him, and if he gets excited, I can't stop the pain."

"That would be wonderful if it's possible."

"It's possible. I just have to learn all the ways . . ." He paused. "You told Caleb what I wanted you to tell him?"

"He told me you two were a lot alike. He said to tell you he understood."

"I knew he would. I'm going to check on Tomas and then go to sleep. Bye, Jane . . ."

He hung up the phone.

Of course Michael realized Caleb would have no trouble understanding him. They were linked in ways that Jane would never fully comprehend. But that didn't mean that she should give up as she'd done before when she'd pushed Caleb away. That would never happen again. There were deeper, more profound links that she had to believe were already in place between them. She just had to explore them and make Caleb believe in them, too.

But that was down the road, and there were other problems to face in the next twenty-four hours. So think on the bright side as she'd tried to do with Michael. Be positive.

Luca was on the move, and he'd taken Tomas with him as Caleb had demanded. That meant he was at least going through the motions of a trade. And the boy was no longer at Tower House where they'd been helpless to help him. Surely they had a good chance to keep him alive if Joe could find that house in the Highlands. That was good news.

She only hoped the remainder of Caleb's plan for staging the removal of Cira's treasure from the bank would prove as successful. Which could depend entirely on Angus Wilson, who might be totally impervious to Caleb's skill.

Well, Caleb said they'd know soon.

Another three hours . . .

———◆———

It was over five hours, not three, when she heard Caleb come into the house.

She jumped out of bed and ran into the living room. It was still in darkness, but she could see his familiar shadow near the front door. "Well?" She turned on the lights. "Yes, or no?"

"No," he said. "With an infinitesimal chance of yes. That's why I spent the extra time with Angus tonight. But I won't know if there will be a payoff until tomorrow night." He began stripping off his clothes. "So I suggest we get a few hours' sleep and get ready to face the new day. Smythe and Campbell will be no problem. Angus Wilson might be a nightmare."

"I can see it." Her gaze was searching his face. "You look very tired."

"No, I don't. That's your imagination." He smiled teasingly. "Expressions can be controlled by blood flow and I'm an expert. I fooled Luca with no problem at all when he called me that first night he had you at Tower House."

"And then smashed your fist into a mirror." She took his hand and led him toward the bedroom. "And it's not my imagination. I can *feel* how tired and on edge you are. Who knows? Maybe it's because you've lowered your defenses and are letting me step into your world. It's about time." She pulled her sleep shirt over her head and threw it aside. "Now come to bed and let me hold you."

He smiled. "*Persuasion?*"

"No. That's taking, not giving for me. And I'm in a mood for giving." She pulled him into bed and cuddled close to him. "Now tell me what you meant about Wilson, and then take anything you want from me. There's so much I'm willing to give. Understanding. Peace. Love. Whatever. Just relax and take."

"That's quite a smorgasbord you're offering." He was stroking her hair. He was silent a moment and then said, "I don't know if I can pull it off with Wilson, Jane. I was able to enter a few post-suggestions, but I don't have even a clue if they'll work. Other than that, I'll be working blind."

"Then we'll play it by ear. You'll figure it out." She nestled closer. "Michael called me. Luca took Tomas away from Tower House, and they're on their way here. You were able to get Luca that far along; now we just have to get him the rest of the way. It's not as if we're alone in this. Luca said he'd had that property in the Highlands for eight months. I called Eve and she said that Joe was already talking to Scotland Yard and having them check records on any house or property in that area rented during that period. If he gets lucky, we might know where Luca's heading before he even lands in Scotland."

"All wrapped up, with no problems? I don't think that's very likely." He suddenly chuckled. "You're much more optimistic than when I left."

"One of us has to be. You've never let me see you worried before. Since that was a definite first, I felt as if I had to find a remedy. But I admit it was kind of nice and normal and human. It didn't have the least bit of the Ridondos' fierceness and gloom peeking through."

"Don't get used to it."

"Oh, I fully intend to get used to it," she said. "But I'll go slow since you obviously need time and space to adjust."

"I appreciate both the consideration and generosity." He paused and then burst out with sudden recklessness. "But I find it's bringing on an outbreak of honesty and unselfishness that I usually try to keep at bay. So I'll tell you the Ridondo strain is still alive and strong in me. I'll try to make it palatable for you, but it's who I am. I'm not nice and I'm not normal, but I'm very, very human. And sometimes that's not good, either. You probably think you're going to change me, and I'll let you go on thinking that you can. Because I can't do without you. But don't trust me."

She went still. Something had been revealed in the rawness of those last words that might have consequences, and she had to be very careful. Then she stopped analyzing and just relied on instinct. "Too late. I do trust you. And, because I have confidence in my own judgment, I won't pay any attention to you." She raised herself on one elbow and looked down at him. "As for changing you, I wouldn't presume. That's in your court if you want to do it. But you might have noticed that we've both begun to change since we've known each other. When you care about someone, it happens automatically and there's nothing either one of us can do to prevent it. And just the fact that you're concerned about it is a sign that maybe it's not such a bad thing." She met his eyes. "So stop worrying about it. I'm not. And besides, it's getting in the way of what I wanted to do tonight."

He was silent a moment, then smiled. "That's right, giving, not taking. I wouldn't want to spoil that mood. I've had my moment of unselfishness for the decade." His fingers were stroking her back with a feather-light touch. "But let's go back to the smorgasbord. Do you suppose out of all that sweetness and light, you might add a little more fire and brimstone to the mix? Since you want to make me happy, you know it would add enormously to me feeling more comfortable considering my wicked Ridondo streak."

She couldn't breathe. Heat was traveling down her spine, the muscles of her stomach clenching.

"That might be okay," she said shakily. "As long as you're taking and not giving. That's important to me, Caleb."

"I guarantee it's going to be impossible to tell the difference." He slid into her with one deep thrust and she bit her lip to keep from screaming at the fullness. She could feel it in every muscle, every breath. She clenched and then moaned as he went even deeper. "But I promise I'll take, and take, and take . . ."

———◆———

"Mom. He's there. Tomas is *there*. I saw it."

Eve jerked awake to see Michael standing in the tent doorway. Lord, he looked tired. She glanced at the clock. It was nearly five in the morning. She hadn't thought she'd be able to sleep after he'd left her, but she must have drifted off. Evidently Michael had not. She held out her arms to him. "Come here. Tell me about it."

He ran across the tent and cuddled down beneath the blanket with her. "Dad's not here yet? I should tell him."

"It may take a little while for him to get here. He had to stop in Edinburgh. He has to go over a list of houses with several real estate companies that had been rented in the Highlands during that period Luca told Caleb he'd arranged it. He should be here this afternoon." She drew him closer. "You actually saw the house? Can you describe it?"

"I think so. Tomas was all confused. He was hurting and he's always so scared . . ." He moistened his lips. "What I was seeing was through his eyes, and I don't think the house could have been that big or scary. It was brownstone, and it had a porch in the rear where the helicopter landed. But he saw a landing strip at the front of the house, too." He frowned. "The house looked really old and kind of crumbly, but the landing strip looked clean and new." He paused.

"But there were nine or ten other men waiting when they landed. So it's not going to be just those few people who came from Tower House for Dad to fight." He shook his head. "It must have seemed like an army to Tomas. They carried him out of the helicopter and through the house, but that was all blurry and dark, too. Then they shoved him into a room under the stairs and he had to crawl onto the bed himself." He whispered, "That hurt him, too, Mom. Everything was hurting him and strange and scary. We've got to get him out of there."

"We will. You drew sketches for me before when your dad was hurt last year. Do you suppose you can draw a picture of the outside of this house?"

"Yes, and a little of the inside, too. But like I said, it might not be exactly right because I probably didn't see it as Tomas saw it." He shook his head. "What he saw was like something from one of those spooky movies you don't like me to watch. Maybe that's how everything looks to him now."

"Maybe it does." It wouldn't surprise Eve that everything seemed terrifying and filled with horror to the child. "Well, you can only do what you can, Michael. When we compare your sketches with your dad's photos from the real estate company, that may help a lot."

"Then I'll start right away." He sat upright. "I'll have them done by the time Dad gets here."

"No." She tried to pull him back down. "Rest. I don't think you've slept since they put Tomas on that helicopter. You can wait until your dad gets here and then you can try to get together on the location of that house."

"I can't wait, Mom." He broke free and jumped to his feet. "I don't know how much time Tomas has. I promised him that I'd take care of him. I'll go get Jane's sketch pad and start working."

"How much time he has?" She raised herself on one elbow. "What do you mean?" She was afraid she knew what he meant.

"It doesn't matter what Jane or Caleb do." Michael's voice was unsteady. "Luca is going to kill Tomas. After he gets the treasure, he'll have a way already set up to do it. He wants to kill all of them, but he said Tomas will be first because he's easiest and it will hurt Jane the most. Tomas heard him say that to Alberto when they were carrying him into the house tonight. That's why they just threw him into that room. They didn't care if they caused his wounds to break open." His eyes were glittering with tears. "They didn't care..." He had to clear his throat. "But I care. I know Caleb and Jane will do the best they can, but I have to help, too. Luca is a terrible, terrible man, Mom."

"Yes, he is." And it was terrible that Michael had to feel that he had to do battle against him. But all she could do was help him where she could. She motioned him to leave. "Go do those sketches. I'll send your dad to come and see them as soon as he gets here."

He nodded and ran out of the tent.

———————

Joe spread the four sketches Michael had drawn beside the photos on his phone he'd downloaded from the Edinburgh real estate firms. "You've got to understand," he said quietly. "These rental properties are all just old farmhouses that have been around for decades, Michael. Most of them have the same floor plan and look pretty much alike. Nothing much distinctive about them." He pointed at the third real estate photo. "This one is very similar to one you drew, but it doesn't have a landing field." He pointed to another one. "And this one is similar, but it looks larger."

"But it's how Tomas saw it," Michael said. "And the houses all do look alike. But that one did have a landing field. Tomas saw it. Couldn't Luca have had one built after he rented it?"

"Yes, he could," Joe said. "And that's what might have happened if Luca decided that he'd need a larger aircraft than a helicopter to accommodate the treasure." He hesitated. "We just have to be careful not to make a mistake when Tomas might be the one to suffer for it."

Michael flinched. "I know that. I'd be able to tell which house it was if I was there and could see it for myself and not how Tomas saw it." He tapped four of the photos in the real estate brochure. "It's one of these. I *know* it. Couldn't we go and look at them all and then just go in and get him when I find the right one?"

Joe shook his head. "These properties are spread all over the Highlands. We don't have the time to do that—and if we did, there's a good chance Luca's men might spot us and decide to hurt Tomas. That's the last thing you want."

Michael nodded. "But I'd know which house, Dad. I'd feel Tomas there. Just let me get a look at it, and I'd know it."

Joe had known where this was going. "I couldn't take you with me, Michael. This isn't only about Tomas, it's about Jane. I'm going to go up to the Highlands with Inspector Tovarth and his team and see if we can find that house and capture Luca, but it's no place for you."

"You *have* to take me with you. Tomas knows me, and he won't be afraid if I'm there." Michael's finger jabbed at the photos again. "Just these four houses? How long would that take?"

"Too long." He looked him in the eye. "I'm sorry. The answer is no, Michael." He turned and started for the door.

"Dad."

He turned to look at Michael. His son's face was pale and his eyes frantic and glittering with tears. "Yes, it's about Jane and Tomas, and I have to help both of them. And I know I can do that. I can't let you stop me."

Joe shook his head. "I've just done it. Leave this to me, Michael."

"We're zeroing in on four farmhouses," Joe said curtly when Caleb picked up his call ten minutes later. "All very similar brownstones. None of them that close to each other, and we don't have time to investigate all of them in the time frame you've given me. I'm going to split up the team and send one of them to check out the location that's the farthest away. But other than that, all I can do is try to get in two or three and hope to get lucky. I'm leaving here in the next twenty minutes with Tovarth and twenty of what he assures me are the best men the Yard has to offer. We'll do everything possible. I'll try to take out Luca before you get there, but if I don't, let me know as quickly as you can where Luca is sending you." He paused. "And Michael wanted you to know that Luca is planning on giving you a welcoming party of nine or ten of his closest friends when you land there tonight."

"I suspected as much," Caleb said. "He's a bit upset about the new arrangements. Thank Michael for the warning for me."

"At the moment, we're not communicating. I'll let you know when and if we dig out Luca. Take care of Jane. Good luck tonight." He ended the call.

Caleb turned to Jane. "It seems Joe is having a few problems."

"Of course he is. It's the Highlands," Jane said jerkily. "We both know what that means. It's wild country and, even if Joe finds that blasted house, Luca could still manage to take off and lose himself if he got even a hint of warning." She was silent a moment before she added, "And you know he'd kill Tomas before he did it."

"Yes, I do," he said quietly. "But I prefer not to think about it at the moment, and neither should you. We'll just trust that Joe can handle his problem and concentrate on taking care of our own." He turned and headed for the library. "I believe I'll just check and see if Angus Wilson is still planning on joining us tonight..."

KENDRICK CASTLE
FRONT COURTYARD
4:15 P.M.

"This place looks like a staging center for an antiterrorist attack," Eve said to Joe as her gaze traveled over the collection of sleek black vans and the uniformed policemen who were receiving their final instructions. "Everything moving like clockwork. But then the British are used to dealing with terrorists." She turned to face him. "But Luca isn't a terrorist, he's a vicious psychotic and we don't know what to expect from him. According to Jane, he can be totally erratic." She shivered. "He could kill that little boy with no warning. He could kill Jane . . ."

Joe shook his head. "Tovarth's a good man and he has me along to strike the balance. No one can say I ever operate with clockwork precision. I learned in the SEALs that every situation can change in a heartbeat." He frowned, his puzzled gaze on her expression. "What's this about? I thought we agreed that we needed Tovarth. You don't want him to go with me?"

"I didn't say that. I want very much for Tovarth's team to go with you. I wish you had the entire British army to go with you." She had to steady her voice. "Because I want that much protection to surround Michael."

He froze. "What are you saying? I told you that I'd refused him permission. It would be crazy to take him, Eve. Did he come running to you?"

"Yes." Then she shook her head. "No, he wasn't playing you against me. He was very quiet. He just said he didn't want to make either of us unhappy, but he had to go." Her hands clenched at her sides. "It was almost like a damn goodbye."

"I'll talk to him again."

"What can you say? What can you do? Lock him up and put a guard on him? I told you how he ran away from the lake cottage last year when he thought you were in danger. You probably don't remember all of it because you'd been shot and were unconscious most of the time." She added fiercely, "But I remember every single second of it. Michael traveled hundreds of miles until he found the cabin where you'd been shot. He'd do that again for Tomas or Jane." She took a step closer to him. "He'd find a way, Joe. And I don't know what else he's learned and taught himself while he's been working with that poor boy, Tomas, but I don't want to force him to show us."

"And I don't want to risk his life because I wouldn't say no to him," Joe said roughly.

"He'd find a way," she repeated. "I *know* it, Joe. And you won't be the one to say yes to him, I will." She stepped back. "I've already done it. I've told Michael that I'd go along with him, and he agreed to stay in the car at all times. I even told him to run and get Lisa and bring her down here." Her lips twisted. "You see? I'm not only willing to risk Michael, I'm going to let Lisa come and help me guard him. Because I knew she'd actually jump at the chance to put her life on the line. That's pretty ruthless of me, isn't it?"

"Pretty desperate," Joe said hoarsely. "I can see it's tearing you apart."

"It's *killing* me. Everything about this is killing me."

"Then change your mind. We can talk to him. We can work through it."

"You're wrong. It's too late. You said once that Michael might have gone beyond us while we were trying to hold him back. I hope that didn't happen, but I'm not going to take a chance on losing him now. Not physically, not mentally, not spiritually." She turned away and headed for Joe's vehicle. "I know this isn't the way you'd like it to be, but that's the way it is. You just concentrate on keeping yourself alive and getting Jane back, and leave Michael to me."

NORTH ATLANTIC SAVINGS AND LOAN
3:05 A.M.

"Okay?" Caleb nudged Jane down the row of mulberry bushes that bordered the back entrance of the bank. "Your cheeks are flushed, and I can feel your body trembling. Do you want to back out? Say the word."

"I can't back out. You told Luca that you had to have me down there to give MacDuff a reason to go down to the vaults. And it's not nerves, it's excitement," she murmured. "I've never robbed a bank before. But I'm trusting you to make it a memorable but safe experience."

"Really?" He smiled crookedly. "I believe you're embracing all this a little too eagerly."

"I'm not entirely without apprehensions." She looked at the glass door ahead. "The thought of Angus Wilson has been haunting me since last night."

"Rightly. But nothing he does will affect you. If the *persuasion* doesn't work, I'll just have to go in another direction."

"That's what I'm afraid about. I don't want you to go in another direction with an honest, straightforward man whom I'll probably like and respect."

"I didn't say I meant anything fatal," he said absently as he glanced to the right of the path. "And maybe I'm better than I think I am. Don't worry about it." He raised his voice. "Isn't that right, MacDuff?"

"Yes, don't worry about it, Jane." MacDuff was grinning as he stepped out of the shadow of the bushes. "Though I didn't catch all you said, I caught the word 'fatal,' and I'm sure Caleb has that under control."

"Good heavens, you look like a cat burglar." Jane shook her head as she looked him up and down. He was entirely in black from turtleneck sweater and jeans to expensive black-leather loafers. "What's that about?"

"I believe I'm insulted. I was trying to dress appropriately. There's really no dress code for what we're doing, is there?" He looked critically at Caleb's jeans and jacket. "He looks entirely boring and common and so do you."

"Since these guards will recognize you as an important client, that wouldn't be an entirely bad thing," Caleb said dryly. "But I should have known that you'd take advantage of the opportunity to make a unique experience even more bizarre."

"I'm supposed to be going down to catch Luca in the act of stealing my fortune, aren't I? My role should be both dangerous and threatening. I believe I'm entirely in character." He looked down the street. "And, as I think I see a couple vans down the block that are probably Luca's men keeping an eye on us, I think this absurd apparel conversation should be cut short." His gaze was still on the vans as he added coolly, "And you said that you wouldn't let Luca know until the last minute about the transfer of my funds here to North Atlantic, Caleb. I trust you kept your word."

"No, you don't. You never trust me," Caleb said. "But I called Luca right before we left the house tonight. He was most upset and distrustful that I hadn't let him know about the switch before. But he decided he had no choice but to let our arrangement go forward." He met MacDuff's eyes. "Ask Jane."

"No, she wouldn't be here if you'd done anything that might have upset her. It was just amusing me to goad you." He moved toward the door. "I just hope that Joe Quinn has done his part to make my participation in this charade worthwhile. What have you heard from him?"

"He's doing the best he can," Jane said. "He has several valuable leads."

"That doesn't sound promising."

"He's always come through for me."

"I know," MacDuff said as his pace quickened. "Let's just hope this time isn't the exception that proves the rule..."

———————

WICK, SCOTLAND
HIGHLANDS

"I need a decision." Tovarth got out of his van and strode toward where Joe was parked on the side of the road. He unfolded his map down in front of Joe and shone the beam of his flashlight on the two roads ahead. "Two choices," he said brusquely. "The road to the left leads toward the foothills of Ben Nevis. The road to the right will eventually get us to Skye. But we're going to run out of time if we pick the wrong one. We took too long on those other farmhouses that proved to be duds." He pursed his lips. "And I'm not going to be the one to choose. Your decision, Quinn."

Joe felt like cursing in frustration as he gazed down at the map. He had no clue if he had a better chance with either of these destinations. The farmhouse near the island of Skye was small but it had all the same general proportions as the other property of St. Giles House in the foothills of Ben Nevis. And he wasn't certain they could reach either house before Caleb's and Jane's situation would prove critical.

"Left." It was Michael's low voice from the backseat. "Take the road to the left, Dad."

Joe turned to look at him. "Believe me, you don't want to make this decision, either, Michael."

"No, I don't. And I know you're upset with me and don't want me to interfere. But I guess I have to do it." He drew a deep breath and said, "You have to turn left, because it's going toward the hills. The hills are important."

"Why?" Eve asked.

Michael shook his head. "I don't know. You just have to turn left, Dad."

"We need to make a decision, Quinn," Tovarth said sourly. "And you'll excuse me if I ask it not be based on the fact that your son likes the idea that one direction has a few hills."

Joe was silent. Then he said, "You heard him, Michael. You've told me that you had to come along because you'd be of value if you did. Now you're going to have to prove it. Are you willing to do that?"

"Joe," Eve murmured.

"Do you think I want to put him in a spot like this? But he chose not to act like a kid, so he has to accept all the ramifications that implies. He said we could trust him." He met his son's eyes. "I'm trusting him. Can I do that, Michael?"

"You can do that," Michael whispered. "Turn left, Dad."

Joe immediately turned to Tovarth and thrust the map back at him. "Left. Toward the foothills of Ben Nevis." He started his car. "And get a move on, Tovarth. I need at least a chance of taking down Luca before he manages to find a way to kill Caleb and Jane."

CHAPTER
17

NORTH ATLANTIC SAVINGS AND LOAN

MacDuff looked back over his shoulder at Jane and Caleb as they reached the front entrance. "What do you think, Caleb?" He was staring with curiosity at the glass doors. "Do I have any chance of finding this experience at all exciting? So far you've disappointed me."

"Exciting?" Caleb repeated, gazing warily at the eagerness on MacDuff's face. Jane could tell just by the amusement and catlike anticipation in MacDuff's expression that he might prove to be more trouble than any of the employees Caleb had so carefully programmed for tonight. Evidently Caleb agreed, because he said, "Not at all, MacDuff. I promised Jane I'd make it as boring as possible for those guards we're using. You just make your appearance and I'll handle the rest." He added, "The only person you might regard as a challenge is Angus Wilson. You know him very well and he likes you. I'd really appreciate any help you can give me to take care of him."

"My, my, that actually sounded vaguely humble," MacDuff murmured. "I wonder why..."

"I'm sure you'll dig and probe until you discover the reason," Caleb said dryly. "Feel free. Angus will be on the lower level and you'll have to be very convincing with him. I've told the guards and Angus that the bank is running a security test of the high-tech facilities here in the North Atlantic bank annex. You've kindly volunteered your time and are even allowing a portion of your treasure to be used in the test."

"Yes, I'm very kind," MacDuff said silkily. "But I don't have the reputation of being a fool and I don't intend to acquire one. This had better work, Caleb."

"As I said, I'll handle it." Caleb stepped in front of the glass door and showed himself to the guard on the other side. "Let us in, James," he called. "Let's get this party started."

Jane tensed and then tried to relax. It was beginning. They'd done all they could; now they had to just react to any emergency that occurred.

The door swung open and James Smythe smiled at Caleb. "Hello, sir, I've been waiting for you. I have to admit I'm a little nervous, but I'm happy you chose me for the job."

"It was really my assistant, Jane, who chose you." He gestured to Jane. "She said the job needed someone who had your reputation for hard work and honesty." He nodded at MacDuff. "And Lord MacDuff agreed with her. So you also have him to thank." He looked around the foyer. "Now, where is Sergeant Campbell?"

"When I saw you out there, he went to the audiovisual room to set up the automatic faux feed to go in effect to all the bank cameras." He looked at his watch. "In exactly four minutes. We're to meet him at the elevators." He led them toward the bank of elevators and smiled at Jane as he pressed the button. "I appreciate this opportunity," he said in a low voice. "Mr. Caleb said that it would make everyone sit up and take notice when promotion time came around."

"You're welcome. And I assure you he was telling the truth." She met Caleb's glance. "It will be a night that will give you nothing but rave reviews, James."

"As promised," Caleb murmured. He turned to a fiftyish, uniformed man with a black mustache who was coming down the hall
toward them. "Isn't that right, Sergeant Campbell? It's not often a
young man just starting out in security gets a chance to spread his
wings like this."

Campbell nodded brusquely. "But we'll have to make sure everything about the work tonight is well documented. No one can say
that the tests tonight are going to be anything but unusual. I'm
surprised that we're being allowed to run them." He punched the
elevator DOWN button. "Mr. Wilson isn't a man who likes to take
chances, and I've found him a trifle...stubborn."

"Bullheaded," MacDuff substituted. "But I've always liked that in
a man who's taking care of my money."

"Yes, my lord," Campbell said. "I'm sure he was glad to cooperate
with you this time." He turned to Caleb. "While you deal with the
vaults, James and I will go get the chests and prepare them as we
discussed. Unless you have a change for us?"

"Not unless Angus Wilson has some objection," Caleb said. "As
soon as we get off the elevator, you go and tend to your business
while I go talk to Angus at the vaults. We'll meet you back here at
the elevators in thirty minutes." The elevator door was opening, and
Caleb stood aside to let Jane and MacDuff get off before he strode
toward the bank of vaults at the end of the corridor. A man in
black-rimmed spectacles and a neat, sandy-colored beard was sitting
at a desk and looked up as they approached. His glance went past
Caleb to MacDuff, and he frowned as he got to his feet. "I couldn't
believe when I got the email that you'd actually agreed to be a part
of this, my lord. It's neither conventional nor safe. I don't wish to be
disrespectful, but I have to speak up and tell you that you should not
have agreed to do this."

Jane tensed, her gaze flying to Caleb's face. Worst-case scenario?

MacDuff smiled. "Ahh, I'm having second thoughts, too. I admit
if I hadn't known you were going to be involved, I might have

refused. But I've always trusted you, Angus, and I've decided we have to keep pace with the times." His smile deepened. "So let's get this over with and then have a few drinks before we go home and prepare to deal with the paperwork and all those technical superstars who will be asking us questions tomorrow."

"I don't like it," Angus said. He gave Caleb a cool glance. "Mr. Caleb was very persuasive, but as I was sitting here tonight, I began to think it was something that shouldn't be done."

"Just tonight?" Caleb asked. Jane caught a flicker, a sudden intensity in his expression. Then he took a step closer and stared Angus straight in the eye. "That's very interesting that only now are you having second thoughts. Then can I urge you to think again? MacDuff seems to think it a workable plan, and after all it is his money."

Angus frowned, but his gaze slid away from Caleb's. "True. However, it's my duty to care for it." Then he glanced at MacDuff and hesitated. "Though I wouldn't want to disagree with you, sir."

"Then don't," Caleb said as he took a step back and gestured to the vault. "He's told you what he wants us to do, so let's do it." He moved to stand before the vault. "Providing you'll come over here and give us the benefit of the infinite trust that the bank has placed in you. The first door is handprint with DNA analysis? Both parties have to enter their ID simultaneously." He looked at MacDuff, who was just gazing at him with a bland smile on his face. "Perhaps MacDuff will oblige us by coming over here and setting an example?"

"Perhaps he will," MacDuff murmured. "I'm thinking about it." Then he strolled across the room and placed his hand on the vault door. "But I guess I *should* join my friend in this nonsense. Come along, let's do it, Angus."

"As you wish, sir." Angus Wilson crossed the room and placed his hand on the vault panel beside MacDuff's.

The panel lit with a green glow.

"Satisfied?" MacDuff murmured to Caleb. Then he taunted softly, "But don't think that you're off your knees yet. There's still that retina ID to go."

"MacDuff," Jane whispered. "*Stop* it."

"Oh, very well." He sighed. "But baiting him is probably the only amusement I'll receive tonight other than that fine whiskey I brought with me."

"I believe you'll survive," Caleb said. "And we're wasting Mr. Wilson's time when all we need to do is get into that vault. That retina ID has always fascinated me. What about you, MacDuff?"

MacDuff nodded. "And this one is particularly sophisticated. Not only identification, but the ability to signal an alarm just by blinking twice into the camera. I insisted on it. I understand you did, too, Angus?"

Angus nodded and strode over to the vault. His fingers played down the complex series of keys, then he stood in front of the vision scan with MacDuff until the green light came on. "It's as good as it can be, but it has fallacies. I'd prefer not to have the human factor enter into it."

The vault door slid open.

"There it is." Angus shrugged. "I'll wait here for you. Then let's get this foolishness over and get out of here." He went back and sat down at his desk.

"I'm in complete agreement," Caleb said as he and Jane entered the vault. "Whew, close," he breathed once they were inside. "And by all means we'll definitely get out just as quickly as we can."

"How close was it?" Jane asked. "What happened with Wilson?"

"Very close. And it seems we got lucky. Angus *is* susceptible to the *persuasion* on a minor level, but evidently it wears off after a time and has to be redone. That last reinforcement I did out there should last for a few hours at least before he comes to realize that this whole scenario is bullshit." He opened the next door of the vault and gave a low whistle as he gazed at several chests overflowing with jewels and artifacts. "Stunning. And tempting. Jane, can you find the Judas coins?"

"Yes. MacDuff and I discussed vault placement when he first deposited the treasure at the Royal Bank of Scotland after we found it." She went to the wall units and pulled out the first drawer. "Numero uno importance." She tucked the coin drawer in her briefcase and fastened it shut.

"A matter of opinion," MacDuff said as he strolled toward them from the vault opening. "I've always preferred inspiration to betrayal. Do you need anything else?"

"No, you'll be relieved to know we leave the rest safely here in the vaults," Caleb said. "Campbell and Smythe are packing up two chests containing what will appear to be a magnificent collection of gold and jewels identical to the ones here. They'll carry it out and put it in the van tailing us that you were so suspicious about, MacDuff. It should be parked out in front by now. Then we're gone and over to you." He turned to Jane. "Are you ready?"

She nodded. "I'm ready." She headed for the door. "MacDuff, you take care of Angus and the others. They only did what they thought they should."

"He'll have no trouble," Caleb said. "The guards have their orders that will keep them safe and remove any post-command that I inserted in two hours. You'll only have to worry about Angus, MacDuff. Give him those couple of drinks you promised, and then take him home. That last post-suggestion I gave him may take three to four hours to erase. Stay with him until you're sure he's forgotten what happened tonight."

"I'll handle it," MacDuff said quietly. "I've had enough fun putting you through hell for one night. Now I'll play lord of MacDuff's Run and do my duty to queen and country for a while." He suddenly smiled recklessly. "I'm fully capable of making sure Luca doesn't know that, instead of lying dead in this vault, I'm trying to drink Angus under the table." He looked at Jane. "You just take care of her. I'll see you later, Jane." He strode out of the vault, blocking Angus's view as Caleb and Jane moved toward the elevator. "Okay, Angus. I gave Jane one of my minor treasures to show security that the theft could be done. Come in and give a glance around to see that nothing else of value was taken." He clapped him on the shoulder. "Then we'll lock up and break out the whiskey. Sound good?"

He nodded. "I didn't mean to be difficult, sir."

"You're not difficult. You're an honorable man, Angus. I'm sure Caleb appreciates that as much as I do now." He grinned. "Now, will you look around quickly so that we can have that drink?"

"Aye, my lord." Angus smiled back as he stood next to MacDuff at the vision scan and then ducked into the vault. "I won't be a minute . . ."

———◆———

Jane watched Campbell and Smythe as they slammed the rear door of the van after depositing the two chests inside. She was breathless as she turned back to Caleb after the two guards walked back into the bank. "Done?"

He put his finger on his lips as he took out a small metal box and pressed a button. He waved it around the car and then studied it. "Done." He put the device away. "I just had to make sure that Luca hadn't bugged the van." He pressed the GPS. "We'll probably be followed by that other van, but I don't think we'll be stopped as long as we head for the airport."

"It went well, didn't it?"

He nodded. "His men saw us with two crates of supposed treasure. They also saw us with no troublesome MacDuff, which presumably means we killed him. We're on our way to the airport to get our flight plan to go to pick up Tomas and deliver Luca's booty to him. In short, we've given Luca everything he wants." His lips twisted.

"Of course, the major problem might be the check-in of the treasure chests with Luca's man at the airport."

Jane's gaze flew to his face. "But you said you had it covered." She frowned. "And I *hate* it that you wouldn't tell me how we're going to be able to do it."

"I think I do have it covered. We'll have to see when we get there. Have a little patience..." He looked down at the GPS. "Ten more miles..."

⬥

The GPS led them into the cargo section of Diarmid Airport and straight to a large hangar occupied by a blue-and-cream-colored Cessna twin-engine plane.

But no one was in the hangar and Jane instinctively stiffened.

"Trap?" she whispered.

"Maybe. But I don't believe Luca would be that stupid. He'd know I wouldn't blunder into a trap with a cargo full of treasure without making sure I could get out of it." He opened the driver's door and got out of the van. "Just in case, stay in the car until I check it out."

"Which means you're doubtful about exactly how stupid he might be," Jane said. She was opening her door as she spoke. "I don't believe he's stupid, but he's egotistical and likes power plays. He might get carried away." As she got out of the car, her hand slipped into her pocket and closed on the handle of her gun. "And we can't let him do that."

"Jane, this is not a good—"

"Be quiet. You're trying to keep me as far away as you can from all of this. But you're doing this for me and Tomas. I won't let you do it alone." Her eyes were flying around the hangar. "There's a camera on the wall over there. That's not a good sign, is it?"

"No one ever said Luca was a trusting soul," Caleb said. "I thought that he might want to check up on whoever he sent to verify his treasure. He didn't disappoint me." He gave a derisive wave at the camera. "Let's see if he gives the go-ahead to his person of choice to come out and do his duty."

A moment later the utility door in the rear of the hangar opened. "Let's get this over. Luca is getting impatient." Russell Davron strode over to the van and opened the rear door. He loaded the two chests onto a cart and wheeled them toward the Cessna. "Stay away from me, Caleb," he said nervously. "Luca said that you have a deal and that I was in no danger. But he needs me to check these and he won't be happy if you interfere."

"And we do want him to be happy." Caleb stepped forward and helped Davron load the chests into the plane. "See how cooperative I'm being?" He stepped to one side. "By all means examine MacDuff's treasure, which will soon be Luca's. With a generous portion to go in my own pocket, of course. After all, no one would have been able to claim any of it except for me." He looked up at the camera and said softly, "You would have been totally helpless, wouldn't you, Luca? I do hope it's making you feel totally inferior?"

"Everything seems to be in order." Davron was shining a light on the interior of the first chest. "Incredible... This necklace alone is worth a king's ransom, Luca." He opened the other chest and shone the light once more on the interior, tilting it toward the camera. "You can see for yourself that it's all totally amazing..." He suddenly frowned. "It all seems to be in order, but I don't see the Judas coins."

Caleb was no longer smiling. "That was not in our arrangement." His tone was ice-cold. "Those are *mine*."

Davron shook his head. "I was told to make sure they were included." His eyes flew pleadingly to the camera. "Unless Luca has changed his mind?"

"Caleb, no." Jane was at his side, her hand grasping his arm as he took a step toward Davron. "It's going so well. Don't risk Tomas's life now."

"I *want* them."

"Please." Her eyes were glittering with tears. "Can't you try to negotiate those damn coins later? Take something else instead?"

He hesitated and then shrugged. "Give them to him. But I *will* have them, Jane. I won't let Luca cheat me. It's only a matter of time."

She quickly took the coin box from her briefcase and thrust it at Davron. "Verify them, and let us get out of here."

Davron quickly opened the padded box, took out one of the coins, and examined it closely. "Authentic." He turned the box around and displayed the coins for the camera. "Age is correct. You'll need a numismatic expert to tell anything else." He let it remain on view for another moment and then closed the box. He opened the lid of the treasure chest nearest him and slipped the coin box inside.

"May we go now?" Caleb asked impatiently.

"One more thing." Davron turned to Jane. "Before you board the plane, I'll need to have your gun."

She tensed. "What?"

"Luca said that Caleb is a rather unique case, and removing his weapons might not be of value." He held out his hand. "But to have you without any way to defend yourself could be of benefit. Luca said to tell you he not only likes to see you helpless, but it might be the very best weapon he could use against Seth Caleb."

She hesitated and then slowly took her gun from her jacket pocket and handed it to Davron. "If Luca keeps his deal with Caleb, then there won't be a need for weapons. Now may we leave? Tomas must be terrified alone with Luca and his father."

Davron jumped down from the plane and was already hurrying toward the door of the hangar. "The flight plan is on the pilot's seat." He turned to Jane. "Don't fight Luca. He might let you live if you don't make him too angry." Then he was striding quickly out of the hangar.

"Let's go." Caleb was lifting her into the plane. The next moment he was climbing into the pilot's seat and taxiing out of the hangar.

He didn't speak until they'd taken off and reached altitude. "I wasn't expecting him to take your gun. I don't like it."

"Because it proved that you're not able to completely pull every string? We both should have expected it. I *am* a weapon against you." She drew a long, shaky breath. "I just have to figure out a way not to let it matter." She looked over her shoulder at the chests in the back of the plane. "I take it we don't have to worry about the plane being bugged? You said that you had it covered, but would it have hurt you to explain that you had Davron in your pocket?"

"Probably not. But I wanted your every expression to be perfectly natural, and you have a tendency to let your feelings show."

"And of course you don't have that issue."

He nodded. "Though I do have my moments. This couldn't be one for either one of us. Nothing could go wrong." He glanced at her. "And it didn't. You handled the Judas coins just right."

"It might have gone better if you hadn't caught me by surprise. All you told me was that you expected a confrontation and you wanted me to distract."

"It gave Davron a chance to keep Luca from not thinking of anything but the coins and not demanding a closer inspection of the other treasure chests." He smiled. "You did beautifully."

"And you sound patronizing. How did you know he'd choose Davron to authenticate the treasure?"

"Davron was as close to an art expert as Luca had among his men. Also Luca obviously had a vast contempt for him and thought he wouldn't have the guts to ever betray him."

"Except when he did," she murmured. "He was trying to warn me when we were at Fiero."

"Don't get all soft. He helped Luca bring you to Tower House. But I knew he was probably ripe for Barza to get him to come over if we pushed hard enough." He added, "And he did, and that's all that's important." He was gazing down at the automatic pilot. "No, *this* is more important. That location to give Joe..." He quickly scrolled through the autopilot menus to see the program's end point. "It's north, toward the mountains..." Then his eyes narrowed on the screen. "*Yes.*"

He swiftly punched in Joe's number.

"It's about time," Joe said when he picked up. "Where?"

"St. Giles. How quick can you get there? We're about twenty minutes out."

Joe was muttering a curse. "Not as bad off as we could be. We're almost to the foothills. But it will be at least forty-five minutes before we can get there. You'll have to stall." He paused. "And you'd better do it damn well. I told you Luca is going to want to kill Tomas in front of Jane. And Michael says he's so eager to do it that he'll pounce on you as soon as he can."

"We'll stall." Caleb glanced at Jane and then reached over to take her hand as he saw her expression. "But it might be a trifle difficult to do. So we'd appreciate if you'd put on speed to keep us from looking foolish in front of Luca." He cut the connection and smiled at her. "Not that we ever would, but I thought I'd light a fire under Joe. Mustn't let him get too complacent."

"Complacent?" She was shivering. "You heard him. Luca wants me as an audience. It would surprise me if he hasn't rigged up another crucifix for Tomas on the runway."

"It's possible. But we need to give Joe a little time to get there and take the heat off the boy. Let's see, right now Luca will think he's on his way to getting everything he wants. He'll be heady with triumph." Caleb's gaze was narrowed thoughtfully on the horizon. "He'll believe killing us and Tomas will be the icing on the cake, his final act before he flies off into the sunset with his treasure and his great destiny."

Jane's eyes were focused on his intent face; she could see he was thinking, plotting, planning. "Then how can we stop it?"

He didn't speak for a moment. Then he suddenly smiled and

snapped his fingers. "Why, by pulling that comfortable rug right out from under him." He released her hand and nodded at her briefcase. "And make him think that fate has taken a nasty hand in spoiling everything for him. Go check your computer and see what you can find out about the St. Giles area."

"What am I looking for?" She was quickly flipping up the lid as she spoke, her shaking fingers accessing Google. "I'm sorry, but I don't believe there's any useful listing here under fate, Caleb."

"Sure there is. It's under a subheading of Mother Nature. You know I have a home up here in the Highlands and there's no territory I'm not familiar with here. Including the countryside around the St. Giles area. I don't remember any mountains..."

"No mountains. Though there are foothills a little to the north." She had found the topographic map of north Scotland. "Most of it looks like flat farmlands right before the foothills start. Is that important?"

"Infinitely." He was checking the autopilot and running it to the final destination. "And no lakes near the property." His gaze went to the darkness beyond the windows. "It should be almost dawn by the time we reach St. Giles House."

"What are you looking for?" She reached out and grasped his arm. "Tell me. I went along with you keeping that bullshit with Davron a secret from me. Maybe you were right, and I might have given something away to Luca. You appear to know him better than he knows himself these days." She held his gaze. "But this is different. This is Tomas, and I won't be left in the dark."

"I wasn't going to leave you in the dark," he said quietly. "We have to delay at least forty minutes for Joe to get here. The plan was to have Joe, Tovarth, and his men from the Yard take out Luca's men before we hit the tarmac. Because if I land this plane on that runway, we'll probably be surrounded in a heartbeat. If I don't land it, Luca will go into a rage and kill your friend, Tomas, out of sheer frustration."

"I knew all that," she said impatiently. "But you're not going to let that happen. You're smarter than Luca and you've already thought of a way, haven't you? Now I want to know what it is."

He was looking at her intently. "I believe you do trust me."

"Of course I do. And I always will. How many times do I have to tell you? You can be very obtuse, Caleb."

"Point taken." He smiled slowly. "Permit this obtuse individual to tell you how we're going to give Joe and Tovarth the time they need to rescue us without raining down fire and brimstone on the boy."

Her grasp tightened on his arm. "How?"

"Lies, trickery, and your old friend at which you proved so adept in that hangar, distraction." He was already banking the plane as he started to lower the altitude. "Most particularly distraction. In short, we're going to do what I promised Joe and stall..."

ST. GILES

"The house is right ahead," Caleb told Jane. "I'll make contact with Luca when I'm ten minutes away from the property. Be ready."

Jane was peering into the half darkness out the window. "It's still not entirely light. Will you be able to see well enough to land?"

"Maybe. Probably." He was gazing down at the fields below. "But I don't promise I won't run over a few black sheep or fine Scottish cattle."

"Not funny."

"I can only try." He smiled. "I'll promise you if I get low enough to see there's a threat, I'll avert and go in another direction. It's good that it's still not that light yet, because we don't want Luca's goons to be able to see exactly what we're doing. Blurring is good, Jane."

"If you don't run over sheep or cows. Then blurring would be—"

"It's time," Caleb interrupted, his hands on the controls in front of him. "Let's have a little atmospheric noise to start off…" He sharply pulled back on the throttle. The engine started to sputter and cough noisily.

He pressed the button on his phone that he'd just pre-dialed. Luca answered immediately. "You're making good time. How close are you, Caleb?"

"What do you mean how close am I, you son of a bitch?" Caleb asked harshly. "You put me in this Cessna that you rigged to fall out of the damn sky and thought I wouldn't suspect you'd done it?" He pulled back on the throttle and jiggled it, once again forcing the engine to cough and sputter. "Listen to that. What did you do? Sugar in my fuel line?"

"I don't know what you're talking about," Luca's voice was suddenly frantic. "I didn't do anything to that plane, you idiot. Why would I? I want you down here so that I can get my hands on my treasure. How close are you to the landing strip?"

"Not close enough." The plane shuddered as it began to lose altitude. Jane instinctively grabbed the strap of her seat belt and shot Caleb a nervous glance. Did he really know what the hell he was doing?

Caleb lowered his window a few inches, flooding the cockpit with cold air and the sound of the sputtering, gasping engine. "I'm at least ten minutes away. I'll have to crash-land." He jiggled the throttle back, bringing the engine to the verge of a complete stall. He cursed viciously. "But don't think I'm going to let you kill us and waltz away with MacDuff's treasure after all I've gone through to get it. Buckle up, Jane."

"This is all your fault, Caleb." Jane's voice was trembling. "We're going to die, aren't we?" It was a performance, but the fear was very real.

"Not before I show Luca he can't cheat me of those Judas coins and then try to kill me." He lowered his voice menacingly. "I'm a very experienced pilot, Luca, and I've gotten out of worse spots than this. We're going to live, and you're going to have to beg me on your knees for your share of the treasure in the back of this plane. Do you hear—"

The Cessna shuddered, and its engine abruptly stalled.

Suddenly there was no sputter, no roar. Just the sound of the icy wind whistling through the cockpit.

Jane's breath left her. "Caleb . . . ?"

He pushed the yoke and the nose lowered. Then the plane drifted to the left, then slowly circled into a corkscrew spin toward the ground!

Jane was gasping, her heart beating crazily as the spins grew faster, tighter.

The ground rushed toward them as pens, maps, and every loose object flew around the cockpit.

"What the hell is going on up there?" It was Luca's voice, almost a screech of sound. Other excited chatter on his end of the line. He'd obviously spotted them.

They hurtled ever faster toward the ground.

"Are you *trying* to kill us?" Jane asked.

He shook his head. "That's not the plan." Caleb punched the starter, and the engine roared to life.

But still the plane spun toward the ground!

"Pull up!" Jane yelled.

"Not yet. We need more speed."

"*More* speed?"

"It's the only way to regain control." He pushed the throttle forward, sending them even faster toward the ground. "Just a few more seconds . . ."

She didn't know how many seconds there were until they hit the ground. "Now, Caleb!" She turned in her seat, trying to orient herself as the cold air whipped over her face.

Caleb pulled the yoke and the plane's nose lifted. A second later, they finally turned out of the spin.

Luca's voice crackled over the phone. "What the hell happened? Caleb?"

Caleb cut the connection and nodded toward a flat patch of land ahead. "That should do."

They landed in a field several miles distant from St. Giles House. The wheels touched down and the plane bounced over rough terrain of brush, rocks, and occasional bales of hay.

It finally came to a stop. Caleb released his seat belt and turned to her. "How are you? Not hurt?"

She shook her head. "Other than the heart attack I suffered when you went into that spin?" She was quickly undoing her seat belt. "I hope it looked effective from Luca's viewpoint because I never want to do it again."

"I did warn you." Caleb jumped out of the cockpit and ran around to open her door. "And if it helps, I think it was everything we wanted it to be. The light was good enough for him to see us hurtling toward death and then me pulling us out and saving the day." His gaze narrowed on the brownstone house in the distance. "And that's a truck leaving the property and heading in this direction. Which means we've got to get the hell out of here." He was back inside the plane and pulling one of the chests out of the interior and throwing it a few feet away from the plane. Then he tossed his jacket soaked in oil onto the other chest, still occupying the rear. He threw a match after it and it immediately exploded into flames. He glanced over his shoulder and saw Jane still standing there. "What are you doing? It's going to blow any minute. Start running for those foothills."

"When you do."

He muttered a curse and was out of the plane and grabbing her hand. "Run!" He pulled the Judas coins out of the box he'd first removed from the plane, then tossed a match onto the chest and watched it flame up. Then he was running, pulling her, heading for the foothills in the distance.

She glanced behind them to see the Cessna totally engulfed in flames. It was a miracle the fuel tank hadn't blown yet.

And then it did!

KABOOM.

———◆———

Joe jammed on his brakes as he saw the explosion light the dawn sky. "There it is," he told Eve. "Caleb said to watch for a fire that would distract everyone from the house and let us go after Tomas." His lips tightened grimly. "I'd say that's one hell of a fire."

"But where are Jane and Caleb?" Eve said hoarsely. "It's all very well to lure everyone from that house, but we both know who they're going after."

"Then we'll just have to go get them," Joe said as he raised his binoculars to his eyes. "There are at least nine men in the back of that truck that's headed for the wreckage of the plane. Caleb definitely got their attention."

"Tomas is alone there." Michael's eyes were fastened on the house. "He's scared, Dad. We have to go get him."

"We will," Eve said suddenly. She opened the car door and jumped out. "I'll take Tovarth with me and go get Tomas. You go and make sure Jane lives through this, Joe."

"No, Eve."

"Don't tell me no. All her life Jane has never been certain she comes first with us. I'm not letting her think she's taking second place this time." She turned to Michael. "Tomas is alone in there? You're sure?"

"I'm sure." He suddenly flung his door open and was pushing Lisa aside to jump out on the road. "He's by himself. I'll take you to him. Lisa, you go get Tovarth." He streaked across the grass toward the front door. "It's okay, Mom. We just have to get him out of there."

"Michael!" But he'd already disappeared into the house. Eve whirled on Joe. "Well, he always said we had to trust him," she said unsteadily. "Now we don't have a choice." She was running toward the house. She gestured to Lisa standing beside Tovarth, who was getting out of one of the police vans. "Come with me. Both of you. I need you!"

She didn't wait for an answer. The next moment she was inside the house.

———◆———

"Get that fire out!" Luca shouted as he jumped out of the cab of the truck. He was cursing helplessly as he gazed at the burning plane. He knew that it was useless to try to save anything within that cacophony of flame. All he could do was hope that Caleb and Jane were burning a slow, painful death inside that plane with his treasure. All his dreams, all his plans, and they'd ruined it for him.

He stiffened. He'd caught sight of a burning chest that must have been thrown out of the plane by the explosion. It was on fire but not to the extent of the rest of the plane. "Get over there," he shouted at the men, pointing at the chest. "Everyone. Put that fire out!"

"There's no water," Alberto said. "We can't do—"

Fools. He wasn't going to lose this chest, too. There was no telling what treasures might still be in it. "Use shovels or your shirts or rifle butts. Anything. I want that fire out!"

He watched frantically as they pounded and worked until they finally got the burning flames under control. Then he pushed Alberto aside to look down in the chest as they tore aside the lid and blackened first layer. "How bad is it? How much damage did the fire—"

"No damage." Alberto looked down at his burnt hands in rage and disgust. "There's nothing in this chest but books and a few shiny necklaces draped over them. It was a trick. Seth Caleb made a fool of you."

Luca was looking at the interior of the chest, stunned. "Shut up," he said fiercely. "It's not true. It couldn't be true." But why couldn't it have happened when that asshole, Caleb, had been the unknown element from the very beginning. Luca had planned and worked for his destiny to emerge intact and as glorious as he'd dreamed it was going to be. He couldn't believe Jane and Caleb had ruined everything for him.

"It's true," Alberto said contemptuously. "The plane never crashed. They just wanted to keep us busy. They're still out there in those hills somewhere."

"Then we'll go after them."

"Not me." Alberto jumped into the cab of the truck. "I'm done with your promises. I'll do what I want to do." He stomped on the accelerator and took off across the field toward the house.

Luca stared after him, outraged. Everything was falling to pieces around him. He whirled to Pietro, who was staring very uncertainly after Alberto. "Don't pay any attention to that traitor. I'll pay double for you to bring Seth Caleb and Jane MacGuire to me." He looked around the field and then to the foothills in the distance. He *had* to believe in his destiny that might still be waiting for him in those hills. "No, I'll pay triple."

"You shouldn't be here, Ms. Duncan," Tovarth said when he followed Eve into the foyer of the house. "Neither should I. I should be with your husband, hunting down Luca and his men. I have to do my duty."

"Tell that to my son." Eve was striding through the hall. "And that little boy Luca tried to crucify. I'm sure they'd love to hear about your duty. But right now I need your help to get Tomas out of this house. He's only eight and he'll have to be carefully moved. After he's away from this place and safely in your van outside, I'll be glad to let you chase Joe down and round up everyone else."

"I meant no offense," Tovarth said quietly. "It's just that I'm concerned since this has not gone down as we'd expected."

"Things rarely do with Caleb." She called out, "Michael!"

"Here." Michael was standing at the door ahead. "I just wanted Tomas to see me and know that we were here for him."

"Well, he did see you," Eve said. "And you know you shouldn't be in here. I told you that you should stay in the car."

He nodded. "But you knew I had to be here with Tomas. He needed me."

That was just what she'd told Tovarth, she thought wearily. "We'll talk about it later. Right now we have to get Tomas out of this place. They haven't hurt him since they brought him here?"

He shook his head. "He's only scared right now. But I told him that he was safe."

Inspector Tovarth nodded. "Then let's get the lad out of here. Do you suppose you could run interference for me since I'm a stranger to him?"

"I'll try. He doesn't like men. His father hurt him." He led him toward the bedroom door. "I'll tell him you're a policeman. That might help. Though I don't—" He abruptly stopped as he reached the doorway. He inhaled sharply.

Then he whirled toward Eve, his face pale. "Mom, you know I told you that there was no one here but Tomas? It was true. But it's not true now." His eyes were big with fear as they went to the front door. "There's someone else here..."

FOOTHILLS OF BEN NEVIS

"Run!" Caleb was pushing Jane up the steep incline as he glanced over his shoulder at Luca's men scattered in the foothills behind them. "Once I get you past the tree line, I'll be able to leave you and circle behind those bastards."

"And then what?" Jane asked fiercely, trying to catch her breath.

"You're going to go after all of them? Pick them off one by one? Don't be ridiculous. You saw how many men Luca managed to send after us once that plane exploded. I hate to call it to your attention but you're not a miracle man. No, you stay with me until Joe and Tovarth's men come riding over that hill and can give us a little help. Otherwise, I'll follow you wherever you go."

"That's not going to happen," he said coldly, his expression tight. "I won't have you interfering. I know what I'm doing, Jane."

"So do I, and I don't like it. So choose stay or go. Either way we'll be together."

He drew a deep breath, and then his expression changed, softened. "I've noticed that that appears to be the case no matter how I fight it. I'll have to decide which way is best for us." He smiled. "Though I don't like you scoffing at the idea that I might be a miracle man. My wicked forebears would be most insulted when they went to such a lot of trouble to convince everyone that they were."

"Stay or go?"

He didn't answer the question. "And I wasn't going to pick them all off. Just one or two so that I could get at Luca. That's all I'd have to do. Take down the top dog and the others would have no reason to fight. Since they weren't on the helicopter coming from Tower House, most of them were probably paid goons, not his regular cult followers. Remove the money and they'll disappear." He paused. "Since I'm not going to attempt miracles, couldn't you be more reasonable?"

"No." She was gazing down at the foothills. "But I do feel more comfortable about you doing it. You're the hunter, so I imagine you've been watching, planning, making sure that you're ready even while you were pushing me up this damn hill." Her gaze shifted to his face. "Do you know where Luca is located down there?"

"At the moment he's near that creek on the other side of the plateau halfway up the hill. He's not leading the charge because there's no way he's a warrior; he prefers to let his men run any risk. I guess he thinks getting killed might seriously interfere with his destiny." He glanced to the right, considering. "I'd probably take out the man in the blue windbreaker first, then wait until the man in jeans and a hoodie moved into the trees to get rid of him." He shifted his gaze back to her. "So easy and then I could move in and take out Luca. Wait here," he coaxed. "It would be much safer for Joe and the Scotland Yard team not to have to deal with him."

"I can see that. I just don't like the way it might come about." She turned back and said, "Therefore we'll change that part of the scenario. Staying is no longer a choice. I'll go with you and let you stash me near those rocks where you set up to go after Luca. I'll remain there until you've removed him. I promise I won't get in your way, but I do want you to give me the gun that you take from that first goon you're planning on taking down so that I can use it if needed. I didn't like it that Davron took mine away from me in that hangar."

"Neither did I." He was frowning. "But I like you doing this even less..."

"I've never been helpless, Caleb. I can defend myself. But being without a weapon makes me feel as if I am. And hiding out up here in the trees while I worry about Luca trying to kill you would be even worse." She started back down the trail and then turned to look at him. "You managed to spot most of Luca's men down there. Did you see Joe or Tovarth anywhere in sight?"

"Not yet. But Joe's much sharper than Luca or anyone else on his payroll. There's a good chance I might not have been able to see him. He has to be out there somewhere, Jane."

She knew that, and it was really a good thing if Luca's men hadn't been able to spot Joe.

But there was one more question she had to ask. "Alberto," she said. "Did you see Alberto down there with Luca?"

Caleb didn't answer at once. "No." He muttered a curse as he saw her expression. "But I did see him in the back of the truck leaving the St. Giles House when we were running away from that burning plane. So Luca didn't leave him behind. Joe would have had his chance to get Tomas out of there."

"If he got there in time."

"*We* gave him the time. Even a little more than he needed. Joe would have been there when said he would. You've always trusted him before—trust him now."

She nodded. "I do trust him." She swallowed hard as she started back down the trail. "I just wish you'd seen Alberto down there with Luca."

CHAPTER
18

ST. GILES HOUSE

W hat do you mean someone is here, Michael?" Eve's gaze
followed her son's eyes to the door. "*Tell* me. Luca?"

He shook his head. "I don't think so. Worse. I think it's..."
He turned away. "We've got to get Tomas away, Mom. He's almost
here."

"Tomas's father?" He was the only person she could think of who
might be worse than Luca. She hurried toward the bedroom and
threw open the door. "I'm afraid we have a problem, Inspector. We're
going to have visitors. Let me help you get the boy out of here."

"Visitors?" Tovarth glanced up with a frown. "What do you—"

"No! You can't do—" It was Michael's alarmed voice behind her!

Eve whirled to see Michael being lifted and thrown to one side
as if he were a rag doll by a huge man with blunt, coarse features.
Alberto? It must be.

She instinctively stepped forward to help Michael, but Alberto
was already next to her, reaching for Eve as if she was as small and
helpless as her son. He hit her with the butt of his gun before he
hurled her at full force against the wall.

Pain. Shock. Darkness.

No, don't let go. Hold on . . .

She forced herself to keep her eyes open as she saw Tovarth reaching for the gun in his holster.

Too late.

Alberto turned and fired at the inspector.

Tovarth crumpled to the floor.

She was vaguely aware of Tomas screaming and crying frantically in the bed across the room. She had to help him . . . The gun in her purse . . .

"Mom . . ." Michael was beside her, tears running down his cheeks. There was a bruise on his cheek, but he didn't appear too badly hurt. "Your head is . . . bleeding. He hurt you—like he did Tomas." She was vaguely aware he'd pushed the handbag that held her gun toward her, blocking the movement with his body. "He mustn't do it again . . ."

"I told you I'd make you pay, brat." Alberto was standing over them, glaring down at Michael. "Your whelp got in my way before, bitch. But now I can take care of him at the same time I finish with Tomas."

"You won't take care of anyone." Eve put her arm protectively around Michael. "You just shot a police officer. They'll hunt you down for that. Is he dead?"

He glanced indifferently at Tovarth. "Maybe. I don't know. I don't care. I've got to finish up here and get back to where I belong." His smile was savage. "I thought I'd put Tomas on a crucifix on the door to welcome Luca when he comes back here. Don't you think it's a good way for him to find out that I'm the one in charge now?"

Michael had pushed Eve's handbag close enough to her so that it would take only the slightest movement of her hand for her to reach for the gun. She carefully avoided looking at it and instead held Alberto's eyes. "I think it's a fitting way to let him know you're as much a brute as he is."

"I'm more than him in every way. I was meant to be the Grand Master." His hand lashed out and he slapped her, hard. "And I told him that I could show him how to punish a woman who spoke out of turn. It starts like this."

She could feel Michael tense against her, and her hand closed warningly on his arm.

Her lack of response must have bored Alberto for he turned impatiently back to Tomas. "You thought you got away from me by all that sniveling and crying? I always finish what I start." He strolled back to the bed. "Shall we talk about what happens next...son?"

Eve's hand slipped into her handbag and closed on the gun.

But she didn't get a chance to use it.

The open door was sent crashing against the wall.

Lisa!

She burst into the room and streaked across to the bed where Alberto was standing. "You son of a bitch. Pick on women and kids?" She dived down, grabbed the pistol from Tovarth's holster, and came up aiming it at Alberto. "What kind of weak asshole are you? Make a move and I'll pull this trigger. Maybe even if you don't make a move. I owe you for taking Michael from me that night at the tent. And all those poor kids who lost everything in that fire..."

Lisa looked so tiny standing next to that Neanderthal giant, Eve thought. "Watch him. Be careful, Lisa." She got to her feet and pulled Michael closer to her. "He just shot Tovarth."

"Yes, be careful, Lisa." Alberto was smiling maliciously. "You're only a woman and I might take that gun away from you. Women always hesitate to pull the trigger. I'm not afraid of you." He took a step closer to her, lifting his own gun. "Do you think I'd be afraid of a slut who—"

Eve shot him in the right kneecap.

He screamed in pain and fell forward, trying to lift his gun to point it at Eve.

She shot him in the other kneecap.

He was panting, but still trying to aim his gun.

Then Eve blasted him in the throat, killing him.

Lisa was staring at her blankly. "Eve?"

"He said he wasn't afraid. He should have been afraid." She looked down at Alberto wearily. "Monsters should always be afraid. He threatened Michael and his own son and so many others. It had to end, Lisa."

"But I was here," Lisa said quietly. "I could have done it. I promised Caleb I'd take care of Michael. I would have been here before, but I was digging a first-aid kit out of the police EMT van. You didn't have to be the one to do this."

Didn't she? Eve wondered. But if Eve hadn't done it, how did she know that Lisa wouldn't have been drawn back into the blood talent she'd been fighting against using all these years? "He threatened my son," Eve repeated. "It's done." She came forward and started to examine Tovarth. "Unconscious. Not bleeding severely. Strong heartbeat. We can only hope it's not too serious. I'll have to call for help right away. Lisa, you said you have EMT training, can you get Tomas and Michael to Tovarth's van and then come back and help me check out that wound?"

"I'll help with Tomas," Michael said as he crossed to the bed. "It's all over, Tomas." He smiled gently down at him. "You're safe now. We'll even get you back to your mama soon. Everything's fine."

Except that she'd just deliberately killed a man in front of her son, Eve thought wryly.

But Michael had lifted his head from speaking to Tomas and was meeting Eve's eyes. "Everything's fine," he repeated. "He's alive and he'll get well." He was helping Tomas out of bed, trying to bear his weight. "Don't worry, we can make the rest of it right..."

FOOTHILLS OF BEN NEVIS

"As ordered," Caleb murmured as he crawled through the brush and around the rock to hand Jane the 9mm revolver. "One down, and a weapon to guarantee that you'll not feel helpless. Now stay here, don't move a muscle, and I'll go after number two."

The next moment he was gone, and Jane moved forward to try to watch him. But he was too fast and made no sound as he moved through the grass and brush. He wanted her not to feel helpless? How could she not, when he was out there, and she wasn't with him? Now she could no longer even see him in the—

"Not a word." The cold barrel of a pistol was pressed to her temple. "Not a whisper." Luca cocked the gun. "Hello, Jane. Surprised?" He took the gun Caleb had just given her and tossed it on the ground a few feet away. "I promised my men a fat fee to bring you back, but then I realized I had to be the one to do it. I'm the only one who is clever enough and knows you and Caleb well enough to judge what you'd both do next." He threw his hand out toward the trees where Caleb had disappeared moments before. "He's out there, isn't he? Leaving you where he thinks you'll be safe to go after me. I deliberately sent one of my men to lay a false track for him to follow, but he's very good and he won't be fooled long. He'll be coming back here to make sure you're okay. Not that he'll be too worried, because he believes that no one can really touch him. But I can touch him, Jane. Just watch me."

"Clever?" Could she make it to that gun that Luca had just tossed away into the brush? "Are you talking about your glorious destiny again? You should've realized by now that that's a figment of your imagination. Caleb has beaten you at every turn."

"Liar!" Luca muttered a curse and his fist lashed out at her stomach. "It's all your fault. Everything would have gone just as I planned if you'd been what you were supposed to be."

Pain. She fought the dizziness. "Or what you thought I should be. Same song, different chorus. Do you know how pitiful that sounds?"

"I'll still get what I want. You're just a challenge I have to overcome. Do you think the Medicis didn't have their own challenges?" His eyes were blazing down at her. "This is just another. I'll go back to Italy and the cult will accept me with open arms and hide me away until I can start over."

If Jane had ever had a doubt he was completely delusional, it had vanished in these minutes. Yet she felt a terrible dread as she gazed at him. He had managed to bring horrible blood and gore into existence once; it wasn't impossible he might do it again. "And I'm just another challenge you have to solve? I suppose you're going to kill me?"

"Eventually. You and Caleb will both have to die, of course. That's why I had to be the one to come after you. Pietro and Alberto and the others would never have understood how arrogant and overconfident Caleb could be. They might have let him get away when it would be so simple to bring him down." He smiled. "You're right, he did fool me for a little while, but in the end he went right back to where I first thought he'd be when I saw you together all those years ago. He went back to *you*." His voice held a note of triumph. "So that proves I was right all along. And how can he resist attempting to keep you alive when he knows he might be the only one who can do it? The arrogant son of a bitch thinks he can do anything he sets his mind to. Not this time. Because he surely knows that he can't trick me or fool me again. That time has passed." He raised his voice and called out, "Isn't that right, Caleb? You realize that she will die. It's just a matter of when and how long it takes. If I take long enough, she might even manage to stay alive until she can convince me she's able to provide me with entertainment. But not if you don't let me take my chance at you. I know how fast you are, what a killing machine you can be. I've studied you for a long time. But I also know I'll be safe from you as long as I keep the correct distance between us." He tilted his head consideringly, his gaze raking the terrain. "I'd judge that will be until you reach the clearing. So here's how it's going to go down. You'll walk slowly toward me out of those woods and I'm going to enjoy enormously putting a few bullets into your body. If you threaten me in any way, I'll put a bullet in our lovely Jane. If you haven't fallen by the time you reach the clearing, I'll have my men fire their weapons at you and take you down. My own personal firing squad." He added maliciously, "And Jane will live for a while longer, though you won't be alive to notice. How is that for a plan, Caleb?"

Silence.

"Oh, you don't approve? I'll have to show you I mean it." He swung his gun and pointed it at Jane. "Her upper right arm. I do hope I don't hit an artery." He pulled the trigger.

Pain. She could feel the hot streak of agony in her upper arm. Don't shout. Don't draw Caleb to her.

"I believe it's only a flesh wound," Luca called out. "But she's hurting, and she doesn't want you to know. How brave. Should I make her scream?"

"Not necessary." Caleb was walking out of the stand of trees. "You've got what you want. Now let's have it over."

It was a nightmare and Jane couldn't believe it was happening. "Don't do this, Caleb."

"But he knows it's the only thing that will keep you alive," Luca said. "And I do want my pound of flesh." He was aiming carefully at Caleb. "I've been waiting for this for a very long time. Left shoulder…"

"No!" Jane jumped forward toward the gun, but Luca knocked her aside with a karate chop to her neck.

Then Luca aimed and took his shot. He watched with satisfaction when Caleb staggered as the bullet pierced his shoulder. "First blood," he said softly. "Do you know that I've learned to appreciate that concept since I've taken over the leadership of the cult?" He aimed again. "Now the stomach...So painful...so deadly." He fired!

He smiled as Caleb flinched and jerked as the blood gushed from his abdomen. "You're getting a little too close to that clearing, Caleb." He raised his gun again. "But I think I have time for the lungs..."

"No..." Caleb was staggering forward, his head hanging down. "Always told you...that you didn't know...everything about me." He raised his head and Jane could see a rivulet of blood pouring out of the corner of his mouth. A savage smile was suddenly on Caleb's lips. "You...waited too long...You let me get too close....I didn't need to reach...that clearing." Then he was running, tearing across the ground toward Luca.

"What?" Luca's eyes widened in bewilderment as he tried desperately to get off another shot before Caleb reached him. The bullet went wild as Caleb's arms closed around Luca's body.

Luca's eyes bulged in his livid face as he struggled to breathe. "Stop...Hurts." Blood was gushing from his nose and then from his eyes. "You can't...do—this to me. Not supposed to be—this way." The blood was pouring from his mouth. "I—have a—Destiny."

Caleb's arms tightened around him, his hands spread on his chest. "Screw...your destiny."

Luca screamed in agony as his heart exploded!

And the next moment Caleb collapsed on top of him.

No...No...No...

Jane crawled frantically across the ground toward Caleb.

So much blood. She had to stop it.

Shooting...

Who was shooting?

Were Luca's men shooting at Caleb as Luca had told him would happen? Personal firing squad...She instinctively tried to cover his body with her own.

"Okay?" Caleb whispered.

All this blood pouring out of him and he was asking if she was okay? "Of course I am," she said shakily. "You shouldn't have done this craziness. You should have tried to bluff him or something."

"Too late . . ." His eyes were closing. "Only thing . . . left . . ."

He was unconscious.

And she was tearing off her shirt and trying to bind the wounds.

Stop the blood. Stop the blood. Stop the blood.

"Jane."

She looked up to see Joe kneeling beside her. Relief poured through her. Joe would help. Joe would make the blood stop. "Luca shot him, Joe. I have to stop the blood."

"I know you do," he said gently. "If you'll move out of the way I have one of Tovarth's men who's trained as an EMT here to help." His gaze went to the flesh wound on her arm. "You're not bleeding, but it should be cleaned and bandaged. Will you let me take care of that for you?"

"Not now." She moved to one side to let the EMT work on Caleb. "He needs a transfusion." He was trying to stop the blood, but Caleb had lost so much already . . .

"We might still be in time," Joe said. "I called for a medical trauma helicopter when we closed in on the hill. They carry blood with them. It should be here any moment now, and then we'll get him out to a hospital."

"When you closed in on the hill," she said dully. "Caleb said that you might be here even though he hadn't spotted you yet. And he thought we'd given you enough time to get Tomas away before Alberto got back. Was that true?"

"Everyone's safe, Jane. You don't have to worry about anyone."

"Except Caleb. How long have you been here?"

"An hour or so. We were trying to take down Luca and his crew without endangering either you or Caleb."

"You should have come in sooner." She was starting to shake. "Look what Luca did to Caleb."

"Yes, I can see that," he said quietly. "It was a judgment call. We were worried about what Luca would do to you."

"It was the wrong call. No one ever worries about Caleb. He always comes last." Her voice was breaking. "It shouldn't be that way, Joe."

"I'm sure you're right. We'll talk about it later." He was motioning to a couple of policemen with a stretcher. "But the helicopter just arrived, and you'll want to get Caleb to the hospital."

He was treating her with great gentleness and agreeing with everything she said. She suddenly realized why. He thought Caleb was going to die. He thought Jane was going to lose him.

She stiffened and her gaze flew to meet his eyes. "No, you're wrong, Joe. He's going to be fine. Naturally he's unconscious after going through so much. But that doesn't mean he's going to die."

"No, that's not always what it means."

That gentleness again, and it was terrifying her. Joe was so smart. What if he was seeing something she wasn't?

Her gaze went slowly down to Caleb's still face and she inhaled sharply. "He's not breathing!" Could Joe be right? She was frantically checking Caleb, her fingers on his throat. "No, I feel a pulse. But we have to get him to that hospital right away."

"We will." Joe motioned for the EMTs to put him on the helicopter. "And as soon as they get him settled, I'm going to have an EMT bandage your arm. Let him do it, Jane. You're not going to do Caleb any good if that gets infected. I have to take care of things here, but we're going to fly him to Glasgow for treatment. MacDuff practically owns that hospital. They'll take good care of Caleb."

"Yes, they will. I don't know how many times Caleb's gone to that hospital when the surgical teams called on him to help with a case. Now they have to help him. They *have* to do it." Her hands tightened on Caleb's. "They'll make sure he lives, Joe."

"He's lost a lot of blood, Jane," he said gently. "And there's no telling what damage those bullets did. Shock alone is a danger."

"Don't *tell* me that. He's strong, and he replaces blood quickly. Everyone knows he's not like anyone else. He's not going to die."

"Of course he's not." Joe was standing beside her. "Caleb is much too stubborn to allow himself to do anything so common. He'd consider it a defeat. We'll take care of him, Jane." He helped her to her feet. "Now let my men get him into the helicopter and we'll be on our way. I'll call a specialist to meet you at the ER when you get there."

She nodded jerkily. "Let's go. Tell Eve I'll call both of you when I know something more." She headed for the helicopter. "But let her know Caleb is going to be all right. He'll be fine. I won't let anything happen to him."

"I'll let her know," Joe said quietly as he turned away. "Take care of yourself, Jane. We'll be with you soon."

He was still worried about her, she realized dully. He didn't believe Caleb would live and wanted to find a way to cushion the blow. But he was wrong. It couldn't happen. She wouldn't let it. She jumped on the helicopter and settled on the floor beside Caleb's stretcher. She took his hand as the helicopter took off.

Stay with me. You reached out and saved me. Now all you have to do is save yourself. Easy. Now do it.

No movement. No expression.

Stay with me.

Then she stiffened as she thought of something else. Stupid. Why hadn't she thought of it before?

She quickly reached for her phone and started to punch in the number.

———◆———

GLASGOW HOSPITAL

"Where is he? And why the *hell* did you let Luca do this to him?"

Jane turned around to see Lisa Ridondo striding down the

corridor toward her. Lisa's eyes were blazing in her pale face, but Jane could see that her lips were trembling with fear. She gestured to the hospital room behind her. "They put him in there. They wanted to send him to ICU, but MacDuff pulled strings and got permission to put him in a private room as long as he was closely monitored." Her lips twisted. "I don't believe the ER doctors thought it made much difference. They think Caleb's going to die anyway."

"No!" Lisa had reached her, and Jane could see the agony in her face. "They're fools, that can't happen to him. You shouldn't have let Luca—"

"Shut up. Do you think I don't know that? Caleb stepped right in front of those bullets to save me. I watched him do it. Do you think I don't want those minutes back? But we don't have time for looking over our shoulders." She grabbed Lisa's arm and jerked her into Caleb's room. "We don't have time for anything but making sure all those doctors are wrong. I was hoping Joe would get you here sooner than this."

"I should have been on the helicopter with you when they took Caleb. That's your fault, too."

"You're right. I didn't think about you. I didn't think about anything but him." She was pulling her over to Caleb's hospital bed. "I tried to arrange for Joe to get you here as soon as he could get another helicopter when I realized how stupid I'd been. I know he tried, but he's like everyone else. He thinks Caleb's going to die." She was looking down at Caleb's face, and she had to stop before she could go on. "Which, of course, he is not. Because now I have you here, and you will *not* permit it." She tore her gaze from Caleb's face and shifted it to Lisa's. "Because you have the blood talent just as he has, and you can help him. I've watched him heal and save lives dozens of times over the years. I know that the blood talent works. While all those doctors are just shaking their heads and waiting for him to die, you can keep him alive."

Lisa's eyes widened in shock. "You expect me to do it?"

"You *will* do it," Jane said. "You have no choice. I won't let you have a choice."

"I don't know if I can." Her expression was suddenly panicked. "I'm not like Caleb. I never wanted to be. I saw how it had hurt him. He taught me just enough of the blood talent to protect me. I don't know anything about the healing."

"What did Caleb tell you about it?"

"Not to worry about it." She reached up and rubbed her temple. "Only that it would come when and if I needed it. Otherwise, just call him."

"That's like him," Jane said in frustration. "Don't worry, and he'll take care of it. Only he can't do that now, can he?"

"No," Lisa whispered. She reached out and touched Caleb's cheekbone. "I've never seen him like this before. It . . . hurts."

"Then do something to make it stop hurting us," Jane said. "And the only thing that will do that is if you make him well enough to get out of that damn bed. Start doing it."

Lisa's lips lifted in the faintest smile. "You're being very bossy. What if you're wrong about me?"

"I won't permit it." She met her eyes. "I'll keep everyone away from this room as much as possible. I'm the only one you won't be able to get rid of. But I can't do anything but *will* him to live and act as guardian at the gates. You sit down in that chair by his bed and begin working. Concentrate. All this blood talent and *persuasion* has to be worth something. He told you that it would come? Then let it come to you. Heal him, dammit."

Lisa nodded slowly. "But it's the blind leading the blind. I have to try to remember what Caleb did when he was healing me that time I was shot. But I was the one who was wounded then, everything in reverse. I don't know if I can do it."

"I don't believe that. You don't, either. Between us we can do this." Her voice was trembling. "Because neither of us could bear it if we didn't."

"No, we couldn't." Lisa dropped down in the chair and took Caleb's hand. She didn't speak for a moment as she looked down at him. "You did at least one thing right when you got Joe to bring me here." Her voice was trembling as she added, "So try to do another and be quiet and let me get to work to keep my brother alive."

"Right." Jane nodded and tried to fade into the background as she sat down in a chair across the room from the bed. She wanted to be there beside Caleb, but it wasn't her place right now. She'd chosen Lisa to save him, and she had to give her the space to do it.

Because as she'd told Lisa, it would be unbearable to do anything else.

SEVEN HOURS LATER

"You're doing that wrong, Lisa. The artery will tear."

Lisa stopped in shock and drew a deep breath. *"Caleb?"*

"Who else? There's no one but us here. Unfortunately, since you appear to be trying to cause me to bleed out."

He was back! Reaching out to her after all these hours of darkness they had shared while she'd tried to heal him. *"It's not my fault. I don't know how to do this. You should have taught me, not just let me wing it."*

"I thought I'd probably be here to do it for you."

"You always think that. Jane said it was just like you."

"Jane . . . She's okay?"

"Of course. You took those bullets. You shouldn't have done that. I was angry."

"You always are. But you can't be angry. You have to take care of her. I'm too tired . . . right now."

"No, I don't. She wouldn't let me. She's the one tossing orders around.

You'll have to take care of her yourself, if you want it done. But you'll have to stick around to do it. She's not going to let you die."

"I never said I was. Just . . . tired."

"Too bad. Suck it up, Caleb. You said I almost made you bleed out. Since it's your fault for not teaching me, you'll have to stay around and tell me how to do this bullshit."

"You could probably do it yourself. You were doing pretty well until you came to that last artery."

"I'm not going to take a chance. You're too fond of saying I told you so. You're going to stay until I get you patched so that I don't have to face Jane and have her go hysterical."

"She never goes hysterical."

"Well, maybe I was talking about me." She swallowed. "This is pretty hard for me, Caleb. It would help if I had you here."

"Then I'll be here," he said simply. *"Aren't I always, Lisa?"*

"Yes." Don't let the tears come. She cleared her throat. *"When you don't do stupid stuff like get yourself shot. And then you just lie here all these hours and let me do all the work. You were gone far too long before you showed up with that snide crack about the artery."*

"Sorry. I always like to make an entrance."

"I suppose I'll forgive you."

She added brusquely, *"If you'll tell me what to do to keep me from destroying this artery when there are all those others that are so close to it. Don't get slipshod. I want this step-by-step, Caleb . . ."*

———◆———

Something was happening. Jane tensed, her eyes on Lisa as she bent closer to Caleb. Bad or good?

Good. There was an eagerness, an excitement, to the line of Lisa's body as she gazed at Caleb's face.

After all these hours he had to be coming back to them.

Yes! The relief soaring through her was dizzying, and her hands clenched hard on the arms to her chair. *It's about time, Caleb. Now open your eyes and let me see that you're all right. Say something. I can't take much more of this silent treatment.*

She was being idiotic. Patience. She could take anything as long as he was alive and getting better. Lisa would tell her when Caleb was safely out of the woods.

Jane's gaze fastened on Lisa, trying to read every nuance on her face and in her body language. *Tell me it's not my imagination.*

Tell me you've brought him back to me.

———◆———

"You...look...like hell," Caleb whispered. "I told Lisa...to take care of you."

Jane's gaze flew to his face, and she saw that his eyes were open. Thank you, God. She had to wait a moment before she could answer. "Then you should have told her not to spend the last three days trying to keep you from dying on us. She was a little busy. She only felt comfortable letting me throw her out of here this morning." She struggled to keep her voice steady. "How do you feel?"

"Fine. Lisa did a good job after she got the hang of it." He smiled faintly. "Though I did get tired of her complaining because I hadn't taught her anything useful. I didn't want to tell her that even if I'd given her lessons for years, those were wounds that could have gone either way."

"No, they couldn't." She reached out and took his hand and said fiercely, "Because we wouldn't have let it go any other way than where we wanted it to go. I wasn't going to let you get away from me, Caleb."

"That's what Lisa told me. She said I wasn't going to be allowed to die because you wouldn't permit it."

"That's right. You said you'd die for me, and this time it came too close. I'm having to rethink ways and means to keep you alive. One thing is that Lisa proved to be an asset I don't want to do without. She *saved* you. So I think she has to stay close to us no matter how much you want to keep her free from the dreaded taint of the Ridondos."

"We'll talk about it later."

"Which means you'll probably try to talk me out of it later." She shook her head. "Go ahead. It won't work, but we'll put the argument on hold for the time being. You need mega rest and healing, and I don't want to rock the boat."

"I'm already on my way back. The healing will go very quickly from now on." He paused. "Luca's dead?"

"You know he is. You couldn't have been more lethal."

"I had to be sure. I wasn't in very good shape during those last moments."

"Tell me about it. Eve killed Alberto after he shot Inspector Tovarth. Joe said Tovarth is going to be all right. No other problems. Except that you managed to get yourself shot."

"Now you sound like Lisa. Tomas?"

"Bewildered but on the upswing. He's been in the pediatrics wing at this hospital since the night of the raid. MacDuff has been flying in specialists to examine him, and Eve and Michael have been there to see him through it. Joe is bringing his mother from Tower House to be with him tomorrow after he and Tovarth do a final cleanup of those cult members there." She added firmly, "Now that's all I'm telling you. You can find out anything else later after you wake up from your next nap. Go back to sleep, Caleb."

"Don't push me, I told you that I'll get stronger from now on." His gaze was searching her face. "But you could use a little rest yourself. Go to bed. I don't need you, Jane."

"Oh, that's right, you said I look like hell. Well, you'll just have to put up with it. And you probably don't need me. But I need *you*. I had to sit there in that chair across the room after I turned you over to Lisa and I couldn't do *anything*. It nearly killed me. But now I can at least watch over you, pretend to guard you." Her lips were trembling as she tried to smile. "Do you always have to have everything your own way? You saved my life. Will you just shut up and let me do this?"

He didn't speak for a moment; then he nodded. "By all means, a little more loss of sleep won't hurt you. It might be good for you." He added mockingly, "I should have known you'd be suffering major guilt feelings about me taking a couple of bullets on your behalf. Soothing my feverish brow will be excellent therapy."

"Stop joking. Nothing about that moment was amusing," she said hoarsely. "You just kept on coming toward him and you wouldn't stop. All I could do was watch it happening and pray. You had no right to try to sacrifice your idiotic neck for me. I'll never let you do it again." She drew a shaky breath. "Now close your eyes and go back to sleep. You'll be rid of me soon enough when Lisa wakes up and comes running back to you. You should appreciate the fact that I've gotten very good at being so quiet that you never even knew I was in the room while Lisa was doing her magic."

"Have you?" He closed his eyes. "Maybe not that good...Because I'm sure I remember being aware of you every moment, every second, since those bullets struck me..."

<hr/>

FOUR DAYS LATER
PEDIATRICS

"What can I do here?" Jane asked the minute she saw Eve in the hall outside Tomas's room. "I'm frustrated as hell. Give me something to do."

Eve's brows rose. "Unless you've suddenly acquired more experience than those two new doctors who are examining Tomas in his room, I can't imagine what that would be. They kicked me out and only permitted Michael to stay because Tomas was getting upset." She sat down on the bench in the hall. "So why are you getting frustrated? Has Caleb taken a turn for the worse?"

She shook her head. "He looks like he's almost back to normal. But how would I know? I hardly ever see him. Lisa is always with him during the day, and he won't let anyone stay with him at night. He's being... Caleb."

"Which is singularly difficult," Eve said. "I understand your problem, but I don't know how to solve it." Her lips quirked. "Unless you want me to tell you that you should leave him as you did once before. But you've already told me that's not an option."

"No, that's never going to be an option." She dropped down on the bench beside Eve. "I just don't have an idea what to do right now." She moistened her lips. "I can't read him. He seems almost... cold."

"Cold?" Eve shook her head. "Not Caleb. Go back and start over." She took her hand. "Look, you and Lisa almost brought him back from the dead. What's a little stumbling block compared with that? Go kick Lisa out of his room and make him talk to you."

Jane's hand tightened on Eve's. "Yeah, what's a little stumbling block? I'm sorry I ran up here to whine to you. But then I always did do that, even when I was a kid."

"You never did it enough. You always were too grown-up." She smiled. "And I was glad to help with pointing out the possibility of a random stumbling block. I don't want to risk the family losing Caleb. I'm feeling very grateful to him for saving you."

"I am, too. But then it's not the first time, is it? He always seems to be there for me." She got to her feet. "I'll come back and visit Tomas this afternoon. But now I believe I'll go and have a chat with Caleb." She waved and started down the hall toward the elevator. "Thank you, Eve."

She smiled. "My pleasure."

"She's upset about Caleb," Michael said from the doorway behind Eve. His gaze was on Jane getting on the elevator. "Is he okay?"

"I'm sure she'll find out. But she says he's healthy enough." She gazed beyond him to the closed door. "Did you get kicked out, too?"

He shook his head. "Tomas wanted me to leave. They were hurting him, and he didn't want me to see him cry." He added gruffly, "I couldn't make him understand that it didn't matter. It's different now that I'm trying to keep out of his head and just be a friend."

"How is that working?"

"Okay, I guess. Since he doesn't need me in that other way any longer, it's easy for him to think what we had together was just a dream. Because he doesn't know about friends, I have to keep explaining it to him." He frowned. "But I was listening to those doctors in there and it sounded to me like it's going to take a long time to fix his wrists. So I wondered if we could take Tomas home with us."

Her eyes widened. "What?"

"Not to live with us. We're strangers to him and that would only confuse him. He's had such a lot of bad stuff happening to him that he doesn't understand. He needs something solid and familiar to grab and hold on to. Was I right about how long it will take those doctors to fix his wrists?"

Eve nodded and said gently, "From what I can gather it might take several operations, but there's a good chance he'll eventually be fine."

"But he'll need to be with his mom while that's going on. She's the only one he loves and is sure loves him." He shook his head. "But at the same time he feels like he has to take care of her. I guess they'll both have to learn how things work when there's no Alberto messing up their lives for them. That's kind of confusing, too."

"I can see how it would be." Her eyes were narrowed on his face. "So just what are you asking, Michael? What is it that you want?"

"I'd just like to be around Tomas when he needs me," he said quietly. "I thought maybe we could rent a house for him and his mom somewhere near the lake cottage and help them get a new start. Maybe show them what a family could be like? Could we do that?"

"It would be difficult." It obviously didn't seem too difficult to Michael. Just transplant two broken people and try to put them back together. Let them heal their own wounds, yet keep their roots and independence. And then show them how it could all be possible. How long had Michael been thinking, planning, trying to find the best way to save Tomas and his mother? Yet Eve could see problems looming, and she didn't want Michael to believe that it would be that simple. "They're foreign nationals and there could be all kinds of roadblocks to prevent them from entering the U.S. even on a temporary basis. Particularly since Tomas's father was guilty of several gory homicides."

"It wasn't their fault. It wouldn't be right to blame them."

"Sometimes bureaucrats don't pay attention to what's right. They only see what's in their rule book. It could be a hard battle."

"But we should do it." He smiled. "We should fight it, if it would help them. You know that, Mom. And if we all do this together, you know we could win."

She looked at the eagerness in his expression and then slowly nodded. "We'll do our best." A brilliant smile suddenly lit her face. "What am I talking about? No, we'll do better than that. You're right, together we're totally unbeatable." She held out her hand to him. "Now let's go call your dad and discuss how we're going to find a way to make it happen."

———◆———

"He's gone?" Jane stared blankly at the orderly who was taking the linens off Caleb's hospital bed. She whirled on Lisa. "What do you mean he's gone? He just checked out of the hospital? When? Why?"

Lisa held up her hand. "I can only answer one question at a time." She was drawing Jane out into the hall. "And some of them I can't answer at all. All I know is that when I came to see Caleb this morning, the head nurse told me that she'd had notice he'd already checked out of the hospital." She made a face. "She was as bewildered as I was because he'd not been dismissed by any of his physicians. Shortly before midnight last night, he just told the floor nurse he was leaving, and she wasn't to tell anyone until the head nurse came on duty in the morning."

"And of course she'd do as he wished." That damn *persuasion* again. "You didn't know he was going to do it?"

She shook her head. "I told you, I didn't know until this morning. I left him at eight last night and he never mentioned that in four hours he was going to blow the place. The closest he came was telling me that he'd received a call about some offer of a hunt he might accept. At first, I was mad as hell that he didn't trust me." She shrugged. "But then I realized he might have thought I'd tell you. He'd been avoiding you recently, he wouldn't even talk about you. So it might have been about you and not me."

Pain. Even through the bewilderment and rejection, Jane was feeling the pain twisting inside her. "Yes, it sounds like it might have been about me," she said unsteadily. "That must have been a great relief to you."

"You're right, it was a relief. Because trust is everything between Caleb and me. But then I realized he only did it because he knew I might have told you, if I'd known." She was frowning. "Because he was *wrong*. He shouldn't have hurt you like this. I don't know why he did it, but he was wrong."

"I think so, too." Jane swallowed to ease the tightness of her throat. "But I'm surprised that you believe it's true, when Caleb is always perfect in your eyes."

"Not this time. He made a mistake. He's entitled, but I saw how you fought to save him. You're *good* for him. He shouldn't walk away when you're so good for him." Her gaze was on Jane's face. "And he hurt you. I can see it. You're my friend and I don't like him hurting my friend. He mustn't do that."

"I'm in complete agreement. But I'm glad that you're on my side this time." Jane took a deep breath. The pain and shock were gradually fading, and she was left with bewilderment and yet perhaps the start of a vague notion why this had happened. "And I have an idea Caleb might have deliberately handled this abrupt departure just the way he intended, with all the brutality and cruelty those early Ridondos would have shown."

Lisa frowned. "I don't know what you mean."

"Neither do I. But I'm going to find out." She turned and started down the hall toward the elevator. "Right after I find Caleb."

"You might not be able to find him," Lisa called after her. "Not if he's on a hunt."

"You don't think so? Believe me, Caleb's never had anyone as determined as I'll be on his trail. He doesn't stand a chance." She added grimly, "Don't worry, I'll find him."

———◆———

OUTSIDE PAPHOS, CYPRUS
THREE WEEKS LATER

He was close!

Jane was half running, her eyes narrowed on the shadowy trees that bordered the trail. He could be anywhere.

But Caleb had already left the hotel, so that meant he would be heading down this hill toward the sea.

Move fast, before he reached the cruiser he'd stashed in the cove. She couldn't let him—

She fell to the ground as a tackle from behind brought her down! She instinctively started to struggle.

"Stop," Caleb said roughly. "We don't have time for that. I have to get off Cyprus in the next ten minutes, and now I'll have to take you with me." He got off her and pulled her to her feet. "Run, dammit."

"That's what I was doing," Jane said as she tore down the hill. "And you didn't have to tackle me. All you had to do was stop and let me catch up."

"Which was difficult when there might be three goons coming down the hill from that hotel who might want to shoot me...and you, on sight." He'd reached the cruiser in the cove and he lifted her onto the deck. "Just keep low until we get out on the open sea." He untied the boat and started the engine. "This was totally idiotic, Jane. I can't believe you did it."

"Yes, you can." She sat down on the seat as the cruiser tore out of the cove. "You might have even expected it. Oh, not that I'd actually follow you on a hunt itself, but that I wouldn't let you go easily. You know me well enough to realize how determined I can be. That's why you crept out of that hospital in the middle of the night."

"Crept?" His lips twisted. "Really, Jane. And it wasn't the middle of the night."

"Close enough." She looked back over her shoulder at the hotel on the hill. "There are lights all over that driveway now. You timed it right. Ten minutes. Why did you think there would be pursuit? What happened up there tonight?"

"I kept a promise."

She was silent. "Prey?"

"I think you realized that I was on a hunt." His eyes were narrowed on her face. "But I don't know how you knew where to find me."

"Joe. You mentioned a hunt to Lisa. I told Joe that I had to know where you were going right away. You know how many contacts he has with law enforcement and agencies all over the world. I asked him to sift through them and give me the most logical location for you." She shook her head ruefully. "He exhausted all of his own contacts and then started on yours."

Caleb was swearing beneath his breath. "Palik."

She nodded. "Palik knew you were working with Joe to get Luca. I guess he didn't think there would be anything wrong in telling Joe you'd be here tonight. He even gave him a few details." She looked back again at the hotel, which was almost out of sight. "What promise did you keep, Caleb?"

"To Nicco Barza. I promised him that a very ugly crime boss named Santo would never trouble him again. Barza was the one who talked Davron into betraying Luca at the airport. It was time I kept my word."

"How?"

"Santo had a massive heart attack tonight after returning from dinner at his wife's parents' home." He tilted his head. "You see how considerate I've been? I'd rather have chosen a far more bloody and painful death for the son of a bitch, but there was no use upsetting his wife and children."

"But you still thought there might have been pursuit."

"I wasn't sure I wasn't seen. Santo had men all over that hotel." He put the cruiser on auto and turned to face her. "And they wouldn't have thought twice about shooting you or anyone else on the hotel property after they found Santo's body. They've been trained to shoot first and ask questions later."

"He sounds very unpleasant, and if he was dead, then I don't see why anyone would want to avenge him. I think you tackled me for no good reason."

He frowned and then reluctantly smiled. "I admit I enjoyed it. I was pissed off at seeing you there. You shouldn't have come."

"You shouldn't have left. I wasn't pissed off, I was hurt. Which I believe to have been the purpose of the entire exercise." She looked him in the eye. "Wasn't it, Caleb?"

"Why should I have gone to the bother? I had a job to do and I decided to go do it. I don't answer to you, Jane." He smiled mockingly. "Remember, you promised me no commitment. Maybe I found our relationship a little taxing after you almost got me killed. Everyone knows how self-centered I can be."

"Bullshit."

His brows rose. "Really, Jane. I'm disappointed in you. Where's your pride?"

"Where it's always been." She got to her feet and moved closer to him. "Pride is all very well, but it can get in the way. I'm proud of who I am. I'm proud of who you are. I have no intention of letting either fool me into losing what we can be together." She reached out and grasped the edges of his jacket. "But I do want to hit you for giving me a bad few minutes when Lisa was telling me that I was the one you were trying to escape."

"Maybe you were." His face was now without expression. "How can you be certain?"

"Because I *know* you." She shook him. "Because I love you. Because you're the one who's the idiot. Because I realized after I thought about it that I was the one you were trying to let escape. You almost died for me, and you thought that was a tie I'd never be able to break. You've been saying that you'd never let me go, and this would have sealed it, wouldn't it? Yet when it came down to it, you walked away from me because you thought I wouldn't be able to leave you."

"And I'm so noble that I'd do that?" he asked sardonically. "You must be thinking of someone else. Not likely, Jane."

"Very likely. Call it whatever you want. I've seen you with Lisa and I know you'd give up everything for her." She paused. "And I think you feel the same way about me. You wanted to give me a chance to walk away if it was gratitude that was holding me to you. You didn't mind plotting and planning and using *persuasion*, but you didn't like the idea of gratitude. Heaven forbid that I be grateful to one of the wicked Ridondos for anything. Did it make you feel like a wuss?"

"It might have." He tilted his head, thinking about it. "There's something very milquetoast about gratitude. It could totally ruin my image."

"No way," she said unsteadily. "There's nothing milquetoast about you." She paused. "I was right, wasn't I? Tell me I was right."

He didn't speak for a moment. "You might have been right," he finally said jerkily. "I do detest gratitude, and the worst thing I can imagine is having you chained like that."

"Good. I *knew* it." She pulled him toward her and kissed him.

"Oh, shit." He jerked her into his arms and he was kissing her, stroking her, his hands on her breasts. Heat. His tongue moving, making her . . .

She finally broke free and gasped. "Definitely not milquetoast." She swallowed. "Though you have a lot of other faults. I'm getting very tired of you assuming that because you have all the talents of the Ridondo brothers, you've also inherited all their sins. That's bullshit, and I want you to stop."

"Then of course I'll do it. You're right, maybe not quite *all* their sins." His hand was caressing her throat. "Though I think I should probably confess that it was only two days after I left the hospital that I decided I wasn't going to be able to follow through with my good intentions. I was only going to give you a month's trial period without me before I went after you again." He made a wry face. "Not exactly noble. *Very* Ridondo."

"But also very honest—a move that strikes a balance. I can handle the wicked brothers easier than all that noble bullshit." She went into his arms and held him fiercely. "And now I want you to hold me and tell me that you won't ever do this again. I want a promise. It wasn't fair. It *hurt* me."

He was silent a moment, gazing down at her. "I won't ever do it again," he said hoarsely. His arms tightened around her, and he buried his lips in her throat. "Though God knows I shouldn't promise you. Maybe someday I might actually be able to walk away and that would be the best thing for you."

"Too late. I've got you. And you don't break your promises." She pushed back and looked up at him. "Now one more thing. Considering that you nearly died for me, it's not too much to ask that you tell me it was for a damn good reason. Do you love me, Seth Caleb?"

"Extravagantly." He added lightly, "Though I believe you said it wasn't at all necessary. You said no commitment."

"That was before you sent me wildly hunting after you for these past weeks. I needed the reassurance. I had to be sure, because I think there's only one way you'll ever be sure I love you, trust you, and want to stay with you." She drew a deep breath. "And it's a hell of a commitment. Because you know what family means to me." She cradled his face in her two hands and looked him in the eyes. "I want to be your lover for the rest of my life. But I also want you to be part of my family as I'm going to be part of yours, Caleb." She paused before she could say the words, and then they came out in a rush. "Will you marry me?"

His smile faded. "What are you saying?"

"You heard me. You said you loved me?"

"God, yes."

"Well, I want everything that means. I don't want half measures. Will you give me what I want?"

He turned his head and his lips brushed her palm. "You don't know what you're asking. You should know by now that half measures are safer for you where I'm concerned. I'd be a constant complication in your life. I shouldn't do it."

"Yes, you should. I'm being very selfish. I've decided there's no one in the world better for me than you. Why do you think I ran after you?"

"You're crazy?" He shook his head. "But it doesn't matter any longer. You're not getting away from me." He pulled her closer and whispered, "All I want to know is how the hell am I ever going to convince Eve and Joe that you're doing the right thing?"

"You won't have to convince them. They'll know after our first child is born." She could feel him stiffen against her, and she moved still closer. "Because that's part of the deal, Caleb. Don't you dare draw back from me. I know the blood talent isn't passed down to every child, but whether it is or not, it will be our child. We're not going to be cheated because we might have to contend with a child who is special. Michael is special and difficult and full of wonder. Any child you give me will be the same because you'll be the father. You'll protect him and guide him and love him as you did Maria and Lisa and me. It will *never* be like what you went through growing up, whether he has a talent or not."

"You have no idea what you're talking about," he said hoarsely. "You don't *know.*"

"And neither do you, because it's all going to be new to us." She stared him in the eyes. "But I do know that we're going to make this work, because I won't have it any other way. And I'm betting that you love me enough that in the end, you'll give me what we both need and want."

"We'll talk about it later," he said warily.

"Yes, we will." She lifted her hand again to his cheek, her eyes twinkling. "Constantly. Forever. And I'll be gentle with you for a while. But just remember that if you think I was completely relentless in tracking you down after you tried so idiotically to abandon me, you haven't seen anything yet. I'm going to get my way, Caleb."

He looked down at her for a long moment, his eyes glittering with a multitude of emotions. Then he took her hand on his cheek and moved it to his lips. He smiled but his voice was thick with that same emotion as he said, "I'm very much afraid you will, Jane MacGuire. I don't believe I have the slightest chance in hell. Lord save me from an obstinate woman."

"You won't have to be saved. I might not know anything about *persuasion*, but I guarantee I'm going to work very hard on making both of us enjoy every minute of our time together." She drew still closer and added unsteadily, "Every day. Every way. Count on it."

ABOUT THE AUTHOR

IRIS JOHANSEN is the #1 *New York Times* bestselling author of more than 30 consecutive bestsellers. Her series featuring forensic sculptor Eve Duncan has sold over 20 million copies and counting, and was the subject of the acclaimed Lifetime movie *The Killing Game*. Along with her son, Roy, Iris has also co-authored the *New York Times* bestselling series featuring Kendra Michaels. Johansen lives near Atlanta, Georgia.